THE
RIGBY
FILE

THE
RIGBY
FILE

Hodder & Stoughton

LONDON SYDNEY AUCKLAND TORONTO

British Library Cataloguing in Publication Data

Heald, Tim, *1944*–
    The Rigby file.
    I. Title
823'.0872

ISBN 0-340-50207-X

First published in Great Britain 1989

Published by Hodder and Stoughton,
a division of Hodder and Stoughton Ltd,
Mill Road, Dunton Green, Sevenoaks, Kent TN13 2YA
Editorial Office: 47 Bedford Square, London WC1B 3DP

Photoset by Rowland Phototypesetting Ltd,
Bury St Edmunds, Suffolk

Printed in Great Britain by Biddles Ltd,
Guildford and King's Lynn.

Contents

INTRODUCTION

I first heard about Dorothy Rigby over lunch at White's. My host was a high-flying Brigadier in Military Intelligence whom I'd known for years without being able to say precisely how, or why. It's one of the characteristics of the Old Boy Network: some belong, some don't. The reasons for this are tantalisingly difficult to pinpoint which is partly why the Network is so effective and, in the eyes of its enemies and detractors, so deadly.

It was the beginning of 1988 and the *Spycatcher* row was at its height. Prime Minister Thatcher, her law officers and the Cabinet Secretary were spraying injunctions all over the place and being liberally economic with the truth. A vindictive little spat which should have been glossed over ages before, the crux of it was that this old British agent had published his memoirs of life in the British Secret Services and the Government didn't like it. But because the old boy was holed up in Tasmania he could cock a snook at Mrs Thatcher and any other members of the British Establishment he chose. It was clear that nothing like this would ever be allowed to happen again. Mrs T. would see to that.

The Brigadier sawed off a cube of lamb cutlet and spread it with redcurrant jelly.

"At any event," he said, "it'll put the kibosh on the Rigby thing."

"The Rigby thing?" I was eating lamb too. Welsh, I guessed.

"The Rigby thing." The Brigadier chewed, swallowed, took a mouthful of claret, swallowed that and then said, "There's no way Ma T. will let Rigby blow the gaffe. Not now. Not that you can ever underestimate Rigby. Even so . . ."

He took another mouthful.

"Rigby?" I enquired, trying to make the question seem offhand. I've operated around the fringe of government and officialdom long enough to know when I'm being set up. I was being set up now, but that didn't worry me unduly. Provided you know what's going on, you can usually turn it to your own advantage.

"Yes," he said, "Rigby."

"Sorry," I said, putting down my knife and fork, "I'm not with you."

He gazed at me thoughtfully, still chewing.

"You're not?"

"No."

"Funny," he said, "I rather thought you were on to the lady. She's got quite an 'in' at the *Telegraph*."

"Well I haven't," I said, "I hardly do anything for the *Telegraph* these days. And it's a day trip down to the new plant on Dog Island."

"You really don't know what I'm talking about, do you?"

"No," I said, beginning to be irritated. It's galling to be bamboozled by brigadiers, even when they are in Intelligence. "Not the foggiest."

"I'd have thought you'd have come across her at some point," he said, "you really ought to. She's a remarkable woman. You'd like her. Terrific copy though now, of course, out of the question. Thanks to Mr Wright. Pity. It would be worth having Rigby's story on paper."

He poured more claret and it was my turn to smile.

"She a friend of yours?"

"A cousin of my aunt's. Her father Harry was . . . well, you don't want a family pedigree. We're a complex clan. And I did run across her in a professional capacity – her last case and one of my first. One of my first in a senior position that is; the first time I ran an important op for real. But that's classified, of course."

The waiter cleared away the plates.

"Cheese or coffee?" asked the Brigadier.

They're a curious ritual, those lunches. It's like watching the courtship dance of two exotic birds on a B.B.C. wildlife programme: one step forwards, two steps back. First one plays hard to get, then the other. Every little cluck and quack has about three separate meanings.

By the time I got home there was a message on my answering machine: "Rigby would like you to have tea on Saturday. We'll send a car to pick you up at three."

* * *

The cottage was in Sussex though, for obvious reasons, I can't be more specific. It was just this side of picture postcard pretty, with a garden meticulously bedded down for winter: wallflower plants in line along the front path, roses pruned, fig tightly tied to a redbrick wall. Full of character, it was well preserved, with crucial features intact and utterly English. Just like its owner.

"You must be Humphrey's friend," she said, straightening up from some gardening task and removing gloves to shake hands. Then to the driver, "Thank you, Sidey. Call back around six and take Mr Heald back to London, if you would".

Then back to me, "Come on in. There's Twining's Earl Grey or servants' tea. Or something stronger if you'd prefer".

I settled for the Earl Grey. Sam Twining vouched for it.

"So," she said, when we were settled in front of a log fire with mugs – not cups – of strongish black tea and lumps of sticky home-made ginger cake from a friend in the village. "So you're chairman of the nation's Crime Writers."

"'fraid so," I said.

She laughed, an unexpectedly deep brown throaty sound, and crossed her legs, then smoothed her tweed skirt. Remarkable legs in a woman of sixty plus. She reminded me a little of Katharine Hepburn. Only English. Lady Hester Stanhope would have recognised a kindred spirit. She had high cheekbones, a still generous mouth and eyes that could kill across a crowded room. A class act.

There was a long pause, broken only by the crackle of burning wood, the purr of a Burmese cat on the hearth and the tick of a rather good, I guessed, grandmother clock.

"I have an idea," she said at last, "which I think might amuse you and some of your colleagues . . ."

I liked Rigby's idea. It took her much the best part of two hours to outline it in detail and it was well after six before Sidey and I drove back towards London. The more I thought about it, the more I liked it. It was a plot and I'm fond of plots. It would almost certainly embarrass the Government and that's a noble aspiration. Above all, it was a great story. Or, more accurately, a whole series of great stories. My part in it was to use my contacts among 'crime writers' – a loose term which includes thriller writers as well – and persuade them to join the Brigadier, Rigby and me in the conspiracy. Oh, I realise, there was one other totally compelling reason for accepting Rigby's proposal: from the moment I set eyes on her, I absolutely adored her.

By February I had selected a suitable team of writers – men and women I could trust implicitly and who had the proven ability to write the sort of material Rigby and I were looking for. This, with a personal covering note, is what I sent them:

Dorothy Rigby, daughter of Colonel H. R. F. Rigby, D.S.O., M.C., and Mayotte Rigby (née Plouviez) was born on January 28th, 1920 in Madras, India. She was educated at a number of schools in a variety of different countries before being recruited into the French Section of the Special Operations Executive.

After a distinguished war during which she twice parachuted behind enemy lines, she was recruited into the British Intelligence Services where she eventually became Director of Operations (Europe). For most of her life, however, Miss Rigby was a field officer, sometimes working as an officially accredited Foreign Office employee at a variety of foreign embassies but, more often, unattached and alone, using a wide number of completely different identities.

Informed sources within the security world on both sides of the Atlantic (and on both sides of the Iron Curtain) are unanimous in saying that, until her retirement in 1985, she was probably the most respected member of the British Intelligence Services. She was also, without question, the single most brilliant and important operational agent of the post-war years.

It seems probable, for instance, that without Rigby's infiltration of the Kennedy White House, the Cuban missile crisis might have come to a very different conclusion. Her intervention in Paris in 1968 during the so-called student revolution is universally acknowledged to have been decisive, though her attempt to prevent Gamal Abdel Nasser's seizure of the Suez Canal in 1956 has to be accounted one of her rare failures. She 'shopped' Kim Philby in 1952, but was ignored until it was – just – too late. There have been critics of the part she played in the campaign against E.O.K.A. in Cyprus, but none of her role in the Mau Mau revolt in Kenya, nor as Field Marshal Templer's 'eyes and ears' during the Malayan emergency.

Introduction

It is not overstating the case to say that at almost every crisis point in Britain's post-war history Rigby was there. No one is better qualified to tell the story of what really happened.

Like her colleagues, including Peter Wright, of whom she has a caustically low opinion, Rigby signed the Official Secrets Act and, until recently, felt herself bound by the confidentiality implicit in her employment as a Government agent. Recent events, however, have persuaded her that she is no longer bound by either of these but has a positive duty to speak out, to put the record straight and to defend the reputation of the dead.

In the present climate, however, there is no serious prospect of the Government letting her get away with any revelation of any kind whatever. The only solution is to present her story in a 'fictional' form. In order to do this most effectively, she has decided to allow some of the country's leading mystery and thriller writers to have access to her papers and memories. She is prepared to offer any co-operation necessary for them to provide the most plausible possible account of her life – but disguised as fiction and therefore exempt from Government prosecution.

Miss Rigby has negotiated the arrangement through the good offices of the Crime Writers' Association of Great Britain, to which practically all British writers dealing in espionage and intelligence matters belong. She has delegated the editing of the book to the present Chairman of the Association, Tim Heald.

Each writer will be invited to write about a particular episode in Rigby's life, allowing enough artistic licence to protect all concerned from the grasp of Her Majesty's Government and the courts.

I am happy to say that the response was enthusiastic though you'll see, as you read the book, that one or two of the incidents I mention above are not covered, whereas others are. For example, when Rigby and James Leasor started working on their chapter, it soon emerged that Jimmy knew a fair bit about the mysterious disappearance of Commander Crabb in Portsmouth harbour during the visit of Bulganin and Khrushchev in the Fifties. As Rigby was crucially involved, it seemed more appropriate for them to work on that rather than the Hungarian Revolution, as I'd originally intended.

Similarly, when she told John Ehrlichman about herself and Henry Kissinger at the time of Nixon's great China initiative, it seemed more appropriate to deal with this rather than Watergate, in which she only played a peripheral role. It's interesting, incidentally, that although Ehrlichman was a key part of Nixon's White House, he had never even heard of Rigby until he got my first letter!

For security reasons none of the writers actually met Rigby and it was I who acted as go-between. Every so often I would drive down to the little cottage with a briefcase of written notes and requests, as well as tape recordings. Rigby would answer them in whatever way seemed appropriate and then, when she was ready, I would go down, collect the material and direct it to the various writers. Not ideal, but it worked well. Of course, the writers supplemented what Rigby had to tell them from their own knowledge and experience, but in all important respects the stories are hers. Each writer has filtered and filleted the material so that it reads like an entirely original piece of their own fiction. That was always what Rigby and I intended.

At the time of writing I've had no interference from the Security Services or Government in any shape or form. I've lunched with my friend the Brigadier from time to time, and occasionally he looks up from his good plain clubman's food and says a shade quizzically, "I hear you were down at Aunt Dot's last weekend?" But he never spells things out. He tends not to when it's important. "Some things better left unsaid, old boy!"

It may be that after *Spycatcher* they have decided, after all, that making a fuss about this kind of revelation is counter-productive. Besides, what Rigby has to say redounds entirely, well, almost entirely, to the credit of the British Government. You can't doubt her patriotism. At least, I can't.

Anyway, that explains all the background that's needed. And it's as much of the story as I'm prepared to tell for now. For the rest of it, read on and judge for yourself.

T. V. H.
Richmond-upon-Thames
February 1989

H. R. F. Keating

IN DISGRACE

Rigby's mother, Mayotte, had a difficult labour, not improved by her husband Harry's absence on the frontier where he was commanding a detachment of Waziristan militia.

The Colonel seems to have been away a lot during Rigby's childhood and her exotic mother was often otherwise engaged as well. The most constant influences in her early childhood were, therefore, a series of ayahs and bearers, who had some difficulty in checking her tomboyish excesses. She was an athletic child and at the age of nine was taught cricket by the great Ranjitsinjhi, Jam Sahib of Nawanagar, who also took her tiger shooting and presented her with a gold-tooled Purdey sixteen-bore shotgun for her twelfth birthday.

Shortly afterwards she was sent, P. & O., to England to stay with the family of her Aunt Lavinia in Tunbridge Wells. Lavinia was married to Ernest Browning, a sub-editor on *The Times* where he had been a colleague of the novelist Graham Greene, a frequent visitor to the house who was later to be one of the main reasons for Rigby joining the Intelligence Services. A series of more or less famous boarding schools failed to contain her. She was consistently good at games (especially cricket and lacrosse), languages (living but not dead) and personal relationships (with contemporaries of both sexes, but not with her teachers).

The last straw, at Cheltenham Ladies' College, was when Rigby was seventeen years old. H. R. F. Keating, who not only shares Rigby's father's initials, but also his intimate knowledge of the Indian sub-continent, takes up the story as Dorothy and her friend Camilla Trefusis return to India in disgrace.

"'When in disgrace with fortune and men's eyes',"
Rigby said, "'I all alone beweep my outcast
state'."

Camilla looked at her. The half-melted lumps of ice in the
tin tub between their seats in the grunting and shuddering
train swished to and fro, clinking faintly.

"Beweep?" Camilla said. "For gosh sake. I mean, I know
we're in disgrace and all that, but you don't have to utter in
quite that way, do you?"

"Idiot," Rigby replied. "It's Shakespeare. Sonnet 29."

"Oh, Shakespeare. Honestly, Dottie."

Rigby's eyes froze.

"I've warned you, Trefusis. I'm never to be called Dottie.
And I'm never to be called Dorothy. And, even more, I'm
never to be called Mayotte."

"No, Rigby darling. I'm sorry. Sorry. Cross my heart."

There was a real note of alarm in Camilla Trefusis' voice.
In their earliest days at Cheltenham Ladies' College (before
the disgrace) she had learnt, painfully, what it was to cross
the girl who preferred to be called by her surname alone.

A short silence fell. The train, the Kalka Mail, chuntered
slowly onwards towards Simla, Hot Weather capital of the
British Raj. Outside its triple windows – glass to ward off the
quiveringly hot air, mesh that will admit the cooler evening
air but not, in theory, insects and finally stout slats to keep
out thieves and beggars – the dusty plains beneath the Hills
passed slowly by. Occasionally mud-hut villages were to be
seen, scarcely distinguishable from the ground around them.
Then there might be a burnt-dry field of sugar-cane or a
sudden glaring yellow patch of mustard, its oil highly prized.
But there was nothing really to catch the eye, only the far
immensity of the land ruled over by a few thousand Britons,
the cream of them up now in the cool heights of Simla,
clustering round the august presence of His Excellency the
Viceroy.

"Anyhow," Camilla said at last, "it's pretty grim of you to know any Shakespeare, Rigby, let alone what number of sonnet it is. Even if we are, well, actually in disgrace."

"Daddy's mad on the Sonnets," Rigby answered equably. "Every time I come out here for the hols I get snippets. You can't help picking them up."

"You couldn't help it, Rigby. With your brain. With me they'd go in one ear and out the other. I mean, what use are they?"

Rigby gave the small secret smile that over the years had deeply bothered her best friend.

"Use?" she said. "Perhaps you'll see."

Camilla knew it would be no good trying to extract from Rigby what it was she had been thinking. You couldn't extract anything from old Rigby, she said to herself, if she didn't want to tell you. Not even under the most frightful torture.

"But listen, Rigby," she said, "it is going to be all right in the end, isn't it? I mean, for us? We won't be stopped going to dances or anything, will we? Or not for ever? Otherwise it won't really have been worth me coming all this way to stay with your parents. Not if your mother's going to take a fearfully dim view."

"Mummy's not like that," Rigby answered. "She's half French for one thing. I get that beastly Mayotte from her. And then she had a pretty good time before she met Daddy. Hearts broken all round. She danced with Lifar, you know."

"Yes. Super."

"No, it's Daddy who's going to be difficult. I mean, he's terrifically hot on discipline. If any subaltern under him's caught poodle-faking he's on his way to the Frontier p.d.q."

"But . . . But if there aren't any poodle-fakers about . . . Well, what sort of a time are we going to have? I mean, one does like to have a bit of a swarm of, well, men around one."

Rigby smiled enigmatically.

"We'll see," she said. "After I've been hauled up in front of Colonel H. R. F. Rigby, D.S.O., M.C."

"Damn it, Dorothy," Colonel Rigby said, "is this true? What the damn headmistress told me in her letter?"

"Well, Daddy, it depends what she did tell you, doesn't it? I haven't seen the damn – the letter, you know."

The Colonel looked down for a moment at the toes of his gleamingly polished riding-boots.

"Hm. Yes. Well . . . Damn it, the woman says that you and your precious friend Camilla Trefusis sneaked out of your dormitory at night and were reported to have been seen at an hotel in Cheltenham in the company of two Guards officers."

"Well, yes then, Daddy. That's true enough."

"By God, girl, you've been guilty of damn disgraceful behaviour and I'm dashed if you get away with it, you and Camilla."

"Well, what can I say? 'Alas! 'tis true I have gone here and there, and made myself a motley to the view, gor'd mine own thoughts, sold cheap what is most dear . . .'"

Again the Colonel regarded his boots. "A motley to the view, eh? Sonnet 110. Yes, well . . . In any case, never thought much of that damn headmistress of yours. Not since she took you off the cricket team because you bowled too fast. Unfair to other schools, what tommyrot."

Colonel Rigby coughed.

"Well, look here, my girl," he said, "promise to be decently discreet for the future, eh? And we'll say no more about it. Hrumph."

"And the same goes for Camilla, Daddy?"

"Suppose so. Though I don't think the girl's got a tithe of your sense, my dear. But there it is. Can't confine one to barracks and let the other go scot-free, eh? Oh, damn it, now I'm starting another damn nose bleed. Bloody Simla air."

And Colonel Rigby was reduced to temporary impotence.

But, perhaps because Camilla Trefusis had not been 'up before the Colonel' in person, once granted the freedom of Simla society she showed little sign of being 'decently discreet'. Which was what led to the trouble, and to Rigby's opening brush with the Great Game.

The game that was first to the fore, however, was not the one played for often deadly stakes (and always out of the sight of simple John Citizen back at Home reading the *Morning Post*) between the imperial might of the Indian Empire and the Russian steamroller ever poised beyond the towering

Himalayas. It was instead the more rules-regulated, though hardly less important, game of cricket. Cricket was very much the talk of the town in Simla at that time. Because a challenge had been issued. A daring, even an impudent, challenge.

His Highness Maharajahdhiraj Raj Rajeshwar Major Sri Sri Sri Sahib Bahadur Mahapundit Mahasurma Sir George Singhji, Maharajah of Bhopore, had gathered together his own team and had challenged any Eleven the Viceroy himself might choose, provided always, of course, that his team consisted of gentlemen and not players, whether professionals imported from England or others in India. The challenge had been seen at once for what it was: an assertion on behalf of Native India against the Paramount Power itself.

So, a lot hung upon it. However, all should be well, it was generally considered. The Viceroy, or those who advised him, had got together the makings of a very decent team. It was strong in batting, with Colonel Rigby one of the pillars in that department, and it was also unexpectedly strong in bowling. There had recently been posted to the Viceroy's staff, entirely by coincidence, a young I.C.S. officer, Lance Vulliamy who, in his final year at Haileybury, had been responsible for skittling out most of the Eton XI and the whole of Harrow's. Now he had been recruited, in conditions of some secrecy, to the Viceroy's team, a concealed weapon of which much was hoped.

Nor were the hopes that hung on this newcomer seriously diminished in the following weeks when Camilla Trefusis was observed to be hanging on his ever ready arm. Flirtation was the very air of Simla, especially by night when the stars shone with more glowing brilliance than ever they do in northern climes and the moon seemed larger, more lustrous, more apt to bathe man and woman in soft, enhancing light. And so it was thought right by everyone, almost without exception, that pretty Camilla Trefusis should be escorted here, there and everywhere by the darkly handsome Lance Vulliamy.

Simla gossips, ever ready with disparaging talk of 'the Fishing Fleet' when unmarried girls arrived from England and quick with a sharp 'poodle-faking' when young men paid them attention, appeared to be content with the possibility even of an engagement. There was, in fact, only one person not in favour of a formal arrangement: Lance Vulliamy.

Lance, from the first moment he had been introduced to Camilla and Rigby, had made it plain that Rigby was the one who really attracted him. Rigby, however – for reasons she could not quite put her finger on – was not attracted to Lance, though he was, in a different style, every bit as handsomely masculine as the young Guards' officer – on account of whom she had been expelled. Not that her rebuff had left Lance forlorn. If he was unable to secure Rigby, he was happy enough to take what pleasure there was to be had with Camilla.

And Camilla, 'disgrace' all too easily forgotten, was more than willing to give Lance all the pleasure he asked for. Not with him simply the romantic hand-in-hand stroll along the shaded length of Simla's Lovers' Lane. Hardly more than a week had passed before it was the slippery slopes of the *khuds* – the literally slippery slopes of Simla's precipitous ravines – with all that the seclusion of the pathless, wild and shading deodar trees could lead to. All, too, without the smallest hint of any permanency, even to the extent of one of those long engagements, product of the discouragement by both the Indian Civil Service and the Indian Army, of officers marrying under the age of thirty.

Yet Camilla's willingness was apparently not enough for Lance Vulliamy. Nor were his energies, it seemed, depleted by frequent, semi-secret practices at the nets where batsman after batsman succumbed to his deadly turn of speed. He still had eyes, meaningful eyes if ever there were such, for Rigby.

So it was that one afternoon – it was at a croquet party at Elysium House, the official residence of the Bishop of Simla – Lance contrived, with discreet cunning, a private word with Rigby.

By letting his ball lie in such a position that Camilla could hardly fail to send it shooting across the smooth lawn, deep into a herbaceous border in all its glory of massed pinks and poppies, sweet peas and fuchsias, and thus giving her the inescapable task of running through hoop after hoop herself, he was able to escort Rigby into the seclusion of the towering rhododendron shrubbery. There he was charmingly persuasive. And Rigby had almost overcome her unaccountable reluctance and agreed to a midnight stroll that evening during the ball to be given by the Governor of the Punjab and his lady at Barnes Court, when something Lance said, almost by chance, brought her up short.

It came about in the simplest of ways. Rigby, to gain a little time before finally consenting to that stroll, said something about the Bishop's garden and how wonderfully English it was.

"Oh, come on," Lance said. "You'll be blathering away about Shakespeare and the white cliffs of Dover in a moment."

He nearly learnt then, as Camilla had discovered in her first term at Cheltenham, what Rigby, when roused by any aspersion on her native land, could do in the way of physical violence. But something made her bite back the sharp retort that would have preceded the physical lesson. Afterwards she worked out what that something was, though at the time she had checked herself it had been out of pure instinct. What her instinct had told her, more quickly and more persuasively than any rationalising, was that the gibe on Lance Vulliamy's lips came not from the man she and Camilla and everyone in Simla knew, and even admired. It came from a hidden Lance, who must be a very different sort of person from the outward one.

And she decided there and then that the hidden Lance Vulliamy needed to be explored. There was something wrong there and Lance, after all, was in the confidential employ of the Viceroy whose task it was to rule the immense dowry of British India. To rule over it, and to protect it. And Lance – she knew from the gup that ran through all Simla – was concerned with matters of security.

So she said, instead, that, yes, she would take a stroll at midnight from the Governor's ball. She would try to teach Lance to appreciate the pretty flowers there, dark though it would be.

She planned next day how, during the midnight adventure, she could lead her suspect on and discover enough about him to learn whether the disquiet she had felt was justified.

In the event, however, she found Lance a tougher proposition than she had anticipated. True, she succeeded in learning a certain amount. How his parents had been in India all through his boyhood and how, because his father had been one of 'the twice-born', as members of the Indian Civil Service were called in imitation of the Brahmins they ruled over, he himself had been sent Home to school. There he had spent every holiday with a clergyman cousin of his mother's who was unmarried, frugal and moralistic.

That knowledge gave Rigby an inkling of why, perhaps, someone brought up to be a pillar of the Empire and all that was good in it could have become soured and secretly vindictive. But, press as she might, she got not an inch deeper into the psyche of the man at her side.

Only one other, possibly telling, fact was let slip during their walk in the soft darkness of the Simla night. Rigby learnt that Lance was a great student of languages, busy acquiring one more to add to the French, the German, the Spanish, the Urdu and the Punjabi already under his belt. But when, all innocently, she asked what language this was Lance had laughed and said only, "When I can speak it to perfection I'll come and astonish you".

She had also learnt that, duties at Viceregal Lodge not being all that onerous, Lance spent every afternoon alone in the bachelors' 'chummery' he shared, working at his hobby. So she made it her business, on the afternoon after the ball, to drop in unannounced with the object of catching a glimpse of whatever language book Lance was studying.

He was considerably put out when Rigby, jumping from her rickshaw, knocked vigorously at the door of Honeysuckle Cottage, as the chummery was called. The look of alarm on his face – hastily converted into a not unlascivious smile of welcome – gave her a good deal of inward pleasure. But, look casually about her as she might, she failed to spot any sign of what Lance had been working at. If he had had any book in front of him, he had succeeded in hiding it before, in the absence of any servant, he had come himself to the door. Yet, after all, was that not in itself a suspicious circumstance?

But she did not have long to weigh the possibilities. She was too busy fighting off Lance's exploring hands. Or, conceiving it on second thoughts her duty, co-operating with those hands.

Would Daddy think I ought to be in disgrace again? she caught herself wondering. Or would he feel I am doing the right thing?

A little later she realised that Lance was feigning sleep.

Why is this? she thought. The answer came at once. He wants me to fall asleep too, as I have in fact been on the point of doing these last five minutes. And if he wants me to fall asleep, it is because he plans to do something he doesn't want me to know about.

She produced the lightest and most delicate of snores.

At least, she thought, I can feign sleep better than Mr Vulliamy, even if so far he has outwitted me.

In a few minutes she had her reward. She sensed her partner slide carefully from the sofa at her side. She heard him, still keeping her eyelids lightly closed, put on again such clothes as he had thrown off. She heard him go into the study and make a slight sound in looking out to see that no one was about. And then she heard him leave.

She was up in hardly more than a minute. Then she, in her turn, was looking out. But it was to see in which direction Lance Vulliamy was hurrying.

She did not find it difficult to follow him. She knew that this was no tribute to her skill as a shadower, an art she had practised out of sheer fun from the time she was ten years old, as Lance was plainly in too much of a hurry even to think that he might be followed. And why, she wondered, was he carrying that bundle? It looked like two or three garments rolled up together, something that certainly ought to have been given to a servant.

His destination, too, somewhat surprised her. Barely ten minutes after setting out, he halted in front of a tin-roofed cottage rejoicing in the name of 'The Grotto'. Why should he be going there? It seemed to be no more than one of the many places rented to Simla visitors during the Season.

She was yet more surprised to see her quarry, once he had carefully examined the lie of the land, go round to the back of the house to where there was only the servants' quarter. But she worked out rapidly that, if she crept along beside the cottage's compound and shinned up a pine tree, she would in all likelihood see just what it was Lance Vulliamy was up to. And one thing was certain now: he was up to no good.

She was yet luckier than she had expected. From her vantage point, lying like a leopard along a thick branch of the spreading pine, she was able to see Lance standing outside one of the huts of the quarter talking to a man she recognised from the heavy brass iron he held in one hand, its top glowing with the hot charcoal inside, as a *dhobi*. The fellow was evidently in the middle of doing the household ironing and Lance, after a moment, handed him the bundle he had been carrying.

Rigby felt a jolt of disappointment. Was it just, she asked herself, that Lance was getting his *dhobi*-ing done on the cheap by someone else's servant?

As he set off again in the direction of his chummery – what would he think when he found her gone? – she almost accepted this prosaic explanation. But then better reasoning prevailed. No one would have taken such precautions as Lance had done just to deliver some laundry, however extraordinary by Simla standards carrying one's own dirty washing might be. No, the *dhobi* to whom Lance had given the bundle must be worth watching, and to hell with any thoughts of racing back to Honeysuckle Cottage before Lance, strolling on his way, could get there.

But the *dhobi* did not seem to be behaving in a manner any different from her parents' *dhobi* or any other of the dozens she had watched during the times she had been in India. He had left the door of his hut open and she was able to see him quietly wielding his heavy iron.

No doubt, in a moment, she thought, he will do what all *dhobis* seem to do, despite stern admonitions to the contrary from many a memsahib. He will take a swig of the rice-water starch in that bowl beside him and then spew it out in a fine spray on to that shirt. The custom was beyond curing.

But then, to her surprise at first, this *dhobi* behaved out of character. He sprinkled his rice starch by dipping his fingers in the bowl and ineffectually shaking them. That shirt, Rigby thought, is not going to be anything like as evenly starched as it should be. So why is the fellow doing his starching like that?

In the next instant she had a likely answer.

The *dhobi*, well disguised though he was, could not be a real *dhobi*. He must be, in fact, a link in a chain leading from Lance Vulliamy, privy to viceregal secrets, to – to where?

Then she got confirmation of her hypothesis. The '*dhobi*', his ironing finished, went to the bundle Lance had brought, rapidly searched through it and extracted a small roll of papers from a pair of white drill trousers. The fellow read the contents hastily, tucked the roll into the top of the loincloth that was his sole garment and prepared to leave.

Rigby slid from the pine's concealing branch.

Now she knew she would need every bit of the craft she had begun to learn as a slip of a schoolgirl if she was to follow this man without being seen. He had read the papers Lance had delivered to him at lightning speed. He was plainly a thoroughly literate individual, and a clever one. If it had not been for his disdaining to spit starch on to that shirt, she herself would never have taken him for anything else than the washerman he appeared to be.

Now he was slipping expertly along the crowded Mall, keeping well clear of the roadway with its English sahibs on high-mettled horses, its memsahibs on neat ponies and its occasional rickshaw with four trotting, sweating *jampanis* in smart, if sometimes stained, uniforms bearing some heavy-weight lady to bridge or afternoon tea. It was all Rigby could do, forced from time to time to exchange a wave or a smile with an acquaintance, to keep him in sight.

But at last he slipped off from the road down a path leading to the leafy depths of a *khud*. It went, Rigby knew from one of Camilla's ecstatic descriptions, to a waterfall far from the customary haunts of Simla walkers and inaccessible by any other means of transport. Following the figure of the disguised *dhobi* in this changed setting, Rigby tossed away the wide, white hat that protected her complexion as Miss Rigby, the Colonel's daughter and Simla socialite. One glance backwards from the quarry and she would be betrayed. Nor was her frock as dull-toned as she would like. She stooped, seized a clump of fern by the pathside, tore it away from its roots and held it in front of herself.

Not a moment too soon. The false *dhobi* came to a stop. Rigby dived for cover. The *dhobi* turned and gave the path behind him a long and careful scrutiny. Rigby, who had managed to push herself halfway behind the trunk of a massive deodar, stood absolutely still, her bunch of fern drooping beside her.

It seemed she had been quick enough. Her quarry turned

back and walked on for a few yards. Then, just before Rigby, with every precaution, prepared to follow once more, he slipped from the path and scrambled up the steep side of the *khud*, pushing his way through the thick vegetation. Reckoning he was making too much noise now to hear other sounds, Rigby abandoned the path in her turn. She made her way as swiftly as she could up the side of the ravine till she could look at her quarry from above.

She had only just taken up a position behind a sprawling wild rhododendron bush, panting from her exertion and aware at the edge of her mind that one good afternoon frock was ruined beyond repair, when she saw the *dhobi* carefully part a thick tangle of underbrush. Then he simply disappeared.

At once Rigby began to squeeze and worm her way along the steep bank. The distance she had to cover – it was not much more than a hundred yards – took her a considerable time, conscious as she was of the need now for maximum quietness.

At last she reached a point only just above where she had seen the *dhobi* vanish. And when she looked down she saw at once what had happened. There was a narrow cave or cleft in the side of the *khud* and he had stepped into it. But it must be, she realised suddenly, a pretty shallow affair, because she could distinctly hear coming from it a familiar sound. The sound of Morse code, the Morse she had learnt even before the age of ten.

And that little bleeping sound – Rigby felt the thrill of a hunter with a tiger in the sights – was in Russian. It was the Russian Rigby had taught herself during Miss Spinkerton's utterly boring French classes, compulsorily attended although the French she had learnt at her mother's knee was a sight more idiomatic than Miss Spinkerton's and twice as well pronounced.

But then Rigby realised that her situation was not quite that of the hunter up on a tree-perched *machan* platform with the tiger in the line of a rifle's sights. She had nothing with which to stop her prey. And stopped he must be. He was sending by wireless, beyond doubt, information which Lance Vulliamy – he must be contaminated with communism: it all fitted – had extracted from the Viceroy's secret files. Every second this *dhobi* tapped his Morse key, the secrets of the British Raj were darting into Russian ears.

Yet how to stop him? She could try direct attack. But it was hardly likely to be successful. For one thing the fellow – he must be a Russian: in her mind she named him Oleg – was young and looked pretty powerful, and for another, merely getting at him in that narrow cave would put her at a tremendous disadvantage. But she must not let that signalling go on one second more than she could help.

Then an idea came to her.

She jumped to her feet and banged down the side of the *khud* taking no care to be silent. Then, turning, she let out a loud halloo and clutched hard at the nearest slim tree-trunk.

As she had expected her Oleg appeared instantly at the mouth of the cave.

"*Achcha*," she said in loud, deliberately crudely pronounced Hindustani. "I thought I saw someone in the bushes there. Now, my man, I have taken a tumble and hurt my ankle. Run as fast as you can to the Mall and ask the first sahib you see to come and help me."

'Oleg' stood looking at her. From the very way he was holding himself she guessed he had at least a strong suspicion that she was not all she seemed. Would he act on it? Would he have taken in her dishevelled appearance enough to realise it came from no simple fall? And then . . . ? Then what would he do? Could he have a pistol under that loincloth? Unlikely, but not impossible.

"*Jaldi, jaldi*," she said imperiously. "Do you not see Missy sahib is hurt? Hurry. Run. Run."

And 'Oleg' lost his nerve.

"*Ji haan*, memsahib," he muttered, and left at a trot.

It took Rigby only some ten minutes of active work, as soon as she was certain 'Oleg' was well out of hearing, to wreck his wireless for ever. But, as she made her way back to her parents' house, taking good care the man she had faced and outfaced was not lying in wait for her after all, she realised her bout of happy destructiveness could not be the end of the business.

No doubt 'Oleg' would give no message to any sahib riding along the Mall. He was bound to think it likely she had looked into his cave and seen his wireless set, and he would be off

In Disgrace

now across the Hills heading for the Russian border. But that hardly mattered. His work had been brought to a halt.

What was probably going to be a good deal more tricky, she thought, was bringing to an end the activities of Lance Vulliamy. Because it was quite possible her father would think that the Vulliamy part of her story was no more than the romantic nonsense of the schoolgirl she still would be, had she not been asked to leave in disgrace. And even if she could convince her father, would those in highest authority believe it all, believe a mere Colonel – even if he was a good enough bat to be a mainstay of the Viceroy's XI? After all, he would have to include in his report the fact that sweet-seventeen Dorothy Mayotte Rigby had deliberately allowed someone she thought might be up to no good to sleep with her, so as to worm his secret from him. Would His Excellency credit that? Would he even want to?

Yet, in the event, everything went smoothly. Rigby, bracing herself a little, told her father what had happened. Everything that had happened. And Colonel Rigby did no more than raise one eyebrow at certain parts of the narrative. But when she had finished, instead of worrying about how he could put the affair to those in highest authority, he simply said, "My dear, there's a chap just come up to Simla I think ought to hear your story. Old school friend of mine, as a matter of fact."

So, an hour later Rigby was introduced to a Mr Denham. "In India to look at a few miniature paintings. Pahari School, you know," he said, while the servants were still present. But as soon as they had left he turned to Rigby.

"And I'd like to hear your tale, young lady," he said. "Every detail, if you don't mind."

When Rigby had told it to him, every detail, something which she found unexpectedly easy because of the way he listened, he said one thing before he left.

"Have to see young Vulliamy is shipped off Home. This evening, I rather think."

He must have seen the look of surprise on Rigby's face then, because he gave her a little crooked smile.

"We'd hardly want his activities to become the gossip of all India, would we, my dear?" he said.

"No," said Rigby. "No, I suppose that wouldn't be a very good idea."

But then an awful thought occurred to her.

"There's only one thing though," she blurted out, turning to her father.

"Yes, my dear?"

"The Viceroy's XI. You'll never beat Bhopore's team without a bowler with a decent turn of speed."

Colonel Rigby looked grave. He explained to his old schoolfriend just what was at stake in the seemingly friendly match due to start next day. Mr Denham nodded, and even he looked a little perturbed. Rigby began to wonder whether Lance Vulliamy was going to get a short reprieve and how she would feel seeing him play, as it were, for England.

But an idea came to her. An idea as daring, in its way, as learning the covert Communist's secrets in his bed.

"Daddy," she said, "do you think I've got a cousin? A boy called Donald? Donny? Who arrived in Simla this evening, and who's not bad as a pace bowler?"

The Colonel looked momentarily bewildered.

"About as fast as your darling daughter?" Rigby said.

For a long moment the Colonel pondered. Then he spoke.

"Do you think you could do it?" he said.

"I'll have a bloody good try," Rigby answered.

It remains only to record that the Viceroy's XI, despite the unfortunate absence of Mr Lance Vulliamy on urgent official business, won the match against the Maharajah of Bhopore's XI, by one wicket. Young Donny Rigby – his appearance was the first time Rigby worked in disguise – took six wickets for forty-nine, sending that of the Maharajah himself spectacularly flying. And it was she – or rather he – when at the tensest moment of the game Colonel H. R. F. Rigby had to retire (nose-bleed) who scored the necessary single to settle the matter.

After that Rigby was never in disgrace again.

———

This was not the last time that Rigby managed to play more than one game at a time, though I think Harry Keating is inclined to credit her with an unlikely degree of sexual precociousness. The escapade which led to her expulsion from Cheltenham would have been considered almost charmingly naïve and innocent today. When I quizzed her later about her relationship with Vulliamy she admitted that she 'led him on' but there was no question of her 'going all the way'.

Camilla was another matter altogether.

I only mention this to allay any suggestion that Rigby was a flibbertigibbet. She always had a healthy interest in attractive men and there were times, later, when she may have used her sex as a professional weapon. But always with discretion, even fastidiousness. She found Camilla's comparatively indiscriminating sexuality amusing or upsetting, according to her mood.

Poor Vulliamy, by the way, never made it back to England, but disappeared overboard in a force ten gale in the Bay of Biscay.

The girls stayed on in Simla for the remainder of the Indian summer, then accompanied the viceregal court back to Delhi where Camilla's increasingly risqué behaviour began seriously to embarrass Rigby's parents. Rigby herself was anxious to get back to Europe where, she felt, exciting things were afoot. Deeply shocked by the Fascist bombing of Guernica, she toyed with the idea of joining the International Brigades in the Spanish Civil War. She also tried to persuade her father to let her help him and the young John Masters put down the violent revolt of the Fakir of Ipi.

Colonel Harry, alarmed by his daughter's restlessness and her friend's scandalous behaviour, decided, with his wife's rather bored consent, to pack the pair of them off to England and the safety of Tunbridge Wells. Some sort of finishing school seemed the answer.

Peter Lovesey

THE MUNICH POSTURE

Tunbridge Wells between the wars was not – as anyone who has read that magical memoir, *Still Life*, by my friend and former tutor Richard Cobb, will know – quite as safe as it sounds. Indeed Rigby remembers Richard, who was a few years older than she, as a mildly sinister and solitary youth who once took a pot-shot at her with his air-gun. Characteristically he missed and has no recollection either of the incident or, more unexpectedly, of Rigby.

Among the surprising number of foreigners who came to that ancient English watering place was a German family called Schnabel, one of whom, Countess Schnabel, ran a finishing school in Munich. When this fact came to light during one of Miss Meade-Waldo's bridge sessions in her large house on Grove Hill, Lavinia Browning wondered if the school might be the answer to her prayers. Her niece Dorothy was proving more than a little 'tiresome' and as for her friend, Camilla . . .

True, the war clouds were gathering. Air Raid Practice had started, even in Tunbridge Wells, but Lord Halifax had been to see Herr Hitler and the Brownings were convinced that alarmist talk was mere warmongering. Nice Mr Chamberlain who had just taken over as Prime Minister would sort everything out. Ernest listened to the leader writers at *The Times*, and they *knew*! Besides, the Schnabels were good Germans *and* titled.

Rigby, for her part, had a very good idea of what was going on in the Fatherland and she was anxious to see for herself. Camilla, who showed signs of being a bit of a Unity Mitford and thought jackboots incredibly sexy, would go along for the ride. Both girls thought it might be rather jolly.

Adolf Hitler stared across the restaurant.

Camilla, blonde, eighteen and English, succeeded in saying without moving her lips, "He's looking, he's looking, he's looking!"

"For a waiter, not you, dear," Dorothy Rigby remarked. Rigby was, at this formative stage in her life, less flagrantly sexy than her friend Camilla. Rigby's appeal was subversive and ultimately more devastating, as the business with young Vulliamy in Simla had begun to suggest. Here in Munich, in September 1938, they had made a fresh start – with no questions asked – at the Countess Schnabel's Finishing School. Rigby's lightly permed brown hair was cut in a modest style approved by the Countess, so that a small expanse of neck showed above the collar of one's white lawn blouse.

It was Camilla who had dragged her into the Osteria Bavaria. Their table was chosen for the unimpeded view it afforded of the Führer and his party, or rather, the view it afforded the Führer of Camilla. Flamboyant Camilla with her blue Nordic eyes, her cupid's-bow pout and her bosom plumped up with all the silk stockings she owned. She was resolved to enslave the most powerful man in Europe. It wasn't impossible. It had been done by Unity Mitford, the Oxfordshire girl turned Rhine-maiden, who had staunchly occupied this same chair in Hitler's favourite restaurant through the winter of 1935 until she had been called to his table. From that time Unity had been included on the guest lists for Hitler's mountain retreat at Obersalzberg, and for the Nuremberg rallies, the Bayreuth Festival and the Olympic Games.

Until this moment, Camilla had unaccountably failed to emulate Miss Mitford, though she was just as dedicated, just as blonde and, by her own assessment, prettier.

Until this moment.

"Oh, my hat! He's talking to his Adjutant. He's pointing to this table. To *me*!"

"Calm down, Cami."

Camilla gripped the edge of the tablecloth. "God, this is it! The Adjutant is coming over."

Undeniably he was. Young, clean-shaven, cool as a brimming *Bierglas*, he saluted and announced, "Ladies, the Führer has commanded me to present his compliments . . ."

"So gracious!" piped up Camilla in her best German.

". . . and states that he would prefer to finish his lunch without being stared at." Another click of the heels, an about-turn, and that was that.

"I'm dead," said Camilla, after a stunned silence. "How absolutely ghastly! Let's leave at once."

"Certainly not," said Rigby. "He wants to be ignored, so we'll ignore him. More coffee?"

"Is that wise?"

They remained at their table until Hitler rose to leave. For a moment he glared in their direction, his blue eyes glittering. Then he slapped his glove against the sleeve of his raincoat and marched out.

"Odious little fart," said Rigby.

"I hope Mr Chamberlain spits in his eye," said Camilla.

"He'll have Mr Chamberlain on toast."

Outside, in Schellingstrasse, heels clicked and the young Adjutant saluted again. "Excuse me, ladies. I have another message to convey from the Führer."

"We don't wish to hear it," said Rigby. "Come on, Camilla. We're not standing here to be insulted."

Camilla was rooted to the pavement. "A message from him?"

"This is difficult. The message is for the dark-haired young lady."

"*Me?*" said Rigby.

Camilla gave a sudden sob and covered her eyes.

"The Führer will dine at Boettner's this evening. He has arranged for you to join his party. Fräulein er . . . ?"

"I am not one of your Fräuleins. I am *Miss* Rigby."

"From England?" The Adjutant frowned and reddened.

Rigby said off-handedly, "Actually I was born in Madras. India, you know. I expect he thought I was a starry-eyed little Nazi wench. Will you be there?"

He stared back. "I beg your pardon?"

"I said, will you be there?"

"As it happens, no."

"A night off?"

"Well, yes."

"How convenient. You can tell Herr Hitler that when you found out the young lady's dusky origins, you did what any quick-witted officer of the Reich would have done – arranged to take her to dinner yourself, thus saving your Führer from sullying his snow-white principles."

His eyes widened. First they registered shock, then curiosity, then capitulation.

His name was Manfred, he told her in the candlelight at Walterspiel that evening. "It's strange," he said. "I took you for an English girl."

"Oh, I am, by blood. Daddy served in India with the Army."

He frowned. "Then why did you decline the Führer's invitation – such an honour?"

"I didn't care for the way it was communicated, as if I was biddable, to put it mildly."

"But I think your friend was biddable."

She laughed. "Still is. She's stopped talking to me. She can't understand why she was overlooked. Frankly, neither can I. Camilla has the fair hair and blue eyes, and much more."

He leaned forward confidentially. "With respect, Miss Rigby, I think you misunderstood the Führer's motives. He is not in want of female companionship. There is a lady at Obersalzberg."

"Eva Braun?"

"Ah. You are well informed."

"Then why did he ask me to dinner?"

Manfred took a sip of wine. "Some years ago there was a girl, his stepniece actually, who died. He was very devoted to her, more than an uncle should be. No, I mean nothing improper. Like a father. She was eighteen when she came to Munich. He took her about, to picnics, the opera, paid for singing lessons, rented a room for her."

"What was her name?"

"Angela Raubal, known to him as Geli. She looked remarkably like you. The dark hair, the cheekbones, the whole shape of your face, your beautiful hazel eyes. This, I think, is why he wanted to meet you."

"I see. And you say she died?"

"Shot herself with the Führer's own gun." He paused. "No one knows why. I think perhaps it was best that he did not meet you. But please understand that it was not because you are English. He likes the English. The Führer and Mr Chamberlain are much in agreement, wanting to keep the peace in Europe."

"Neville Chamberlain does, without a doubt," said Rigby with a quick, ironic smile.

"So does the Führer."

"Yes – if the other powers allow him to march into Czechoslovakia."

He frowned. "You speak of international politics – a young girl?"

Rigby decided to take the remark as a compliment. She was a great reader of newspapers. She'd often been told that comments on international affairs came oddly from a girl of her age, but she wasn't perturbed. Crisply she analysed the crisis over Germany's claims to the Sudeten regions of Czechoslovakia and the dangerous effects of Hitler's *Lebensraum* policy. Manfred used the stock German argument that something had to be done about the crushing restrictions imposed at Versailles after the Great War.

"It won't wash," commented Rigby. "It's transparently clear that Czechoslovakia is next on your Führer's list. God help us all."

He gave the grin of someone with inside information. "But it will not lead to war."

She said, "You're very close to him, aren't you?"

He nodded.

"He thinks he has the measure of our Prime Minister, doesn't he?"

He gave a shrug that didn't deny it.

Patriotically casting about for something in the Prime Minister's favour, she said, "You tell him that Neville Chamberlain may be almost seventy, but he forgets nothing. His memory is phenomenal."

"Is that important?"

She said, "Hitler relies on people having short memories, doesn't he?"

He said, "I think it is time we talked of something else. Shall we walk in the Englischer Garten?"

There they followed the twists of the stream among the willows until almost midnight. They sat on a bench, listening to the trickle of the water, and she allowed him to kiss her.

She murmured, "What would the Führer say about this?"

He laughed softly. "What happens tonight is nobody's business but yours and mine."

Resting her face against his shoulder, she said, "Manfred, if I were very bold and made a suggestion, would you do something to please me – something really daring?"

"What is it?"

"It's a practical joke. I need your help to make it work. It will be enormous fun."

He said, "If you wish". Then, bleakly, "I thought for a moment you were going to suggest something else".

She smiled and nestled closer. "That's not for me to suggest."

It was a measure of the priorities at the Countess Schnabel's Finishing School that the Countess herself took the deportment class. "Upright in body is upright in mind," she repeatedly informed the seventeen young ladies in her care. "Perfect posture is perfectly attainable. Cross the room once more, Camilla, if you please. *Ooh! Grotesk*! Don't rotate the hips so."

The lesson ended at noon. The Countess clapped her hands. "Before you leave, I give you a thrilling announcement. Tomorrow the school is to be honoured by a visitor, a visitor so important that I am not yet at liberty to mention his name. No finishing school in Munich has ever been so favoured. Suffice to say that you will all be perfectly groomed, immaculately dressed and silent unless spoken to."

Camilla told Rigby sourly that it was obvious who the V.I.P. was. "And I can't bear to face him when it's perfectly clear that he's coming to ogle you. I shall report sick."

So when the Countess swept into the gym at ten next morning and triumphantly announced the Führer, only sixteen girls were present to say, "*Heil*, Hitler!" and salute.

Rigby had no eyes for the strutting figure in the black mackintosh with his Chaplin moustache. She gazed steadily at Manfred, standing a pace to the rear, feet astride and arms folded, wearing his brown uniform with the swastika armband. He appeared twice as handsome this morning. He had more than proved his daring. This stunt was incredibly reckless and he had engineered it himself, simply because she had asked him.

She rather thought she had fallen in love.

"Dorothy, I hope you are paying attention," said the Countess.

The timetable had been adjusted. Deportment again. A chance for the Countess to make an impression. For twenty minutes the class went through its paces, breathing, balancing and walking gracefully, all without a noticeable hitch. Then the Countess turned, curtsied, and asked if the Führer would graciously consent to present the posture medal to the girl with best deportment, and certificates to the others.

It was a pleasing little ceremony. Of course, the Countess nominated her favourite for the medal, an obnoxious girl called Dagmar who was one of the Hitler Youth, but everyone else stepped forward in turn for a certificate.

His handshake was damp and flabby, Rigby noted as she collected hers.

At Manfred's suggestion, the certificates had been typed that morning in the school office. They read simply: *Presented by the Führer for Good Posture.*

And now the Countess was asked whether every girl in the school had received a certificate. She had to explain that one of the girls was unfortunately in the sick-bay. The Führer insisted on going upstairs to meet Camilla.

Rigby almost purred, things were going so well.

The official party moved out.

Frustratingly she couldn't contrive to witness the scene upstairs. But she imagined it vividly: Camilla saucer-eyed as the Führer entered and approached the bedside; speechless when he asked if she was the young lady he had seen in the

Osteria Bavaria; and flabbergasted when he grasped her hand, leaned close and whispered that he wouldn't mind climbing into bed with her.

Rigby shook with silent laughter.

Then her daydream was shattered by gunfire.

Panic.

Girls screamed.

Rigby dashed to the staircase. On the landing she met Portland, the fellow in the black mackintosh who had posed as Hitler. He was a limpet-like admirer she had dragooned into this performance after he'd followed her to Munich. His Hitler impersonation had been a highlight of the Chelsea Arts Ball.

"What happened?"

Portland was ashen. He peeled off the moustache. "She must be barmy, that friend of yours. She drew a gun before I said a damned thing. She tried to blow my brains out."

"Oh, God! Are you all right?"

"I shoved the gun aside but she put a bullet into your German friend."

"Manfred! No!"

All caution abandoned, Rigby rushed up the remaining stairs and into the sick-bay, into mayhem. Camilla, sobbing hysterically, her nightdress spattered with blood, knelt by the motionless body of Manfred. The Countess was at the medical chest, grabbing boxes and bottles and throwing them down as if they'd been put there to thwart her.

Rigby went to Manfred and turned his face. It was deathly white.

"She shot him!" wailed the Countess. "She meant to shoot the Führer, wicked girl, but the Adjutant got in the way. I don't know what will happen to us all."

"Is he dead?"

"Passed out. The bullet went through his foot. Did you pass the Führer on the stairs?"

"No," said Rigby truthfully.

The Countess handed her a bottle. "Smelling salts. Do your best. I'm going to find the Führer."

"That isn't possible, ma'am."

In the next five minutes, everyone became wiser. Rigby

confessed to the practical joke that had misfired – literally. The Countess made a great show of being scandalised but couldn't suppress her relief that there had not, after all, been an assassination attempt on the Führer in her school. It wasn't from want of trying, Camilla rashly told them. Far from hero-worshipping Hitler, she had planned cold-bloodedly to rid the world of him. The vigil in the Osteria Bavaria had been her attempt to entrap him.

"Enemy of the Reich!" cried the Countess. "She-devil! You are expelled from my school!"

"Then I shall go to the newspapers."

"On second thoughts, I see it as my duty to reform you."

Then Manfred opened his eyes and groaned. "Help me to stand, please. I must leave at once."

"Out of the question," the Countess told him. "I'm going to put you to bed."

He said with desperation, "I report to the Führer at noon. It is the four-power conference with Chamberlain, Mussolini and Daladier. I'm on duty".

"With a shot foot? Don't be idiotic!"

He propped himself on an elbow, moved the leg, grimaced with pain and immediately passed out again, giving the Countess the opportunity to make good her promise. With Rigby's and Camilla's help she lifted him on to the bed, then instructed them to look the other way while she stripped him of his uniform. The doctor who usually attended the school arrived to dress the wound. He injected Manfred with morphine. Nobody told the doctor who Manfred was; by a process of nods and shrugs he formed the impression that Manfred was on the staff of the school and had shot himself by accident while investigating a noise in the cellar.

"Rats," said the doctor, with a knowing look.

The rest of that morning was torment for Rigby as she speculated what would happen to Manfred. Soon enough his absence would be noticed – absence without leave. What explanation could he give? He was going to be on crutches for weeks. Hitler, a man utterly devoid of humour, would take it as treason. Manfred would be lucky to escape with his life.

Her own fate, as the instigator of the stunt, paled into

insignificance. So, it must be admitted, did Camilla's, as the would-be assassin of the Führer.

That afternoon Rigby missed the German lesson, saying she had a toothache, and slipped upstairs to the sick-bay. She found Manfred semiconscious, too drugged to move, but capable of recognising her. He smiled. She stroked his forehead. How much made sense to him was difficult to judge.

"I've thought about this for hours and something drastic has to be done, my darling. I'm going to speak to your Führer. He expressed a wish to meet me, and now he will. I shall make a personal appeal to him. He's got to be told that this was just a practical joke got up by some high-spirited girls who tricked you into taking part. You were injured heroically trying to put a stop to it. All I want from you is the pass you carry, or something to get me into Hitler's flat. I must see him alone – it's no use with all those aides around him. How will I gain entry? Is there a password?"

Manfred gazed at her blankly.

She went to the wardrobe and searched his uniform. In an inside pocket was a wallet containing various identification documents.

Munich buzzed with stories about the Conference. Hitler had pushed Europe to the brink of war over the Sudeten question. Germany was set to occupy the disputed territories on October 1st and it was now September 29th. Chamberlain had flown in that morning from London for his third meeting with Hitler in a fortnight. Daladier, the French premier, was already installed at the Four Seasons Hotel. And Hitler had gone by train to the German-Italian border to escort his ally, Mussolini, to Munich. The talks at the Führerbau had started soon after lunch and were likely to last until late.

About six-twenty p.m., a taxi drew up at the building in Prinz Regenten Platz where Hitler had his private apartment. Rigby, dressed in a black pillbox hat with a veil, a bottle-green jacket with velvet revers and a black skirt, got out and approached the guard. She gave the Nazi salute.

"I am here on the personal instructions of the Führer. I am to go up and wait for him."

"Your identification, Fräulein?"

"Examine this. It is the pass of his Adjutant, Oberleutnant Reger."

"Do you have some identification of your own?"

"This is sufficient. My presence here is highly confidential. Mention it to nobody. Nobody. Do you understand?"

Her voice carried authority. He saluted, stepped aside and swung back the iron gate of the lift.

At the door of number sixteen, she repeated the performance for the benefit of Hitler's housekeeper. She got a long look before she was admitted to a modestly proportioned flat, furnished with ornate dark wood furniture and insipid oil-paintings. She sat in a chintz-covered armchair and listened to the clock for a time.

About seven p.m., the housekeeper returned and said she was going out to her sister's. "Are you sure the Führer wished you to wait?"

"Absolutely."

"Then it is better, I think, if you sit in my apartment. There is a connecting door."

So Rigby transferred. The adjoining flat was more agreeable; for one thing, it had a kitchen where she was able to make coffee for herself. After two hours she made a second cup and there came a time when she had made four. She had resolved not to leave without speaking to Hitler, but the possibility now arose that he had gone elsewhere to sleep, because it was past two a.m. Apparently the housekeeper wasn't coming back either. In the next hour or so Rigby twice dozed until her head lolled uncomfortably. She got up to look for somewhere to stretch out.

She didn't care to be found in the housekeeper's bedroom. If there was a guest room, she would use that. She tried a door opposite the bathroom and found it locked, but the key was in place. She turned it and reached for the light switch. How charming, she thought, and what a surprise! Pastel colours. White, modern furniture. All very feminine. A single bed with the sheets turned back as if for airing. A pale yellow night-dress tossed across the pillows. A pierrette's carnival costume with black pompoms hanging from the white wardrobe. Dance programmes and invitation cards ranged along the mantelpiece. Rigby picked one up. The date of the dance was September, 1931.

1931?

She looked at the other cards. All were dated 1931 – *seven years ago*.

She crossed to the bed and picked up the nightdress. It smelt musty. Horrible. She'd heard of this morbid custom before. When some loved one died, their room was preserved exactly as they had left it. On Queen Victoria's orders, Prince Albert's room at Windsor had been left intact for forty years after his death. Rigby had just walked into a shrine.

Feeling the gooseflesh rise, she turned to leave. Something else caught her eye, a photograph in a silver frame on the dressing-table. Out of some intuition she picked it up. A young girl was pictured beside Hitler. He had his hand on her shoulder. Rigby stared at the picture. The girl could have been herself. The face was her own. The photo-frame slipped from her fingers and hit the floor, shattering the glass.

She gave a cry, not merely from shock. Footsteps were coming fast along the corridor, the heavy tread of a man. She spun around to face the open door. Hitler stood there in his braces, an older, more strained Hitler than the photograph had shown.

For once he looked unguarded, vulnerable, not in command. He said in a whisper, "Geli?"

Rigby shook her head.

He stepped towards her, hands outstretched as if to discover whether she was flesh and blood. His eyes glistened moistly. She shrank from him.

Suddenly words gushed from her. "I'm not your Geli. I shouldn't be here, I admit. I'm English. My name is Dorothy Rigby and I came to see you to explain about your Adjutant –"

Terrifyingly, he became the Führer again, shouting her down with his tirade. "You have no right in here! Nobody is allowed in here. You've smashed her picture, defiled her memory, mocked me, the Führer. What are you, a spy, a witch, a streetwalker? You'll be punished. How did you get in here? Who let you in?"

She said, "You asked to meet me. You spotted me in the Osteria Bavaria." And it sounded appallingly lame.

He grabbed her arm. "Out of this room! Out! I spend fifteen hours settling the future of Germany, of Europe, dealing with old men and popinjays, and I come home to this. I shall call the Gestapo."

Rigby shouted back, "If you do, my friend from the finishing school – remember her, with the blonde hair? – will go to the British Ambassador and tell him you importuned me. You – the Reich Chancellor – importuned a foreign schoolgirl in a restaurant. Pick up that telephone, Herr Hitler, and your reputation is scarred for ever."

He let go of her and flapped his hand. "Ach – this is nonsense. Be off with you. I'm too tired to take this up."

It was a crucial moment. Manfred's fate was still paramount in Rigby's plans. "I refuse to leave until you've listened to what I have to say."

Hitler marched away towards his own apartment, but she followed him, talking fast, making sure that he heard her much-rehearsed, much-doctored version of the practical joke she had played on Camilla, in which Manfred was blameless because he had answered a summons supposedly from the Führer, and had been shot in the foot, heroically trying to prevent an assassination.

Hitler spun around and faced her. "How can you prove one word of this horse-shit?"

She felt the blood drain from her head. How *could* she prove the story? He was calling it horse-shit, but he wouldn't have asked her the question unless he gave it some credence.

With a flair that would serve her well in years to come, Rigby picked her handbag off the chintz armchair she had first sat in, took out her posture certificate and handed it to Hitler.

He stared at it for longer than he needed to read it. Finally he handed it back and said in a tight, hard voice, "Go back to my housekeeper's quarters. Tonight you will remain there".

Rigby obeyed. She heard the key turn in the lock behind her. She didn't need telling that every exit would be locked. She pushed two armchairs together, climbed into them and curled up, praying she had done the right thing for Manfred.

"Last night you said you were English."

She opened her eyes to Hitler, in uniform, leaning over the

back of the armchair. It was daylight. In the background were the voices of others in the flat.

"Yes."

"You speak good German also."

"I like languages."

"This morning I am to receive your Prime Minister on a private visit before he returns to England. You will assist my regular translator, Dr Schmidt. Tidy yourself."

Rigby collected her wits. "I see. You want to pass me off as your interpreter."

"Do as I say."

She saw presently that the two apartments throbbed with activity. Aides, secretaries and domestic staff had been hastily summoned after word had come through from Neville Chamberlain that he wanted one more session with Hitler. Clearly, Rigby's presence in the place wanted some explaining, so a job had been found for her.

When the British delegation arrived, Rigby was in the room, at Schmidt's elbow. She knew nothing of the agreement signed the previous night, so it shocked her to glean from what Chamberlain was saying that Hitler had run rings around the English and the French. Czechoslovakia now had ten days to hand over the Sudetenland to Germany. In the cold light of morning, Chamberlain was looking for something to save his face when he got back to England.

That face, which Rigby had never seen except in photographs, looked strained and anxious. The Prime Minister expressed the wish that the Czechs would not be 'mad enough' to reject the agreement. He said he hoped it would not be necessary for Germany to bomb Prague; in fact, he had hopes of an international agreement to ban bomber aircraft.

Hitler listened impassively to the translation. Finally, when it was clear that no more progress was possible, Chamberlain took two sheets of paper from his pocket and asked if Hitler would be willing to sign a statement on the future of Anglo–German relations.

"What is it?" asked Hitler. He passed it to Rigby. "You can translate."

She asked if she could have a moment to draft an accurate version in German. She took it to the writing-table, the famous 'piece of paper' that Chamberlain was to proclaim as the evidence of 'peace for our time'.

When Rigby's translation was ready, Hitler gave it a glance. "Yes. I'll sign."

Chamberlain stepped forward to add his signature below Hitler's. Rigby blotted each copy of the document. She handed Hitler his, and then turned her back on him. This was her opportunity. Dextrously she made a substitution and handed Chamberlain a note she had jotted on the reverse of her posture certificate: *SOS. Essential I return with you to England with a man who has vital information.*

To his credit, Chamberlain gave it a glance and placed it smoothly in his pocket. He shook hands with Hitler. Then he turned to Rigby and said, "And how charming to meet you once more, my dear. Perhaps the Führer will allow me to drive you home if your duties are over."

"They are," said Rigby.

The British had come in two cars and Rigby travelled in the second. It made a detour to the finishing school. On the advice of one of the diplomatic staff she didn't go in. It was possible that the Gestapo were inside. But her heart pounded when a figure presently emerged on crutches and limped towards the waiting car.

Only it wasn't Manfred.

It was Camilla, disguised as a man. She sank beside Rigby, slammed the door and said to the driver, "Start up, for God's sake! The Gestapo are on the way". To Rigby she said, "Manfred's safe".

"What happened? Where is he?"

"Rigby – I'm sorry to tell you this. His wife collected him."

"His *wife? Manfred is married?*" The world caved in on Rigby.

"I know. It was a complete shock. There were two young children. Absolute sweeties. He doesn't deserve them. She arrived in a car twenty minutes ago. One of Manfred's colleagues had tipped her off that Hitler had ordered a raid on the school. I think they'll make it to the border. I dressed up like this in case the place was being watched. To put them off, you see."

Rigby was numb.

Even when the plane took off she felt no sense of relief at escaping. She would never trust a man again.

Fifty years on, that flight home is still a void in her memory. She does have some recollection of the landing at Croydon, when Chamberlain stepped off the plane to make his famous announcement to the press. In some of the photographs Rigby can be seen in the background, standing beside Camilla, who is wearing a trilby. She remembers the moment of horror when Chamberlain produced his famous piece of paper and waved it triumphantly. She recalls opening her handbag and checking that it still contained the agreement that Hitler had signed.

Chamberlain was holding up a piece of paper with the words *Presented by the Führer for Good Posture.*

How was it, then, that shortly after, he appeared to read out the text of the agreement? As Rigby had observed, you could say one thing for Neville Chamberlain – his memory was phenomenal.

Peter Lovesey, who wrote that section, says he was "behind bars in the year in question, confined to his playpen", but several of his novels are set in and around World War Two and, as fans of Sergeant Cribb will know, he is keen on historical research. Rigby was surprised and impressed to discover how much he knew about, for instance, Croydon Airport in the 1930s.

It took Rigby a long time to recover from her handsome young Nazi Lieutenant. Perhaps she never fully recovered?

The idea of returning to Tunbridge Wells was more than she could bear and a reluctant father and mother agreed that she and Camilla could live in London. The girls took a long lease on a top floor flat in a house in Marylebone High Street. Rigby stayed there throughout her working life. They both took jobs – a series of jobs, since employers proved no more understanding of either girl than schoolteachers. Mayotte asked one of the Jesuit fathers from Farm Street to 'keep an eye on them' and he used to come round once a week for supper, after which the three of them drank malt whisky and played gin rummy. Father Keen sent regular and reassuring reports out to India. Occasionally the girls went to his church for Mass; they liked the music. Afterwards Father Keen took them for lunch at the Connaught Hotel and they liked that too.

Rigby was almost in love with Leslie Howard and Jean Gabin because celluloid heroes were safe. In real life poor Portland, the Hitler impersonator, persevered and a series of men took her to nightclubs and made advances in the backs of taxis. They didn't get much further than Portland.

But the highlight of those years was cricket. Rigby was at the Oval when Len Hutton made three hundred and sixty four against the Australians. She saw every ball and she got his autograph.

Paula Gosling

A LITTLE LEARNING

Most of the jobs, in and out of which Rigby drifted, were uninteresting. The fortnight teaching French at a boys' preparatory school in Weymouth had its moments, but Camilla ruined that by turning up late one night with a houseparty of drunken friends and suggesting they all go for a midnight swim. The headmaster – a nice and reasonable man named Randall Hoyle – had been very understanding but explained that if any parent got to hear of it there would be no end of trouble. There was also a giddy moment when they both signed on as hat check girls at a new night club in Half Moon Street, but even Father Keen drew the line at that.

One job which lasted longer than most was in the Foreign Propaganda Section of the Ministry of Information. Rigby had always enjoyed making up stories and this gave full rein to her linguistic abilities, her powers of invention and her devil-may-care bloody-mindedness. It had been Father Keen who suggested it after the night club *débâcle*. He said a parishioner of his had mentioned that there was this new department on the look-out for bright young people who were good at languages. Subsequent investigation led Rigby to believe that the man in question could have been her old Tunbridge Wells acquaintance, Graham Greene, but she remains uncertain.

She signed on at the Ministry in March 1939 and was soon busy writing satirical lyrics for such popular German songs as "*Wir fahren gegen England*" and "*Bomben auf England*". She even claims that she and two colleagues were responsible for the ribald new words for Colonel Bogey, the ones about Hitler only having one ball, while Himmler had something similar and Goebbels had no balls at all.

But I have my doubts. That summer, however, something quite unexpected happened on holiday . . .

T he speedometer read sixty-three when the tyre blew.
       She was on the coast road, notorious for its blind
       curves and sudden dips, but so tempting because of the
views.

And now temptation had led her, as it so frequently did, to
disaster. Rigby was shocked by the sudden sound of the
blow-out and the bone-cracking wrench of the Singer Le Mans'
wheel from her hands. After an instant of horror, she took
hold again and fought hard against the suicidal desire of the
motorcar to swan-dive over the unfenced edge of the cliff on
to the rocks below.

The car bucked and careened into the up-slope at the cliff's
edge on her right and then slithered back across the gravelled
road to the wall of stone on her left. Sparks flew, metal
crunched and clattered, tyres screamed.

She screamed, too.

But she held on.

Now her speed was dropping: fifty, forty, thirty.

That was good – but every swerve brought her closer to
the edge of the cliff, the wheels skidding on the gravel,
the occasional pothole deflecting them without warning.
If you're going to crash, do it *your* way, she told herself.
Keep control. Don't slam on the brakes! Touch, lift, touch,
lift, wait, wait, wait until the nose is in, is tight, tight in
and . . .

Handbrake!

The Singer jerked and shuddered. Gracefully, with what
seemed like infinite slowness, it pivoted around the locked
wheels and then slammed side-on into the overhanging bluff,
facing the way it had come.

Rigby blacked out momentarily from the shock of the impact, and then her vision cleared. A shroud of dust hung over
the road along which she had just fought for her life. The late
afternoon light turned the billowing clouds into a shimmering
curtain. The sound of the waves snarling over the rocks beyond

the cliff seemed very far away and, amazingly, she heard a blackbird singing on the hill above her.

Otherwise, all was still.

A sudden cascade of earth and sand beside her brought her back to reality. The car began to settle, with groans and pings, into its final misery.

Cautiously, Rigby moved her arms and legs, flexed her neck, took a deep breath or two, and waited for the grate of bone on bone. There was none. Her forearms and wrists ached abominably, and her throat was raw from her lusty screaming (always the best way to get through a physical crisis, she'd found), and every muscle was protesting, but she was alive and whole.

Then she felt the blood trickling down her face.

"Damn!" She leaned forward and looked into the last remaining shard of the rear-view mirror that hung askew from the mid-rib of the windscreen. There was a cut on her forehead – rather nasty – that was bleeding steadily. Blood had run down the side of her face and there was already a stain on the collar of her new Molyneux frock. "Damn and blast!" she said.

Blood was absolutely *impossible* to get out of crêpe de chine.

Half an hour later she was standing in the middle of the road, making a decision.

She had mopped up the cut as best she could, tying a handkerchief compress against it with a red and blue scarf, achieving a rakish and not unpleasing effect. Not a single car had passed in either direction and she expected none. There was a much better and faster road inland, and it was the hour for high tea, sacrosanct in Scotland. She had changed from her dress and court shoes to a more sensible ensemble of blue hiking shorts, red cashmere pullover, white silk shirt, thick wool socks and a stout pair of brogues. She stuffed some absolute essentials into her rucksack – how fortunate she had intended to do some walking on this holiday, she thought.

One up to Tony Whyte.

Everyone in the Ministry said Tony Whyte was a scaremonger (they called him 'Worry-Whyte'). Some had taken to teasing him about it, telling him they'd seen Nazis in the most unlikely places, the latest candidate being the Gents' attendant at the Dorchester. Tony smiled – Tony always smiled – and went on warning.

"Do it because you're there, Rigby. Because it's a golden opportunity. Because it could make a difference. It won't hurt you, will it? Nobody notices hikers in July," Tony had said, over her protests. "They're everywhere, looking at everything. It's the latest craze." (She'd snapped back that in her opinion people were getting altogether *too* hearty. The real future lay in the dry martini. But he kept on . . . and on.)

She sighed. Night would soon be here. Forward lay Scudaugh, approximately fifteen miles on this road. Still, it was a more tempting goal than the definite twenty-two miles back to Invercrairie.

Taking a torch from the glove box and a thick jacket from her suitcase in the dickey, she made a last regretful survey of her little Singer and then resolutely turned her back on it and set off. The car was an old problem, now. The next problem lay ahead.

Three hours later she was trudging through the lingering northern dusk. Though it was late she could still make out the vista of frosted pewter waves that crashed, out of sight, at the foot of the cliffs, and the hummocky folds of the boulder-strewn moor rising on her left. She had stopped several times to sit on a rock and smoke a comforting Abdulla while gazing out to sea, but it was too cold for such soulful pursuits now that the sun had gone.

The road was, very gently, sloping downwards, and the going was easier. She had paced herself to a nice, even stride, putting her whole body into the task of walking, stretching the muscles and joints that had taken the full jolt of the crash. All those afternoons of tennis, golf, and cricket had served her well today – she would never have managed to control the car without that extra strength in wrist and forearm. But she still hurt.

Probably only another two miles or so to go, now.

Suddenly the sound of the waves was overlaid with another, sharper noise – the engine of a small boat. A late fisherman, heading home?

Rigby crossed the road and, leaning forward through a cleft between two large rocks, looked down. About forty feet below her, the cliff curved back to form a small, white-beached cove. Several hundred yards out, there lay a small fishing boat running without lights.

Even as she watched, it cut its engine.

Rigby frowned. Either the vessel was in trouble – or it *meant* trouble.

"You've been infected by Tony Whyte's paranoia, my girl," she told herself, severely. "You're becoming suspicious of everything you see and hear. The worst it could be is a spot of smuggling."

Still, this sign of life – however odd or sinister – was encouraging. As she watched, a small dinghy detached itself from the shadowy side of the boat and made for the cove. There were three people in it, silhouetted against the silver gleam of the water. Perhaps the boat was in trouble, perhaps they were coming ashore to seek help. At least she'd have company for the last few miles, gruff but companionable fishermen with jokes and tales to tell.

But something about them made her stay silent, and in shadow. Something told her to wait.

Suddenly, from beyond the rocks that hid her, there came a beautiful sound – the throb of a large engine. A car was approaching! She wouldn't have to walk, after all!

Immensely cheered, she stepped into the roadway and prepared to wave down the approaching vehicle.

But it never arrived. The engine was abruptly stilled, and she realised it had stopped at the landward mouth of the small, hidden cove.

The people in the dinghy were being met.

Rigby moved back to her vantage point between the rocks. The boat was nearly beached, now. Across the sands came two figures. One carried a lamp and lit it at the last moment to aid the disembarking passengers, who splashed ashore through the shallows, while the third man remained in the dinghy.

As one of the men on the beach reached forward to help the landing party, his shirtcuff slid back. The lamplight shone on the back of his right hand, revealing the scarlet pucker of an old burn. A moment later it was out of sight as his hand was grasped by a smaller, more slender one.

The lamp moved upward, revealing the face above – and Dorothy gasped. "Good God!" she whispered to herself. "It's Frisky Fritzi!"

Fritzi Baum had been one of the leading socialites of Munich, much pictured in the newspapers – glamorous, charismatic, and fanatic in her devotion to the new religion of National Socialism.

Both passengers were ashore now, and the dinghy itself was pulling back toward the fishing boat that waited offshore, dark and silent. The smallest figure on the beach turned toward the rower and raised a hand in farewell, calling out thanks in a phrase that turned Rigby's spine to ice.

"*Heil* Hitler!" The words came clearly, carried by a wind that bore no good that night.

Rigby felt sick. Tony had been right, after all.

Working as they did in the Foreign Propaganda Section of the Ministry of Information – interpreting and analysing everything that came by radio, print and whisper across the Channel – they were more aware than most of the extent of the German machinations. Once war was declared – and Herr Hitler seemed determined to precipitate that declaration one way or another – the coasts would be watched and everyone would be alert. Now, when everyone was complacent and careless, *now* was the time for them to get their agents in place. Tony Whyte had told her to look out for it – and here it was.

Her lip curled. At least the two from Germany were driven to act by blind fanaticism. What name was there but traitor for those who welcomed them to this dark, isolated and vulnerable shore?

From behind the rocks she watched as the figures walked across the sand and disappeared. Moments later the heavy throb of the powerful car engine could be heard again as it turned on the narrow road and then headed back up the coast.

Rigby lifted her arm and looked at her watch in the moonlight – nine o'clock, and another two miles to walk. "Well, old Worry-Whyte was right," she muttered to herself. "Now, are you going to close your eyes and cling tight to your nice safe life, or are you going to do something about it?"

* * *

Scudaugh was no more than a huddle of buildings at the throat of Scudaugh Bay. There was no pub, and the Post Office was dark. Rigby walked slowly down the road, looking at each house in turn, hoping to see something that indicated a telephone within.

She spotted the spider's thread she was searching for leading to a large house set well back from the road. In the drive an Alvis crouched like a dark, sleek panther, its chromework glimmering in the moonlight. On impulse, Rigby slipped in and laid a hand lightly on the bonnet of the car. It was still warm.

Stepping back, she looked at the house again. Now she could see threads of light around the edges of thick curtains. They must be inside, now. Probably they would stay put until morning – but then where would they go? What plans had been laid, what guise would Fritzi and her 'friend' take as they began their secret, deadly work?

Well, it was secret no more – Rigby would see to that!

She went back to the road and continued her search. It was not until she had come nearly to the end of the village that another house showed a wire connecting it to a tall pole by the side of the road. Flicking on her torch, she read the words on the brass plate set into the gatepost: 'Dr B. Ruff, General Practitioner'. In the drive beside the house there stood a small blue Riley. Its bonnet was quite cold. Salvation was at hand.

The housekeeper who opened the door was a kindly-looking woman who listened sympathetically to Rigby's tale of her car crash and led her to the telephone that stood on a table in the hall.

She rang her parents. Harry and Mayotte were home on leave. They had taken a place near Loch Dour for the summer, and had expected her in time for tea. Her father, once he had ascertained her whereabouts and state of health, promised to send someone to collect her and the car in the morning.

"Daddy, darling?"

"Yes?" Harry Rigby was always very brisk on the phone – a result of his long years in the Army.

"Could you do something else for me?" She heard the housekeeper in the kitchen – a little too close for comfort. No sense babbling her suspicions and starting a panic – better to be discreet.

"Settle your dress bills again, I suppose?" he said, but there was a smile in his voice.

"No, that's fine. Could you be an absolute sweetie and ring Camilla for me and give her a message?" The Colonel didn't approve of Camilla but she *was* Rigby's oldest, dearest friend.

"Tell her that Tony was right, and to pay him the fiver I left in the sugar bowl. During my walk along the coast I saw two Yellow-Backed Warblers and two Sooty Cuckoos. He should check up on them for himself." She hoped it sounded convincing – Yellow-Backed Warbler was the current Ministry joke term for Nazi sympathisers, and Tony had once referred to secret agents as Sooty Cuckoos – song birds that hide behind the chimney.

There was a silence, and then Harry Rigby spoke in a dry tone. "You did say you had a bang on the head, didn't you?"

"Oh, Daddy, *listen*, it's really important. Tony is Camilla's latest and he's an absolutely *frantic* birdwatcher. He writes articles for the Royal Society and *everything*. We had the most frightful argument before I left and –"

"You want me to send a nature report, is that it?"

"Daddy, *please* – I have to *work* with Tony, and Camilla is already livid with me as it is. I don't want to come back to an *atmosphere*."

Harry Rigby's voice changed. He knew very well where Rigby worked – he had tried repeatedly to talk her out of taking the job 'with all those damned bureaucrats'. "Tell me the names again, then."

She repeated them. "And say that I'll ring him myself tomorrow with the details of habitat."

Harry made an indescribable noise. "You are a most exasperating child, if I may say so," he said. "What was your last craze? Becoming the world's greatest fastbowler? Before that it was motor racing, the circus, and that slimy damned yogi chap, Rambojambo –"

"Rama San Tal."

"The Devil take him. My dear, you are a worry to us. You can figure the odds in poker and blackjack but you can't pass a simple mathematics exam. You spend a fortune on clothes and can't sew on a button. And now it's *birdwatching*."

"Sorry, Daddy," she said, meekly.

59

Her father sighed, heavily. "The things I do for my darling daughter. Good night, Dorothy. Behave yourself." He rang off.

As she stood there with the receiver pressed against her ear, she thought she heard breathing. "Hello?" Probably the exchange, listening in. "Hello?"

There was a slight click, as if a receiver had been replaced, and then the girl at the exchange answered. Dorothy asked the amount of the call, replaced the receiver, and turned.

A tall, white-haired man was standing a few feet away, watching her. He had a ruddy complexion and bright blue eyes that twinkled at her. "I'm Dr Ruff," he said.

"An automobile smash on the coast road, Mrs MacGillivray tells me. And you've walked miles, by the look of you. Sit down, girl, before you fall down."

As Rigby described the blow-out, Dr Ruff untied her scarf and slowly peeled the handkerchief from her forehead. The blood had dried as hard as glue, and pulling the cloth away started the bleeding afresh.

"Nasty. Is this all?" He handed her a clean bit of gauze to stem the flow and turned away to gather things from a cabinet. "No broken bones or loose teeth anywhere about you?"

"No, just the cut and a few bruised ribs." Rigby watched the efficient movements of his hands.

He turned back and nodded. "Well, I'll do my best for you, but it will hurt like billy-oh, and I can't promise there won't be a scar. No fancy surgery up here – I'm more accustomed to stitching up shepherds and fishermen than pretty young women."

He was right – it did hurt like billy-oh but Rigby managed to maintain her composure as he stitched the wound.

"I saw a beautiful Alvis Phaeton parked in front of a house back down the road," she said. "Do you know who owns it?"

Dr Ruff smiled down at her. "Keen on motors, are you?"

"Very," Rigby said. "That's a new model, I was surprised to see one so far north."

"We do have occasional contacts with civilisation up here," the doctor said, wryly. "However, that particular house and car belong to a new chap in the neighbourhood – a Mr Delahaye."

"Oh. Has he been here long?"

"A few months. I've not had the pleasure of meeting him – presumably he's a healthy type." He put down his forceps and looked down at her approvingly. "There's the good girl," he murmured. "Never a whimper." He covered his handiwork with a neat dressing, then began to clean up. As he reached out to turn on the tap in the sink, his sleeve moved back to reveal the bright pink pucker of a burn scar.

Rigby drew in her breath sharply, and Dr Ruff glanced at her and then down at his arm. "An old souvenir," he said, sliding his cuff forward. He moved through an open door and she heard the clink of glass. When he returned he had a gleaming hypodermic syringe on a tray, along with a small vial. "I'm afraid I'll have to give you a tetanus injection, my dear."

Rigby stood up quickly. "That won't be necessary, really."

"You don't mean to say you went through all that stitching without a murmur, only to balk at a tiny prick in the arm?" The twinkle in his blue eyes had, she saw, turned to ice. "We can't risk complications, can we?"

"No, really, I don't need –" She should never have mentioned the Alvis.

"Such a long road, the coast road, with so many animals wandering along it –" He put down the tray and thrust the needle into the vial, holding both up to the light as he measured out the clear liquid. Was it tetanus antitoxin? Or something else?

"I had a tetanus injection last year –" Rigby stammered, backing away.

"While you were in Munich, *ja?*" came a clear voice from behind her. Rigby whirled around.

Fritzi Baum stood in the doorway. She was not smiling.

Rigby came awake all at once, to a throbbing headache. She had fainted – the result of exhaustion and shock. But Ruff had obviously gone ahead with his injection for there was a bruise on the inside of her elbow. Not a tetanus injection at all, but a strong sedative. There was an unmistakable metallic taste in her mouth and a familiar brightness to the light overhead.

Her recalcitrant metabolism always had a reverse reaction to certain forms of sedation – where others slept she became hyper-awake.

Slipping off the couch – for she was still in Ruff's surgery – she moved to the hall door and opened it quietly. The hall beyond was dark but further along she could see a line of light around what was probably the lounge door.

What a fool she had been to trust anyone! She could imagine Tony Whyte's scholarly tones listing the precautions any sensible person would have taken. Well, she was not a sensible person – never had been – and she was unaccustomed to lying, untrained in intrigue.

Anybody would be better at this than she.

But she was the only one around.

Bending down she removed her brogues and tied them together, then slung them around her neck. She crept stocking-footed down the hall and pressed her ear against the door. All those nights of sneaking out of school had been excellent practice for such an occasion, she smiled to herself. Oh Camilla, if you could see me now!

The murmur of voices beyond the door was muffled, but clear enough. Although the conversation was in German she had no trouble whatsoever in following it. Heaven bless Countess Schnabel and her insistence on 'practize, practize'!

"We don't know if she saw anything!" That was Dr Ruff.

"And *I* tell you she is familiar to me!" Fritzi – the clear, nasal voice as imperious as ever. She had been known to reduce a rival to tears at a distance of half-a-ballroom. "Something in that face I recognise and do not like."

Rigby's mouth twitched. You have good reason not to like, Miss Fritzi Baum, she thought. I made sure of it, for Camilla's sake. Or did you never know why the Prince suddenly refused to see you?

Fritzi went on. "Her being here, now – it cannot be a coincidence. That talk of birds on the telephone, I do not like it."

"She's a birdwatcher, there are hundreds of them around at this time of year," Ruff protested.

"No – she is something else."

I only wish I were, Rigby thought. Then I might know what to do next.

"She must have seen something on the road. The timing would be right." This was the voice that had said '*Heil* Hitler' on the beach.

"Then she must be eliminated." The third man, patently English though his German accent was good, but cold – cold as ice. Was this Delahaye – or had that been a lie, too? "She must die of her injury, which was more serious than you believed, Doctor. A clot on the brain due to concussion, that sort of thing."

"I cannot do that," Ruff protested. "I refuse to do that."

"You gave her the injection."

"That was a simple sedative to keep her asleep and give you time to get away."

"Another injection – that's all we ask. The end justifies the means." Fritzi's companion, again. "We cannot risk any witnesses to our arrival. If you are not with us, you are against us."

"But murder . . . I am a doctor . . ." Ruff's protests were growing weaker. It was only a matter of time before the implacable intentions of the others prevailed over what seemed to be his rapidly diminishing devotion to the cause.

Rigby decided there was no point in listening any further. She moved away from the door and down the hall to the kitchen. There, watched by a sleepy cat, she slipped the latch on the back door and crept outside. She put on her shoes and started down the road.

The little Riley was easy to push out once she had released the handbrake. Rewiring the ignition had been the work of but a moment – blessings on Camilla's cousin Jack at Brooklands, who'd taught her to fix them as well as drive them. There was a downgrade from the Doctor's house that allowed her to roll a good fifty yards before letting in the clutch and starting the engine.

And the Alvis would never start, now. She opened the window beside her and tossed its rotor arm out into the darkness. "*Auf Wiedersehen!*" she muttered, and pressed the throttle to the floor.

But within ten minutes she saw headlights behind her. Unbelievably, but unmistakably, those of the Alvis – huge beams like the luminous eyes of a monstrous insect. She cursed her own carelessness. Why hadn't she done more to the larger car? She should have realised they'd keep a complete set of vital spares up here where service would be difficult.

The lights of the Alvis were coming closer, bearing down on her inexorably.

Time to think again.

She had originally planned to take a turning somewhere past Scudaugh that would have joined the highway to Inverness.

But where was the turning?

The moon was hidden and the night was dark. The Riley's headlights revealed only the endlessly curving road, now turning away from the sea and wrapping itself around the shoulders and boulders of moorland. Occasionally the luminous eyes of sheep roused by the noise of her car glowed in the heather, but otherwise there was only the road, the road, the hypnotic –

There!

On her left, a narrow road with a signpost beside it, long dismasted. But a signpost it was, and that meant the road led *somewhere*. The lights of the Alvis were momentarily obscured by an intervening rise and she took the opportunity to swing the little Riley hard left, cutting her lights and changing down to avoid using the brakes. A sharp turn quickly hid her from the coast road.

A minute later, to her relief, the Alvis swept by behind her, the beams of its immense headlights swinging up into the sky as it climbed a rise and then sweeping down like twin scimitars as it rolled into another dip and turned away.

She put on the Riley's lights again and pressed the throttle to the floor.

Five minutes later the little car was up to its radiator in the peat-brown skirling waters of a rocky burn, and Rigby knew what the sign on the post must have said when it was intact – 'No Through Road'.

It was head and footwork from now on.

She got out of the car and looked up at the stars in the sky. Why hadn't sailing and navigation ever been one of her

enthusiasms? Even the moon was only a mottled milky circle
– she had no idea in what direction it rose and fell at this time
of year. Standing there in the icy waters of the burn, with only
a rug snagged from the back of the traitor doctor's car around
her shoulders and a rucksack full of useless cosmetics and
couture clothes, Rigby realised how little she knew about
anything.

"Oh, damn, Damn, DAMN!" she shouted. In the distance
some sheep protested at this noisy intrusion into their peaceful
dreams. She turned towards the noise – and saw the lights of
the Alvis poking up into the sky. They were coming back!

Panic seized her. Any direction would do – as long as it was
away!

She sloshed out of the burn and began to run, but soon was
reduced to a shambling walk for the springiness of the heather
mat made walking resemble progress across a feather mattress.
Within minutes her calves and thighs began to ache. She came
to a tiny, winding path and followed it, relieved to be free of
the heather, but was soon assailed by the stench of crushed
sheep droppings. The path led nowhere in particular – just
the shortest distance between one ewe and another.

And she had always thought spies and their ilk led glamorous
lives. "Hah!" she announced, bitterly. "Dorothy Rigby,
beautiful girl spy, cold, wet, scared to death, and up to her
ankles in –"

Now she could hear the throb of the Alvis engine behind
her, coming closer. It stopped – presumably they had found
the Riley. How many had come after her? One? Two? All of
them? She hoped she wouldn't find out too soon.

Keep moving, keep moving, she told herself.

And promptly fell into a ravine.

She lay on her back and cursed.

The shorts were Schiaparelli, the shirt was Hartnell, the
pullover was Chanel, and the whole outfit was a total ruin.
She could feel icy water flowing over her legs and under her
shoulders, gravel biting into her back, mud squeezing behind
her socks and she just wanted to *spit* she was so angry.

Instead, she got up and peered over the edge of the ravine.
The beams of the Alvis' headlights were poking up like search-
lights into the sky, and she saw a figure silhouetted against

their glare. Dr Ruff – his white hair fluttered in the same light breeze that was making her teeth chatter.

On either side of him were two torchbeams, moving away. Fritzi's companion and the faceless Delahaye? Probably.

Ruff seemed to be hesitating – she didn't think his heart was in this. It was one thing to be drawn to the seductive Nazi Dream of a 'new' world, another to realise that at its heart there lurked a nightmare. Too quickly he'd had to face the willingness of the fanatics to kill and destroy anything and anyone that lay in their path.

Rigby began to make her way along the ravine in the dark, feeling the sides with outstretched hands. Treacherously, the floor began to rise until what had been a protective trench became only a shallow indentation in the wide stretch of moor.

And there, not twenty yards away, was silhouetted the shape of one of the men. Rigby stood stock still, afraid that he had already heard her thrashing progress among the rocks and heather. He had his head on one side, listening. She could practically hear him breathing . . .

Something touched her shoulder and she yelped involuntarily. The searching torch immediately swung towards her, illuminating her white face and the benignly curious expression of the sheep that had nudged her companionably. Rigby ducked down and began to retrace her steps down the ravine.

"There is no use to hide, Fräulein. I have you, now."

The hell you do, Rigby thought, and bent to pick up a rock, just about the size of a cricket ball. There was little room for a decent run-up but the torch gave her the range and the target.

It was one of her better overarm deliveries.

There was a yelp. The torch flew in a high arc and disappeared into the thick heather and a body thudded after it. "Howzzat?" Rigby muttered, and climbed out of the far side of the ravine.

But no sooner had she emerged from the ravine than the other man – Delahaye – had her by the arms.

"Now then, little Miss Trouble," he said. "This has gone far enough."

"Too far, if you ask me," Rigby retorted, struggling in his grasp. "You traitor, you sneaking –"

66

"So you *did* see something, after all," he grunted as she wriggled and fought. "I knew it. I told the others – why else would you run away?"

"I couldn't stand the stench," Rigby said, aiming a kick at his knee and connecting with a satisfying crack. He swore and lurched to one side, but held fast to her left arm.

This was a mistake.

Rigby pivoted on her heel and took hold of his throat, her fingers searching for the tell-tale chords that would guide her to the vagus nerve in the side of his neck. As he swung the torch towards her temple, she pressed down, hard. Harder. They stood poised for an agonising moment and then he crumpled and lay at her feet.

"Thank you, Rama San Tal," she gasped, her chest heaving and blood thundering in her ears. "Lesson Fourteen – the Pathways to Higher Consciousness. I always thought there was something fishy about it – especially when I woke up and found my knickers on backwards. Never did get to Lesson Fifteen, did we?"

She managed to overcome her impulse to kick Mr Delahaye's head into touch, and searched him instead. After extracting his wallet and all other papers, she rummaged in her rucksack and found a black lace suspender belt with matching brassière, and a soft Russian leather belt. By the time she had finished, Mr Delahaye – if that was his real name – was trussed up. Very beautifully.

That left only Dr Ruff.

She stood and brushed her hair out of her eyes. It was obvious that she couldn't go blundering about on this godforsaken moor for the rest of the night. If she could sneak up on Ruff she might be able to knock him out and get away in the Alvis – the keys for which she had just extracted from the beautifully tailored tweed overcoat of Mr Delahaye.

But Ruff was gone when she got back to the burn. The little Riley and the Alvis stood there, but there was no one around. She suddenly realised that she could see the two cars more clearly, gleaming against the background of gold and purple heather. Several sheep had come to stand around and make comments, and the sky had begun to show the first signs of approaching dawn.

She'd managed to make it through the night – now all she had to do was make it back to the road! She'd vanquished two enemies, frightened off a third, and was definitely going to arrange the capture of a fourth. She hadn't done badly for an amateur! Why, there was nothing to this espionage business, nothing at all! With a light heart and not a single backward glance, she climbed into the Alvis, keyed it into throbbing life, turned it expertly, and started off.

As she came around the first bend she saw Dr Ruff lying sprawled in the road. She slammed on the brakes. At the same moment a shot rang out on her right and the big car swerved to one side, nearly going over into the heather. Shakily Rigby climbed out.

Fritzi was sitting on a rock, smoking a cigarette, wearing an immaculate lilac suit and smiling. Fritzi was also holding a small, chrome-plated revolver, from the barrel of which there spiralled a tiny wisp of smoke.

"*Guten Morgen*, Fräulein Rigby," said Fritzi.

Rigby stood absolutely still, staring at the round black eye of the gun's muzzle. She raised her eyes to Fritzi's. "So you remembered me, after all?"

"Oh, yes, I remembered you. And, unlike those fools, I do not underestimate you. Men do not think a woman has brains, or can be physically strong, but I know better, do I not? I am a woman and I am as clever and as strong as you. I am also something else."

"Rotten to the core?" Rigby suggested.

Fritzi laughed. "Only in your terms, my dear little Rigby. But determined to succeed. You are only determined to stop me – and that is not enough." The rising dawn light brought a glow to the perfect waves of Fritzi's ash-blonde hair. An errant breeze brought the scent of her expensive perfume to Rigby who stood in the road knowing she was filthy, ragged, soaked to the skin and scented only with sheep manure. It was a disadvantage only another woman could comprehend and Fritzi not only understood it, but was enjoying it.

Fritzi shrugged her elegant shoulders. "When the New Order rules, women will take their rightful place in it."

"No doubt you will be in charge of sewers," Rigby said, sweetly. "It's where rats belong."

Fritzi laughed again – it was really a most irritating laugh, Rigby thought. "But you are so bitter when you lose, you British," Fritzi said. "Really, it is unbecoming."

"Are you planning to shoot me or simply sit there giggling all morning?" Rigby asked.

"Oh, shoot you, of course," Fritzi said, brightly. "You can join the foolish doctor." She gestured with the gun. "The cowardly fool thought to stop us. He had no backbone, only foolish dreams. We need practical men now, not dreamers. We have left our dreams behind and are moving on."

"And what will you do after you have shot me?"

"I will find my two stupid companions whom you have left somewhere in the heather –" She paused. "Dead?"

"No," Rigby admitted.

"I thought not. You are so *humane*." She made it sound like a filthy habit. "When I have rescued them we will continue as planned. It will probably be some time before you and the stupid doctor are found down this track. By then we will be gone away."

"And the explanation?"

Fritzi shrugged. "You had a head injury, you were crazy from it, you ran away, the doctor came after you, you shot him and then, in a fit of remorse, shot yourself. What does it matter to me? I will not be here."

Rigby sighed in defeat. "All right. But may I tidy myself up a little, first?"

"So in the end only vanity remains, *ja*?" Fritzi smiled. "I think it would take hours, but you may have a few minutes."

"Thank you," Rigby said humbly. She removed her ruck-sack and knelt down on the road to rummage through it. Muttering something about finding a comb, she surreptitiously opened the new box of face-powder that Marie of Maison Bleu had blended especially for her.

Then, with a quick, snake-like twist of her arm, she flung it full in Fritzi's smug face. She followed through with a rugby tackle that would have made her father proud. He'd always wanted a boy, after all, and had taught her well.

There was an explosion that nearly took her head off (but only nicked an ear) as the gun flew out of Fritzi's hand and was lost in the thick heather. That was followed by a sound of ripping cloth as Fritzi's Chanel skirt parted company with its Chanel waistband. Rigby was left with a handful of lilac gabardine.

Trailing a string of German curses, Fritzi was already running down the road, nimbly skirting the corpse of the fallen doctor.

Grabbing her rucksack Rigby followed.

Fritzi was hampered by her neat little heeled shoes and slowed to kick them off. Glancing behind her she saw Rigby coming on quickly. With a shriek, Fritzi turned from the painfully gravelled road on to a dirt path. Branches of heather ripped and clawed at the delicate lace of her petticoat, soon reducing it to filthy tatters. Still she ran on, and Rigby ran after her.

There was a roaring, a steady thunder that grew louder and louder. Rigby thought it was the blood pounding in her ears but suddenly Fritzi stopped. Rigby stopped too, and stared at the white churning water that lay before them, stretching out of sight on either hand. The burn that had halted the cars had been running down to this – a broad, rock-clotted expanse of water hastening to the sea in a turmoil of rapids and falls.

"How now, Moriarty?" shouted Rigby, who had been weaned on Conan Doyle. Fritzi, unfamiliar with the scene by the Reichenbach Falls, stared at her in confused dismay.

Then, her lips drawing back in the snarl of a cornered animal, she leapt screaming at Rigby's throat. Rigby pushed her body forwards to counter the impact and they both slipped down the bank into the sucking whirl of the water. They went under and then rose as they were dragged along by the erratic current. Now pressed against a moss-slimed rock, now tossed into a whirlpool, spun and slammed and sucked down and spewed out and choking for breath, they still struggled against one another.

This was no place for odd abilities or couture clothes, for social repartee or intellectual cunning. This was survival, one female animal against another, and they spat and screamed and clawed and kicked mindlessly while the water roared around them.

Rigby, her lungs bursting, caught both hands in Fritzi's hair and dragged her head under as they approached a pool. But wet hair is slippery, and Fritzi twisted away and caught Rigby around the legs, then burst up out of the water and pressed a hand between her breasts, forcing her back until the water closed over her eyes and mouth.

Rigby rolled like a trout and slid away under the water, then surfaced behind a rock and tried to catch her breath while clinging to the rough granite. The current pulled at her and it was all she could do to hang on. Where was Fritzi?

There she was – on the far side of the stream, soaked to the skin and laughing triumphantly. "So, now – *auf Wiedersehen*!" she shouted over the noise of the rapids, then turned and began to move away. The sunrise was turning the sky to a pearly pink, tinged with gold. It was beautiful – but Rigby was filled with despair.

If Fritzi got back to Delahaye's house and made contact with whoever was in charge of the network, she could disappear into the unwary population and get on with her evil work. That mustn't happen!

Rigby dragged herself from the water. She was stiff with cold. Her rucksack lay back along the bank, slumped and nearly empty. Was there nothing more she could do? Desperately she ran back and began to rummage, turning out the last delicate bits of lacy lingerie, a handful of silk stockings and a perfectly wonderful new silk tussore nightgown from Brussels.

Useless stuff, just as she was. She stared at the mound of soft pastels, looked across the tumbling water at the fast-disappearing Fritzi and almost gave up.

Then she saw the broken shepherd's staff caught up by the water's edge. And remembered Colorado Red.

The rocks that breached the burn were widely spaced but the tricks of balance she had learned when she'd run away to that travelling French circus two years before stood her in good stead, now. She gained the far bank, tossed down the staff she had been using as a balance bar, picked up a few small rocks and began to run after Fritzi. As she went, she twisted the silk stockings together and used the rocks to weight them. Now she was getting closer – she could hear Fritzi's voice raised in anger. Then she saw her.

The blonde girl was slightly below her, surrounded by grey and white mounds. Fritzi was struggling through a group of sheep, pushing them aside wildly and cursing them. Benign and friendly, they crowded back around her, curious and unafraid.

Rigby took a deep breath. "Yippee ki ay!" she shouted – and let fly.

"You didn't!" Harry Rigby stared at her.

"I did. You said you never knew when a bit of Indian rope trickery would come in useful, that summer when you taught me the Pathan way with a lassoo. Before Fritzi knew what had hit her, I'd lassoed her, pulled her out of that herd, and roped her down ready for branding. Very strong, silk stockings." Rigby leaned back against the pillows and grinned back at her father.

Mayotte Rigby shook her head and tidied the coverlet which was the best the cottage hospital had to offer. "It's disgraceful, all this running around. It's so unfeminine, Dorothy. So rough. Why must you do these things?"

"I hardly volunteered for it, Mother," Rigby said, wryly. "I just stumbled into it and had to do my best using what I knew."

"You are *always* just stumbling into things," Mayotte murmured fretfully. "You are incorrigible." She bent to kiss her dangerous daughter.

Rigby winked at her father who winked back over his wife's beautifully coiffured head. "We're lunching with the Alexanders, but there's someone waiting to see you. Shall I trot him in?"

The 'someone' proved to be none other than Rupert Denham whom she had first met in Simla when she had helped uncover the duplicity of Lance Vulliamy. Rigby regarded him with caution.

After he had thanked her on behalf of the Government (very embarrassing) and had told her what had happened to the two unwelcome German visitors and their traitorous host (very satisfactory) he leaned back in his chair and was silent, just staring at her, until she became uncomfortable. "You have showed intelligence, resource, strength of character, patriotism, cunning and courage," he said.

Rigby felt herself blushing. This was awful. "I only did what anyone would do," she said, wishing he would go away.

"No – you did much more than that," he said gravely. He stared at her a moment longer, then spoke half to her and half to himself.

"I wonder . . ." he said.

———

"There's no point," Rigby said to me more than once at our regular meetings at the cottage, "in being wise after the event."

Rigby tended to be fatalistic. If Dr Ruff had slipped a really lethal dose into his hypodermic syringe . . . If Fritzi had not allowed her time to titivate . . . "If, if, if" Rigby would say, "it's just hypothetical, Timothy." (She always called me Timothy after our first meeting.) *"Que será, será!"* My own view is that our Intelligence people talent spotted her from a very early age indeed. Maybe – and that would be a joke – while she was at Cheltenham Ladies. Perhaps Miss Beale and Miss Buss were paid by Sir Vernon Kell! It's a nice line in speculation, even if not one Rigby herself was ever keen to pursue.

One incidental point. As I re-read Paula's piece I noticed how observant she'd been about clothing and scent and appearance. Cashmere and Chanel. Men tend to be bad about that sort of thing and I know I'm as guilty as the next person. It never occurred to me to ask Rigby where she bought her clothes, or what scent she preferred. Rigby noticed that too – and she also guessed rightly that Paula, who succeeded me as Chairman of the Crime Writers, was American. Don't ask me how. All Paula's questions were in writing and, as Rigby conceded, she knows Scotland really well – it's one reason I asked her to work on this episode. But though she's lived in England for years she is American and Rigby spotted it. Typical!

Michael Gilbert

THE RULES OF THE GAME

And so war came, as Rigby knew it would. Her father fought with Slim's 'Forgotten Army' in Burma. Her mother nursed and helped fighting men forget themselves. Valuable war work!

Rigby herself, as Michael Gilbert reveals, swiftly became an integral cog in the British war machine. He doesn't, incidentally, mention that Camilla became a dashing A.T.S. despatch rider, speeding about the country on a khaki Norton motorbike. When the chips were down, you could count on Camilla.

Gilbert himself had a different sort of war. The one hiccup came when he fell into the hands of German parachutists in North Africa and was held for six months in a prison camp. "Since," he says, "the camp was, fortunately, in Italy, not Germany, I was able to remove myself when the Italians called 'time' in 1943." He adds, "I was never parachuted into enemy territory (thank the Lord), nor was I ever a paid or unpaid member of MI5 or 6 or 7 to 12 inclusive; though for reasons now lost in obscurity some back-room boffin once insisted on my signing the Official Secrets Act, by which I am still, no doubt, bound. Nevertheless it was impossible not to come into touch from time to time with what is euphemistically called Intelligence and to gain at second hand an impression of how the wheels went round."

They went round for Rigby, all right. Slowly at first, but after a while she was caught up in them and they went faster and faster. The war was a boon for Rigby. It suited her age, her temperament, her need for danger and excitement and for pitting her wits against all adversaries. She was always a fighter and always game for anything. Or anyone.

D orothy Mayotte Rigby lay in bed, listening to the bombs. By the spring of 1941, the Germans had abandoned that indiscriminate scattering of high explosives over London, christened the Blitz. Now their bombing was more selective. Tonight it was the docks that were catching it.

If anything did happen to her, in her flat at the top of the house, it would happen with merciful speed. An old friend of hers had been trapped in a ground floor flat in Paddington and had been burned to death before the rescue squads could reach her. For the last half hour, as they cut their way through to her, they had heard her screaming.

The thud of an explosion, a little closer.

She was also an old-fashioned patriot. When the unemphatic Midland-businessman's voice of Neville Chamberlain had told them that they were at war with Germany, her wish had been, simply, to help her country to the fullest extent of her ability. So many people had felt the same that it had not been easy. In the end she had secured two jobs. By day she was one of a team of secretaries who worked for Hugh Dalton in the Ministry of Economic Warfare; unaware, as were most people, that he was also the founder and head of Special Operations Executive.

At the end of a long day's work in the office she went to help in an inter-services canteen in Westminster. This kept her busy until midnight. By the time she got home she was usually so tired that sleep came easily.

On this occasion she had something else to take her mind off the bombs. The message had come from none other than Portland, now one of Dalton's P.A.'s. If she was interested in a special and rather important job, would she present herself, at noon on the following day, at the Northumberland Hotel?

Special and important. Certainly she would do so. She went to sleep happily.

When she arrived, the custodian checked her name on a list and she followed a Boy Scout messenger up two flights of

77

stairs. The room she was shown into might have been, once, a second-class bedroom. The peace-time furnishings had been removed and replaced by a trestle table and three hard chairs.

The man who got up as she came in was a surprising contrast to the room. His beautifully cut pin-striped suit, cream shirt with thick gold cuff-links, his Rifle Brigade tie and the glimpse of a thin platinum watch chain across his double-breasted waistcoat would all have been very much at home in the ante-room of the Savoy Grill or propping up the Berkeley Bar. It was Denham.

"Miss Rigby?" The voice matched the clothes. "Rupert Denham. Simla – Scotland. And now Whitehall. Glad you decided to come."

"I could scarcely refuse," she said, "when the job was described as special and important."

"Yes. Both those things, certainly. Dangerous, too. I should make it clear that you have every right to say 'No'."

"Perhaps I had better hear about it first."

"Of course. Not reasonable to blame a horse for refusing a jump before you have even led him up to it."

In years to come she sometimes looked back on this as the beginning of a long association. They were weighing each other up.

"I shall have to start by explaining to you something of what is going on in France. For reasons that you will appreciate, I will keep much of this information general, not specific."

"Of course."

"The organisation which I represent has succeeded, in the months since France fell, in establishing circuits of men and women who are helpful to our cause. Twelve of them operate in the Unoccupied Zone, where life is somewhat easier. Five in the Occupied Zone. And of these, four are heading for disaster."

Saying this he had slid into French, smooth, unaccented, adorned with the occasional piece of slang. His mind seemed to run on horses. When speaking of impending disaster he had called it 'falling at the fences'.

"The exception is the Oberon circuit. It operates in both zones. In the Nevers-Dijon area just north of the dividing line and around Vichy to the south of it. As to why it has proved more successful than the others, I must be frank with you: the other circuits are amateurs, despatched from here, brave and well-intentioned. All the members of the Oberon circuit are professionals nominated by de Gaulle himself, before he came to this country, from the lower ranks of the French Army intelligence service and the police. Two of them certainly have criminal records. They owe their prime allegiance to the General, but they are administered by us and they report to us. The flow of Intelligence material they have given us, to say nothing of their active help to escaping prisoners, has been quite invaluable. To lose them would be a major set-back."

"And is there some danger," said Rigby, also in French, "that this circuit may fail?"

Since he seemed fond of race-course language she used the word '*se dégonfler*', a piece of argot applied to a horse which refuses a jump. Denham listened carefully while she was speaking. Like an oral examiner, she thought. She was not worried. His French was smooth but hers, she was confident, was as good. And possibly more up-to-date.

"Until recently," said Denham, reverting to English, "one would have said that the Oberon circuit was operating in complete safety and would continue to do so. Our confidence stemmed from the method in which it had been set up. The other four groups I mentioned were composed of friends, known to each other and operating as a team. In sending them into the field we had underestimated the techniques and the brutality of the Gestapo. First they picked up one member of the group and got to work on him. Sooner or later, according to his power of resistance, they extracted the names and particulars of all the others. These could then be rounded up at leisure. That is precisely what has happened to two of our circuits and is a constant threat to the other two. You follow me?"

Rigby nodded. She was finding speech difficult as she faced up to the expression 'got to work on'. If Denham noticed this he refrained from comment.

"The Oberon circuit on the other hand is formed on what they call the '*méthode d'échelle*' – the ladder system. Each member of it knows only one other, his 'contact'. If any member of the circuit were taken, his 'contact' would be removed, if possible, to a place of safety – probably to Switzerland, thus preventing the infection from spreading. Only the head of the group would know everyone, but in this case he was above suspicion: a retired state prosecutor, a cosmopolitan with as many friends in Germany as in France, a landowner in the Digoin area, conveniently situated almost on the dividing line between the occupied and unoccupied zones – Henri d'Espagne."

"Of the Château de Belle Espérance?"

"Correct. And I fancy you knew his daughter, Claudette."

"Very well indeed. She was a great friend at school and afterwards I stayed with the family in France. Are you telling me that she is involved in this?"

"She is indeed involved. When d'Espagne, who died last month of his third and most massive heart attack, was setting up the circuit for de Gaulle he used her as a messenger and intermediary. His own health was already making travelling difficult. She was his eyes and his voice. She went everywhere and knew everyone. When we understood this, we had one paramount objective: *to remove Claudette from France.*"

"And she has refused to leave?"

"It is difficult to argue and to persuade when one's only contact is by coded message, passed through different hands. We have concluded that the only method likely to succeed is by personal contact."

"So when do I start?"

The directness of this took even so imperturbable a character as Rupert Denham by surprise. After a long moment he said, "It was certainly our intention to offer you this assignment. You seem to be uniquely fitted for it. But normally we should have advised you to sleep on it."

She said with a smile, "A night's sleep is unlikely to change my mind. And a well-placed bomb might remove your candidate."

"True."

"I imagine that speed is important."

"It is vital. Circumstances might direct the attention of the Gestapo to Claudette at any moment."

"Then you may take it that I am ready to go immediately."

"I wish that were true. Unfortunately it is not. It will take a fortnight, probably more, to give you the minimum training. And that will mean compressing into two weeks a course which normally takes two months. However, there are a number of items which can be dispensed with in your case." He ticked them off on his fingers. "Parachute training. Unnecessary. Entry by parachute is a one-way operation. In your case we aim to get you out with Claudette, so a different method will be chosen. Wireless and code drill. Unnecessary. General commando and fitness training. I have young Portland's word that you played five games of squash with him recently, and left him on his knees."

"Leslie's fat and chair-borne. But yes, I am reasonably fit."

"Then that leaves three items. First, tactical training. What to expect when travelling in France. What help to look for, what action to take in emergencies. Second, your own cover story. You are Madeleine Lamotte, travelling throughout the Haute Loire district, getting orders for your uncle's glassware and china business. Finally, and most important, you must be taught how to kill. Both with knife and gun and with less conventional weapons. Above all, how to kill silently."

"That seems a moderately full fortnight's work," agreed Rigby.

Exactly three weeks later she was occupying the corner seat of an 'omnibus' carriage in a train which, if it ran to time, would reach Le Donjon in half an hour.

Of those three weeks the first two had been as hard as she had expected them to be. It had not been so much the physical training which, in her case, had mostly been swimming length after length in the Olympic Baths at Hammersmith. Excellent exercise for all her muscles. And she had enjoyed the pistol practice and the unarmed combat on which her instructor, a male chauvinist, had reported 'Remarkable progress – for a woman'. It was the classroom work which had tired her. The advice and instruction which had to be memorised, the ceaseless repetition of names and places.

She wondered whether her life, up to that point, might have produced a hard body and a soft mind. A disquieting thought, if true.

At the end of the second week a Sunderland flying-boat had

taken her to Gibraltar. After a wait of forty-eight hours on the Rock she had boarded a submarine with an amazingly youthful skipper which had surfaced, after an unexciting interval, off a beach some way east of Toulon. She had been ferried ashore by a French sailor who had removed his sailor's cap as soon as he landed, put on a chauffeur's cap and led her to an aged green Citroën which was parked in the sandhills. In this he had driven her to a villa on the outskirts of Toulon where he had handed her over to a comfortable, middle-aged lady whom he addressed as 'Duchesse'. This, she guessed, was a cover name, not a title.

She was, by now, sufficiently well instructed in the etiquette of clandestine travel not to enquire her hostess's real name, but there was one matter which she had to pursue. She said, when they were sitting together in the *art nouveau* lounge that evening, "I was told that, once I was in France, all my instructions would come from a certain Michel. Ought I to make contact with him?"

"Ah, Michel!" Duchesse said. "What a man!"

Feeling, perhaps, that this had not fully dealt with her point she added, "It is not easy for him to communicate, as I am sure you will understand. However, I heard from him, through a friend, this morning. You will be going from here by train to Le Donjon, but not today. Today a special control has been imposed by the police. On the orders of the Germans, it is said."

"Do you know why?"

"Maybe they are looking for someone. Who knows? Meanwhile, make yourself comfortable. Tomorrow I hope you will be able to go forward."

It occurred to Rigby that, even if there was a control on the train, her papers being in perfect order and her cover watertight, it need not have stopped her. She was beginning to feel that she was part of a machine which was moving at its own pace, not at hers, and she was not entirely comfortable about this.

By the following morning it seemed that the control had been relaxed. Before she left the villa Duchesse gave her a handsome cockade in the form of a spray of fern leaves. "Wear it when you arrive," she said. "It will bring you good fortune."

Rigby gathered that it was some form of recognition signal. The green Citroën appeared with the same driver and she was deposited in the forecourt of Toulon station where she acquired, without difficulty, a ticket for Le Donjon and a seat on the Lyon express. At Lyon she changed on to a slower train which dawdled across country to Vichy where she changed for a second time, on to a train composed entirely of half-empty omnibus-class carriages. The slow rhythm of the train matched her thoughts.

Her main preoccupation was the invisible Michel. Perhaps he would meet her at Le Donjon. She had pinned the cockade ostentatiously on to the lapel of her smart jacket. But when she stepped down from the carriage it attracted the attention only of a schoolboy, who sidled up and said, "M'selle Lamotte?" and, when she nodded, "Can you ride a bicycle, *ma mère?*"

She said, "I was riding a bicycle before you were out of your nappies".

The boy grinned and led the way out through a door labelled 'Personnel de CNF'. Here two ancient bicycles were propped against the wall. The boy strapped the capacious waterproof shoulder bag which held all her possessions on to the back of his own machine and pedalled off through the maze of back streets behind the station.

Her destination this time was a top-storey flat in a new looking block. The door was opened by a brown-faced middle-aged man with an impressive white moustache. An ex-soldier, she guessed, and was not surprised to find that his cover name was 'the Colonel'. He apologised for the absence of his wife, who was out shopping, and showed her her room.

From the window Rigby could see the low ridge of hills behind which, as she knew, ran the upper waters of the Loire. She got out the Michelin map and studied it. She felt that it was high time that she took charge of her own destiny.

Later that afternoon, when his wife had still not reappeared, the Colonel suggested that they walk out to meet her. Rigby agreed willingly. She had had enough of sitting about. Also it amused her to realise that the old buck was delighted at the thought of parading with her.

The streets were full of shoppers and strollers.

"No Germans in uniform here," said the Colonel. "We are south of the line. Plenty of the other sort. Grey slugs." He indicated a party of three who occupied a table in front of the principal café. "*Vert-de-gris*, we call them." He inspected them with distaste.

They were a curious trio. Two of them were bulky, pale-faced, soberly dressed men who might have come from a business or civil service background.

"Gestapo, without doubt," said the Colonel. "I can smell them."

Between them sat a French youth whose outfit contrasted sharply with that of his companions. He was wearing a long jacket with slits in the back, tight trousers and two-tone shoes. His blond hair was a great deal longer than the Army would have approved.

"A *zazou*," said the Colonel. "A nancy boy. The Germans use them as spies. They should be exterminated." He had not troubled to lower his voice. "Ah, here is my dear wife, at last."

The Colonel's lady was encumbered with her shopping and Rigby hastened to relieve her of some of it. The Colonel did not assist. Evidently he believed that soldiers did not carry parcels.

That evening, fortified by an excellent dinner, Rigby decided that the time had come to make her feelings clear to her host. She was grateful, she said, for the careful organisation which had brought her so far on her journey. But the time had come for her to cease being carried like a registered parcel. She must stand on her own feet.

She explained some of this to the Colonel, who listened courteously. She said, "From the map I see that we are twenty kilometres from Digoin. From there, perhaps, another seven to my destination, the Château de Belle Espérance."

"I regret that you should have told me that."

"You didn't know?"

"In our trade, knowledge is only shared when it is necessary. My part is to look after you until I get further instructions."

"From Michel?"

"From him, or through him."

"But why must we wait? I could reach the château from

here on foot and return the same night with the girl I have come to fetch."

"You forget one thing. There is a frontier to cross. The line between the Unoccupied and the Occupied Zones. At this point it runs along the Loire. There are bridges, of course. Large ones at Digoin and Dompierre. Smaller ones in between."

"They are guarded?"

"Some of them, some of the time. However, there are men who regularly make the trip across the line. Food is still plentiful in this zone. It is becoming much scarcer in the other."

"Then these men are blackmarketeers. And I am to attach myself to them?"

"It would seem logical. They have the necessary knowledge and skill. I think that Michel will arrange matters in this way."

"Michel!" said Rigby, trying to keep the impatience out of her voice. "Who is he? Have you ever met him?"

"Never. But in the circles I move in, his suggestions are treated as orders."

"*My* orders emphasised that speed was important. I am prepared to wait until tomorrow night, but no longer."

The Colonel awarded her a tolerant smile.

As it fell out, her patience was not to be tried to breaking point. At dusk on the following day a vehicle drew up in the back yard of the block. It was an old army three-tonner, designed for transporting goods but adapted for carrying people by the insertion of a bench along each side under the canvas tilt at the back. The driver, a bird-like Provençal, hopped down and entered into earnest conversation with the Colonel. It was clear to Rigby that she was the subject of it.

She half hoped that she might secure the seat by the driver, but this was occupied by a fat, red-faced brute – a Belgian by his accent – who clearly had no intention of giving it up. She moved round to examine the back. There were five men already in it, three on one side and two on the other. The space between their feet was crammed with bales and bundles. While she was hesitating, a friendly hand helped her and her shoulder bag over the tailboard. She had barely time to lean out and say goodbye to the Colonel when they were off.

It was a curious journey. Avoiding the *route nationale* they stuck to the smallest of side roads. At every crossing they halted and an animated discussion took place between the driver and the Belgian. He had opened up a corner of the curtain between the front and rear of the truck, thus involving the other passengers in the debate. It seemed to Rigby that he usually had the last word.

She had memorised the map very carefully and a glimpse of the word Talent on a signboard told her that they must be intending to use the bridge at La Varenne. This would suit her well. As soon as they were across the river she could complete her journey on foot.

It was in the hamlet of St Radegonde that she changed her mind.

They had drawn up in the square opposite an *estaminet*, and this time the driver had dismounted and was talking to someone who had been standing in the doorway. The Belgian, who seemed to disapprove of this, was leaning across the driver's seat prepared to dominate the discussion. The other passengers were craning forward to see what was happening.

At this moment a van came into the square from the north. As it swung round its headlights lit up the doorway. The man who had been standing there drew back quickly, but not quickly enough.

It was the blond youth who had been sitting with the two Gestapo men in the café.

A tactical precept which had been drilled into Rigby said: if you are heading for disaster, do something unexpected and do it quickly.

She muttered to the friendly man on her right, "I alight here," lifted the canvas, slid down over the tailboard on to the cobbles and took to her heels.

Behind her a volley of voices had broken out, but she was already clear of the square and dodging round the church. She was confident she would not be followed. The truck had its own programme and would not hang about.

As soon as she was out of the village she abandoned the road and took to the fields. Thank God for S.O.E. training. No need for a compass. The pointers of the Great Bear and the bright eye of the Pole Star showed her the way. By keeping north with a little west in it she must reach the Loire downstream from Varenne.

When she slid down the bank on to the shingle Rigby saw that the river, though nothing like as formidable as in its lower reaches, was broader than she had imagined. She stripped naked, packed her clothes into the top of the shoulder bag, drew the string tightly and fastened it across her shoulders.

The water still had the chill of winter in it. She struck out, swimming a sedate breast stroke to keep her bag out of the water. Ten minutes later she was crouched on the north bank, drying herself on a scrap of towel. It was ten o'clock.

The Château de Belle Espérance, when she had stayed there in peace-time, had not been notable for early nights. In war-time it might be different. However, when she arrived, she was relieved to see lights on in many of the rooms.

It had been quite an easy approach march. She had halted once, at the sound of gun-fire away on the right, but she had met no one. A grey-haired man who answered the door peered at her and said, with a mixture of surprise and alarm, "M'selle Rigby!"

"Indeed, Gaston. I have come to see your mistress. On business," she added sharply when he seemed to hesitate.

"M'selle Claudette is in the small salon. But –"

"No need to announce me. I know the way."

After a moment's hesitation the old man stepped aside and she ran up the stairs, opened the door of the smaller of the two salons and stepped in.

Claudette d'Espagne, who had been sitting at her desk, writing, swung round in her chair. She did not, as she would have done in the old days, jump up and embrace Dorothy. She seemed to have aged ten years. The eyes were narrower, the mouth was harder. It was no longer the face of a girl. It was the face of a wary and disillusioned woman.

She said, in a voice which matched her expression, "What in the world are you doing here? How did you get here? What do you want?"

"To persuade you, I sincerely hope, to come back with me to England."

A long silence. Then, "I see. A follow-up to two rather curious messages I received, whose object I found it difficult to understand."

"The object was very simple. It was to save you from the attentions of the Gestapo."

Claudette laughed. It was not a pleasant sound. She said, "Perhaps you would be good enough, my dear Rigby, to explain why *I* should be afraid of the Gestapo. They are policemen. The only people who are afraid of policemen are criminals."

It was clear to Rigby by now that her mission was in tatters. This new Claudette had no intention of leaving France. To discover how far the change had gone she said, with an edge in her voice, "You realise that it was not you alone that we wished to protect? It was the members of your father's organisation."

"As I thought. Then let me tell you that I have only recently discovered how my father was duped. The men you are speaking of are not patriots. No. Many of them are criminals. And all of them are traitors. Avowed followers of the self-styled Général Charles de Gaulle."

Rigby was aware that many Frenchmen disliked de Gaulle, but she had never heard his name pronounced with such venom. Claudette must have noted the look on her face because she said, speaking more rationally but just as bitterly, "How can you, sitting smugly at home, have any idea of our feelings? When your army ran away at Dunkirk, it was father Pétain who came to our assistance. He is not only the lawful head of our Government, he is our hero. We do not forget the victories and sacrifices of Verdun. He is the living symbol of our last victory. It is to him that we owe our loyalty and our obedience. And I must warn you that he has decreed that anyone who assists or conceals a traitor is himself a traitor."

"And so," said Rigby coldly, "you would defile your father's honour by handing over his friends to imprisonment and torture?"

"A fate which they have brought on themselves."

"And me, too, no doubt?"

"Certainly not. I have no quarrel with you. You have been duped as my father was."

(The gun was in its holster, under her left arm. Her duty was now quite clear.)

"Also, I promise you that I shall not say a word until you

have had every chance to return to your own country."

(But she was capable of carrying out, in cold blood, the execution of someone who had been her friend? Even if that friendship had, sadly, been lost?)

By hesitating, she had forfeited any chance she might have had. Someone had come into the room. Rigby was unsurprised to see the blond youth. He had a gun in his hand, an obscene-looking weapon, with its bulbous silencer.

He said to her, "Turn round and face the wall". She had no thought of refusing. Then he fired, twice. Out of the corner of her eye she saw Claudette rise on to her toes, as though she was dancing, and then crumple on to the carpet.

The boy bent forward and shot her carefully through the back of the neck. He said, "I did not want you to see that. She was, I understand, your friend. I think it will be best if we go now? Yes?"

When Rigby tried to think about it afterwards, she was unable to recollect with any clearness the events of the next few minutes. She knew only that they left the château by a side door and started across the park at a brisk trot. By the time they reached the wall and the aged car which was parked outside it, the night air and the exercise had combined to restore her senses.

"If we encounter trouble," the blond youth said, "we abandon the car and run in different directions. It will be for you to make your own way back to Le Donjon. The Colonel will take care of you."

"So I am to be posted back? A returned empty?"

"You are blaming yourself? There is no reason to do so. Training can teach you how to kill. It cannot nerve you to pull the trigger. That comes only with experience."

Seeing him now, at close quarters, she realised that he was older than she had thought. Older and much more formidable. "You are Michel," she said. It was a statement, not a question.

"I go by that name. And since it was I who asked London to send you, it was naturally my duty to look after you. Not," he added, "by any means an unpleasant duty."

She let this go. It was not a moment for small talk. Rigby wanted the truth, however unpalatable.

"So I was sent to provoke Claudette into declaring her true feelings?"

"Correct. We could not move until we knew where she stood. Her father, you understand, was a most respected figure. It would have been inconceivable to have condemned her without the clearest proof. Which you obtained for us with considerable skill."

"I might have done better," said Rigby stiffly, "if you had seen fit to take me into your confidence."

"It is the unbreakable rule. Tell no one anything they do not need to know. And see how well things have fallen out. Gaston will talk. It will be learned that Claudette was killed by a female agent sent from London. No reprisals will fall on our organisation."

"I'm glad you're satisfied."

"More than satisfied. And might I predict that when you have had more experience you will be a very successful operator? For you possess the one faculty that counts above all others. An instinct for danger. It led you to leave the *camion* and take to your heels. If you had not done so you would be dead, or captured. The crossing of the bridge at Varenne had been sold to the Germans."

"By that Belgian?"

"Correct. He did so to gain their tolerance for his trade. The Germans were aiming to kill the driver. He was one of our best men. The machine-gun is an indiscriminate weapon. The Belgian was killed too. If he had not been, we should, of course, have executed him ourselves."

As the car started she was conducting an internal debate. The compliment he had paid to her was very agreeable. Should she tell him that it was based on a total misconception planted by the Colonel, who probably assumed that any well-dressed male in Le Donjon was a member of the Gestapo?

It would be honourable to confess this and she was on the point of doing so when a further thought stopped her. After all, he *didn't need* this information.

When she laughed Michel heard her, above the rattle of the car, and asked her what was amusing her.

She said, "I'm just beginning to understand the rules".

Claudette's betrayal was yet another of those dagger thrusts which Rigby had to endure in early life. She says she was not suspicious by nature, but life taught her to be frugal with her trust. It made her wary – never cynical. She never lost a passionate patriotism and an almost equally intense optimism about her fellow man. (Man meaning 'mankind'. Rigby was a walking embodiment of female emancipation, but irritated by self-proclaimed 'feminists' who, she maintained briskly, were 'nothing of the sort'.)

After the incident at the Château de Belle Espérance, Rigby was passed along the chain from one Resistance group to another until finally being flown out in a Westland Lysander, a small high-winged monoplane which only needed five hundred yards of grass or clover to take off. Rigby's was one of just seven hundred such 'pick-ups' conducted by the Special Operations Executive.

Back home she found that she was now accepted into the small, shadowy little world of Intelligence as a proven professional. Denham had indeed been observing her from afar ever since the Vulliamy affair in Simla. He knew all about Manfred and the Führer and now, in his view, Rigby's promise was fulfilled. She remained as a secretary in the Ministry of Economic Warfare and she continued to help out in the canteen at night, but more and more often she disappeared, sometimes for months at a time.

Camilla and her other friends and colleagues were naturally suspicious, but they never dared ask. Somehow people never did. Oddly enough what she remembers best of those years was a popular song called, 'I got it bad and that ain't good'. She would catch herself singing it at the oddest moments.

Richard Martin Stern

THE BOMB

On December 7th, 1941 the Japanese bombed Pearl Harbor. Later that month Churchill visited Washington with Denham in tow. When they returned Rigby was summoned to Denham's office.

"I think," he said, "it would be wise if you started to familiarise yourself with our American cousins. They're going to be rather important from now on. Know any Americans, Rigby?"

Rigby blushed. "I had a bit of a pash on Ambassador Kennedy's son Jack. We went riding in the park once or twice before his father was recalled."

"Joe Kennedy's nothing but a bloody bog-trotter," said Denham. "Not that I've anything against the boy but his father's no friend of ours. There's a new film out called *Citizen Kane*. Tells you a lot about Americans. Go and see it. And read some American books. Raymond Chandler, John Steinbeck, William Faulkner. I'll give you a reading list."

And so it was that Rigby became an instant authority on the United States of America. She would infuriate poor Denham with such conversational gambits as "Max Baer hasn't a prayer against Joe Louis" or "Do you fancy Oregon State or U.S.C. for the Rose Bowl?" She started to build a collection of Aaron Copland 78s; she knew by heart the U.S. Supreme Court Action bought by the Jehovah's Witnesses to reverse the 1940 ruling on children saluting the national flag; and she cultivated a string of admirers at the U.S. Embassy, so successfully that she practically cornered the black market in nylon stockings.

Finally the work paid off. "Northolt airport, Friday at nine," said Denham. "Take an overnight bag and a handful of dollars. You're crossing the pond."

P assing through the eye of the proverbial needle, Rigby decided, would have been nursery play compared to finding, reaching and getting into what was locally called The Hill (though it was only rarely even referred to), a place more properly named Los Alamos, located in the wilderness of New Mexico, U.S.A.

After the bucket seat flight to Gander and on to Chicago, there was the troop train journey on the Atchison, Topeka and Santa Fe railroad which did not, in point of fact, ever reach Santa Fe. Rigby was let off the train in early morning darkness at a place called Lamy – pronounced Lame-y, despite having been named after a French priest.

Seventeen miles away, in the clear air of Santa Fe at an unlikely elevation of 7000 feet, she passed through the cordial, informal, but definite scrutiny of Mrs McKibbin, called Dottie by everyone, who smiled a great deal while her eyes carried on their careful assessment.

Rigby received documents already prepared and was provided with transport on unsurfaced country roads through early morning landscapes of wind-and-water eroded rock formations in which it was easy to believe that ancient people had once dwelt, as indeed they had, in cliffside caves facing southward for the sun's warmth.

Los Alamos itself was perched on the side of a mountain at an elevation of 7500 feet, surrounded by chain-link fence and guard houses in one of which Rigby's documents were scrutinised carefully, a hushed telephone call was made and, finally, entrance allowed.

Inside, her first, overpowering impressions were of mud, temporary buildings and an air of quiet excitement – in the order named.

Antony Hobbs, thank Heaven, was there to meet her. "Welcome to this organised madness," he said, and bussed her soundly. "One is not allowed, I assume, to ask what brings you here?"

"The usual muddle," Rigby said, and left it there. At this point she could scarcely have told him that it was he himself she had been sent to scrutinise.

Back in London, Denham had made the point obliquely, but quite clearly. "There are faint indications," he had said in his easy, precise way, "that the British contingent working at Los Alamos is not, shall we say, wholly leakproof. You and Antony Hobbs have known one another well from time to time, so it seems logical that you would be the person to pay him an official visit."

"Surely you don't suspect Tony?"

When Denham smiled he was very much the father figure. "Let us say that we will put our trust in your instincts, my dear. Your clearances and transport are already arranged. *Bon voyage.*"

There was, it turned out, a cocktail bash that first evening at one of the new, temporary houses located in what was known as Bathtub Row – for obvious reasons. Rigby met, and filed away in that precise memory of hers, a number of men, scientists all, some of whose names were familiar, and some not.

Among others, there were Robert Oppenheimer, Enrico Fermi, Edward Teller, an amusing little man named Heyne-mann, Hans Bethe, George Gamov, Carson Mark, Louis Rosen and Norris Bradbury, and the conversation ranged from the quality of the martinis Robert Oppenheimer mixed (high) to the ubiquitous mud (reminiscent, someone remarked, of Passchendaele in the 1914-18 War).

Rigby also gathered that some of the scientists, in particular those who had only recently arrived, were not exactly sure why they were there, or exactly what they were supposed to be doing. No one mentioned the atomic energy that, it was hoped, might be packaged in a small enough container to be carried in an aircraft and dropped as a bomb. Nor was the term 'Manhattan Project' ever mentioned.

Later that evening, over a nightcap in Tony's quarters, it was Tony himself who brought the subject up. He studied the liqueur in his glass thoughtfully and then turned on Rigby a crooked, somehow self-deprecating smile. "Do you know what we are doing, or trying to do here?" he said.

"Vaguely."

Tony nodded. "Quite," he said, and studied his glass again as if trying to make up his mind. He said at last, "If we are successful —" He looked again at Rigby. "Note that I say *if* —" He paused. "It is my belief, no, my conviction that the world will never again be the same. Robert Oppenheimer shares that view. How many others do, I cannot say."

Rigby said quietly, "Are you hoping for failure, Tony?"

"No, dear girl, I am not. I am hoping for success because there is no alternative. And yet I fear the results." He sipped his liqueur. "A distressing paradox." He showed again that crooked, self-mocking smile. "Because I happen to be a bit better than ordinary physicist, this is the position I find myself in. I could wish it were otherwise."

"What, precisely, do you fear, Tony?"

Tony closed his eyes for a few moments. When he opened them again, they seemed filled with sadness. "What I fear is unwise use of what we are trying to accomplish. The Americans will have a monopoly. Whether they use it wisely and well is the question." He stood up suddenly and drained his glass at one gulp. "Forgive me. I have kept you up far too long after what must have been an arduous journey."

Rigby smiled. "It was worth it, if only to see you – and this place." She saw the instant change in Tony's attitude, and added quickly, "No, I am not, as the Americans say, still carrying a torch for you, Tony. But we were very good friends once, and I have not forgotten that."

Despite her fatigue sleep did not come easily for Rigby that night. Tony was a man of principles; that she had known for a long time. And it was not for the first time that she found herself wondering how far and in which directions principles could lead a man. Or a woman. Damn Denham, she thought – also not for the first time – for sending her on this particular mission. On that thought, sleep finally came.

She met General Groves, the man in overall command of the project, the next day. "I dislike the feeling that people are looking over my shoulder," he told her straightaway, "although by now I suppose I ought to be used to it."

"I am friendly," Rigby said, "and I certainly do not intend to interfere in any way. I was sent here merely to assure our

British contingent that they are not forgotten in London."

The General smiled. It seemed to be an effort. "Well," he said, "I must say they sent an attractive messenger."

"Why, thank you kindly, sir." Rigby's smile had been known to reduce far more formidable men to friendliness.

She saw Tony again that afternoon. "I have been looking for you," he said, "and I must say you do leave a trail. At the mere mention of your name I get immediately nothing but smiles."

"Something on your mind, Tony?"

"In point of fact, yes. My mind is in a complete muddle. It happens. I stare at a problem too long and the knowns and unknowns become inextricably entangled. So I need your help."

"Doing what?"

"Going for a trudge with me in these lovely mountains." Again the self-deprecating smile. "Maybe breathing this clean air in your company will clear away the cobwebs. Are you on?"

Rigby showed her full, brilliant smile. "Lovely," she said.

"Ponderosa pines," Tony said as they walked up a dirt path among the big trees. Their pleasant scent filled the air. "Their thick, platelike bark is protective. They are quite happy if a modest fire sweeps through here every nine or ten years. It cleans out the undergrowth and fallen branches and leaves the big trees unscathed."

His interests had always ranged widely, Rigby thought, and he took the trouble to learn about whatever caught his interest. He was a comfortable man to be with and had always been, but last night's thoughts still nagged.

"This entire mountain," Tony said, "is what remains of an ancient, extinct volcano. Caldera, really. What is called the Valle Grande is the vast centre of the caldera which in geologic times erupted and then collapsed. A fascinating place."

"The entire place is fascinating," Rigby said. "I have rarely heard so many different accents and even some foreign tongues." She kept her tone strictly conversational.

"To my knowledge," Tony said, "there has never been a

single scientific project as vast as this one. There are scientists from Middle Europe and a number who fled Hitler's Germany, along with men from our part of the world and from all parts of America."

"From Russia, too?"

"No, dear girl. Definitely not from Russia. They are our allies, but I am afraid they are viewed with considerable distrust, regardless." He walked for a time in silence. Then, "And, as I said last night, America is determined to retain its monopoly – *if* we succeed."

"Is that a bad thing, Tony?"

"Stunning view," Tony said and waved one hand at the vastness suddenly visible through a break in the trees. "Let us sit here for a few moments and enjoy it." He waved his hand again as they sat down. "Over there is the mountain range called Sangre de Cristo, Blood of Christ. Named by the Spaniards, of course, because sunsets turn winter snow on their slopes to shades of pink and red. *Alpenglühen* they call it in the Alps."

He picked up a small stone, looked at it briefly and tossed it aside. "Is monopoly a bad thing?" he said, and looked at Rigby. "I am not sure. An ideal world would be one in which all knowledge is disseminated freely. Unhappily, the world we live in is far from ideal. Particularly now. You agree?"

"How can I not?"

Tony nodded. "Quite. Even in war-time, and among our allies, we draw our borders jealously and seek our own advantages. Pity."

"Do many feel the same way? Here, I mean?"

"I think so. Robert thinks internationally, but his is a mind that refuses to accept limits. Others have their own reasons. A friend named Klaus, for example, fled Hitler's Germany in 1933 and came to our island where he completed his studies. When war broke out, he was in Canada and was interned as an enemy alien. Later he obtained British citizenship. So you can see that he might be pulled in many directions."

"Klaus? Did I meet him?"

"Klaus Fuchs? No. He is not as gregarious as some of us are."

99

"I seem to have heard the name," Rigby said, "but I cannot remember where." Not true; she knew very well where she had heard the name.

Tony stood up and, reaching down, pulled her to her feet. "Shall we walk on?"

War-time America was quite different from war-time Britain, Rigby had already discovered. There were shortages, yes, but not on the scale of Britain's war-time shortages. Petrol, for example, was not readily available, but there was constant motorcar traffic between Los Alamos and Santa Fe nonetheless, and arranging a lift was quite easy.

She had tea with the woman, Dottie McKibbin, who had received her in Santa Fe that first day and through whose hands, she had learned, everyone assigned to or merely visiting Los Alamos had to pass. It was an instructive interlude.

"Tony Hobbs?" Dottie said and produced her ready smile. "Oh, dear me, yes. He was one of the first. A great friend of Robert's. A very thoughtful man, don't you think?"

"Very."

"As Robert is thoughtful, far beyond the scope of what he is doing at the moment."

"Considering the consequences, perhaps?"

"I think," Dottie McKibbin said, suddenly thoughtful herself, "that there are a number who are already considering the consequences. I have heard Robert say that the consequences are incalculable. Do have another brownie."

"Do you know a man named Klaus Fuchs?" Rigby said, keeping her voice entirely uninflected.

"Yes." There was a little hesitation. "Not well. I don't think anyone knows him well."

"A theoretical physicist," Rigby said.

"So I understand. In Carson Mark's group," Dottie McKibbin studied Rigby's face. "British," she said.

"Technically, yes. Originally German."

"There are a number who were German," Dottie said. She did not elaborate.

Rigby sipped her tea and nibbled on another rich brownie. "Your American intelligence – F.B.I. isn't it? – must have a great deal of screening to do. All those people up on The Hill."

Dottie's smile did not reach her eyes. "I imagine they must."

"Or," Rigby said, "are our people, for example, accepted as having been vetted by British authorities?"

"That is outside my purview," Dottie McKibbin said. "But I understand our policy is not to appear obstructive, particularly since we seem to need all the scientific help we can find." She smiled again. "May I ask what prompted the question?"

Rigby smiled in return. "Sheer curiosity. Security appears to be tight, and yet with so many –" She spread her hands.

"If one listens to rumours," Dottie McKibbin said, "one can hear all sorts of stories."

"Just as you see all sorts of people passing through here."

"Exactly." Dottie smiled. "And it is not my job to judge them. More tea?"

Rigby left Mrs McKibbin's and walked back to the old plaza. It was there, in front of the Palace of the Governors, that she first met Jim Forrest.

He suddenly appeared, a medium-sized, smiling young man. "Miss Rigby," he said. "I have been waiting for you."

Rigby studied him carefully. "Do I know you?"

"I hope not." He was still smiling. "Maybe a short walk out into the centre of the plaza?" The smile spread. "I'm harmless. Honest."

"I am meeting someone," Rigby said.

"Yes. Your ride back to Los Alamos. I will see that you get back, safely, whenever you want."

"Who are you?"

"Jim Forrest, F.B.I., and I believe we have an interest in common. His name is Antony Hobbs." His hand disappeared, re-appeared, palm up, displaying a shield in a leather case, and disappeared again, all in the blink of an eye.

Rigby said, "Do you do other magic tricks, Mr Forrest?"

"Afraid not. That's why I need your help. May we talk?"

They sat on a bench in the plaza. "It's not news to you," Forrest said, "that there appear to be leaks on The Hill."

"And your people suspect Tony Hobbs?"

"Let's say he's a likely possibility."

"Enlarge on that."

"He makes no bones about his philosophical views on what they are trying to accomplish, and he has been heard to say that an American monopoly might be . . . awkward, even perhaps dangerous."

Rigby said nothing.

Obviously Forrest took her silence as reluctance to accept his thesis. He said, "He is also one of the few at Los Alamos who are in a position to see the broad pattern of the project and to know precisely where it is at any given time."

Rigby said, "Those are hardly compelling reasons for deep suspicion of what amounts to treason."

"Between us," Forrest said, "I agree. On the other hand, there are leaks."

"Going in which direction?"

"East, and not to the Reich."

Rigby thought about it. "In the early Thirties," she said, "Tony, like a great number of other young intellectuals, admired the Soviet experiment. That is on record."

"We're quite aware of it."

"But some of Stalin's . . . excesses changed his view."

"Can you be sure of that, Miss Rigby?"

Rigby took a deep breath and let it out slowly. "No," she said, "I cannot read another's mind, but I believe that Tony's change of heart was sincere." She smiled sadly. "And, frankly, I don't want to think that Tony could turn traitorous for any reason."

"Understood." Forrest was silent, thoughtful.

Rigby said, "Do you know a man named Klaus Fuchs?"

"I'm afraid not. Why?"

"German," Rigby said, "and when war broke out, he was interned as an enemy alien in Canada. There he made no secret of his Communist sympathies. I was in Canada then, and was told about him. He is now at Los Alamos as a theoretical physicist. I've been wondering how closely he has been studied."

Forrest shook his head. "I wouldn't know. My assignment is Hobbs, and I've been told to keep my nose on that trail." He smiled suddenly. "You may not know it, Miss Rigby, but in the Bureau we do what we're told."

Rigby matched his smile. "I am completely familiar with the concept," she said. "Now what do you have in mind as regards Tony?"

Forrest looked uncomfortable. "There is a . . . plan."

"Entrapment?"

Forrest looked even more uncomfortable. "We're at war, Miss Rigby, and what's happening up at Los Alamos may play a large part in determining who wins that war. So, well, yes, anything goes. Even entrapment."

"Quite." Rigby's tone was cold. "Where do I fit in?"

"Would you be willing to keep Hobbs busy for an hour or two, say tomorrow night?"

"You mean away from his quarters?"

"Exactly."

"So you can plant what I believe are called bugs?"

"I'm afraid that's just what I do mean, Miss Rigby."

Rigby stood up. "There is my transport," she said, and waved.

Forrest said, "You haven't answered my question." He too was standing.

"No," Rigby said, "I haven't, have I?" She paused, unsmiling. "What time?"

Forrest relaxed visibly. "Bless you," he said. "Say from seven-thirty to nine-thirty?"

"I'll want to hear the results of your bugs," Rigby said. "I'll have to make a report too."

Was there faint hesitation? "Of course," Jim Forrest said, smiling.

"Done," Rigby said then and walked across the plaza to the waiting car.

There was a film the following night in the makeshift auditorium. "There is a glut of films," Tony told Rigby. "I assume that being in the same country as Hollywood accounts for it."

"The last film I saw," Rigby said, "was interrupted by an air raid. I never did find out how it ended." She produced her smile. "But if you would rather not, then how about a walk? There will be a moon."

"You are determined upon my company?"

"I'm lonely, Tony." Her smile turned wistful. "It happens

even to me. Lonely, and depressed by this damnable war."

"I take your point." Tony too was smiling. "A walk in the moonlight it is."

Once they were away from the glare of the lighted buildings, the black night sky seemed to close in and the stars appeared in all their brilliance. "To be considerably less than original," Tony said, looking upward, "they seem close enough to touch, do they not? Orion there, and Rigel and Betelgeuse, the Pleiades, Auriga – we know so little about them, really, even about the mysteries of our own galaxy, let alone the other billions of galaxies in the universe."

A gibbous moon rose from behind the neighbouring mountains and the stars seemed to diminish in brilliance. "We have never even seen the dark side of our own moon," Tony said. "One day we will, but will we ever be able to see, and control, the dark sides of our own natures?"

"Your ideal world again, Tony?"

"Precisely. All knowledge freely disseminated. One world, perhaps even a single language. We have one universal language now – music. No, two – music and mathematics."

"But not knowledge freely disseminated," Rigby said.

"More's the pity, yes. You shiver. Are you cold?"

"Someone walked on my grave. I'm not cold."

Tony said without warning, "I am the reason you were sent here, am I not?"

"As I told General Grove," Rigby said, "I was sent to assure all our British contingent that they are not forgotten."

"I am afraid I don't quite believe you. My antennae tell me different."

Smiling, "Perhaps you'd better have your antennae adjusted".

They walked on in silence.

It was ten o'clock when Tony delivered Rigby to her quarters. Tony seemed strangely ill at ease. "I have an enquiring nature," he said. "Some might call it a suspicious mind."

"Enlarge on that, Tony."

"I am wondering about the purpose of tonight's walk." He made a small hand gesture of dismissal. "Goodnight, dear girl." He kissed her cheek and turned away.

Rigby lay awake for a considerable time that night, staring

up into the darkness and seeing only her own dark thoughts. Well, she told herself finally, there is no way of hurrying anything. I can only wait. On that note she fell asleep.

There was a letter for Rigby two days later. It was postmarked Santa Fe and it had come through the Santa Fe P.O. Box 1663 that was the only address for Los Alamos. It read merely: *The plaza at noon Friday.* It was unsigned.

She saw Tony that Friday morning. "I am going into town," she told him. "Shopping, what else? For lovely, available things to take home."

Tony smiled. "Happy hunting," he said.

Jim Forrest was waiting at the plaza precisely at noon. "You wanted a report."

"I did indeed. And do."

"Better than a report," Forrest said with his easy smile. "Come along."

It was an inconspicuous house quite like so many other old Santa Fe houses, one storey, flat-roofed, tan adobe, with thick walls and small windows. The main room of the house had large round ceiling beams called *vigas* and smaller peeled sapling logs called *latias* above set in a herringbone pattern. The floor was brick, polished with age.

There was another man, who wore glasses. The smile with which he greeted Rigby did not reach his eyes. "Ted Sommers," Forrest said. "My boss. Sit down, Miss Rigby. We have a wire recording for you to hear." He busied himself with a complicated machine.

Suddenly Tony Hobbs's voice came clearly. "The information has been sent," it said.

"You are sure?" This was another, unidentified voice, harsh and commanding.

"I sent it myself through the customary channels."

"My information is that it has not arrived."

"In war-time, my dear fellow," Tony said, "mail delivery is frequently delayed."

Closing her eyes, Rigby could see clearly the expression that would have been on Tony's face, a blend of tolerance and mild amusement at having to explain the obvious.

"I am under certain pressures," the other voice said, "and

we cannot accept delays. The matter is too important."

"I am aware of its importance, perhaps even more aware than you. But it is out of my hands."

"That is all you can tell me?"

The amusement in Tony's voice now was obvious. "I could tell you in detail what the information is, but I doubt very much that you would be able to comprehend it. Are you a physicist?"

"You know I am not."

"A mathematician?"

"You know that too."

"Then what can I tell you except what I said in the beginning? The information has been sent."

"I cannot report failure."

"Then I can only counsel patience." There was a short pause. "No," Tony's voice said calmly, "threats will accomplish nothing. Surely even you must appreciate that. I suggest that you simply report to your masters what I have said."

"Is it more money you want?"

"My dear fellow, money has nothing to do with it. I have no control over the delivery of mail."

"Could it have fallen into other hands?"

"If it does, no harm will be done. The information is in such a form that it will not be readily recognised." There was another short pause. "Now," Tony's voice said, "if you will excuse me. I have work to do. I am rather deeply engaged in this project, you remember?" His amusement was plain. "If I were not, I would hardly be of any use to you, is that not so?"

There was the sound of footsteps and then of a door opening and closing again. A short silence followed, broken at last by the sound of a telephone being dialled.

Forrest shut off the machine and looked at Rigby. "Satisfied?" he said.

"Whom was he telephoning?" Rigby said.

"Someone in the lab." This was Ted Sommers. "The conversation is technical and almost certainly not to be revealed."

Rigby sighed. She said in a sad voice, "It does seem conclusive, I must admit. And I am deeply disappointed. He, Tony, has been my friend for ages." She stood up. "Thank you both for your co-operation." Her smile was wan. "I am afraid I am not grateful for finding out what you have shown me."

"We understand," Forrest said.

Rigby walked back to the plaza. She was, she had to admit, close to tears, which was ridiculous, but there it was. Denham, back in London, she was sure, would be as shocked as she was, and as sad because Tony's stature within the scientific community was high and his reputation, until now, beyond reproach. That he –

Her thoughts stopped there abruptly, and resumed on a different track. She quickened her pace and walked along the east side of the plaza to the Hotel La Fonda where she found a public telephone. She stood in front of it for long moments, eyes closed, checking carefully in that memory of hers to make sure exactly what she had heard.

Satisfied at last, she put a nickel into the telephone slot, listened for the dial tone and quickly dialled a seven-digit number. When a voice answered on the first ring, she hung up and began to smile, feeling, for the first time since she had arrived in New Mexico, free of all doubts.

Tony said, "Back so soon? Shopping all accomplished? I must say you do look happy, so you must have found exactly what you were after."

"I did," Rigby said, "but it wasn't shopping. Let me tell you about it."

Tony listened quietly while she told him where she had been and what she had heard. And when she was done, he said, "What I do not understand is why you are telling me this". He shook his head slowly. "You do not believe what you heard? Why?"

Rigby said, "As soon as the man left, you dialled the telephone".

"Yes."

"I asked Forrest and Sommers whom it was you called."

"Go on."

"They told me it was someone here at the lab and that the conversation was technical and probably not to be revealed."

"It was pure jargon. Telephones are too easily tapped. You still have not made yourself clear."

"The first three numbers you dialled were 982. I counted the clicks automatically. That is the Santa Fe exchange, not the one up here."

"My dear girl," Tony said in slow wonder, "I have always admired you, but not nearly enough." He was smiling.

"I remembered the remaining four numbers," Rigby said, "and called. The man answered C.I.C., which I believe is American Army Counter-Intelligence."

"It is."

"And so the entire conversation with the man was planned?"

"A rather nasty fellow," Tony said. "We are all most anxious to see who is behind him."

"And the F.B.I. – if they are indeed F.B.I. – had no idea."

"You of all people," Tony said, "should certainly understand that the right hand frequently does not know what the left hand is doing. Call it departmental jealousy. Have you not heard of that?"

"Too, too often," Rigby said. "But it never really entered my mind. Oh, Tony, I am relieved."

"So am I," Tony said. "I thoroughly disliked being under your suspicion. But I had my orders, just as you had yours."

Rigby's report to Denham included mention of Klaus Fuchs, whom she had never met but whose pro-Communist sympathies, expressed during his internment in Canada, had aroused at least her curiosity.

Her mention of Fuchs was ignored and it was not until 1950 when Fuchs was head of the theoretical division of the Atomic Energy Research Establishment at Harwell, that solid information concerning his espionage activities was supplied by the F.B.I. from testimony of confessed Communist agents in the U.S.A. Fuchs confessed and was imprisoned. He was released in 1959, whereupon he went to East Germany and became director of the Institute for Nuclear Physics.

Richard Martin Stern, who collaborated with Rigby on that section, is an old Santa Fe hand who has lived in New Mexico for years and knows that wide, wild landscape like the back of his hand. Los Alamos is still there, a brooding, sinister presence up on the hill near the Bandelier National Park and when Dick was doing his research there were plenty of old Los Alamos hands like Dottie McKibbin herself who could corroborate Rigby's own testimony.

After her return there was a move to have her shifted to the Japanese theatre of war. Her father was briefly on Mountbatten's staff and was able to confirm what Lord Louis had already heard about the Colonel's daughter on the grapevine. Instead the Americans got in first and she was seconded to General Eisenhower's staff to work on Intelligence and liaison between him and the other Allies. She had a tough time explaining Ike to the irascible Montgomery. And vice versa. She thinks Monty never quite forgave her and the signed photograph on the desk at her cottage is teasingly inscribed, "For Dorothy, a far more indomitable foe than Rommel himself, with love and respect, Bernard Montgomery". It sounds to me as if her magic worked with Monty as it did with everyone else.

On 'D' day she actually took part in the landings, accompanying Lord Lovat's Commandos – the only woman to do so. She was also the first woman to enter the Belsen concentration camp – an experience which seared her soul and refined still more that steely professional desire to battle for her country which, in her view, was the one true and reliable repository of civilised and humane values in the world.

William Haggard

THE GREAT DIVIDE

With the end of the war, many Intelligence officers who had signed up 'for the duration' skipped back to civvy street, but Rigby stayed in. What's more, she managed to persuade Denham to take on Camilla as his secretary. She sensed that Camilla would be surprisingly good at it. And she wanted a friend at court.

Despite the cessation of hostilities there was still plenty to keep the adrenalin flowing: she was an unofficial observer at the Nuremberg War Crimes Tribunal where she raised doubts about the true identity of Rudolf Hess, and she was instrumental in persuading Sir Charles Brooke, last of the white Rajahs of Sarawak, to cede his country to the British crown. Rigby served briefly in Palestine where she formed a lifelong, and not entirely platonic, affection for Moshe Dayan and an implacable, and equally long lived, hatred for Menachem Begin. She played mixed doubles in Hyannisport with Jack Kennedy and Jack Kramer, the 1947 Wimbledon tennis champion, but she missed the atomic bomb tests at Bikini and the election of Juan Perón to the presidency of Argentina. South America was not her thing.

In many ways she seemed busy and fulfilled, but there was also a sense of sadness and loneliness about her. There was no shortage of men in her life – an opposite number and sparring partner at the U.S. Embassy called Wayne Perkins; Richard 'Dickie' Daniels, the suave character who had congratulated her after the Buchanesque pre-war episode in Scotland; even the indefatigable Portland. There were others too, but no one who seemed quite right.

Perhaps it was the fault of Colonel Harry. Rigby always worshipped him and when, in 1946, he was killed trying to protect a party of Nepalese schoolchildren from a marauding tiger, his canonisation was complete. For Rigby he was an ideal with whom no suitor could compete.

When Rigby and Camilla Trefusis were peremptorily recalled from leave, both were surprised but neither was stricken. After a spell of particularly gruelling action, Denham had given Rigby a gracious little speech of thanks and two months' special leave to rest, and since Camilla had leave coming up anyway, the two old friends had gone together. Denham had insisted that their holiday be without distractions – both of them must unwind completely – and had himself arranged that they did so properly. A villa in northern Majorca would see to that.

The island was then unspoilt and, indeed, rather boring. This was as Denham had coolly intended, for he knew both women's habits perfectly: both could live without men and were sometimes glad to (when, in his experience, they did their most effective work), but sooner or later they'd feel the need of one, and that spelt the end of a peaceful unwinding. But in northern Majorca men would be hard to find. There was the Resident Great Man of Letters, but it was whispered that his tastes were unorthodox, and there was also a naval college quite close. But the cadets would be provincial and callow, quite uninteresting to experienced women, and the instructors married men with jealous wives. In any case, Dorothy spoke no Spanish, and though Camilla could get along in Castilian, enough to run the villa and order meals, that would scarcely cover a serious engagement with a man who spoke a debased Catalan. Denham had worked it all out very carefully with the result that, when he recalled them suddenly, they came with an almost unseemly alacrity.

In the days before a pleasant island had been ravaged by package tours and hourly flights, the journey had meant a sea-passage by night and then, unless you were lucky, a train. Both women were tired when they reached Victoria, but both went to Denham's office at once.

"You're looking very well," he said. The women were looking jaded and knew it.

Camilla said, "We've had a bit of a journey, you know. What's cooking?" She had an experienced secretary's right of plain speech.

"Enough for me to need you back badly. Enough for another job for Rigby."

"An agreeable change from darkest Majorca."

"Wait to say it," Denham said, and watched her. He hadn't wished to spring bad news suddenly, and as her expression changed from zest to alarm he wondered whether she'd guessed the worst. Apparently she had, for she asked, "Not India?"

"I'm afraid it is."

She winced. "So many memories," she said, "I vowed never to go back."

"Sorry. May I give you the outlines?" he asked.

She nodded.

He spoke lucidly, for he had prepared his brief. The Prime Minister and his attendant progressives were determined to let India go. As Denham saw it, that was wholly inevitable. It might be held by suspending the rule of law and by heavily reinforcing the garrisons, but to suspend the rule of law was unthinkable and to keep British troops in a country they hated would bring even the best quite close to mutiny. So basically it was a question of how. The Cabinet didn't want to split India; it wanted to bequeath a single country, Hindu-dominated since that was the arithmetic of it, but with consti-tutional safeguards for Muslims caught in the new state. The Muslims, naturally, wouldn't wear that. They wanted partition and were fighting hard for it.

"And you're pro-Muslim?" Rigby asked.

"I am. But not for the usual reasons – far from it. There's a certain sort of old India hand who's pro-Muslim for the worst of reasons." Denham mimicked an Indian Army voice. "They're so much politer and so much more manly." His voice returned to his own as he went on. "That's prejudiced middle-class rubbish, of course. Are Gurkhas unmanly, or Mahrattas, or Dogras? My reason for wanting partition is better since it's political and therefore amoral." Denham leant forwards in deliberate emphasis. *"The new Hindu state will turn to Russia so we do not want this state too big."*

"I follow that, but what's the local form?"

The Great Divide

"Our present and slightly improbable Viceroy, Veronica's bemedalled husband, would like to hand India over intact. He'd stay on as Governor General of all of it and maybe get his marquisate thrown in. He gets on well with the Hindu Misra, who's an upper-class Brahmin, a Wykehamist too. Just the type to have His Excellency on a string."

"And on the other side, the unfortunate Muslims?"

"There's Ali Khan, a quite different kettle. He isn't really a Khan by blood – it's just a kind of family name. He's a middle-class lawyer, hard as nails and, from what I hear, very tough to talk to. He puts his demands on the table and sticks to them, not the sort of thing a full General much likes. Most of the British officials detest him." Denham added in a cool aside, "From what I've seen of them that inclines me towards him. So he isn't on an easy wicket, but he does have one thing going for him. He has Veronica's ear, and some people say more."

"I've heard rumours," Rigby said.

"Discount them. The practical difficulties make a liaison near-impossible. But Veronica, bless her, has not been discreet. Her interest in the underdog is real. When she puts on one of those beautiful uniforms she isn't the Great Lady slumming. She gives money – God knows she has always had plenty of that – and she chivvies lethargic officials to get things done. So she let Ali show her how Muslims lived. Not being stupid, she's seen Hindu slums too but Misra didn't go with her. Oh, no. And she's been to Ali Khan's house for dinner. Naturally his wife was there and other suitable female guests. But her husband hasn't eaten with Misra."

"It does sound something short of protocol, but why do you obviously think it's dangerous?"

"Because it could be used to smear Ali. That sort of thing in India can be even more lethal than it often is here. A little more rumour, something half-concrete, and Ali's fall is not unthinkable. And there's nobody to replace him, no first-class man, nobody whom the Muslims quite trust and nobody to hold them together. Partition would in effect be dead and Misra would scoop the all-India pool. The Prime Minister may want that but we don't. I told you why."

"And where do I come into this?"

"Through Veronica, of course."

"You want me to spy on her? That won't be easy."

Denham didn't laugh often but did so now. "Nothing so grotesque or corny. I want you to go to New Delhi and hold her hand. Particularly when it begins to get sticky. You're going to be her lady's maid."

"Will she accept me as that?"

"She has. I suggested you be a Lady-in-Waiting, but she said that she had two already. Both dull as ditchwater – probably selected for that reason. I told her something of what you do and how you think. She said that another civilised woman was the nicest present I could possibly make her."

"You must know her pretty well."

"I did once." Denham saw the two women exchange a glance and added smoothly, "It was some time ago, as you probably realise."

"She sounds a very nice woman."

"She is. You'll get on together or I wouldn't be sending you." His manner returned to the briskly businesslike. "So any more questions?"

"Only the obvious. I take it I'll have no formal back-up, so what do I do if the going gets tough?"

"You go to Wayne Perkins if you need any heavy stuff. He's in Delhi too and I've fixed it up." Denham raised his hand as he saw her stiffen. "Yes, I know that you've brushed with him more than once. You don't quite trust him and nor do I. He's as passionately American as you yourself are devotedly British and if it comes to a conflict of interest he'll cross you. But in this case there isn't one – quite the reverse. America no more wants Misra all-powerful than I want an undivided India. And for exactly the same reason – Russia. For once I think you can trust him entirely."

"What's he doing in Delhi?"

"He's at their embassy. Ostensibly as a Cultural Attaché, but in fact doing much the same as we are."

"Then when do I start?"

"Tomorrow morning. R.A.F. Dakota. Three stops. It won't be comfortable but you'll have interesting male company. And I'll give you a thorough brief on Veronica."

"But I haven't any tropical clothes."

"Then buy them in Delhi."

Denham saw the two women smile, and flushed. He knew what they were thinking precisely . . . Men were impossible, wholly impossible, impractical, insensitive animals. But *pace* the sillier sort of feminist, they could make a woman's life much more interesting.

The journey had indeed been uncomfortable, but the company less amusing than Denham had thought. The crew of three had been polite and obliging, but the passengers resentful and surly. They were long-service soldiers, a replacement draft for India, and most of them had fought in Europe. They thought this posting unfair and said so; they talked, in fact, of nothing else, and the single young officer who nominally commanded them was clearly a very anxious man.

Rigby had had time to read her brief. A husband was part of Veronica's life, but there was surprisingly little solid about him and what there was seemed deliberately, almost cagily, neutral. The marriage had been the social event of the year: the youngest Brigadier in the army, ambitious and cosily well-connected, certain to race up the ladder to high command; and the biggest heiress of the decade. There were first-class minds who had reservations about Alfred, but then first-class minds had reservations about most things. He also liked money and didn't have any. That was all about Alfred and quite enough. Not everybody admired him slavishly, but nobody wished to make him an enemy.

On Veronica the brief was more detailed, but its essence could be put as shortly. The marriage had been one of convenience in the sense that it had pleased the worldly and by now had become, well, the best word was 'open'. But mostly with the greatest discretion. Divorce would have been unthinkable and Veronica held the purse strings firmly.

Rigby nodded contentedly. This woman she was going to serve would freewheel when she fancied, which was something they had in common. Denham had said she was a very nice woman and Rigby was inclined to think so too. It remained to be seen if she was also intelligent.

At the airport there were more senior officers to march away their near-mutinous drafts. Rigby came down last, alone, and was greeted by the station commander. She hadn't expected a guard of honour and even a Group Captain surprised her. He saluted with a certain deference and drove her in his jeep to another car. It was a Rolls but with normal plates and flew no flag. The driver wore breeches and leggings, and a chauffeur's cap. Another man had opened the door and stood waiting. He had the hard, alert air of a professional bodyguard. Inside the car a single woman sat stiffly. She was wearing a *yashmak*.

"Rupert Denham's friend?"

"I also work for him."

"Then please get in."

Rigby got in with Her Excellency.

"You must forgive this silly veil but it's necessary. If I go anywhere interesting the papers print it and my official social life is a screaming bore. I meet Lady Slip and Lady Gully. Lady Slip is the wife of some Commissioner somewhere and Lady Gully's man runs the police of a province. They both of them bend the knee to me, but both would pull my eyes out happily."

"I'll bet they would."

"You know the type? You've been in India?"

"Not for years. But I've met it elsewhere and I don't get on with it."

"Then you're going to get on well with me."

Something rather rare had happened: the two women had struck an instant empathy, one which lasted till the elder died. The rigid back began to relax and the Vicereine said, "I saw you had only one bag – you'll need clothes. I'd love to come with you when you do your shopping, but it's exactly the sort of thing I can't do. I'll give you the least stupid of my various women. At least she knows which shops aren't phoney."

"That's very kind."

"It's only sensible. We can't have you walking about in London clothes, which brings me to a point of some delicacy. I take it you're not really a lady's maid?"

"I'm afraid I'm not."

"It doesn't matter – you can go through the motions. Lay out the clothes I need for some rattle. There's a laundry, of course, but I don't want *dhobi's* itch. So I've an Indian woman who does my smalls. It's against her caste principles and she giggles obscenely."

"Then how do you get her to do it?"

"Money. In this horrible country money does anything. Except provide attractive men. I'm afraid you'll have to put up with that. We can hold each other's hand when it gets too cruel. And there's one other thing you can do for me if you will. I don't sleep well alone and I take pills. Sometimes I take too many. It frightens me. So you're to give me two at night and take the bottle. If I ring in the night you're not to answer."

They had come to the pretentious palace and Veronica led the way to her sitting-room. She mixed a drink and Rigby looked round the room. The first thing she saw was a framed photograph of Ali Khan. He wore a black astrakhan cap which suited him perfectly and his sharp-pointed beard had been neatly trimmed. He looked very handsome, undeniably male.

Rigby went to bed some hours later, but it took her several more to get to sleep.

Several hundreds of miles to the east of Delhi, in the sweltering slum they called Calcutta, the editor was saying firmly, "We can't print this and you very well know it".

"The Hindu papers have been hinting at it for weeks. Anything they can do to discredit Ali Khan . . ."

"It's not our business to smear Ali Khan, far less the wife of the Viceroy of India. Anyway, where did you get the story?"

"It was brought to us by a man called Gupta."

"Who'll be a Bengali and therefore doubly tricky. He's trying to get us to splash the story, then he'll sell the hard facts to another paper. If there are any, which I do not credit. A discreet little flat in Delhi, indeed! And he with a house there, a wife and children. He's a public figure whose least movement is followed."

"Men have done curious things for women."

"And women for men – I grant you that."

"Shall I put someone on it? Try to get details?"

"Certainly not. It isn't our cup of tea at all."

It wasn't, the other man thought as he left. The editor had his C.I.E. but he wanted to leave with a knighthood too.

* * *

Wayne had asked Rigby to dinner at his embassy, since anywhere else was out of the question. Dine at any of Delhi's hotels and the news that an American diplomat had been seen with the Vicereine's lady's maid would be gossip on every lip next morning. There were Indian restaurants and Chinese too, but Wayne didn't like Indian food and to eat Chinese was a certain tapeworm. Rigby had had one once and didn't intend to host another.

Wayne had begun by re-stating their common interest, which was to prevent a too-powerful Hindu state. Rigby had nodded agreement, but with a certain reserve. She hadn't doubted what Denham had told her – he and his kind thought the Prime Minister an innocent – but the Americans would have more than one motive. They had themselves once been a British colony and the chip on their shoulders was always visible, even on those of sophisticates like Wayne. He was Ivy League but still all-American. She didn't fault him for that; she was all-British herself. Now he was explaining smoothly, "And there's the local side of it too – that's important. Apparently your Cabinet won't see it, but anything short of partition means civil war. Of course, if there's a split there'll be trouble, especially in the Punjab where they're all mixed up. But we don't think there need be general chaos. The Indian Army will probably divide peacefully, each regiment or company to its own people. If there isn't a clear-cut division there'll be bloody civil war."

"Then what are you going to do?"

"Back Ali Khan for all we're worth."

"How are you going to do that?"

"I can't tell you."

"Since for once we're on the same side I don't see why not."

"I put it to my Brass but they said no. They asked a very sensible question: had I ever double-crossed you? I said I had. They then asked another: so why shouldn't you cheat on me?" He looked at her straightly. "And would you?"

"With pleasure."

Wayne managed a laugh and went on. "Anyway, for a day or two, don't believe what the papers tell you."

"I seldom do."

"In this case quite rightly. We can do a lot to boost our Ali,

but we can't save him from political suicide. He's a very poor
negotiator. Some of his demands are outrageous. There'll have
to be two Pakistans and there'll be nearly a thousand miles
between them. Ali has asked for a connecting corridor. A
thousand miles through the Hindu heartland! Naturally that's
out of the question. You British would have to hold it and you
couldn't. Even if you could, you wouldn't. It would mean
British troops staying on in India and that's about the last
thing you'd stand for. And Ali Khan won't get his partition
on the maps he's now waving about like flags. There'll have
to be a Boundary Commission."

"Why are you telling me this?"

He hesitated, but she could see it was calculated. "I know
why Denham sent you here – in fact we talked it over before
he did. And I hear that you've been very successful. Veronica
likes you and talks to you freely. To put it another way, you
have her ear. And so, it is widely believed, does Ali Khan. If
you should ever get an opening or can make one . . . ."

"I'll bear it in mind."

"He is dining at our embassy tonight. And be sure that he'll
be seen to leave it. A little brandy?"

"Make it a big one."

In Calcutta the respected editor was looking at a first pull of
his paper.

MUSLIM LEADER DISAPPEARS

He nodded in approval. That was carefully neutral and
therefore good. Almost certainly, Ali Khan had been snatched
and only one party had a motive to do so. Was Misra privy?
Very possibly not. He had plenty of wild men and couldn't
always control them. Either way, there was going to be trouble,
trouble with the biggest 'T' yet.

Ali Khan came to in a windowless room. There was a light in
the ceiling with a steel grille covering it. His head ached and
his legs were putty, but he wasn't tied up and the sheets were
clean. On a bedside table was a telephone without a dial. He
hesitated, but made up his mind. If he didn't ring they'd
come for him anyway. They'd be Hindus, of course, and they
wouldn't be gentle.

To his astonishment the man who answered was the stereo-type of the Muslim *khitmutgar*. He wore the long white coat of the upper servant, a coloured sash and a matching turban. He bowed deeply and said in formal Urdu, "Will his Honour be taking tea or coffee?"

"Coffee with milk. No sugar, thank you."

The servant returned with both on a silver tray. "A gentle-man wishes to speak with you, sir."

"I'd prefer to receive him properly dressed."

"That has been considered, sir." The servant pointed to a door in the wall. "Beyond that door is your private bathroom. You will find your clothes laid out when you return."

The bathroom too was windowless (whoever had organised this knew his business) and fitted with every conceivable need. Ali took a shower and felt better. Back in the bedroom his clothes had been returned. His linen had been scrupulously washed, his suit pressed and his shoes shone brightly. He dressed and began to feel almost normal, for he was resilient as well as stubborn. He picked up the telephone and said simply, "Ready".

The man who came in was a European though he spoke with a New England accent. "I apologise for the inconvenience."

Ali Khan had thought it out in the bathroom; he'd been kidnapped but clearly not by Hindus. This man was an American . . .

Careful.

"How long have I been here?"

"Part of a night, a day and another night. We had to give you a pretty big shot to have time to be sure things worked as we hoped they would." Wayne had been carrying a sheaf of newspapers; he put them on a table and said, "The Muslim press is boiling over, accusing the Hindus of snatching you". He had charm and was now using it consciously. Ali Khan in turn was half-way to trusting him. "If you're meaning to help me, I don't see how you are."

"Obvious, my dear fellow. Consider. Up to now you've been a party leader, but soon you'll be a Muslim hero and your hand will be better by two aces at least. But you mustn't overplay it, you know. You mustn't say that the Hindus snatched you and that you escaped by fighting your guards with bare hands. Just say that you're not sure who took you – that's the literal truth since you don't know my masters – and that suddenly they let you go. After brutal interrogation, of course. Your people will draw their own conclusions, and when you have time to read those papers you'll see that they already have. When we let you out in a couple of days you'll be very much more than a minority leader."

"Why are you doing this?"

Wayne told him. "Though I must warn you again – don't overplay it. Time isn't on your side, you see. The British are getting impatient and edgy, talking about your intransigence. I wouldn't put it past them to lose their cool. In which case they'll throw the whole thing at Misra and beat retreat. So you'll have to make a few sane concessions. That corridor, for instance – it's out. And you'll have to accept a Boundary Commission."

"And if I don't?"

"Then God help you all."

Her Excellency was chatting to Rigby. "You're the only person I have to natter to. I know that's the reason Denham sent you and it's worked. So who was it who snatched Ali Khan?"

"I can truthfully say I don't know. But I can make a pretty good guess, and I have."

"So have I, but it doesn't matter. Ali now ranks just one step below Allah. Unhappily he also knows it. He's throwing his weight about, being impossible. No concessions of any kind whatever. He wants the lot. My old man is getting distinctly tetchy and he has the power to recommend what's craven. Cut and run. I don't want that and nor do you." Veronica drew a long breath and added, "I'm tempted to take a hand in high politics."

Rigby looked at the handsome framed photograph and then at the newly excited Veronica. She reflected before she asked softly, "You might not find that disagreeable?"

"Some people think he's my lover already. He isn't since it hasn't been possible. But I find him very attractive indeed. That hard black beard all round his chin . . ." The Vicereine very slightly shivered. "After partition is sealed and settled – on terms I'm pretty sure I could get – a bit of a scandal would hardly matter." Veronica made an instinctive gesture with her lean and almost ringless hands. She seemed to be accepting a gift. "You follow me, Dorothy Rigby?"

"Perfectly, and I'd do the same. But 'a bit of a scandal' is pretty cool. What would your husband say if the skies fell?"

"Alfie? He'd be furious but he'd do nothing whatever. In fact there isn't a thing he could do."

"Are you sure?"

"I'm very sure." Veronica looked at Rigby and smiled. "We've never had a joint bank account."

The editor disliked the word but was euphoric under his creaking fan. For one thing he had been offered his knighthood, not in the Order he had secretly coveted, but his wife would be an authentic Lady and that would be good for domestic peace. And for another it looked like peace in India. There were going to be two Pakistans, East and West, and except by sea they'd be unconnected. And the Boundary Commission was arriving tomorrow.

"Peace for our time," he said aloud, and an old god heard him and laughed derisively.

One of the reasons I asked William Haggard to be responsible for writing up Rigby's involvement with the partition of India was that he himself was in the Indian Civil Service and, in his own words, "spent several years in Delhi as a sort of superior clerk unconvincingly disguised as a soldier".

With a civil servant's discretion Haggard (a *nom-de-plume* incidentally) advises me that I won't want to say anything which suggests that his piece is any other than pure fiction. I am content to respect his wishes and say only that if any readers should think they detect any similarity between the characters named in the preceding pages and the real life characters who played the principal roles in the real life partition of 1947 then I'd have a sneaking sympathy with them. Rigby and I agreed from the very first that each writer should have *carte blanche* to present their stories as they themselves wished so here, as elsewhere, I have made only the slightest of alterations.

I should record that, in conversation with me, Rigby always referred to India with much affection. Certainly she mentioned her old cricket coach, Ranjitsinjhi, with great warmth. It's true that she did not suffer a certain sort of memsahib very gladly. Nor many of their menfolk. My own view is that it was the Raj she found objectionable, not India.

It is true, however, that this was Rigby's last mission on the sub-continent.

Duncan Kyle

THE BREATHLESS HUSH

Not all Rigby's work was at the sharp end. She continued to turn up in the most unlikely places. In 1948 she was in Stockholm to see T. S. Eliot get his Nobel Prize and back in New Mexico to watch the Americans send a rocket seventy-eight miles into the sky at 3000 m.p.h. But she also spent time driving a desk, dealing with codes and ciphers, logistics, administration and bumf in all manner of guises. She was adroit at briefing ministers and as easy with the Labour Government as she would later be with the Conservatives. Privately, she wasn't sure she didn't prefer the better type of old fashioned Labour M.P., even though she professed to be completely apolitical. She had a particularly soft spot for Ernie Bevin, the Foreign Secretary, and he for her. He and Mannie Shinwell at Defence.

"You'll be the death of us all, Miss Rigby," Shinwell used to say, as he dismissed yet another of Denham's madcap schemes. Denham always got Rigby to present them. She was so persuasive.

Duncan Kyle was an obvious choice for an episode which took place in the far from glamorous surroundings of G.C.H.Q. at Eastcote, the codebreaking centre which was the descendant of the brilliant Government Code and Cipher School at Bletchley Park. It was the Bletchley team who cracked the Germans' Enigma and – some say – did as much to win the war as the boys in blue or khaki. Kyle was posted to G.C.H.Q. as a young national serviceman at the same time, 1949, that Rigby paid her momentous visit.

Oh, one other crucial qualification. During National Service he once bowled his medium pacers at P.B.H. May.

The first time I saw her she coasted by me in running kit, somewhere between Eastcote Station and G.C.H.Q., all brown legs and long smooth muscles. By the time I reached my desk she was sitting at it and I knew her for what she was: one of Sillitoe's advance skirmishers down from Curzon Street to have a little gnaw at the ankles of our security. They descended on us from time to time. Sometimes word reached us beforehand and there'd be general hysteria. ("Sir Percy, oh, Sir Percy – Sillitoe's coming!" The dread news hissed and yelped along corridors, across refectories and up and down stairs.)

She was showered and changed by now and looked quite unnecessarily at home in my chair. I hung up my hat and brolly, and she rose as I walked towards her and held out her hand for shaking. Nice smile, level eyes, a steady sort of woman. "You'll forgive me, I hope, Mr Cartridge."

"Know my name and face, do you?"

"Well . . ." Nice grin, too.

"Yes, you would. Mr Prince warn you about all the splinters in the kneehole of that desk?"

"Er, no."

"Maybe Sir Percy can get something done about it. I can't. Coffee?"

"Mmmmm."

"Get it or show you?"

"Show me, thanks."

So I did and in the process became a kind of guide. She had my desk because it stood on a little foot-high platform at one end of the Call-Sign Hall, and from it she could See Everything, which meant sixty or seventy backs, male and female, all ages, bent over sheaves of schedule forms, or 'skeds'.

I sat at a spare desk and got on with my work and watched her idly. She also pretended to work, of course, but observed everything and everybody, not that that could have been highly exciting. Occasionally she'd get up and stroll about like an invigilator in an exam room. I was waiting for The Fuss. This was the third descent of the security Assyrian upon our particular fold, and on the previous two there had been A Big Fuss. The first time, the appropriately red-bound Soviet Master File had vanished from Reg's desk; the second time somebody'd pinched Linda's wallet from her bag. The general idea must have been to see who did what under the pressure of suspicion.

So when Reg suddenly went barmy at about eleven o'clock, I simply thought it was now Fuss Time. What's more, I was right, in a way, though this turned out to be Fuss of another order altogether: Fuss in Hearts, doubled and redoubled.

Ten minutes earlier Reg had stopped at my desk. "Score for us on Sunday?"

"No."

"Be a good lad, John. Kitty's going away." Kitty was his termagant wife, theoretically scorer for our Sunday cricket; but Kitty was a shrew who, beforehand, had to be persuaded and more persuaded, and afterwards thanked and thanked again.

"What's the fixture?"

"Combined Services Sunday Side."

"Anybody good playing?" Those were the days of National Service and it was not unknown to find very good cricketers indeed taking to obscure and faraway fields.

He shook his head. "But I'll buy you a half of bitter."

"Make it a pint of mild."

"Very well, if I must."

Miss Rigby must have had ears like a bat's. Reg had barely turned away before she was at my side murmuring, "Did he say Combined Services?"

"Sunday Side," I said. "The S.S."

"This weekend?"

I nodded. "At Swakeleys. F.O. ground. You're bound to know where it is."

She laughed and laid a forefinger against her nose. "See you there."

Then, as I said earlier, Reg went barmy. Somebody whinnied and shot over to his nook and began waving paper under his nose, then someone else did the same. Morning delivery of Ministry mail, including the overnight skeds, had just arrived for sorting and . . .

And – wait for it! – the bloody Russians had changed everything! Yes, everything. All in one go.

You'll forgive me if I now state the blindingly obvious, but some things do have to be explained. If Admiral Sodov in his cruiser wishes to send an order to Commander Rufskin in his destroyer, he does not transmit: "Cruiser Lenin to Destroyer Stalin, serve cabbage soup for dinner again", at least not in clear, because he knows Big Ears is not only all over the place, but has direction-finding equipment, and is keen at all times to know the positions of both vessels, plus the quality of the soup in case mutiny is becoming a possibility. Accordingly Sodov becomes something like Glint and Rufskin becomes Apple and the message is enciphered and turned into five-character groups so that the message actually despatched is: "Glint to Apple xcbvn lkjjt cfres." Big Ears intercepts it, of course, and sets to work on the cipher, and may even break it, but all this takes time. By then the ships have moved and next time, instead of Glint calling Apple you will (or may) hear Shine calling Grape.

Sailormen being simple souls, these call-signs would be changed regularly, but not too often. The result was that most of the time Big Ears had a good idea of which ships and planes and regiments were where – and why. The whole Order of Battle was neatly drawn up and stuck with drawing pins on office walls and up-dated weekly. We knew, and could forecast, that Glint would be succeeded by Shine, followed by Light, and so on. And all regular as Bile Beans.

Not now. Suddenly three-character call-signs were pouring in from all directions. Something like Q9Z took the place of simple old Glint, and KD3 took Apple's. Wouldn't matter too much in the end if the new call-signs continued in use, but it was as plain as Reg's panic that they wouldn't!

Not fair. I'm doing Reg down and I shouldn't. Reg was one of the old Bletchley Park boys, and brilliant. Reg it was, in fact, who actually began the business of forecasting call-signs and set FW 190s to shooting down JU 88s. Clever feller.

But this really was a facer. Thousands of transmissions were being made and recorded and logged and suddenly we had no way of telling t'other from which. It was important. Less than five minutes after Reg went crackers the phone rang on my desk – the old desk, that is. Dorothy Rigby picked it up and beckoned. I went over and took the handset.

"What the bloody 'ell's goin' on?" demanded an angry, grating voice.

I asked cautiously, "Did you scramble, sir?"

"Oh, 'ell! I 'ave now."

I pushed the scramble button. "They've changed all their procedures, Foreign Secretary."

"I know that much. But tell me this – are they going to bloody war?"

Fact was, the Soviet Black Sea Fleet could be on its way to bombard Istanbul for all we knew, or the Baltic Army sailing for Helsinki and Stockholm (this was high summer, remember). Anything could be happening and maybe was – don't forget that mad Stalin was loose in the Kremlin in those days.

As I hung up, Dorothy Rigby looked at me. "Percy chose a bad day, did he?"

"Not," I said, "if he wants to see how we carry on under pressure."

"Can I help?"

I shook my head. "Don't see how. You'd need tons of briefing and nobody has time to do it."

"Perhaps you?"

"I have to dive into the pond, too."

She smiled at one corner of her mouth. "Speak two sentences."

"What's your clearance?"

"Alpha two."

"Higher than mine. Okay – the Russians have changed all call-signs and all schedules. We no longer know who is where, Army, Navy, or Air Force!"

Rigby said perceptively, "Uncle Joe really could be on the move, then?"

"Anywhere from India to Ireland, yes. And the first we'll know is Nehru telling us Tiger tanks are romping down the Khyber, or Dublin says Malik has shot De Valera."

"Can this be solved?"

I pointed to Reg. "Bloke over there has worked miracles before. They're three-character groups, mixed letters and numerals," I said. "We just have to find how they're linked together."

After that I saw almost nothing of her for several days. I was supposed to be manning my desk and maintaining liaison with the F.O. but until the problem was solved, liaison had no point. By now the rest of the world was going about its business largely unobserved as the whole of G.C.H.Q. concentrated on Russia and on maps and charts showing a rash of three-character call-signs and the straight lines of Direction-Finding bearings. The war being only four years behind us, war-time habits had not yet died, and camp beds were issued from stores so that the Great Problem could be Confronted Throughout The Night (the capitals are those of Prince, head of department, who actually Spoke Like That).

And so the week proceeded. By Wednesday, when forty-eight hours had passed, the feeling of pressure-above-normal came down from about two hundred and forty per cent to perhaps two hundred and thirty-nine point six; we rather felt that if Brer Stalin really had invaded somewhere, we'd have heard about it by now – through different channels, admittedly.

So we toiled on, day and night, night and day in Mr Porter's words, with an oh-such-a-hungry-yearning burning inside of us – mainly behind the eyelids. Intelligence Corps lads assigned to us as temporary clerks were sent out for bottles of Optrex and eyebaths, and about Wednesday one learned that constipation was becoming general and Boots in Ruislip was looted of crates of Ex-Lax and Syrup of Figs.

All sounds funny, but it wasn't. Reg drew up a roster and set people walking briskly three times round the perimeter, taking deep breaths. This may have helped a little, but nothing was noticeable. The call-signs, the skeds, the enciphered messages piled up, and no amount of laxative would shift *them*!

Thursday morning . . . I was in the refectory, holding a cup of black coffee in a less-than-steady hand and keeping my raw eyelids closed, when a female voice asked, "May I join you?"

Dorothy Rigby, fresh as morning's dew, smooth of skin,

white of eye, untroubled of smile, stood beside me, politely awaiting my answer. (I should like to add something, and here's as good a place as any. Dorothy Rigby had absolutely beautiful manners.)

She thought the whole thing horrible, she said. "All these very bright people flogging themselves to death quite at random and getting absolutely nowhere. Oh, by the by, will you be playing this match on Sunday?"

"If it's on," I said pointedly, "they can look elsewhere for a scorer. For me Sunday will be a pint or two of beer, some roast beef if I'm lucky, and a drowse in a deckchair . . ."

She lifted a finger. "Quite right. Over there in the corner, that's . . . ?"

I glanced across. At the corner table the Head of Ciphers was rising, coffee finished. "That's Alexander," I said.

"Someone said he does all three crosswords over coffee every morning – *Guardian, Times* and *Telegraph?*"

"I believe so. Then he leaves them behind. Wait till he's gone and you'll see the jackals pinching them."

"Several people have told me about it," Rigby said, "in tones of utmost awe. Yet I can't imagine it's as difficult as all that."

"I disagree," I said. Alexander's ability was the pride of the place. Secret establishments can, by their nature, barely boast at all; we could boast only of Alexander, our crossword king and chess grand-master.

"The difficulty," she mused, "would be in writing down all the answers. How long is the coffee break?"

"Fifteen minutes, to be formal."

"Then would you be so kind," she asked, "as to time me tomorrow?"

"If I'm spared," I said. "But you could time yourself, surely?"

"Left entirely to myself," she said, "I'm inclined to cheat."

Spared I was. Like everybody else in The Great Call-Sign Confrontation I was in ruins, almost praying for early death. I told Reg that morning that I was off to the refectory and he gave me a bleary nod, and I noticed that the bags beneath his eyes were of the same green shade as, and similar bulk to, the suitcases carried by sailors on leave. I said, "Sunday – the match. Is it on?"

"Oh, my God! What's today?"

"Friday."

Reg said thickly, through a spasm of coughing and his thousandth Senior Service that week, "We ought to let 'em know". I nodded and walked away. I'd gone ten feet when his shout halted me. "Be damned," he roared, "if it's going to be Stalin stopped play!"

He snorted then, and scavenged in his cabinets for a little address book. "To be found at the War House, this blighter is." He dialled and asked for Captain Something-double-barrelled and warned him of the possibility that Sunday's game might be orf, then hung up, looking thoughtful. "Blighter said he wouldn't if he were us," Reg said. "Says we'd be missing something we'd be sorry about."

"Flannel," I offered.

"Very likely. But I wonder who it could be?"

"Not Hobbs," I said. "Nor Hammond. And Bradman's retired now."

Reg grunted and applied the fine edge of his intellect to a splatter of call-signs while I went off to my date with Rigby in the refectory.

"Brought your papers?" I asked.

"In there." On the seat beside me lay a thick manilla envelope which turned out to be sealed with wax and signed by Sir Percy, no less. It all gets damned obsessive, you know. The envelope contained three untouched daily papers, and she did the three crosswords in thirteen minutes and twenty seconds, apparently without extending herself. No grunts of effort and no blanks. I kept the papers to check the answers later, if I had the strength.

Frantic endeavour continued. We'd now had a week of poor coffee and worse tea, of fish paste sandwiches, lukewarm sausages and beans, of artificial light and twenty-hour days, and there was talk of doctors and Benzedrine. Ex-Lax was *washed down* now with Syrup of Figs.

All this and yet – we had not, somehow, contrived to involve Dorothy Rigby! Looking back now, near the end of the

Eighties, and knowing what we now know of her, the thing's absurd – like tackling the Armada without involving Drake! But there it was. She spent all of those days at my desk, the merest spectator.

Then two things happened at midday on Saturday. First came Reg's decision that the match was ON and to hell with it, a decision followed within minutes by the discovery of a repeat call-sign.

"Tee-three-wye," Reg muttered through clenched teeth. "Picked up at . . . ?"

"Habbaniyah," Linda said.

"So was the first one, eh?" His voice rose with interest.

"Yes. And D/F got on to it."

He drummed his fingers and muttered that call-signs are like Mr Heinz's little beans – once they begin to repeat, you've got 'em . . . "Where are those bloody D/F bearings?" cried he.

Moments passed. The Habbaniyah signals were being deciphered; then at last the result was on his desk. T3Y had appeared first from an already identified cruiser off Sevastopol, and the second time from something – possibly a tank – far behind the Urals. Hardly the same source. "Right," said Reg, "they've a system for switching 'em round. That's proved. But what the hell *is* it?"

That was roughly the picture at breakfast in the refectory on Sunday. Alexander sat in his corner, tearing through Mephisto and Ximenes, or whatever those hard Sunday crosswords were called in those days. We, a tableful of call-sign clerks of varied seniority, Reg and Linda among us, sat like corpses at a long table, enveloped in smoke and trying to summon the will to tackle cool scrambled egg and lukewarm coffee. Nine further repeats had so far been identified, but all they did was confirm there was a switching system. Nothing gave the faintest indication of how it might work. The thing seemed entirely random – as though each formation had been handed a little pile of combinations and told to use which it liked, when it liked. But of course, nothing could work like that. There must be a system. If not, chaos. And it could still be part of a deliberate pre-invasion plan!

By the Grace of the God of Courtesy, our procession of cars reached Swakeleys a minute or two before the S.S. bus at ten. We had agreed on an early start. When it came, our tired and anxious eyes scanned the windows for Merchants of Death (one Sunday team that year had found itself facing Aircraftman Trueman on a bumpy pitch in a dismal light). The bus halted and I sensed someone beside me. Dorothy Rigby.

"They don't look too bad," I muttered. "Nothing to terrify our batsmen."

She nodded. "But there's one to put the wind up the scorer."

"What do you mean?"

"On the step now."

I looked and saw a tall young man of pleasant if muscular aspect, plainly shy, and wearing what could be a Surrey tie. "Who –"

"That," she said, "is Writer May. Good job I brought my kit."

I blinked at her. "We have a full side, you know."

"Oh," Rigby said airily, "somebody always drops out. And look, isn't he the most beautiful young man!"

Indeed he was. Writer May was quickly changed and out at the nets: modest, boyish, immaculate, thrumming with power. The ball boomed off his bat and screamed along the netting. This was true class, the genuine article, your real McCoy, and no mistaking it for anything else. I watched in awe for a minute or two until he smiled and gave up his place to somebody else, and then I made for the scorer's box.

And was intercepted. "Got your togs?" Reg cried, rushing towards me. "Morrison's in terrible agony with piles. Can't possibly turn out!"

Well, I had boots and flannels; the rest I borrowed, thinking the while about poor Morrison and his painful affliction, and also of Rigby's prediction: always one short, she'd said. But it hadn't got her a game.

I was watching May at fielding practice – quintessential public schoolboy, though with hands and arms like the village blacksmith – when shouts of alarm came from the pavilion behind me. Poor Burton, it seemed, had tripped and cracked his head. "We're going to be one short," Reg snarled. "Who the hell could play?"

"I could, if you like." Rigby had moved in softly.

"But you're a *woman*!"

"True. But I do play cricket. And I'd love to play today."

Reg looked at the summer dress, at the sandals. "Thank you, Miss er – but really . . ."

"Cricket bag's in my car," she said, ready to scamper off.

"Cricket bag? Here, just a minute," Reg said. "What do you actually do?"

"Well, I can bat a bit. I'm not a bad slip field."

"It's a bowler we need. It's two bowlers we've lost!"

"I dare say I could get my arm over."

"Look here, where have you played and who for?"

"For New South Wales a few times, and Western Province – both women's cricket teams – oh, and for Pudsey. That was men's league cricket in Yorkshire." The name of Pudsey had overtones of Hutton and Sutcliffe. Reg, reluctant to play her, clearly had no option. "Right," he said. "Get changed."

She looked good in whites: well-cut flannels and silk shirt, plus a short-sleeved sweater with green hoops. I tossed a few to her on the boundary edge and she put her left foot to the pitch and swung through a nice clean arc, and I looked at that pullover and wondered. When we stopped, I asked, "That's Australian?"

She avoided my eye and didn't answer. "Where'd you get it?" I demanded.

"I got the previous owner out in a country match one day. He said he'd give it to me for sheer bloody impertinence."

"Who was he?"

Dorothy Rigby beckoned me closer; she whispered in my ear. I will *not* repeat the name. I didn't believe it then and I'm not sure I believe it now. "Not HIM?"

"Did you watch Writer May?" she added blithely.

"Yes," I said, "and he *is* beautiful."

"If vulnerable," she muttered darkly.

Well, it was just a game of Sunday cricket: two innings each side, a lunch of sandwiches, pork pies and beer or lemonade if the sun got hot, with close of play five minutes before the bar re-opened. Reg won the toss and decided to bat. May stood at mid-on, as though with a spotlight on him. He did everything perfectly: heels or knees behind the ball, pick-up on the run, a flat underarm throw that snapped into the wicket-keeper's gloves. And he was running about a good deal, too, because the rest of the S.S. team seemed fairly ordinary and Reg was a pretty fair player (a Cambridge Blue in a good, if distant year) and Prince still better. (Prince was one of those pale intellectual New Zealanders, an old All-Black trialist, who had batted for Otago in his time.) The two of them, faced with a nothing attack on a flat wicket, began to tonk it about.

You'll have gathered already what kind of cricket it was. Our lot had been players in their time; the other lot seemed mainly young and promising, with a couple of elderly ones mixed in – and May, of course. Their opening bowlers were medium-pacers, straight up and down. But then the first-change materialised in the form of a chubby Indian Army captain who had bowled for Uttar Pradesh in the Ranji Trophy, and began to loop up his leg-breaks and googlies and even, occasionally, to turn one. He was through us like the proverbial hot knife. I didn't even see the one that bowled me, and was cross, really quite cross, about it, because Rigby was, by now, at the other end, and I wanted to watch her play, at close quarters. As it was, I watched from a deck chair and she did rather well: seventeen not out when the innings ended, and she'd used her feet to the Indian.

Then they went in and the Indian turned out to be an all-rounder, patting a cultured twenty before his partner ran him out.

The Royal Navy called its clerks Writers so enter Writer May (if he'd been a pongo, the rank would have been Private) and the ball began to fly. One blew past my ear at mid-off and I heard the zeep of the seam in the air. He'd got about forty (five sixes) when the fluke happened and Reg, who'd come on to trundle down some slow droppers, got his hand to a straight drive by May's partner and directed it into the stumps. Writer May, run out, 42.

After that Reg gave Dorothy Rigby an over – left arm, and she bowled, of all unlikely things, chinamen. Not quite like Denis Compton of course: where he was all muscular forearm and wristy tweak, Rigby delivered from a high, slender arm. No enormous spin, but she bowled all three and you couldn't pick 'em. I couldn't, anyway.

At any rate, she bowled very tidily and got three: two bowled and one caught at deep mid-wicket. So off we went again – Good Lord, I haven't given you the scores! We made 146, then they got 128. So we had our ham sandwiches and lettuce at one-forty-five p.m. and Reg said to me, just before we went out to field, "Good, that girl".

"Very fair."

"She's batting four this time."

You'd have thought they were a couple of really good pros, Ames and Fagg, for instance, or Keeton and Harris: singles came off every ball, twos off many and fours pretty frequently. Sweet, handsome stuff it was, with the rooks complaining in the elms and the smell of warm grass and the crack of bat on ball. We were 154 for two before Rigby got to the wicket, and her first over was against the wily Oriental, who kept a cool good length. She didn't face a ball next over, either. Old Prince was in commanding form, in the eighties and hogging the bowling. He could get a century today and it might well be his last and he wanted it. But a slick bit of fielding by May saved a run and left Rigby facing, with two balls left in the over. She danced out impatiently at the first and put it back over the bowler's head. The Indian didn't enjoy it – who does? – and I could see that she meant to do it again, so I reckon he could too. Then, and I can see this moment now in my mind's eye, he was in to bowl and she was footworking forward and he, the crafty beggar, drops it neat as ninepence at her heels. No run there, you'd say?

You'd be badly wrong. What she did was somehow to pivot to her right and smack the damn thing on the half volley as it went by – six over the wicket-keeper's head! Never seen it before or since, and not sure whether it's believable even now . . .

So, Prince got his ton and she was twelve – not out, again, you'll notice. Then Reg declared at 180 putting us 198 ahead. Tea and a wad and we were off again.

In a match like that in those days we'd have a new ball at

the start and by the time innings number four came round it would be scraped and battered, so our opening quicks did nothing with it and Reg had himself on as first change and got their opener caught at long-off. Enter Writer May, tanned and shiny under his private sunbeam, all aglow and virtuous in the afternoon light. Reg vs Writer May was not Bradman vs Verity, not by miles. This wasn't contest, it was murder. Six, four, four, six, four, four. Twenty-eight off the over, two of them high to the elms, the rooks rising and swirling in rage. Reg took himself off and brought on an Intelligence Corps Corporal who claimed to have bowled in the Bradford League, said he was medium-quick, but he was straight-driven, on the up, off ball four, the third having hissed just wide of mid-on.

Crossing at the end of the over, I passed Rigby. "Hits it hard, doesn't he?"

"He's what I want for Christmas," she murmured.

As it happened, he was hers long before Christmas. You don't get too many people tossing-up accurate left-arm leg-breaks and googlies in that class of cricket, and she was a bit better than competent, so after Reg put her on, wickets fell. May's *wasn't* among them.

There's a yawning gap between club side and county, and an even wider gap between county and Test player. May, at this time, was two years away from a century in his first Test. He could cope. The others couldn't. Rigby conned them out, even though the ball didn't turn.

So, between the clatter of wickets at one end and the resonant boom of May's bat at the other, an interesting finish began to look likely. Now Rigby was to bowl a new over to him. Numbers Nine and Ten were already gone, and Jack stood a-tremble at the bowler's end. It was plain she would have Jack for breakfast, and if she didn't, somebody else would.

Henry Newbolt time, then: all breathless hush. Twenty-eight to win, May on 70.

Now, you'll have seen the point at once: the winning stroke must be a six if Writer May was to get his ton. We knew it; Rigby certainly knew it, and Writer May knew it with such intensity that blue lights were flashing from his ears.

"Any bright ideas?" she asked me softly as she walked back to her mark.

"You want one that pitches leg stump and nips the top of the off," I said.

She showed her teeth briefly and walked away, slim and controlled. Then ran in . . .

There were all sorts of options. She *wasn't* going to get his wicket; he *was* going to plaster her all round the ground. But if one clever bit of containment could be introduced, well, *then* . . .

She gave him the off-break out of the back of her hand, and somebody's son caught it proudly twenty-five yards beyond the roller. Six. She walked back thoughtfully, then gave him the same again. May was forward like an armoured brigade and lifted it on the up over mid-on. It didn't fly more than half a mile.

Twelve.

Heaven knows what to say about her third one. It seemed to me that the ball slipped from her grip as she bowled, and what's more she stumbled and went down on one knee. The ball, meanwhile, was bouncing twice on its way to a disconcerted Writer May. His bat picked it up cleanly on the second of those bounces, but there wasn't much way on the ball and, though it sizzled to the boundary, it ran all along the ground.

Sixteen, then. Three balls to go. Two sixes would win the match, but leave the good Writer two short of his hundred. One, therefore, would have to be a four.

She now bowled him a top-spinner. It didn't do a thing except pitch middle stump and find the sweet spot on his bat. Mid-wicket had to find it in the long grass.

Two to go, and if the Young Gent was to have his hundred (and don't tell me he didn't care: all cricketers, always, desperately want hundreds, whatever kind of game it is) the next must be a four.

She bowled him a slow ball of the kind that young lads used to call donkey drops. It came down gently somewhere about the point of his left shoulder: a delivery without danger (you'd say), void of skill, without anything to be said in its favour except that it was five feet off the ground and hard to hit down. Up would have been easy, and oh! was he tempted! But this was a young fellow not only of quality, but of self-discipline. Somehow or other he actually got his bat on top of it, and hit it hard, and prevented himself from smashing the six, but it was a close thing. As it was the ball bounced a mere yard or two inside the boundary chalk.

Four it was.

So now: if May hit the last ball for six, he won the match and got his hundred. Four won the match, but left the Writer fuming on 98.

I watched her walk back to her mark. We didn't know then that this young man was one of the best this century, but he'd already shown us more than enough of his extraordinary command. And she . . . well, whoever else he faced in his career, the Writer could not face a ball so carefully contrived to offer such problems and possibilities. As she turned, she paused, and I saw their eyes meet and lock in a little contest of wills. You could almost hear the click. Then she moved forward. It was a mere five paces . . .

She took three of them, then stopped. And turned. And stared long and hard at the scoreboard. I called, "Don't worry, you've got it right!" But she gave a little shake of the head and went on staring. This little hiatus continued for quite a long time. May had taken his stance and didn't abandon it, and was certainly far too well-mannered to call "Oi!" as you or I might. In the event the umpire (theirs) solved the problem by calling "Play, please", in one of those ringing army-officer voices. And she turned and ran slowly in.

I was strung tight as Yehudi's Strad. I mean to say: it was a match of no consequence whatever, destined to be forgotten by tomorrow, but I've remembered it forty years, so you see how tense it was. What would she bowl? Leg-break, off-break, top-spinner? Little skip, little jump, and the ball was on its way. But round arm, dead on the stumps and pretty quick. A round arm shooter, in fact, of a type probably not seen in public since – oh, since Lillywhite.

Well, nobody could hit a shooter like that for six. Bradman couldn't, Compton probably couldn't and May didn't, though he did his very considerable best as it skated sideways at him, and tried to waft a kind of four-iron shot over extra cover. It was a bat in the Writer's hand, though, not a golf club, and the ball merely tore towards the grateful hands of Reg at deep extra, and he put his throw sweetly in the keeper's hands.

Final result, therefore: Rigby 1, The Writer 0

He, being a sportsman and a gent, managed to laugh lightly and give her a wave of acknowledgment. In his place I'd have wrung her chiselling neck. I didn't think that round arm shooter had been very sporting, even if the laws allowed it, and as she seemed to be grinning very widely as she ran towards me, I thought I'd tell her so. "Dorothy . . ." I began.

But she sidestepped off the left foot like a Welsh stand-off. It was Reg she was making for, Reg for whom her outstretched arms were reaching, Reg whose name spilled from her eager lips.

He looked and nothing moved. No. 3 remained on 96, the total on 196. The groundsman had left the board and was now walking towards his besom broom and barrow on the boundary edge.

"I'm looking," said Reg.

"Then imagine," she cried. "Imagine that that last shot had been a six, and it had been put up! What would have happened? What would have moved?"

"Well," said Reg, plainly humouring this lunatic, "add six and the ninety-six becomes one-oh-two, yes?"

"Yes, yes. What else?"

"Well, the one is slotted in place to make the hundred. Then the wheels are moved. That what you mean?"

"Part of it. That one is the start of another hundred. Agree?"

"Er – yes." Suddenly there was a dreamy quality in Reg's normally bold tone.

"Imagine it's three wheels, not two. Each has A to Z and zero to nine round the circumference. They're printing wheels."

"Hold on," says Reg. "That's twenty-six thousand odd combinations."

"Twenty-six thousand."

"So it'll be pages – one hundred squares to the page and one call-sign per square," Reg gloated. A small smile began and spread; it became a grin and then a laugh; finally it was a deep chortle of enormous happiness. "And ten pages per book equals a thousand call-signs, all picked at random! Oh Christ! And every unit gets allocated its page. 'You Boris,'" he mimicked, "'for your airplane you get on Tuesday Book One

Page Ten, and your permanent coordinates are four and nine. Complete the square and what you haf?"''

"M.V.D., comradeski," said Rigby.

"Tell me," said Reg, "do you like champagne?"

"In view of the Official Secrets Act," said Dorothy Rigby, "Mumm had better be the word."

"I drink any kind," I offered.

"But unfortunately," Reg said, "you have to liaise with Ernie."

Rigby smiled. Everybody knows that smile of hers.

Observant readers will have noticed that there had been a dramatic change in Rigby's bowling style. As a teenager in Simla she was bowling some pretty dangerous fast stuff. Now, nearing thirty, she has switched to slow left-arm and chinamen. It was partly age and partly something she did to her shoulder round about the beginning of the Berlin air-lift. Even she wouldn't tell me precisely what happened. She said it was embarrassing and not important. But it meant she had to develop a new bowling action.

The following year, of course, Klaus Fuchs was finally found guilty of betraying Atomic Secrets to the Russians. He was put away, but we let him out in the end and he went back to East Germany where he headed up their nuclear research institute.

Rigby, always cheeky, couldn't resist sending a postcard to the head of the C.I.A., Allen Dulles, saying, "Told you so!" Dulles wasn't amused and complained to Denham. Denham told him not to be so pompous so Dulles complained to Harry Truman who complained to Attlee about both of them. And, to Rigby's delight, Attlee told Truman and Dulles not to be pompous. "Bloody pompous", he actually said. Attlee wasn't nearly as mild as he looked.

She was happy in these years though she was increasingly concerned about some of her colleagues in Intelligence. She suspected the Philby, Burgess, Maclean *galère*. Despised Peter Wright. Liked, but could not wholly admire, Roger Hollis.

Socially it was the mixture as before. She and Camilla still shared the Marylebone High Street flat. Rigby toyed with men like a dieting mannequin with hors d'oeuvres. She still went, sometimes, to Mass at Farm Street. She was having a good time but she was getting older.

Angela Cheyne

RUN RABBIT RUN, RUN, RUN

Burgess and Maclean got away in '51 and Rigby was furious. "That drunken nancy boy," she said of Burgess whom she had once thrown over her shoulder at a staff party. They had been arguing about the Albanian succession, King Zog and Enver Hoxha. As for Donald Maclean, he had once made a pass at Rigby and been icily rebuffed. "I always *knew* there was something *wrong* about Donald," she said, "he smelt wrong." Rigby was fiercely intuitive!

In '52 Eisenhower was elected President of the U.S.A., which did her career no harm whatever. She liked Ike and Ike liked her. During his presidency she often acted as a courier for really sensitive inter-governmental dispatches. Churchill got quite peeved with Eisenhower saying, "Winston, send it over with your piss elegant Miss Rigby and we can play a round of golf together". Rigby was good at golf, better than the ageing Eisenhower. But she always let Ike win.

1953 was the year Stalin died (no tears from Rigby); the year Hammarskjöld became Secretary General of the United Nations (almost three cheers from Rigby) and the year Everest was conquered and the Queen was crowned. These last two naturally brought out all Rigby's most patriotic instincts. She had climbed in Snowdonia and the Alps with John (now Lord) Hunt and was a friend of *The Times* correspondent on the expedition James (now Jan) Morris.

1953 was also, improbably, the year that Rigby got involved with rabbits.

Snow fell out of the sky in huge soft flakes blotting out buildings, trees and the sounds of the city. Rigby awoke and wondered where she was for a moment. She'd been walkabout in a sunbaked desert and vestiges of an Aboriginal chant still reverberated in her ears. Large quantities of cold beer, fish and chips obviously did not agree with her. Rigby did not imbibe to any marked degree – a single malt or a chilled glass of Sancerre from time to time, but cold beer . . .

She bathed and dressed and was at her desk early. Alice brought her regulation tea and biscuits as she wrote up a succinct and withering report on Mick Larson, Under-Secretary, Australian High Commission.

"Have a good evening?"

She glanced venomously at her employer, draped against the door jamb.

"We had rather a good dinner at the Ritz," he continued, "I'm so sorry you couldn't join us, but I think that young Australian's rather keen. I hope you'll see him again, I hope you'll see a great deal of him over the next three months . . ." He was gone before she could protest.

Nibbling limp ginger nuts, she gazed towards Big Ben. Men and women in overcoats and galoshes hurried across the icy pavements to work. Rigby shivered involuntarily. She had a bad feeling about Larson. There was something about his mouth. She was sure she'd run into a mouth like that before.

"You can't beat Bondi! It's beaut!"

They were sitting in a small bistro, in an unfashionable London suburb, eating goulash. She'd brought Camilla along for the evening. It is, after all, one of the functions of a best friend to interfere with the unwelcome advances of ardent suitors. Camilla was more than fulfilling her duties, gazing raptly into Mick's large blue eyes while he extolled the virtues of an outdoor life 'down under'.

Rigby tried to concentrate. The relationship with Britain and Australia was close. Only a few months had passed since the Woomera test and, although Princess Elizabeth's Commonwealth tour had been cut short due to the death of the King, the Commonwealth summit was coming up soon. Portland hadn't given her any clues. "Keep an eye on Mick," was all he'd said. Why? What was going on? Was Larson leaking test secrets to the Russians? Were the Japanese causing problems? Had the scramble by disenchanted Brits to emigrate for a fiver caused too many difficulties? What? Portland couldn't leave her on a 'watch with Micky' assignment for long. She'd mutiny.

"I hear the wildlife is spectacular!" breathed Camilla.

She had the most irritating way of speaking on little intakes and outtakes of breath. Men found it irresistible. Rigby found it absurd.

"Of course koalas are favourite . . ." Mick grinned and his eyes locked with hers ". . . then there's kookaburras, kangaroos, crocs . . ."

Rigby let the two of them contemplate Australian mating habits while she drifted back to her desert, where she had come across a group of Aborigines standing very, very, still.

A lethal combination of particularly thick pea soupers and increasing industrial smoke had turned the 'smog' into a killer. Thousands succumbed to aggravated coughs and colds. It also did for Lady Annabelle Smythe-Jones' favourite grandmother. Lady Cynthia Hooper-Bolton refused to give up her early morning and evening constitutionals.

"But Gran," cried Annabelle helplessly, ". . . something might happen."

"What?" retorted Lady Cynthia.

"I don't know. You might be attacked, or run over – anything."

"Don't be silly child, I've lived through two wars, *and* prohibition . . ." (Lady Cynthia's family had spent several years in Chicago, something to do with money) ". . . and I'm not dead yet."

Annabelle was racked with guilt that she hadn't gone

with her granny that evening. But she really didn't, very sensibly, want to go out in the fog. The Coroner pronounced death by misadventure and Annabelle found herself rattling around an enormous flat in Bloomsbury all by herself. It was gloomy and rather frightening. She thought about moving, but redecorated and invited her favourite cousin to live with her instead.

Sir Leon Hooper-Bolton was twelve years older than Annabelle, extremely good-looking, with not a penny to his name. He also had a reputation. The Duke of Cirencester's daughter had gone to Switzerland for a 'cure' the previous autumn and everybody knew why. It had only served to increase Hooper-Bolton's mystique. He was becoming something of a legend.

March winds blew away the fog and carpets of crocus scattered the park. Annabelle was enjoying her ride. She was twenty-one today and was giving a party. The decorators had finally finished the flat and she was seriously thinking of taking up interior design as a profession. There were plenty of men waiting to marry her of course, but she found the English, with a few exceptional exceptions (like Hooper) insipid. The fashion for marrying favourite cousins was out of vogue, which was probably just as well as Hooper would never be faithful. She wondered vaguely if that mattered. The French all had mistresses, or so she'd heard.

Annabelle's reverie was rudely interrupted when her mare shied at a passing baby carriage and she found herself eating Hyde Park sand.

"Are you all right?" said a voice.

Annabelle looked up. "I think so." But she gave a cry of pain as she tried to move.

"I don't think you've broken anything," said Rigby as she gently removed Annabelle's riding boot and examined her leg. "You've twisted your ankle."

People talk about their illnesses, but they don't want to see any evidence (men find it especially tiresome, unless they're afflicted themselves). So Annabelle chose a long dress to hide her bandages, with plenty of *décolletage* to compensate for not displaying her legs and arranged herself on a sofa where she was surrounded by suitors all evening.

"Can I get you a glass of champagne?" Rigby looked up into a pair of large brown eyes and felt a weird sensation in her chest. Sir Leon Hooper-Bolton took her by the elbow and steered her away from Larson.

"Annabelle tells me that you rescued her this morning."

"I wouldn't say that."

"I'm terribly grateful. Annabelle's my very favourite cousin . . ."

Rigby experienced another rare sensation, a twinge of jealousy.

"Rigby . . ." someone called her name, ". . . telephone . . ."

Grateful for the interruption, she took the call on the ivory extension in the bedroom.

"Hello?"

"Rigby, glad I tracked you down. All hands on deck, I'm afraid. There's rather a flap on."

Stalin's death was announced on March 5th, although Rigby's inside sources informed her that he'd been dead for several weeks. She waited eagerly for a posting but they sent someone else instead.

"We need you here," was all Portland said.

Camilla was forced to cancel dinner with Mick for ten days and was inconsolable.

"I don't know what you see in him . . ." said Rigby.

"He's so sweet," Camilla breathed.

"But have you found out anything yet?"

"You're the one ferreting secrets. I'm having fun."

Rigby turned away in disgust. Perhaps *she* should have a little fun. Perhaps she would have dinner with Hooper-Bolton after all.

They dined at a small restaurant in Mayfair. They were about the same age and discovered mutual acquaintances. Hooper was extremely amusing and she was surprised to learn that he had a job at the Ministry of Agriculture, Fisheries and Food. He was well informed and very interesting on the subject of land management. Rigby realised what a major setback it must have been for him when his bid for the Duke of Cirencester's daughter (estates), had gone awry. She wondered how he was coping with the bureaucracy of Whitehall.

Rigby was not coping. She was very, very bored but Portland refused to give her any work.

". . . Then you've got to give me leave. You're keeping me in London pushing papers. I'm a field agent."

"The hidden agenda for the Commonwealth summit's been very useful, Rigby." He smiled thinly, "Patience."

It was all politics. She'd been Rupert Denham's favourite and since he'd retired Portland was letting her stew. Patience! She thought she would go mad. There was, at least, the Coronation. She loved the ritual and the pageantry and arranged for a place at the Ministry window to watch and wave. She mused over the rigours and responsibilities of the Queen. That's what she, Rigby, needed – work, and lots of it. The phone rang on her desk. "Rigby, it's Hooper. Can you get over here right away ∴ . . ? Have you had mumps?"

Rigby had had mumps.

When she got to Bloomsbury she found Annabelle in bed – with mumps. There were no two ways about it. The girl could not go to the Coronation. (She and Hooper had invitations as distant, distant cousins of the Royal Family.)

"But we can't let the family down, I've got to be there," she wailed.

"You will be. You will be, Annabelle, my love. I've worked it all out."

Disguise was one of Rigby's talents and she carried off her part as Lady Annabelle Smythe-Jones with her usual aplomb, thanks to a perm, a chestnut rinse, and the family tiara.

Hooper gripped her arm tightly as they took their place beside peers, politicians and crowned and uncrowned heads of State (somewhat the worse for the weather – it was raining on open carriages). The media were having a field day, what with the Coronation, its instant celebrities (notably the large and beplumed Queen of Tonga) and Hillary and Tenzing's conquest of Everest. News of the heroic feat had come that very morning and was being hailed as an omen for the new Elizabethan Age! Rigby searched for the television cameras that were bringing the occasion into the homes of hundreds of thousands of people, including the tumescent Annabelle at home in bed.

Annabelle was still in bed two weeks later, so Hooper took Rigby, Camilla and that 'awful Australian' to Henley. The sunlight sparkled on the river as they wandered about the clipped green lawns, it was a perfect summer's day and Rigby wondered what was going to go wrong.

"Come and meet my oldest and dearest friend, the Duc de Signac," said Hooper. The Duc was attractive and very rich, and invited them all partridge shooting in the autumn. Mick proposed chartering a plane to fly them over, an idea that appalled Rigby but she was outvoted. Hooper and Annabelle, Camilla and Mick and Rigby would go to the Loire for the weekend of the 18th September.

Rigby watched the sun dip behind the trees. She'd enjoyed the day, the champagne and strawberries, the races, and Hooper. Was she getting too fond of him? She wondered idly where he'd got to, when out of the corner of her eye she caught sight of him going into a marquee. There was something distinctly furtive in his manner and her stomach fell to her boots – a sure sign of trouble. She covered the ground to the tent in seconds and through a tear in the canvas saw Hooper, the Duc de Signac and Mick gathered in one corner.

"The Government won't wear it. They're afraid of public opinion," said Hooper.

"We're talking 50 million English pounds a year at least," came Mick's nasal tones.

"Even so," replied Hooper.

"My friends, I have what you need. All you have to do is

let me know if you want it or not. But it must be before the cold weather," said the Frenchman.

"It will have to be unofficial," Hooper sighed, "if the Government finds out there'll be hell to pay."

"What's with them?" asked Mick incredulously. "Why else have they been paying me for the past six months?"

The Count got up. "I leave you to your politicians. Give me your answer when you come to France." He embraced his friend. "*Mon brave.* I see you in September, uh?"

Rigby drove home through the summer evening feeling vaguely depressed. What was Hooper up to? Whatever it was, they were bound to be on opposite sides.

Camilla made a thorough search of Mick's rooms. She found a boomerang, grubby underwear, a photo album of Aborigines and treatises on wildlife. James Hunter, Rigby's inside contact at the Min. of Ag. and Fish., was sunning himself somewhere in the South of France and couldn't be reached. (She and James had been involved with pigs at the Ministry of Defence the year before and she knew she could trust him.) And the trace on the Duc de Signac was clean. He was head of an old Faubourg family – one of the few who'd managed to keep their estates intact by consistently marrying very, very rich wives. The Duc wasn't involved in politics and had kept ahead of the tax man.

She wished she could talk to Denham but what could she say? My boyfriend's up to no good at the Min. of Ag. and Fish. with Camilla's boyfriend, and the Duc de Signac? She had to face it, she had no idea what was going on. Was she slipping? Damn Portland. She'd had almost a year of pushing paper . . . she'd ask for a transfer in December. The Americans would be glad to have her. She could even go back to G.C.H.Q. – at least there she'd be cracking codes.

The White Cliffs looked very white from the air. Snippets of Annabelle's chatter drifted over the engine noise – had she brought the right clothes? Would the Duke and Wallis be there? Rigby looked out of the window and thought how much she would prefer to be in one of the ships down below. Normally she loved flying, but not with Larson at the controls. Hooper was in a bad mood. There'd been trouble at the aerodrome. He'd waved a piece of paper and muttered Min. of Ag. and Fish., but there'd been a problem and she didn't feel like humouring him.

They flew down to the Loire valley and the view from the small plane was spectacular: châteaux, vineyards, farmland and forests. The plane made an aerial circuit of the Duc's extensive estates and then descended sharply on to a small landing strip. Rigby's stomach was in her boots, again. She had a bad feeling about the weekend.

Jane de Signac greeted them on the doorstep. Children hung about her skirts and she carried a baby in her arms. Rigby recognised the young woman from the society columns and whispers of scandal involving an Italian film star came back to her.

"Lunch will be ready in twenty minutes, drinks in the drawing room," said the young Duchess as Rigby followed a servant up the staircase and down a passage hung with Aubusson tapestries. Her bedroom overlooked formal gardens which stretched away to fountains playing in the distance. Her bed was draped with pale blue and pink hangings drawn up into a golden circle of flying cherubs surrounding a trumpeting angel and a Fragonard hung over the dressing table, but there was no running water. A china bowl and water jug stood on a washstand in the corner.

The Duc didn't join them for lunch. He was out with the keeper inspecting the covers for tomorrow. There would be partridge, duck and perhaps wild boar. It was apparently impossible to keep the wild pigs out of the pheasant and partridge covers.

"Isn't that rather dangerous?" asked Rigby.

"Terrifying!" said Jane, "I don't go out these days. The children and I stay and help with lunch. Camilla, Rigby, Annabelle, you're welcome to stay in bed, help me and the children, or go out with the men. Please, I want you all to feel quite at home. Come and go as you like. Oh, and by the way, the front door is always locked at midnight. If you think you're going to need a key please ask the Duc."

*   *   *

After lunch Rigby went into the garden and played with the children. It was a French game involving a ball and numbers. She picked it up quite quickly and they soon became fast friends. Jean-Claude and Janine offered to give her a tour of the stables, aviary and hutches, *or* the gardens.

"The animals are more interesting," said Jean-Claude.

"Let's do the animals then," said Rigby.

"Race you to the stables," squealed Janine.

They both had very white skin, blue-black wavy hair and dark eyes with long, long eyelashes. The girl was a year younger and very striking. Jean-Claude had lean, ascetic features which gave him a serious look. Rigby liked them both and the feeling was mutual.

They pampered the thoroughbreds with carrots and sugar lumps, fed the ornamental birds in the aviary and pushed lettuces, uprooted from the walled garden, through the wire of the rabbit hutches.

"We had a hedgehog called Mrs Tiggywinkle but Monsieur le Duc wouldn't let us keep her because of the fleas," said Janine.

"He says they're vectors," said Jean-Claude. "What are vectors?"

Rigby wasn't absolutely sure.

"I think they're carriers," she said. "You know how bees pick up pollen at the same time as they're collecting nectar and then they drop it off on the next flower . . ."

"Cross fertilisation," said Jean-Claude.

"Exactly right . . . well vectors do the same thing only with diseases. If a flea bites a hedgehog with a nasty disease and then bites another hedgehog, he drops the disease on to that hedgehog and so on . . ."

"That's why we have to keep the other rabbits separate . . ."

"There are more?" exclaimed Rigby.

"Oh, lots and lots – well, quite a few," said Janine.

". . . But . . ." she faltered. "We're not supposed to show you those."

Jean-Claude frowned, looked at his shoes and was saved by the arrival of Mick and Camilla on horseback.

"Hello. We're going for a ride. Hooper's looking for you everywhere, Rigby. And your mother's looking for you two," said Camilla. Rigby looked up at her friend and felt sorry for her. Perhaps Camilla really was in love with Mick and he was going home next month.

The children raced each other back to the house. Rigby followed at her own pace and soon got lost. She found herself in a rose garden and saw what looked like a dead rabbit lying on the gravel path. Moving towards it, she was startled by a voice at her side.

"*Madame, Madame, je m'en occupe.*"

An old gardener bent down and dealt the rabbit a blow behind the ears and swept it into his sack.

"*J'espère que ça ne vous a pas trop dérangé,*" he said and went quietly on his way.

"*Non, non. Pas du tout; ça va,*" Rigby responded and he was gone before she could ask the way back to the house.

Dinner was spectacular. Rigby sat next to her handsome host at one end of a long table peppered with the aristocracy of Europe, most of whom she'd met on one occasion or another. They drank the château's own wine and the Duc promised to take her on a tour of his vineyards. Later they played charades in four different languages and Mick was a great success in Aborigine, promising boomerang lessons on the lawn on Sunday after Church.

In her dreams she was in Australia again. Back to the desert littered with small, grey rocks soft and clammy to the touch. She was chasing Hooper and Larson but ahead was the abyss.

She woke after the shooting party had left and breakfasted alone. Rigby had decided against going out with the guns; she needed to reconnoitre and anyway she didn't much like the sound of boar. She had told Hooper that Jane needed help with the lunch. When he protested that there were plenty of staff to do the lunch, she pointed out that it would be nice for Jane to have company.

"Jane has endless company."

"Not English, female and under fifty-five," replied Rigby, "and anyway Annabelle's dying to come with you."

"Yes," said Hooper, "*she's* not afraid of boar."

Hooper was definitely on edge.

Rigby searched the Duc's study, which revealed nothing but accounts for the vineyard and detailed plans of the estate. But it was there she finally made the connection. The Duc owned estates. Hooper's subject was land management and Mick was an expert on wildlife . . .

At the stables she found Jane and the children setting a long trestle table for lunch. She professed a desire to stretch her legs and walked past the aviary and rabbit hutches on to the fields beyond. There was something she'd seen on the plans of the estate that she wanted to investigate.

She heard the guns in the distance and was glad she hadn't gone with them. Rigby was a good shot, but wasn't enthusiastic about driven game. Stalking was another matter, that was you against the beast, the odds weren't loaded.

She crossed two more fields and turned down a grassy paddock towards a small stream. Golden kingcups glinted in the sun and she walked along the mossy bank through a beech wood. In a clearing she came to a small chapel. The door was locked, but through the window she saw a row of what looked like rabbit hutches.

Lunch was a noisy affair. The morning had gone well. Plenty of partridge and no sign of boar. The bag was laid out in the stable courtyard and Janine took Rigby's hand and squeezed it tight as they stared down at the lifeless birds. A tear rolled down her cheek. The Duc came up behind his daughter and swung her into the air.

"Little one! You must toughen up!"

A young keeper standing next to Rigby said, "You can imagine what she was like about the rabbits!"

"Mademoiselle Rigby! Telephone . . . a Monsieur James Hunter."

"There's a telephone in the tack room," said the Duc.

She cursed inwardly. Hooper's eyes were on her as she walked across the cobblestones. James Hunter worked with Hooper at the Ministry of Ag. and Fish. and she hadn't wanted Hooper to know she and James were in touch.

"Hello, James! What a surprise!"

"Tracked you down, old fish! What can I do for you?"

"I'm staying at the Duc de Signac's – partridge shooting with Hooper-Bolton. I can't really talk now, but I need some information. What's the name of that disease they are killing rabbits with in Australia?"

"Myxomatosis. Why? There's been a hell of a row about it here, I can tell you. The farming lobby's very pro of course and the government's sitting on the fence . . . can't say how I feel about it. Been a huge success in Australia . . . they've saved billions."

Hooper came and stood in the doorway. She smiled at him.

"Listen, James, since you're in the area . . ." she lied, "I thought you might like a lift. A crowd of us are flying back to Lydd tomorrow. We've got a private plane," she said.

"We should be getting back about five-ish, I think. Is that any good to you? No? You're not sure? Well, try and make it . . . Yes. We'll be at Lydd by five. Might see you tomorrow then, glad you called. Goodbye."

Rigby hung up and said easily, "You know James Hunter . . . he's been in the South of France . . . on his way home . . . thought he might like a lift."

"Oh . . . didn't know you knew him . . ."

"Yes . . ."

Rigby went out with Hooper after duck after all. He knew she knew something, and she knew he knew she knew and they behaved as if nothing had happened. It was fun competing and they came out even, same number of cartridges fired, same number of dead duck.

On the way home through the wood Hooper and Rigby brought up the rear. At a turn in the path there was a sudden burst of activity in the undergrowth and then they were staring into the beady eyes of a big, black boar. Split seconds felt like years as Rigby felt for her cartridges and loaded her gun. Afterwards she wasn't sure who hit the ground first, Hooper or the boar. At any rate they both fell at her feet, Hooper in a dead faint, the pig just dead. The Duc was solicitous, apologetic, and delighted to add the boar to the bag. Rigby was delighted too. She had never shot a boar before.

*   *   *

Dinner was another splendid affair, but afforded no chance for uncovering further evidence. Rigby was convinced that the Duc was in possession of the myxomatosis virus. She was also sure that Hooper was planning to take it to England, but how? She had to talk to that young keeper or even the children, not that she wanted to involve them.

The moon was very bright as she took an after-dinner stroll. She wanted to take another look at the rabbit hutches in the chapel. She thought she heard a footfall behind her but there was no one, only the horses moving about in their stalls, blowing softly through their noses. Then she thought about giving Hunter a call from the tack room. She needed to find out how the virus would be transported. What should she be looking for? But the tack room was locked. She only got as far as the aviary.

"Are you all right, Rigby?" said Larson, coming out of the shadows.

"Why, yes thank you," she said, "I came out for some air."

"We were worried about you," he replied smoothly. "After all we don't want any more nasty surprises, do we?"

No, she thought, we don't.

". . . The Duc's about to lock up for the night . . ."

She was extremely annoyed that he'd followed her and that he'd threatened her. Had he set up the incident with the boar? Was the rabbit population of the British Isles that important to him? She thought of using violence, but decided against it. They were obviously worried and it was better to keep them guessing at this stage. So she discussed Australian fast-bowling techniques on the way back to the house. She thought there was a kink in Keith Miller's action. Indeed she had told him as much during the Lord's Test.

It was the young keeper's day off, the children were at early Mass and the Duc's manager arrived early to take her on the tour of the vineyards (the Duc had been called away on urgent business). There was, therefore, nothing more to be done at the château. She left a note for the children, took her leave of Jane and arranged to meet the others at the airstrip that afternoon – they'd opted for church and Sunday lunch.

Rigby learnt a great deal about château bottling, sampled the excellent wine and was presented with two mixed cases for herself and her friends. But the phones at the vineyard were out of order.

The others were already on board when Rigby arrived. She distributed the bottles of wine, which were much appreciated. And then Camilla said, "Look what we've got!" In a brown cardboard box on her lap sat a small brown rabbit. "And here's a present for you from Janine," said Hooper. Inside another brown box was a small black rabbit.

"We've all got them," said Annabelle.

"What about Customs?" said Rigby, without thinking. ". . . Surely it's not allowed, they might be diseased or something . . ." She stopped in mid-sentence as she realised what she was saying.

"It's quite all right," said Hooper brightly, "I cleared it before we left." She knew he was lying.

They didn't go through Customs, and they didn't land at Lydd but touched down somewhere else in Kent, a little further inland. The control tower at Lydd passed the message on to Hunter and the Man from the Ministry, but by the time they reached the spot, Rigby and the rabbits were gone.

They stopped at a pretty pub near Sissinghurst. Rigby slipped out of the back door and walked quickly down the lane to a telephone box. A bent penny piece prevented her from making the call, but on the way back she saw Annabelle in the garden. The girl was depositing a rabbit in the herbaceous border.

"Annabelle . . ." Rigby shouted, "Annabelle, you idiot . . ."

There was a screech of brakes and a strong smell of burnt rubber as James Hunter applied the brakes to his Lagonda, missing Rigby and the rabbit by inches. Rigby emerged un-scathed from the ditch clutching a small, black rabbit by the ears. They all spent the rest of the evening scouring the countryside for four more rabbits, but they'd gone to earth – literally.

*   *   *

There was a good deal of talk about charges and Customs and custody. Hooper lost his temper, Annabelle was in tears. "I couldn't bear the thought of them cooped up in cages," she sobbed. And everyone went home eventually, overtired, nervous and very, very cross.

The tests on Rigby's rabbit proved negative; it was a normal, healthy, pregnant, doe. Was Hooper innocent? After all, the rabbits had been presents from the children . . . Mick Larson returned to Australia and Camilla consoled herself with Rigby's rabbit. She called it 'Beaut' and looked forward to the impending birth. Rigby got her posting to Moscow.

She was in the Kremlin when she saw a copy of *The Times* on Khrushchev's desk. There were two items which particularly caught her attention. An announcement of marriage between Sir Leon Hooper-Bolton and Lady Annabelle Smythe-Jones and confirmation of an outbreak of myxomatosis somewhere in Kent.

The Government passed laws prohibiting the transport of diseased rabbits from one area to another. The fur trade and certain sporting elements were furious, but farmers and the revenue benefited to the tune of £50 millions per year. Ninety-nine point nine per cent of the rabbit population died in infected areas (most of the British Isles), causing a long-term shift in the ecological balance. There is no official explanation as to how the disease came to England. The most popular theory is that a mosquito flew across the Channel and landed somewhere in Kent. After all, rabbits could no more fly than pigs.

Rigby, of course, believed otherwise.

━━━━━━━━

Angela Cheyne claims to have known Rigby personally. According to Angela, Rigby was a protégée of her grandmother, the actress Zena Dare who, with Rex Harrison, Julie Andrews and Stanley Holloway, was one of the original London cast of *My Fair Lady*. On one occasion, evidently, Zena bet Rigby a magnum of vintage champagne that she couldn't take over her part one evening and get away without anyone noticing. As Rigby hadn't made a stage appearance since she played the Archangel Gabriel in a nativity play at Cheltenham, and since she must have been a good thirty years younger than Zena Dare, you might have thought the actress was on a pretty safe wicket.

But Rigby won the bet.

James Leasor

AT REST AT LAST

Not many people realise how influential Rigby was in the setting up of the Duke of Edinburgh's Award Scheme. It was very much her sort of thing – expeditions, the great outdoors, service to the community, putting practically everything before any thought for yourself. For several months in 1955 she ricochetted between the Lake District and Buckingham Palace, the Award Scheme's London offices (conveniently near her Marylebone flat) and Dartmoor. At first not everyone, not even the Duke, was absolutely sold on the idea of girls being included as well. They soon quailed before Rigby and the redoubtable Phyllis Gordon Spencer, first director of the Girls' Scheme.

Portland had now succeeded Denham as Rigby's boss. She could have had the job herself, of course, but it would have meant 'settling down' and that was not Rigby's style. Portland was distinctly beady about loaning his star operative to Prince Philip and Sir John Hunt, and finally insisted on calling her in on the pretext of getting her to try to patch up the dispute between King Hussein of Jordan and Glubb Pasha – Sir John Glubb, Head of the Arab Legion. Rigby failed with Hussein, not least because of a lifetime's disdain for very short Harrovians. This meant that relations between Rigby and Portland were uncharacteristically frosty.

In Russia the short-lived reign of Georgy Malenkov gave way to a double-act known to the Western media as 'B and K'. Marshal Nikolai Bulganin and Nikita Khrushchev were engaged in a power struggle but for the time being they were the Kremlin's answer to Laurel and Hardy. In London they were fêted by everyone except George Brown, the Labour Shadow Foreign Secretary, who got drunk and abused them. Meanwhile Rigby was at work . . .

As the funeral cortège turned slowly into Milton Cemetery, between Edwardian brick gateposts, past newly painted iron gates topped with gold glowing in the rain, Daniels said in the hushed voice people reserve for such occasions, "I bet this is the only time old Brownrigg has ever travelled in a Rolls."

"You may be right," Rigby agreed, her mind elsewhere. She had seen the brief notice in *The Times* about Brownrigg's death, in retirement at Southsea. The name brought back many Special Operations Executive memories – their careers had briefly overlapped. None of the newer crowd had known him but Daniels had, and agreed they should represent the Department. Brownrigg had served it well in his life; at his death he should be remembered.

A smattering of old women in black coats and hats, with a few younger men, were already in the red brick chapel in the centre of the cemetery. No one seemed to recognise anyone else. They could all be strangers drawn together briefly in memory of a man they had once known; maybe one of these women had even loved him?

Outside, they all followed the coffin beneath carvings of scriptural scenes on the chapel wall and the stern admonition in stone: 'Be ye also ready'. The words brought back to Rigby a visit to another chapel in Evora in Portugal. This was partly built of the bones and skulls of people who had died in a plague in the Middle Ages. Above its entrance was a similarly macabre statement: 'Our bones await your bones'.

The coffin was lowered into the damp earth and the mourners drifted away, beneath weeping plane trees, to their cars. It had been a brief, impersonal ceremony, hardly worth the journey from London, but they had kept faith with an old colleague and this was the most important thing – so Rigby told herself. There was also another reason – or maybe the same reason, but for another person – why she had welcomed any excuse to come to Portsmouth.

For years she had meant to make this visit but somehow it had been all too easy to postpone, probably because she felt slightly ashamed of her part in events that had happened so long ago – indeed while Brownrigg was still in the Service.

The cemetery was divided into large plots of grass, each with an initial letter, and separated by tarmac paths. Rigby handed the car keys to Daniels.

"I just want to check on another grave, now I'm here," she told him. Daniels shrugged his shoulders, went back to the car, took a nip of brandy from his pocket flask. Cemeteries depressed him; all reminders of his own mortality had this effect, especially in the rain. He sat, listening to the radio, sipping brandy, waiting for Rigby to return.

They drove out of the gates faster than they had entered them, past the Korner Kafe, along Velder Avenue. A huge Union Jack flew proudly outside an inn with pink canopies over the windows. The name was spelled out boldly: 'The Good Companion'. They passed factories on one side, rows of little boats drawn up on the mud of an estuary on the other, and then they were back on the motorway.

Daniels stretched out luxuriously in his seat; the brandy had cheered him.

"Some friend whose grave you wanted to see?" he asked Rigby conversationally.

"Yes," she said. "I've not been to Portsmouth for years, so I thought I would just check it out. Plot M, Row 16, Grave 10. Even in death we are all neatly listed."

"We? Who was it especially? Anyone I knew?"

"Lionel Crabb."

"Crabb," repeated Daniels slowly. "That *is* a name from the past."

Rigby nodded. It had been raining then, she remembered, just like now, when she had first become involved in the assignment that would end so many years later in Plot M, Row 16, Grave No. 10 . . .

Portland was waiting in his office in the Chelsea house they used for occasional meetings. He stood by the window, drumming the sill impatiently with the tips of his fingers. The roof gutter had broken and water streamed down the window panes. He did not look at Rigby as she came into the room – always a mark of his displeasure.

She looked at him coldly. He was the antithesis of Denham, whom she still remembered with warmth, almost affection. She could not help comparing the two men, always to Portland's detriment. Some men instantly attracted you, she thought. It could be the way they stood, the shape of their shoulders, their smile, their hair. They radiated an indefinable aura of compatibility. At once you felt at ease with them, on the same wavelength.

Portland had never been like this and she knew he never would be, although he tried his best to be pleasant – when it suited him. His suits seemed too tight, the tips of their lapels crumpled. He wore his old college tie with too small a knot, shiny where he fingered it.

"I was expecting you yesterday," he said, half accusing, half resentful. "You had my memo?"

"Yes. But I was out of town. I only got back this morning and saw it. I've come straight over."

"Oh."

The monosyllabic reply was part answer, part apology for his querulous attitude.

Portland opened the window, took from his waistcoat pocket a small crust of bread, broke it, and like a priest giving the sacrament, put the crumbs on the outside ledge. Three pigeons flew down, fluttered damp wings in the rain and squabbled for them.

"They're like people," he said softly, almost thinking aloud. "Like us here."

"Speak for yourself," said Rigby shortly. "I wouldn't fight over bread."

"You're lucky. You've never had to. Cake, maybe?"

She smiled dutifully at his obvious attempt to brighten the conversation.

"Maybe. Eclairs."

He closed the window, turned to her, sat down behind his desk, motioned her to take a seat. She sat in the more comfortable of the two leather armchairs. They must stop trying to score senseless points off each other. No one won that game. Was it even a game?

"I didn't call you here for chit-chat," Portland said now. "There's a job coming up next month, a rather touchy one. We'd like you to handle it."

He paused. Rigby knew that Portland only used the royal or editorial plural when he wished to show the importance of what he had to say.

"You've read about the state visit of Marshal Bulganin and Mr Khrushchev?"

"Of course. The papers print something about it every day."

"So they do. But not that they hate each other, eh? Anyhow, they're coming here in one of Russia's latest cruisers, the *Ordzhonikidze*, a floating shop-window for Communist expertise in gadgetry. We have nothing half its size, and the Americans aren't sure whether the Soviets have caught up, or even over-taken them in the electronic field. The Russians are using the visit, of course, to impress on us – and our allies – where they feel our true interests lie, and what could happen if we ignore them."

Portland paused. Like all insecure people he had to approach a direct request cautiously, in a roundabout way. Then he made up his mind.

"We want someone to go and take a look at the ship."

"How do you mean, take a look at it?"

"Exactly what I say. Underneath. We've had you accredited to a provincial paper as a journalist so you'll get an invitation to a reception they're giving aboard for local big-wigs and so on. That's all taken care of. What we need now is someone outside, and underneath."

"You mean under the hull, in the water?"

"Exactly. The word is that they've got some underwater gimmick that can throw even our newest sonar off course, make its readings a nonsense."

"Who is we?" asked Rigby bluntly. "The Americans or us?"

Portland shrugged.

"I don't know for sure. I only know what I'm told, and I've not been told that. But this must be a freelance job. Then, if anything goes wrong, the Department will be in a three wise monkeys situation – can't see anything, hear anything, say anything. And don't know anything. It's tricky. But, like most dodgy deals in our book, very important. I want you to find someone to do that job."

"Where from?"

"I leave that for you to discover. No one directly involved with the Department, of course, or anyone still in any of the Armed Forces. But there are two or three instructors who have just left the Navy Underwater School and would have the diving expertise for the job."

"Have you their names?"

"Yes," he said. "I will give you them. Then it's up to you. When you find the man, let me know what he wants – in cash. But make sure he can keep his mouth shut before – and after. No loose talk. He will be fully briefed later on, when we've checked out his background. OK?"

"If you say so."

Rigby was having lunch with Camilla and told her the problem; Camilla's brother had been a war-time commander in Motor Torpedo Boats. He knew the first man on Portland's list, and he was in London. They all had a drink at the French Pub in Soho that evening, and afterwards shared a table at Bianchi's. The room was full of cheerful diners, with a background of clattering plates and cutlery and the cries of orders being shouted to the kitchen. It was safe to talk there; no direct mention of names or places, of course, just the general proposition, in the vaguest terms.

"A friend I am involved with would like to hire a diver to have a look at a ship due here in a couple of weeks," Rigby explained casually.

"Red or blue?" the former instructor asked, equally casually.

"The first."

He nodded, sipped his Chianti thoughtfully.

"This official, or on the side?"

"The latter. The person would be paid, of course."

"Have you any figure in mind?"

"No."

"Neither have I," he said. "I appreciate you thinking of me, but I don't really feel there's enough money in the world to make me do it. My wife is expecting our second child next month. The first birth was rather difficult. I think I'll sit this one out, if you don't mind."

"Your last word?" asked Rigby, surprised at such a quick reaction.

"Yes," he said. "Sorry and all that, but I've been involved in one or two of these things already. They all sound so simple and straightforward – and they have a nasty habit of going wrong – and then everyone walks away. They all pretend they never knew anything. Nothing personal, of course."

"Of course."

They changed the subject.

The second possible candidate was not interviewed. At his retirement party he had drunk too much and fallen downstairs, breaking a leg. The break had not set well. He was still walking with crutches. The third candidate had emigrated to Australia.

"I can't go back and tell Portland I've failed," said Rigby.

"Why not?" Camilla asked her.

"Because maybe that's what he thinks will happen. And I don't like to fall down on anything I'm asked to do. There *must* be someone else, surely?"

"Lots of people got decorated for underwater tasks during the war," said Camilla. "Have a look through the Navy List, and pull out half a dozen possibles."

"The war ended eleven years ago," Rigby reminded her. "A man who was thirty then is forty-one now. At that age they won't want to get involved. It's not money we can offer them, simply some sort of adventure. And they've mostly had enough of that to last them all their lives. They're not eighteen and eager to prove themselves."

"You're right, I suppose. Also, things then were all black or white. Now they are grey."

She paused.

"There *is* one man I knew slightly, years ago. Name of Crabb. Commander Lionel Crabb. We called him Buster, after a film star of the silent screen, I think. He did a job for us only last year. Had a look at the Russian warship *Sverdlov* when she came to Portsmouth."

"The present ship is also docking in Portsmouth. It could be a sentimental journey for him."

"He might just look at it that way. Or again he might not. But I'll dig out his address for you."

Next morning, Camilla telephoned Rigby.

"Sorry," she told her. "He left the last address we have for him months ago. And the one after that. Since then I'm told he's had a number of odd jobs. I drew a blank at all of them."

"Anything suspicious in that?"

"Nothing at all. Just the fact that the poor man seemed to be desperate for any work – which could be a plus for you. For example, he has in his time helped get out a handbook for people filling in their football pool coupons. That didn't make his fortune so he took a job with a fishing company trying to work out the size of shoals of fish their trawlers located by echo sounders.

"For a short time, he was actually working in the Admiralty Research Laboratory at Teddington. He left that to join a group who had a plan to raise one of the ships from the Spanish Armada that had gone down off the Isle of Mull. It was thought to be full of gold bars, but whether they ever found the ship, I don't know. Certainly poor Crabb didn't make much out of the venture. Last Christmas there was a chance he was going to be attached to the Iraqi Navy to run their underwater work, but then the political scene changed drastically out there, and that fell through. I think most recently he has been involved with a friend marketing do-it-yourself cupboards, tables and so on. I don't know if that's still going."

"But where can I find him? Is he ever in London?"

"Apparently, yes. He has a bed-sitter somewhere in the Cromwell Road area, I'm told. My informant thinks your best bet could be the Brompton Oratory. The Commander is quite a religious man. Most of these heroic characters are, deep down. Incidentally, he was one of the first frogmen in the Navy in those far-off days when that was all new. They used to dive wearing swimming costumes! To keep themselves down under water they tied weights round their ankles, not around their waists. Research was all by trial and error. He was brilliant – and brave – and awarded the George Medal for taking limpet mines off our ships in the Med."

"And now he's probably doing nothing? It seems such a terrible waste."

"It is. And there are lots like him, brilliant in war and then on to the scrapheap in peace. He retired from the Navy partly because of the defence cuts and partly because he was getting too old. He probably thought he would find a job easily enough, where his talents could be useful."

"I've got one for him," said Rigby.

"I hope you're right," replied Camilla. "For his sake, as well as yours."

For the next few days, Rigby visited the Brompton Oratory in the late morning, then in the afternoon, calculating that these might be the most likely times for an ex-officer, out of work, with time to kill, to go to the church. She had his description – slightly built, walked with a stick, generally wore a white shirt with a starched collar and a Royal Navy Volunteer Reserve tie.

On the fourth afternoon, she saw a middle-aged man with a stick crossing the herringbone parquet floor, past the stone statues of saints. He lit a candle and placed it near the memorial to men who had died during the First World War, reading the inscription as he always did: 'Dulce et Decorum est Pro Patria Mori'. Was it? he wondered, remembering friends in the Navy he would never see again. But what would have happened to them if – like him – they had not died? Would they find it sweet and fitting to be out of a job and unwanted? He didn't.

He paused on the steps in the mild afternoon sunshine, surveying the traffic with the listless air of someone who had nowhere to go, nothing to do. Time stretched ahead, measureless as a trackless desert. The past was where excitement and involvement lay. It wasn't just another country as that writer L. P. Hartley had declared: it was another world.

Dimly, Crabb became aware of a pretty woman standing on the steps a few yards away from him, and looked at her. Perhaps she was a tourist and had lost her way?

"Am I right in thinking you are Commander Crabb?" Rigby asked him.

"Lionel Crabb, at your service," he replied briskly.

"My name is Dorothy Rigby. I've been looking for you, Commander."

"Really?"

He looked surprised and pleased. She guessed that not too many people came looking for Commander Crabb, which was a pity. Maybe their meeting could change this.

"And now that you have found me?"

"I would like to ask you to have tea with me at the Hyde Park Hotel."

"I think I could manage that. But, *why*, if I am not appearing churlish to ask?"

"You are not. I was talking to a friend of yours the other day."

Crabb raised his eyebrows quizzically, as though he didn't believe this. Then Rigby mentioned Camilla's name, and he looked at her more sharply.

"The *Sverdlov*," she said. "Portsmouth. Last October. Remember?"

"I remember. So you're in that line of country?"

"Sort of."

They sat down in the hotel lounge; she ordered lemon tea, hot buttered toast and Patum Peperium.

Crabb seemed a sympathetic character, she thought, and about his courage there could be no question. But was he simply too old? He had a faint air of defeat about him. Had he lost confidence in himself? He must be about forty-seven. That was the age Rudolf Hess, Germany's Deputy Führer, had been when he flew his own Messerschmitt to Scotland in 1941. Crabb needn't be too old. Hadn't Emerson declared that a man only counts his years when he has nothing else to count?

"You've had a number of jobs," Rigby said, trying to draw him out.

"More than you would think," he agreed. "I worked in a gas station in Pennsylvania. I tried my hand at writing advertising copy. I served in the Merchant Navy – but that was before I joined the Royal Navy, of course."

"I meant since you came out of the Navy," said Dorothy.

"You're right. And not one of them led anywhere. Too old at forty. It is a joke – until you are over forty. Then you discover it isn't funny."

He stirred his tea, his face suddenly sad and thoughtful.

"I think I know of a job where your expertise could come in useful."

"Like what?" Crabb asked her sharply.

"Come and see my boss, Mr Portland. He'll put you in the picture."

"Portland? As in Portland Bill?" Crabb smiled at his own mild witticism.

"The same."

They shared a taxi to the house in Chelsea. Portland shook hands formally. Crabb seemed rather smaller and older than he had anticipated from Rigby's brief telephone call. However, he was very competent; he had checked out his record. Also, there were no other takers for the task. Portland had approached several possible candidates without any success before he had passed on the chore to Dorothy Rigby.

"Before we begin," Portland told Crabb pompously. "You have signed the Act?" He meant the Official Secrets Act.

"Of course. For what it's worth."

"On this job it could be worth a lot."

"Tell me more."

"I intend to. But first, let us all have a drink. Gin, I suppose, as you're Navy?"

"Pink," said Crabb. "No ice."

They toasted each other silently. What have we got to celebrate? thought Crabb. We don't know each other at all and, judging from this fellow Portland's appearance and demeanour, I would never make a friend of him.

"This is a difficult one, with all sorts of political risks," Portland began slowly. "Officially we have to distance ourselves from it. That's why we want a freelance like you."

"To do what?"

"To dive under the *Ordzhonikidze* when she docks at Portsmouth. To examine an antenna of some sort she is said to have underwater that can fox our sonar."

"That is all?" Crabb asked him.

"Yes," agreed Portland, surprised. "It's enough, isn't it?"

"More than enough. It's impossible. Tell me, Mr Portland, have *you* ever swum in Portsmouth Harbour?"

"Never."

"I did once, as a boy. And then when I had a look at the *Sverdlov*. The water's filthy. Thick as mulligatawny soup. I'd have to examine this ship inch by inch, literally feeling my way along the whole length of the hull for this antenna."

"We'll give you the best equipment there is," said Portland quickly.

"No doubt. But how can I possibly find anything down there on my own? The ship's huge. I've seen pictures of her in the papers. During the war, when we were taking Italian limpet mines off our ships in the Med – a warm, clear sea then – we had several men, working together, to deal with quite small vessels. For a job like this you'd need maybe twenty divers. And a hell of a lot of rehearsals to minimise the risk of anything going wrong."

"We haven't got twenty divers. We've got one. I hope, you. And we obviously can't have a run-through on site, as it were. I suppose we might manage something with a Navy ship at anchor, but I'd rather not. Someone might see what is going on and put two and two together."

"Then I suggest you call the whole thing off."

"It's not quite so bad as you imagine, Commander. This gadget is probably inside a pretty large protective dome. Plastic or something like that. And right near the propellers, where you wouldn't expect it to be. It shouldn't be too difficult to find. Well, that's the job. What do you say?"

"I say, no. It's far too risky. And I haven't done this sort of thing for years. The *Sverdlov* affair was quite different."

"This is much the same sort of thing, Commander. But a larger vessel, of course, as you say."

They stood in silence, looking at the pink gins in their glasses, not at each other.

"We would pay cash," Portland said, as if by chance.

"How much cash?"

"Two hundred."

"It's very little," said Crabb, disappointed.

"A lot for a dive lasting only a few minutes."

"You're buying a lifetime of experience for the money. Why, it's peanuts. Also, am I right in thinking I am not the first you've asked? And the others all turned it down?"

"Correct. They did. I know the fee isn't great in absolute

terms, but it's all we can offer, Commander. We're not a commercial firm, I am sorry to say."

"Who would back me up if I said I'd do it?" Crabb asked. Portland disguised a sigh of relief as a cough. He was coming round; everyone had their price. With Crabb it could simply be the challenge.

"We'll see to that," he assured Crabb easily. "And give you all the gear you need. Absolutely first-rate kit, as I said, bang up to the minute stuff. A bit different from diving in your swimming trunks, with a clothes peg on your nose, eh?"

"And a hell of a lot more dangerous."

Crabb finished his drink. Rigby thought he looked older, much older than when he had entered the room. Crabb turned the proposition over in his mind. He needed the money and had no other way of making such a sum so quickly. And there was this woman he had met; a gentle creature, not like some others in his life. Two hundred pounds could make a lot of difference to them both. For one thing, it would show her he wasn't finished yet, not by a long chalk. For another, it would give him a psychological boost. Nothing succeeded like success.

"I'll do it," he said at last. "On one condition."

"What's that?"

"That you get me something more permanent. Anything with a regular salary. I've done good work, you know. But somehow I just don't fit into civvy street. Not now. Everything's changed since the war."

"A permanent thing is difficult," said Portland, not meeting Crabb's eyes. "I would promise something if I could, but I have to be honest, I can't. But I'll do what I can."

Which means nothing, thought Rigby. Words. Nothing more. Experience had taught her that when someone said they were being frank or honest, they were invariably being the reverse.

Portland opened a drawer of his desk with a key on a flexible gold chain, took out a manila envelope and removed ten £10 notes.

"You don't have to sign for this," he said. "We'll take your word."

"I'm taking your word, too," said Crabb. "What happens now? When do we start?"

"Give me your address and I'll let you know. We'll book you into a hotel in Portsmouth. A colleague of Miss Rigby's here, name of Daniels, whom I'll introduce you to in a moment, will drive you down when everything's ready.

"Your gear will be delivered to you. We'll measure you first, of course, just in case the wet suit doesn't fit and we can get another one. It's an in-and-out job. No more. You arrive late in the afternoon, have a rest, get driven out to the dockyard, with your suit and flippers and so on, make your inspection and back to the hotel and into the bar. No one need even know you've ever been away."

"I hope you're right. When do I get the other hundred?"

"Miss Rigby will give that to you afterwards. She'll be there, too. Just to see everything's OK."

Crabb looked at Rigby questioningly. She smiled reassuringly. Crabb felt relief flood over him. He trusted her. He had worked before with girls like her in S.O.E.; you knew where you stood with them. They all spoke the same language. Portland didn't; he was a foreigner in such matters.

A few days later, a car called for Crabb at his rooming house off the Cromwell Road; an unremarkable car in need of a wash. Daniels was at the wheel. He was a careful driver, with an irritating habit of humming slightly off-key as he drove. Crabb sat in the front seat beside him, pondering the task ahead. Rigby was in the back.

She hoped Crabb was up to the job. She knew that Portland would do nothing to help him find a permanent job but she had spoken to a friend, someone who ran his own company and needed representatives on the road, men he could trust. Being a commercial traveller might not be what Crabb wanted and, indeed, much less than he deserved, but it could lead to something better. It was a start; in the very last analysis, it could be better than nothing.

Crabb smoked for most of the journey, lighting a fresh cigarette from the stub of the previous one. He wore a blazer, flannel trousers and a white roll-neck sweater. He looked somehow more vulnerable in these casual clothes than when he was formally dressed.

"Penny for your thoughts," Rigby said, making conversation.

"I'm not happy about the job," Crabb admitted.

"*Now* you tell us," Rigby retorted, trying to make light of the remark.

"I have to tell someone."

"Can we make you happy about it?" Rigby asked him.

"Not really. The fact is, I don't like the 13th. I always like to keep a low profile on that day."

"But this isn't the 13th. It's the 17th."

"I know. But Portland offered me this job on the 13th. I accepted on that date. That's when I *started*. That date is the important one in my book.

"Know why I hate the 13th? I'll tell you. I was a member of the diving team that went down to *Truculent* when she sank six years ago. We could do nothing. Everyone on board was drowned. Friday the 13th, as a matter of fact. Then my marriage ended on the 13th. And I took a job searching for that sunken galleon on the 13th. For me it's an unlucky number."

"This will be the exception," Rigby assured him. "Haven't you got a lucky pixie or talisman of some kind to cheer you up?"

"Not now. That's another thing. I used to have a piece of jade. I thought it brought me luck all through the war. But then I lent some money to a friend who didn't pay it back. I was nearly broke. That jade was the only asset I had that I could hock. I had always believed it was worth a lot but all I got for it was £7. However, I have my swordstick." He tapped his stick.

"I thought it was just an ordinary walking stick."

"That's what I like people to think. I feel that in a way it's somehow symbolic of me right now. Outside, it seems only an ordinary wooden stick but inside there's a steel blade, sharp as a spear. Outside, *I* may appear a bit over the hill. But inside, I still have something – or you wouldn't have offered me this job. And I wouldn't have accepted."

They drove on in silence through Kingston, Guildford, Petersfield. Two rooms had been booked in the Sallyport Hotel in the High Street. The rates were not exorbitant: 17/6 for bed and breakfast. Crabb signed the register in his own name, Daniels as Smith. Rigby was booked into the Keppel's Head Hotel in The Hard.

"You'll be all right," she assured Crabb. "I'll come back here about ten o'clock tonight, and we'll all have a drink together."

"I reckon I'll have earned it."

"Three pink gins, then. Large as they come!"

"I've someone I'd like you to meet after all this is over," he said, rather shyly. "A rather special lady."

"I look forward to that."

"So do I. I think you'd both get on."

Crabb was a tidy man, a characteristic that came from years of living in confined conditions aboard a variety of small ships. He locked his bedroom door, put his driving licence, wallet, fountain pen and cheque book in his suitcase and locked it. Then he unscrewed the plug in the U-bend of the waste pipe of the wash-basin, pushed the key inside this and replaced the plug. One could never be certain that some hostile person might not take a quick look round the room. Then he sat down on his narrow bed and lit a cigarette.

He had never drunk alcohol before diving during the war and he could not start now, but he felt he would have given half his fee for a strong gin. I must be getting old, he thought. He had been told to remove the name tag from his jacket, cut his initials off his handkerchieves; all rather pointless, he thought, when he had been booked in under his own name.

The diving gear had been delivered in a suitcase. The wet suit fitted. So did the flippers, but he was not too happy with the mask. The controls were quite different from the ones he had grown accustomed to in the Med, but then that was years ago. Basically they were the same only, no doubt, improved. He'd get used to them. He replaced the gear in the case, lay back on the bed, kicked off his shoes and went to sleep. His wrist-watch alarm woke him at eight-thirty.

Crabb had a quick wash in cold water, combed his hair and went downstairs. As the clock in the hall chimed the quarter hour Daniels came in through the swing door and greeted him jovially.

"All ready for the party, old man? Fancy dress tonight, you know. Got it all there?"

This was Crabb's excuse for carrying a heavy suitcase. He

had told the manager that they had come down for an old boys' reunion. Luckily, the manager hadn't asked the name of the school. They went out to the car. Crabb threw the case on to the rear seat.

Neither of them spoke as Daniels accelerated out of Portsmouth towards the red brick forts covered in ivy and built during the early nineteenth century to repel an expected French invasion. Their windows were shuttered; blind, heavy-lidded eyes above the harbour, where floodlit ships, ablaze with coloured lights, lay at anchor.

Daniels drove through the gateway, pulled up near a small van parked against a wall. A naval Petty Officer, who had been waiting for them behind the wall, stubbed out his cigarette and crossed to the car. He checked its registration number, removed Crabb's suitcase and put it in the van. No one spoke. They could not see each other's faces clearly, which was just as well, Crabb thought. Daniels gave them the thumbs-up sign and drove away. Crabb climbed into the back of the van, closed the doors. It was dark inside, and smelled strongly of petrol. He sat on the suitcase, wished he could light a cigarette, but decided against it.

They crossed the dockyard. Crabb peered out through a side window, saw the giant Russian cruiser soaring like a grey cliff in silhouette behind the roofs of the houses. Her deck bristled with radio antennae and radar aerials. Even at anchor, aerials on her masts revolved watchfully, warily. He felt a great surge of unease. How could one man, in a matter of minutes, and in the foul darkness of a harbour bed, uncover the secrets of such a huge floating fortress?

Twice, sentries stopped the van. Each time, the driver showed a pass and was waved through. The van crossed a mass of railway lines. The driver stopped behind one of the dockyard buildings, switched off his lights. He spoke for the first time.

"You go in here, sir," he said.

"You do a lot of this?" Crabb asked him. Not that he cared, but simply to hear another voice.

"Oh, yes, sir. Underwater diving tests like this go on all through the summer. Every week. Of course, the water's a bit warmer then. You going to change in the back of the van, sir? I've got a rope ladder as the tide's low. I'll fix it while you get ready."

He switched on a small light in the roof of the van. In its feeble glow Crabb undressed, folding his clothes methodically in a neat pile. This was the first time he had undressed that day. Next time, it would be to go to bed. It had been a very long day; he hoped it would not be a long night.

He pulled on his rubber suit and his flippers, and walked clumsily across the dockyard. The Petty Officer was waiting by the rope ladder, which was tied to a bollard. Crabb adjusted his mask, tested the valves on the two oxygen bottles, nodded as casually as he could to the man to whom this seemed routine, and began to climb down towards the water.

The ladder swayed and his knuckles brushed painfully against the slimy dockyard wall. It seemed a hell of a long way down to the water. Of course, the Petty Officer had said the tide was low. That damned ship could be resting on the bottom. He wouldn't have any room to manoeuvre, crawling about in the mud. How could he discover anything in such vile conditions? Portland should have put off the stunt until the tide was high.

It was all right for people like him, sitting in comfortable offices, to say what should be done, or not done. Quite a different matter for the poor devil actually doing it. But was he a poor devil? He had been, possibly, but not now, not since he had met that lady. She would appreciate how he felt, what he was doing – and why he was doing it; not only for himself, but for both of them. She was rare in that he could tell her anything, everything, and she would understand. He'd never met anyone like that before; he was lucky, very, very lucky.

Pieces of wood, empty bottles, orange peel floated past Crabb, touching his arms, his shoulders as he submerged. He turned the valves on the first bottle, and his heart began to steady with the reassurance of familiarity. He had done this sort of exercise so many times before; it was really only routine. Portland had been quite right. Two hundred wasn't a bad fee for a few minutes underwater. Why, in the Navy, that would have been several months' pay. That was then, of course, and this was now, twelve years on. He was a bit tired, that was all . . .

The Petty Officer went back to the van, lit a cigarette. His orders were to wait for half an hour and then to report to his base. If the diver had not reappeared, then he would assume he had surfaced, as often happened, farther down.

The weight of water pressed the rubber suit like a thick, clammy skin against Crabb's body. He struck down slowly, carefully, checking his direction by a luminous wrist compass. He knew when he was near the huge hulk of the *Ordzhonikidze*, more by sense than sight. There was always a feel about a ship's hull as though it was waiting to crush a diver for his temerity in exploring it. Crabb swam on, only feet from the soft, cloying filth on the harbour floor.

Rigby had a bath, changed and checked her invitation to go aboard the *Ordzhonikidze* to their official reception. She put a Press card and a reporter's shorthand notebook in her handbag. It was ironic to think that she would be on one side of the warship's metal hull while Crabb was on the other.

She came up the gangway of the cruiser, showed her pass to two guards waiting with an interpreter and followed him to the stateroom.

"Your first visit to England?" she asked.

"Yes," he replied. "You have been very hospitable to us here. Two hundred and fifty of our sailors have been the guests of your Portsmouth Football Club at the match between what you call Portsmouth Reserves and Fulham Reserves. There is a special dance at the Savoy, a reception at the City Council Chamber. It is all very pleasant. Tell me, have you been to Russia?"

"Briefly, yes."

"And what was your impression of my country, Madame?"

"There are so many countries in one, so many peoples."

"But one creed," the interpreter reminded her sharply. "The teaching of Lenin, as is written on the tomb of Karl Marx in your Highgate Cemetery. 'Workers of all lands, unite. Philosophers have interpreted the world in various ways. The point, however, is to change it'."

"But in what direction?" asked Rigby. The interpreter

frowned and did not reply; it was no part of his duties to become involved in political argument. Why, she might only be leading him on to trap him. He felt a chill sweat of fear on his back.

He opened the door into a stateroom. A babble of conversation against a background of violin music engulfed them both. At the far end of the vast room she could see Bulganin, with his well-groomed, pointed beard, and Khrushchev smiling, showing his stumpy teeth, watching everyone closely with his mean, pig eyes. He was a hard man, fiercely proud of his humble origin.

"My grandfather was a serf," he would explain. "His landlord owned him and could have traded him at any time for a hunting dog." Khrushchev had traded this background for a life of luxury. He had flattered Stalin constantly – when the Moscow Metro was rebuilt he insisted that each station must display a stained glass or mosaic likeness of the dictator. Khrushchev owned a hunting lodge at Zavidovo, on the Volga, and another house on the coast. Here he would swim but, as a cautious man, a natural survivor, he always wore a rubber ring around his waist. Remembering this, Rigby thought of Crabb. Had he accomplished his task yet?

Security men prowled among the guests. Stewards carried trays of champagne and plates with squares of buttered toast, dark with caviare. A voice spoke softly behind Rigby.

"Madame Rigby?"

She turned. 'Oleg' was smiling at her. My God, Simla – almost twenty years earlier.

"I did not expect to find *you* here," he said gently. "Your dossier is remarkable, and compulsory reading for the K.G.B. British section."

"My surprise is as great at finding you."

"You are too kind," he replied, smiling.

The lights reflected the gold in his teeth, but his eyes did not smile; they remained dark and hard as olive stones.

"Are you here as a guest? Or, shall I say, in an official capacity?"

"Both."

She showed him her Press card.

"So you are a journalist now," he said admiringly. "Well, well. You will have much to write about here."

"I hope so. Everyone seems to be enjoying themselves."

"Russia is a happy country. We are a happy people."

A security man in an ill-fitting suit with white bone buttons pushed between the chattering guests to Oleg, whispered in his ear. Oleg glanced at Rigby sharply.

"There is someone in the sea," he said.

"What do you mean 'in the sea'? Bathing? Fallen overboard?"

"I think, neither. Someone who went into the water deliberately. *Under* the water, in fact. A frogman, my friend tells me, a British frogman."

"A *British* frogman?"

Rigby repeated the words as though she could not understand them.

"What was he doing there? Is he one of these people we have on the south coast who bathe in the sea every day of the year, winter or summer?"

Oleg smiled.

"In Portsmouth harbour, Madame Rigby? I think not. But we will endeavour to discover who he is – and why he was there."

"Was? Is he dead then?"

"I did not say that, Madame Rigby. Now, if you will excuse me."

Oleg turned and followed the security man out of the stateroom. Rigby fought down a wish to follow him, forced herself to sip her champagne; it tasted bitter as bile on her tongue.

Daniels sat in the lounge of the Sallyport Hotel, reading the late edition of that day's *Portsmouth Evening News*. Reading did not actually describe his activity; he sat staring at the page, barely able to comprehend the headlines. He was desperately worried about Crabb. The Petty Officer had waited and then gone off duty, after reporting that the diver had not reappeared.

The telephone rang in the hall.

"For you, Mr Smith," said the night porter.

Daniels picked up the receiver. Rigby was on the line.

"I'm back in my hotel," she explained.

"Our friend has not turned up," Daniels interrupted her.

"I know," she replied. "Come round here – now." The lounge at the Keppel's Head Hotel was empty; Rigby told him in whispers about Oleg's news. Had the Russians captured Crabb – or only caught sight of him?

"Either way, we'd better get out of here," Daniels said at once. "Cover our tracks."

"At this hour, no," she replied. "Wait till the morning. Have a look round Crabb's room in case he's left anything. Then we'll go. Nine o'clock. No, make it ten. Something may have happened down here by then. They may have discovered his body – if he's dead."

"I hope for his sake he is. I wouldn't like to be Crabb if the Russians have taken him alive. What went wrong, do you think?"

"I've no idea. Either the Russians had their own frogmen waiting for him, or his gear failed, or he had some kind of fit or stroke."

"He's old for this job."

"There was no one else. You know that as well as I do."

Early next morning, Daniels took the key of Crabb's room from the hook behind the reception desk, examined the bedroom closely. Everything was neat and tidy, the bedclothes still turned down. He packed Crabb's kit in his suitcase, for which he had a second key, carried it downstairs with his swordstick, replaced the key and pressed the handbell on the desk for the manager.

"I'll pay for us both," he told him.

"You had a nice reunion, sir?"

"Great. But it's given me a hangover, like I've been hit by a hammer."

"You do look a bit under the weather, sir, if I may say so. But in a good cause?"

"I hope so. I very much hope so."

Daniels went out to the car. Rigby was sitting at the wheel. They drove out of Portsmouth towards London.

"Anything?" he asked her, when they were clear of the town.

"Nothing conclusive. But there's a rumour going about that *someone's* been found in the sea. I don't know how that started.

Maybe the Russians? Information or misinformation. Anyhow, a launch has been taking sightseers round the cruiser. I joined them."

"Wouldn't you have been recognised?"

"I don't think so. I put on different make-up, glasses, a wig."

"What did you see?"

"Russian frogmen carrying out some sort of search round the stern of the ship from one of the cruiser's own boats. Couldn't discover what they were looking for."

"It's not too difficult to make a guess," said Daniels gloomily.

They drove to the house in Chelsea. Portland listened, grim-faced.

"Lucky he wasn't one of our people on the strength."

"That's the only lucky thing about it," said Rigby. Portland picked up the telephone.

"I'll get on to Five. They'll ask Special Branch to send someone to tear out the page of the visitors' book in the Sallyport with Crabb's name on it."

"Leave it," said Rigby. "That will only draw attention to him."

"No, no. Must cover our tracks."

"That's doing the reverse," Rigby persisted. "Let it lie. No one knows it *was* Crabb, unless he's told the Russians his name."

"We don't know if he's alive. He may be dead. Either way, I'm doing this."

"I beg of you, don't."

"I'll make my own decisions. Ones you've been taking haven't been so bright, have they?"

"It wasn't our decision to use anyone," Rigby reminded him.

"Oh, let's not quarrel about that. Let's just get out of range before the solids hit the fan."

As he replaced the receiver the green telephone rang.

The Head of the Security Service had just heard from the Home Secretary, who in turn had heard from the Prime Minister, that there was the genesis of a grave diplomatic incident at Portsmouth. What the hell was going on down there? Did Portland know anything about it? Some diver had apparently been fooling around near the Russian ship. What could he possibly discover down there? On whose orders was he diving? Or was he just a nutter, acting on his own initiative? They'd put a D-Notice on it, of course, and at once. The Press couldn't publish anything.

Portland replaced the receiver, his face grey.

"A D-Notice won't stop the foreign papers publishing the rumours," said Rigby.

"Heads will roll," said Portland flatly.

A number of other people had reached the same conclusion, and decided that theirs would not be among them. The Admiralty made available to enquirers – but oddly, did not issue – a statement that explained how Commander Crabb was presumed dead after he did not return from completing a test dive in Stokes Bay, involving the trial of underwater equipment. Stokes Bay was about three miles from the Russian cruiser.

Despite this innocuous statement, rumours that a frogman had been seen near the Russian ship now increased. If this frogman was Crabb, how could he then disappear three miles away – far too great a distance for him to swim in full underwater kit? Newspaper reporters learned that a man answering to Crabb's description had been seen with a Mr Smith in the Sallyport Hotel. When they called there, they discovered that four pages, covering the period of his stay, had been ripped out of the hotel register, apparently by a detective superintendent. When they approached the Portsmouth police, asking for an explanation, they were told brusquely that the Official Secrets Act forbade any comment on the matter.

A question about Crabb's disappearance was tabled by a Member of Parliament, and to keep the interest high, the Russian Assistant Naval Attaché claimed that sailors aboard the *Ordzhonikidze* had reported seeing the frogman.

While English newspapers remained circumspect, foreign newspapers showed no such restraint. They printed rumours and counter-rumours that could seriously damage Anglo–Soviet relations – and possibly were intended to do so. Finally, the Prime Minister, Sir Anthony Eden, read a prepared Statement to the House: "It would not be in the public interest to disclose the circumstances in which Commander Crabb is presumed to have met his death. While it is the practice for Ministers to accept responsibility, I think it is necessary in the special circumstances of this case to make it clear that what was done was done without the authority, or the knowledge of Her Majesty's Ministers. Appropriate disciplinary steps are being taken."

Still the Russians did not let the matter rest. In an official note they claimed that the sighting of the frogman had been reported to the Naval authorities in Portsmouth, who categorically denied it. Nonetheless: "The fact that the British naval authorities had carried out secret underwater tests in the area where the Soviet warships were anchored at Portsmouth was confirmed. Moreover, the carrying out of these tests resulted in the death of the British frogman."

The British Government replied that the frogman seen from the *Ordzhonikidze* could well have been Crabb, but his presence so near the Russian ships had no permission whatever. They expressed great regret for the incident.

Ten days after the Prime Minister's statement, Mr Hugh Gaitskell, the Leader of the Opposition, having been apprised of the background, said in the House of Commons: "Whatever may be the circumstances in which he met his death, all of us will agree that this country would be the poorer if it were not for men like Commander Crabb."

In the years since then the Mystery of the Missing Commander had resurfaced regularly. A prisoner released from a Russian gaol claimed to have seen an Englishman answering to his description in a cell. A headless body was washed up along the south coast of England. Some said it was the late Commander Crabb. Others disagreed strongly. But the discovery of an anonymous corpse did not answer the most persistent questions. Did Crabb die in the dirty water of Portsmouth Harbour? Was he captured – and could he still be alive? Or had he been captured and then died in some far-off land and now lay buried in an unknown, unmarked grave? Since Crabb had disappeared, had anyone subsequently discovered anything about the anti-sonar device? Was there, in fact, anything to discover? Was there even such a device?

Dorothy Rigby remembered Hugh Gaitskell's words. Although well meant, they were still only words, like Portland's empty promise to the Commander to help him find something permanent. And how had Portland helped Crabb? To a permanent grave in Plot M, Row 16.

Rigby sat silent for a moment as rain mushroomed off the shining road like a volley of silver spears. The grave had been very simple, just Crabb's name, his decorations G.M., O.B.E., and the inscription: 'At Rest At Last'. A white headstone with small crosses engraved on either side of it, and in front a white marble vase of fresh roses, red for remembrance, put there by someone Rigby had never met, whose name she did not even know.

"Poor old Crabb," said Daniels, breaking into her thoughts. "He didn't get much of a break, did he? But then, from what you tell me, it follows. After all, he was one of life's losers."

Daniels looked at Dorothy Rigby enquiringly, expecting her instant agreement. She shrugged her shoulders non-committally.

"In one sense, yes, he was a loser," she agreed slowly. "He lost his life. But in another, I'm not so sure. He died doing his duty which, for a man of action, must always be a plus. And could anyone claim that a man who, thirty-odd years after his death, still has flowers placed on his grave by someone who must have loved him – who still remembers him – was *entirely* a loser?"

Jimmy Leasor first became interested in Commander Crabb through a friendship with 'a former member of the Security Service'. This shadowy figure was not, in fact, Rigby, but Leasor was keen to test some of his information against Rigby's own testimony. After Crabb disappeared, rumours kept coming in that he was alive and not very well in a Russian prison. Similar rumours, in some cases almost identical, were also spread about Sidney Reilly who disappeared mysteriously on a visit to Russia in the 1920s. Leasor was suspicious.

In 1982 Leasor published a novel called *Open Secret* which included a brief account of the events involving Commander Crabb. As a result a woman friend of his, now dead, got in touch with him. She was strongly of the opinion that the headless body, recovered on the

South Coast long after his disappearance, was not that of Commander Crabb. Leasor adds, "I visited Commander Crabb's grave in Portsmouth Cemetery, which was well cared for. Someone regularly places fresh flowers on it in his memory".

I, fancifully perhaps, wondered if the mystery wreath layer could be Dorothy Rigby herself, but when I put it to her at one of our meetings she said 'No'. She said it just a shade wistfully and, though I couldn't bring myself to ask the question, it occurred to me that she was wondering whether, thirty years after *her* death, there would be anyone laying flowers, anonymous or otherwise, at *her* last resting place.

Anthony Price

THE ROAD TO SUEZ

1956 was a watershed year, or so it seemed at the time. It was the year that Britain was suddenly confronted with the loss of its Imperial role and the year that first revealed signs of a dangerous split in British society. John Osborne's 'kitchen sink drama', *Look Back in Anger*, went on in London and was only half cancelled out by Lerner and Loewe's nostalgic *My Fair Lady*. Colin Wilson published *The Outsider* and Canon Collins led the first C.N.D. 'Aldermaston' march in protest against nuclear weapons.

Rigby was there.

In Cyprus, the E.O.K.A. terrorist organisation continued to defy the British forces and Her Majesty's Government had no alternative but to remove that turbulent Cypriot priest, Archbishop Makarios, and put him into detention in the Seychelles. Rigby sat in on his interrogation and found him unimpressive and physically repulsive. "I have never seen so many stale breakfasts in a man's beard," she said, "let alone a priest's."

She was more impressed by President Nasser of Egypt with whom she had a number of private conversations in the spring of that year. (She was briefed on these occasions by the writer and former Intelligence officer, Malcolm Muggeridge, who had once taught him at school.) The Prime Minister, Anthony Eden, disliked Nasser whom he thought – privately – was a 'wog'. And he disliked him even more because, in the words of his wife, he caused the Suez Canal to flow through his drawing room. Suez was Eden's Munich and not least because, deep down, Britain's rulers thought it a tiresome irrelevance. The Czechs, before the war, had been those 'far away people of whom we knew nothing'. The same was now true of the Egyptians and their maddening claims.

Ironic that the most exciting moments of Rigby's 1956 should have taken place in the City of Lost Causes.

Over the years the routine of her Oxford visits to her godson had settled into an unvarying pattern which only torrential rain (but not snow!) could disrupt: as soon as Rigby settled herself into the guest-room and 'made herself beautiful' (his words, not hers), he'd walk her out of college to inspect his beloved Meadow.

"A breath of air, Rigby? A few moments in which to recollect emotion in tranquillity before dinner? A turn round the Meadow?"

"Of course, John dear." Almost the same words, too. Once upon a time, when his world, if not hers, had been young, he would have addressed her as 'Godmother', or 'dearest Godmother', or even (in moments of extreme crisis) 'God-mother *darling*'. But now, when he had put away childish things, and metamorphosed from Little John and Big John, by way of Scholar John and Don John, to distinguished Pro-fessor John Anstey, she had become plain and equal Rigby. But that was the only change.

The same route, too: past the stately New Library (only two centuries old) and out of Peckwater Quadrangle; along the Great Quadrangle and into the maze of Cloisters and Old Library in the shadow of the Cathedral; and finally through the Meadow Building and into the peace and freedom of Broad Walk and his Meadow.

Already there was a smell of autumn in the air and a hint of mist coming up from the river, and they were at once in the heart of the country although still in the centre of the city. *Rus in urbe*, she thought dutifully as they walked for a time in silence. And then, *Will he confess this time, at last?* as she also always thought.

But once again he held his peace. Instead he was frowning at something.

"What's the matter, dear? You look . . . a little sad this evening."

"I am sad. I am mourning our lost elms." He pointed to

the ground-level stump of a once-great tree, and then to a line of stumps interspersed with saplings. "That damnable Dutch Elm Disease of the 1970s, Rigby! No one alive today will see Broad Walk as it once was, in our age."

"No, dear." She remembered that other time so vividly, if not its trees. "But your Meadow is still beautiful." She paused for a moment, catching only the faintest hum of the traffic in the High Street. "And . . . it's still so quiet here."

"True." He inclined his head, and she noticed the first hints of grey in the also otherwise-unchanged unruly thatch which she had first combed almost half-a-century ago. Then he looked round proprietorially. "This has always been the one great view of Oxford for me. From the hills you see the towers and spires – and the pylons. And the High is full of people and hot-dog sellers . . . and the Radcliffe Camera and All Souls and the Bodleian – they're all very well for the tourists and the Nicholas Pevsners of this world. But this . . . *this* is Oxford, Rigby."

For a moment he filled her view, with his background of the rough pasture of Christ Church Meadow and the distant willows which marked the line of the towpath and the river. Then she turned obediently to admire his Oxford.

The squat medievalness of Merton College held centre stage, its chapel dominating its ancient library, much as the soul had once dominated the mind and the body even in England's first and greatest university: Merton had been old when one King Charles had kept his Queen there in the Civil War, and his son had kept *his* Queen *and* his mistresses there when the bubonic plague had driven him out of London, just as the parliamentary plague had driven out his father . . . But for her it was always the college of Leonard Cheshire, the greatest of all the bomber pilots of her youth, and of Tolkien, the father of all the Hobbits . . .

Then, far away on her right, beyond the green fields but gracing them wonderfully, the lily-tower of Magdalen, slender and golden to its topmost pinnacles . . . Magdalen tower swept her back across Merton to little Corpus Christi, whose sixteenth-century founder had wished it to be like a hive, where, "the scholars night and day may make wax and sweet honey to the honour of God, and the advantage of themselves and all Christian men" (Scholar John's words, from the very first time he'd walked her in his Meadow in his first term, had stuck in her memory) –

And, finally, stately Christ Church (*never* Christ Church *College*, John had warned her that first time: as *Aedes Christi* it could only be 'The House', even though it had started life as Cardinal Wolsey's college, before Henry VIII had nationalised it – or, Henry being Henry, perhaps 'privatised' was nearer the mark).

Christ Church – of course she knew most about Christ Church, because of John – Christ Church beat all comers, far out-pointing Merton's Tolkien with its 'Lewis Carroll' and Corpus Christi's founder of Georgia with Penn of Pennsylvania, and with more Prime Ministers even than Balliol, from Peel and Gladstone to Salisbury and Anthony Eden –

"*Good God Almighty!*" exclaimed John suddenly. "*Talk of the devil!*"

He was looking past her, down Broad Walk, and so fixedly that he would have turned her in that direction even without the exclamation.

A gowned figure – gowned *and* capped, white-tabbed in full Oxford panoply – was approaching them, stalking rather than walking, hands hidden in voluminous black folds.

Rigby frowned, first at the figure, then at John. That *Good God Almighty*! was too strong for such an academic vision, here where such a costume might reasonably be expected before dinner, even though the start of Michaelmas Term was still a full week away. And, in any case, something more than mere amazement sat upon her beloved godson's brow. And, beyond that case, he had spoken of neither man nor devil –

She turned again towards the figure, and saw clearly at last. And, in that fraction of time, understood and instantly remembered everything again: what had been in her mind so short a time ago had equally been in his, of that other time – that long-gone, once-upon-a-time which, in this place, neither of them could ever escape.

That other time –

"Now, dearest Godmother –" Scholar John tossed a lick of too-long uncut hair from his eyes "– what's all this secrecy?

What is it that cannot be said in the pub, *coram populo*, but only in the safety of the Meadow? Is it cloak-and-dagger? You're not going to defect, like the appalling Burgess-and-Maclean duo, are you?"

"That's not funny, John." But, all the same, it was reassuring somehow.

"No." Catching the sharpness of her tone he was instantly contrite. "Sorry, Godmother. Cloak-and-dagger *not* to be mentioned – only admired in secret. 'Let me introduce Miss Dorothy Rigby, my godmother. She's a civil servant ...' something in the Home Office, aren't you, Godmother? Or is it the Colonial Office? Anyway, 'my father was a pimply subaltern when Colonel Rigby was commanding the regiment' – the 43rd Bombay Irish, was it, Godmother? Or Skinner's Horse – 'the Yellow Boys'? On account of the colour of their uniforms, I hasten to add ... Or was it their complexions? Right?" He grinned. "*I* know the rule. And the patter."

Even as a little pitcher he had had big ears, and the curiosity to match them, she remembered fondly. (Not that his coming spell of National Service in uniform would do him any harm; it was just a pity it couldn't be in their fathers' old regiment now.)

"All the same, Godmother . . ." Having made his peace with his patter he unleashed his curiosity again. And (because he was a bright boy too) there was a hint of concern with it ". . . tearing me away from my beer like that? When I'm supposed to be up early, working for my Finals –?"

"Yes, I know, dear." She recalled his most recent letter: *I have had two glorious (or, if you prefer the truth, feckless) years. But now (if I am to get that First, and an eventual fellowship in some minor college) I must buckle down to work before term starts. If you are Oxford-way, you can catch me in the Bear of an evening, around 7, before I burn the midnight oil* . . . "I'm sorry to disturb you."

"No disturbance. I'm still on drinking-time." But his young face was set and serious, giving the lie to his additional patter. "You're in trouble?"

"You might say that." Suddenly she remembered the red-haired Brigadier in S.O.E., who never fudged the bad news he brought. And, in the past, it had always been Dorothy Rigby who had extricated him from trouble. So now, with the roles reversed, she owed him the Brigadier's straight tongue. "I want to break into a college, here in Oxford."

His face cleared. "Only that?" He grinned hugely. "Getting girls – pardon! *ladies* . . . into the House . . . *no* problem, dearest Godmother. 'Your guilty secret is safe with me', as they say – ah-hah-humm –" He stopped suddenly. "Or is it burglary: 'the crime of breaking by night into a house with felonious intent'?" Then he looked around. "Actually, it's not quite dark yet, so we could go for 'breaking-and-entering' if they catch us with the college silver –" The look-around focused on Corpus Christi. "Is it Corpus?" He nodded wisely. "Corpus 'ud be a good prospect, because they never handed over their silver to King Charles to be melted down, during the Civil War. So they've got some really choice stuff." Then he saw her face and stopped even more quickly than before. "Sorry –?"

He knew she wasn't about to burgle anywhere, he was merely nervous. And rightly so. "King's College, John." (That was the red-haired Brigadier again.)

"Ah . . ." He stared at her for a long moment. *"Dick's . . ."*

"Dick's?"

"Ah . . . *yes*, Godmother darling . . ." he added to the moment, then looked at his watch, and continued without looking up ". . . founded by King Richard II . . . albeit in honour of King Edward II, allegedly . . . therefore 'Dick's'. 'Dick' being short for 'Richard' . . . Although there are some who say that it's because Edward was a raving queer." He looked up at last. "You wouldn't prefer King's at Cambridge –? No, obviously not." He squared his shoulders. "Well, then – we'd best be moving, I think –" He pointed vaguely towards Merton across the broad green field which separated the Broad Walk from the old city wall within which that college had been built.

But Rigby needed to know more before they moved. "Isn't it a bit early, dear?" She too looked at her watch. "I mean . . . it's only twenty past seven. And they won't go into dinner until half past. And . . . shouldn't we let them settle down – ?" Then his expression cut her off.

"Godmother *darling* . . ." He drew himself up, and paused to let his emphasis sink in. "Of all the colleges in Oxford – if

you'd named any other one: Oriel or Lincoln, B.N.C. or Teddy
Hall . . . 'a piece of cake', as our R.A.F. heroes would say. But
Dick's – *Dick's*. But I think you know that already, don't you?"
He nodded at her. "Getting into Dick's is like . . . making love
in a hammock, standing up –? Or have I shocked you?" He
pointed. "Let's move, anyway. There's a path between Merton
and Corpus. And they won't have locked the gate yet –"

She let herself be moved. "You haven't shocked me since
you had scarlet fever that time, John dear. But I don't understand why King's College – *Dick's* – has to be so difficult just
now –"

"Oh, that's easy! Have you seen it? The bowler-hatted thugs
on the gate –?"

Thugs? "I was in it not an hour ago, dear. The man on the
door was very polite."

"But he closed the gate behind you – right? After he'd raised
his hat to you?"

"Yes." That was why she was here, after having circumnavi-
gated the college, and observed only its Iron Curtain defences
of iron spikes on high walls, and barbed wire on every drain-
pipe, with ground-floor windows routinely iron-barred. "But
. . . I just don't understand *why* – that's all, dear." Keeping
up with him, first between the wall of Corpus Christi garden
and a green field, and then between railings separating Corpus
from Merton, made her breathless. He was very fit. "It isn't
as though term has started –"

"Doesn't make any difference." He shortened his pace very
slightly. "As it happens, Dick's has always been a difficult
college, getting in after closing time. You have to climb . . ."
He eyed her smart suit critically. "Can you climb, Godmother?"

Rigby thought of Berlin, among other places. "Yes, John
dear. I can climb."

"Jolly good! Well . . . the thing is, they've had a series of
break-ins. Last term. And then during some snooty conference
just recently. And Hobson, the Dean – 'Young Hob', they call
him . . . not to be confused with 'Old Hob', his grandad, who
was Master there for half a lifetime – *Young* Hob – he's gone
on the warpath. Young Hob *alias* Colonel Hobson, D.S.O.,
M.C., as was: the scourge of the Panzers in Normandy,

God-mother. And he's a proper terror . . . especially when added to the equally terrifying Mr Baskerville-the-Head-Porter, who was his Sergeant-Major on D-Day. Between 'em they've slapped an Iron Curtain round poor old Dick's – thugs on the gate by day, doors shut early, twenty-four-hour roving patrols – the whole high-security jazz." But then he grinned at her. "You couldn't have chosen a better place to burgle, Godmother."

The grin reassured her. "Or a better-informed partner-in-crime, apparently?"

"Ah . . . yes, as it happens." As they issued out of the path between Merton chapel and Corpus, he took her elbow and pointed across a cobbled street, up a narrow alleyway. "I have a good friend inside the enemy camp. One Guy Threlfall, senior scholar of the college, who is up at the moment, trying to make up for lost time before term starts, like me – a very *respectable* ornament of the college, since he's reading theology. Head towards the High, Godmother. Yes, *very* respectable –"

"And he's in college now?"

"Yes and no. Meaning – yes, they've given him a room in college until term starts (it's his third year, so he's living out otherwise). And *no* . . . because with any luck we'll catch him in the Turf tavern, hard by New College. Which is his preferred water-hole of an evening, before dinner. And at other times."

"Yes?" She could see and hear the traffic in the High Street now. "So he can get us in, you mean? Will he?"

"Oh, sure! Guy's game for any mischief. So . . . first he gets himself in, after knocking on the gate and saluting Sergeant-Major Baskerville. And then he lets down the jolly old rope ladder for us, like Rumpelstiltskin or whoever –"

"The rope –" Rigby drew breath, partly from breathlessness and partly from the Berlin memory.

"Ladder." He supplied the word as he squired her across the High, unmoved by its majestic curve and glorious concentration of colleges, concerned only for the traffic. "His room's round the side, second floor, over King Richard's Lane . . . so he's got a fire-escape ladder all to himself. They say the room's like Piccadilly Circus sometimes, in term – over we go!" He helped her on to the pavement politely. "Not that it won't be especially hairy tonight, even when we're in –"

"With the patrols?" She followed him into Catte Street, glimpsing the Bodleian ahead.

"They'll be worse tonight though, I shouldn't wonder." He shook his head. "It's the college Gaudy tonight – their old boys' reunion, Godmother. All the surviving relics of past wars and past Governments, and captains of industry – and future relics, too. You've picked the wrong night as well as the wrong college, I must say! 'Gaudy Night', and all that!"

"Yes, I know, dear." She recalled, as she had been leaving the college, the curious mixture of ancient and modern 'old boys' gossiping with each other in the front quadrangle, like long-lost friends and enemies together.

"Yes – so you do!" He looked at her suddenly. "Not an hour ago, you said?"

Now it was coming, thought Rigby. But she couldn't blame him. "Yes, dear."

"Yes, dear," he mimicked. "Just what is it that you're *not* burgling, on this fine evening? Or shouldn't I ask?" The look became more searching.

Breaking into the college and then getting caught would be embarrassing for her, she reminded herself. But Oxford wasn't exactly Berlin, if it came to the crunch. Only . . . for Scholar John and his beer-drinking theological friend, discovery might be something more than an embarrassment, given the reputation of its Dean-Colonel. Being rusticated at the start of one's final year would be no joke at all.

"Once I'm inside you can leave me, John dear. I know where I want to go."

He shook his head. "And you wouldn't stand a chance. Dick's is an all-male establishment. One day . . . when I'm old and grey, or in my grave . . . the colleges may go . . . 'co-ed', is it? But not while Young Hob's alive – not Dick's . . . So, you wouldn't last two minutes tonight. You'd stick out like a sore thumb." He paused. "So . . . ?"

The original question. "I just want to look at something, John."

"Something?"

"A piece of paper. In a briefcase belonging to one of the 'old boys'. In a room in the Fellows Quadrangle – Fellows 3:3. That's the third staircase –"

"I know where Fellows 3:3 will be." He waved a dismissive hand. "'A piece of paper'? Like Neville Chamberlain brought back from Munich that time? A piece of 'peace for our time', that sort of paper?" He made a face. "I know my history – eh?"

He knew *her*, he was reminding her. And, although he'd in fact got it almost exactly back to front, he was also quite dreadfully close to the mark – so close that she shivered as she thought, *How much can I tell him?* And then measured her risk against his, and came to a decision. "Not 'peace for our time', John. Say 'war', rather."

"War?" He stopped suddenly, with Hertford's Bridge of Sighs arching above him.

He was a bright boy, so she waited while he added the word to all the newspaper headlines of the last few weeks, which he couldn't have failed to read, in spite of his own academic imperatives. And thought, as she waited: a bright boy . . . and, being his father's son, undoubtedly a brave one, too . . . And . . . before next year's out, a bright brave boy in National Service uniform. But not a bright, brave boy at war, if I can help it, by God!

"Egypt, you mean? Suez – and all that?" His face cleared as he read her expression. "Phew! I thought for a moment . . . the Bomb – and the Russians, and all *that* . . . But – but just the Egyptians? And Suez – now that what's-his-name – Colonel Nasser – now that he's pinched the canal off us? Are we really going to invade, then?"

"Do you think we should?"

He shrugged, as though it was of small importance. "A chap I know who went down last year – got a First in Maths . . . in the 6th Tanks now – he says they painted their Centurions desert-brown ages ago." He shrugged again. "I guess I don't blame the Egyptians, really. But I wouldn't blame us, either. I mean . . . we can't really let them get away with it – can we?" Then he frowned. "Are we going to invade?"

The 64,000-dollar question! "That's really what I'm after, John dear: the answer to that question."

"On a piece of paper?" The frown remained in place. "And a spy's got it? Or . . . he's trying to get it?" He looked away from her, across Oxford, as though towards King's College.

"They haven't got Anthony Eden in Dick's tonight, surely? He's a Christ Church man ... And it can't be Harold Macmillan – he's Balliol. And Duncan Sandys is Magdalen –" He moved from questions to statements thoughtfully. "Who, then?"

They were all Oxford men, thought Rigby. For better or worse, as always, most of the Cabinet – and many of any future Labour Cabinet which might succeed the Tories one day – had been shaped and educated within a mile of where they were standing, beside a narrow opening which she remembered suddenly was called 'Hell's Passage'.

"I'm not *after* anyone." The Turf tavern was somewhere down Hell's Passage, she remembered additionally: a tiny old-fashioned pub in the middle of nowhere, not on a street at all, but tucked under another surviving section of the old city wall. "But what about your friend – Guy –?"

"He'll keep." He gestured vaguely. "He'll be coming out this way to get back to Dick's, if he hasn't gone already ... But – you're not *after* anyone? Not even whoever is in Fellows 3:3 at Dick's, even?"

Only more would satisfy him. "There's a civil servant staying there tonight. One Cedric Butterworth. He's an old member of the college, up for the reunion – the Gaudy, as you call it. Not that he's exactly 'old'. But ... he's been in Oxford since yesterday, talking to various people. 'Wise men', he calls them. About ... certain issues his particular Minister is concerned with."

"Like Egypt?" He asked for more unashamedly. "And Suez – the invasion? Like getting the answers to the exam questions for his boss, you mean?"

Bright indeed! "Yes. And his Minister is close to the Prime Minister, John."

"I see! The P.M. rates the Minister. And the Minister rates this civil servant of yours. I get the drift, Godmother: it's *our* side you're spying on this time, to see which way the cat will jump! Or ... are you planning to influence the cat too?"

That was enough. He knew too much already. "We just want to know how Butterworth is going to advise his Minister, that's all."

"And he wouldn't tell you this afternoon? Very mingy of

him! So now you want to burgle – pardon! – just take a peek
in his briefcase, or whatever? While he's busy swilling good
college wine in hall – very neat, *very* neat. Except . . . if I
can get you in . . . supposing his room's locked? And his
briefcase –" He stopped suddenly as he saw her expression.

"Just get me in, John. No more questions – and no more
answers."

"Oh – just one more –" He cocked his head at her. "He
wouldn't *also* be a traitor, by any chance? This Butterworth
fellow? Like those Cambridge blighters?"

"Cedric Butterworth?" For an instant she was tempted to
encourage him with a gross slander on a loyal servant of the
Crown. But if things went wrong he would never forgive
such a deception. "Good heavens, *no*. Cedric Butterworth is
absolutely clean: he's just a hard-working civil servant. And
rather clever, too. And –" She stopped as he looked past her
again. And then he grinned and waved.

"*Guy* – my dear fellow! You come most carefully on your
hour, to succour a lady in distress!"

Turning, Rigby beheld a tall, bespectacled young man in a
worn sports coat, polo-necked sweater and shapeless corduroy
trousers.

"Godmother – meet the future Archbishop of Canterbury."
Scholar John ignored his friend's suspicious frown. "Guy –
meet the best of godmothers . . . who can climb rope-ladders
and wants to get inside the sacred portals of Dick's within the
hour. And . . . seeing as you happen to have a rope-ladder of
your own within those portals . . . I have promised your
assistance. Okay?"

The future Archbishop gazed at Rigby. "Oh?" he managed.
"Indeed?"

"I could tell you that my godmother cherishes a secret –
and probably hopeless – passion for Dean Hobson, if not
the Master himself," continued John. "But that would not
be the truth. And I would not wish to lie to you. But . . . the
matter is of some importance – *that* I can tell you. And
urgency."

The future Archbishop tried to smile. "Yes?" he managed.

"Yes," agreed Scholar John encouragingly. "The truth
is . . . that she only wishes to steal the college silver. For the

benefit of distressed gentlefolk and the re-roofing of her club in London, both of which have fallen on hard times."

"Ah . . ." This time a genuine smile broke through. "If it's only *that* – the college silver . . . then how can I resist such a worthwhile appeal?" Poor Guy consulted his wrist-watch short-sightedly, and then the smile returned. "Shall we say . . . Dick's Lane, back of Garden Quad . . . in twenty minutes, Best of Godmothers –?"

Rigby's arm came up, so that she could read her own watch while carefully not looking down into the narrow street below: twenty-one minutes and thirty seconds –

"Easy does it!" Guy fumbled, trying to help her through the narrow window without grasping anything too feminine. "That's the ticket!"

"There was someone passing by – when I was halfway up –"

"Not to worry, ma'am. Just a passing Oxonian. And you were just a climbing girl – woman – *lady*, I mean . . . entering college." He leaned out of the window. "Come on up, Johnnie – on the double!" He gave her another of his shy smiles. "If it 'ud been a policeman . . . before our troubles he'd probably have held the ladder for you. Now, maybe not. But . . . he wasn't a policeman, anyway. And . . . Johnnie was right: you're a good climber, Godmother." He averted his eyes as she straightened her skirt.

Scholar John heaved himself through the window and at once set about hauling up the rope-ladder. Then he looked from Rigby (admiringly) to Guy (smugly). "Didn't I say she was a good climber?"

"I was just saying as much, dear boy." Guy waved him away. "But now comes the more difficult part, with the college more like Stalag 17 than a good medieval Christian foundation – Goons and Gestapo everywhere, with Obergruppen-führer von Baskerville rousting them. I swear they'll bring in the dogs next. And then someone'll get savaged. If not actually *eaten* –" He turned away as he spoke, and returned with a bright red raincoat in his hands. "Still, we have had a slice of luck." He lifted the raincoat. "The perfect disguise, no less!"

Scholar John sniffed and frowned. "It doesn't look perfect to me. It looks more like . . . a lady's raincoat –? Where no lady should be?"

"Right – and wrong, dearest of *godsons*." Guy dismissed his friend, to concentrate on Rigby. "I must say that I'm delighted, albeit a little surprised, that Mr John Anstey *has* a godmother – fairy or otherwise. But, as to this garment . . . I trust that you do not object to donning the scarlet coat of a scarlet woman, Godmother?"

"Her name's Rigby," said Scholar John stiffly.

"Go and keep *cave* out in the quad, there's a good fellow," said Guy without looking at his friend. "I found this garment in this room . . . which doesn't actually belong to me: it belongs to a noted college Lothario who did his National Service in the Dragoon Guards, or the Household Cavalry. A somewhat older undergraduate, is what I mean – with experience of debutantes, rather than female undergraduates –"

"Come to the point." Scholar John hadn't moved.

"I am on the point." Guy raised the red raincoat again. "This belongs to the wife of one of our younger dons – younger, but still middle-aged . . . And she was his pupil not so long ago (more fool him!)." He pursed his lips. "So now he's busy with the War of the Spanish Succession – or the Austrian Succession, or whatever. Because he's an historian . . . And *she's* busy with selected undergraduates, of the more experienced variety." He didn't smile this time. "I do beg your pardon for being somewhat crude, Godmother – Rigby." Now he drew a breath. "But I found this raincoat in this room. Which she must have left one evening, which began wet and ended . . . dry, I suppose. But it's a well-known garment in the college. In fact, it's so well-known that the college servants – and that includes our Mr Baskerville . . . they try *not* to see it, when they see it. If you take my point . . . Rigby? They turn a blind eye –?"

Rigby took his point. And then she took the raincoat and put it on.

"Get out into the quad, like I said," Guy ordered John, Archbishop to Curate. "Keep ahead of us, and meet your godmother outside . . . ?"

"Fellows 3:3," said John.

"And I'll take her to the War Memorial and then watch her back," Guy continued. *"Go on!"*

John moved, and Rigby watched Guy count the seconds off on his watch.

"Now we go." Guy nodded at her. "And put the hood up."

Curiously, it was somehow like Berlin: the bareness of the landing and the stairway outside, with its naked bulb; the bright light outside – or not *very* bright, but too bright all the same.

"That way – under the arch," Guy pointed.

Rigby reached the archway, shrinking back automatically into its most shadowy part. Opposite her, and fully illuminated, was the college Roll of Honour from both World Wars – long enough for 1939-45, but quite heart-breaking for 1914-18; and the second name in that long list was a German one, presumably of some Rhodes Scholar before he became a Lieutenant of the Brandenburg Grenadiers. So, if you were a King's man, that said, it didn't matter which king you fought for, or which country, you were always an Oxford man, first and last.

"Psst!" Guy pointed again as he caught up with her. "The third staircase is on the far side of the quad, in the corner there – see where Johnnie's heading?"

Rigby hesitated for a moment. The lights in Fellows Quadrangle seemed even brighter than those behind her, and the quad was bigger. In the distance, from somewhere in the ancient labyrinth of buildings, she could hear the cheerful hubbub of the reunion dinner. No such sound had attended her final approach to the Berlin Wall that last time, but the stillness and emptiness ahead of her were the same.

"Don't walk across the grass, though," hissed Guy. "But . . . don't creep – walk as though you own the place. That's the way *she* does."

As she launched herself into space Rigby found herself wondering about Guy's suitability for high office in the Church, rather than some more worldly calling – even perhaps her own. But the final disapproval in his voice of the man-eating (or boy-hunting) Red Riding Hood whose coat she was wearing reassured her somewhat as she tried not to hear the deafening *click-clack* of her heels echoing round the quadrangle.

She passed an opening marked '6' – Staircase 6 – just as Scholar John disappeared into a similar one in the furthest corner, across the billiard-table square of grass –

– *Question (in a polite American voice)*: "Say, excuse me, sir . . . but how do you get a lawn like this?"

– *Answer (in a superior Oxford voice)*: "Oh, it's quite easy. You just lay the lawn. And then you roll it for five hundred years."

A door banged loudly in another opening on the opposite side and a bowler-hatted, ramrod-backed figure emerged. Rigby knew that she was being stared at. From within the hood.

God! He was moving now, and in an anti-clockwise direction round the quadrangle which must bring them face-to-face before Staircase 3!

She had passed Staircase 5: her only hope was Staircase 4. But even tha –

"Ah! Mr Baskerville!" Guy's voice rang sharp and peremptory from behind her. "You're just the man I was looking for! I need your assistance."

There was a moment's pause. "Sir?"

"Yes. I locked my room, just like the Dean commanded me to – in that notice about security in the lodge, eh?" Guy strung out his appeal lazily now. "Although I never used to have to lock it. I don't know what the college is coming to. It's getting to be more like a ruddy prison, Mr Baskerville –"

The Head Porter had stopped – no, he was retracing his steps in Guy's direction. And there were two lighted rooms on Staircase 4, just ahead.

"What is it, Mr Threlfall?" Mr Baskerville sounded distinctly irritated.

"Eh? Oh . . . I think I've dropped my key somewhere in the Garden Quad. Have you got a torch with you? Or in the lodge? Or –" The rest of the elongated nonsense was lost to Rigby as she turned decisively into Staircase 4, aware that she was thereby probably compromising the reputations of two hard-working undergraduates who had returned to Oxford before term had started.

First the murmur of voices, then the sound of footsteps on flagstones, died away, leaving only the thump of her heart to disturb the silence of the quad.

Staircase 3 –

"Phew!" whispered Scholar John out of the darkness. "That was a close call! But maybe we should have reckoned Basker- ville 'ud be doing his rounds while all the old boys were making merry in Hall. Only . . . we'd best get a move-on now, Godmother darling – Room Number 3 is first floor right. And there's no light showing under the door, which is locked, naturally –"

Naturally! Cedric Butterworth, with future Cabinet material in his briefcase, would have taken that precaution even without Dean Hobson's *ukase*.

Rigby extracted her pencil-torch and pick-locks from her bag. "Hold the torch, dear – on the keyhole, please."

The lock was old and stiff, confirming Guy's complaint about past insecurity. But, mercifully, it was also unsophisticated.

"Do you always carry the – ah – tools of your trade, Godmother?"

Click!

"Yes, dear." She took the torch from him and opened the door. The layout of the room was as she remembered from the afternoon, but in the burglar's light-and-dark it smelt even more of dust and unwashed linen.

"He's closed the curtains," said Scholar John. "Can I switch the light on?"

"Not until I've closed them properly . . . You can now, yes."

He looked at her strangely. "You are a pro, aren't you? Do you do this sort of thing often?"

"Not if I can help it." The desk was tidier than before, so all the papers must be in the briefcase beside it. And that lock would be even easier – except that she mustn't leave any tell-tale scratches on it –

Click!

Butterworth had almost finished his work before, and now it was complete: just the two bulging files of his own notes and the two slim Cabinet agenda envelopes – *Item One* and *Item Two*. And, as a crowning mercy, neither of them was sealed yet.

John craned his neck across the desk. "Just what are you looking for? Does the look-out man get to see?"

"No, he doesn't –" The thick *Egypt/Suez* file, with the

additional French contribution on command structure, which she'd glimpsed before Butterworth had covered it up, would be interesting. But it was only that *Item One* envelope that she had come for "– it's none of his business –" And . . . Butterworth was a very clever young man (even perhaps brilliant); but, with his career on the line because of the Minister's trust in his judgment, she feared that he would put his mouth on the same side as his bread was buttered –

"Sorry I spoke!" John straightened up, his body as stiff as his words.

Damn! thought Rigby, remembering the red-headed Brigadier again, and his curious gentleness with those of his subordinates who took the actual risks in the field (as Scholar John and future-Archbishop Guy were doing now), however inconvenient their interruptions.

She looked up at him. "I'm sorry, dear –"

"It's okay, Godmother darling." He grinned at her. "Just get on with it – sorry I spoke."

Rigby weakened. "Here –" She pushed the *Oxford Roads* file across the desk, and then added the *Item Two* Cabinet agenda to it as an afterthought, " – have a look at that, John dear."

"Can I?" He perked up disarmingly. "Can I *really*?"

Now she melted. "Be my guest, dear." The future of the Oxford road system was hardly a Top Secret matter, no matter that the Cabinet was discussing it with more weighty topics. And it would shut him up gracefully: he might understand some of it, and keep quiet while she struggled with Peace and War in the Middle East. "It's more your field than mine, actually."

"Oh? Mine –?" His eyebrows lifted in pure innocence, and he was for that instant her Little John again, and as beautiful (from when she'd first held him in her arms at his christening, marvelling at him: '*Such a good baby*!' they'd all said) as he was clever and brave now, twenty years afterwards, as Scholar John (and now she probably couldn't even lift him, who was the nearest thing to the son she'd never had, and never would have!).

"Yes." She cut him, and all that foolishness, off together. The contents of the *Item One* agenda was all that mattered now.

The burden of the envelope's contents swam before her eyes for an instant, simple though it was – simple as she already knew it would be: Cedric Butterworth's Minister believed that all issues, all plans, all controversies could be reduced to five basic questions, to which he required only the briefest and simplest answers:

1. Is this feasible? (The Minister was nothing if not a practical politician.)

2. Is it moral? (That was a joke – but only to those who didn't know that – like Guy Threlfall now – the Minister had aspired to a religious career before succumbing to a political one.)

3. Where does the Prime Minister stand? (Once committed to Question 1, rather more than Question 2, the Minister always played to win.)

4. How does the rest of the Cabinet line up? And the House? (Two-questions-in-one ... and also, in view of Anthony Eden's health in doubt from Question 3, a doubly tricky one, maybe?)

5. In the longer view, what will be the likely verdict of history? (The trickiest question of all – a real dirty one! – dividing success not only by morality, but also by possible eventual discovery of motive? Because the Minister had been trained as an historian, maybe?)

But she knew all these questions already, from when they'd been a private Intelligence joke in the Minister's earlier days. And all that mattered now was Cedric Butterworth's answers:

1. No.

2. No.

"God Almighty!" exclaimed Scholar John loudly, over-printing her own mute astonishment, which was beyond exclamation: Cedric Butterworth was against the invasion of Egypt – on both practical and moral grounds!

"What, dear?" She couldn't ignore his exclamation. But he ignored her so completely that she was able to return to her own happy discovery: the Prime Minister was still undecided – in spite of his background (and that, of course, was Munich, when Chamberlain had given way to Hitler: all the right-wing papers were likening Nasser to Hitler).

"Good God Almighty!" exclaimed Scholar John, even more

vehemently, just as the initialled names were starting to swim before her eyes ('DS' was Duncan Sandys, at present trapped in the boring Ministry of Housing and Local Government, but tipped for Defence in the next reshuffle; and 'HM' was Harold Macmillan – *of Balliol*, she thought irrelevantly – who was hugely influential in the Tory Party, and known to be keeping his options open for the future).

5. Once actioned, this can never be reversed. It will, nevertheless, afford only a temporary solution to the present problem. So –

"This is monstrous, Godmother – Godmother *darling*! Quite *monstrous –*" John threw his envelope and its contents down among the jumbled papers from the file before him. "The blighter's a traitor – an absolute *traitor!*"

She frowned at him. "Cedric B –"

"No!" He dismissed the name contemptuously before she could complete it. *And rightly so*, she added: against expectation Butterworth had taken the braver and longer view of the Middle Eastern crisis, in which each course spelt humiliation, but his at least would not be stained by a useless loss of life in the hard years to come.

"Eden, I mean – Anthony-ruddy-Eden!" John snapped the name at her. "He's a Christ Church man, Godmother. And he's damn-well agreeing to putting a road slap-bang across the Meadow, right in front of his own college! And if that isn't treason-and-treachery, I don't know what is!"

"A –?" She had never seen him so incensed. "Road? What road?"

"The Christ Church Road, of course." He regarded her with astonishment. "The Oxford 'inner relief' road, so-called – the *Meadow* Road – the 'Merton Mall', as that blighter Sharp calls it –" He stopped for breath, but only for a quick breath "– the *damnable* relief road they want to put across our Meadow, where we were walking just this evening . . . where there are foxes and badgers, and wild fowl in the winter, when the floods come up from the river: they want to put cars, and buses, and ruddy pantechnicons and lorries there instead – instead of up the High and round the Ring Road, on the by-pass. And . . . it'll be the absolute *ruin* of Oxford – bloody *ruin!*" He thumped the desk. "And he – *he* – your appalling Butterscotch man . . . *he* thinks it's OK, of course. But he's only a Dick's man, and a civil servant . . . So what can you expect? But Eden – our bloody Prime Minister –"

"Don't keep swearing at me, John." She began to remember headlines and stories she had read in *The Times* and the other quality papers, about Oxford's petty traffic problems. More immediately, she could even recall the idyllic green peace and quiet of his Meadow, which nestled in the midst of the bustling city. But, in the scheme of things, that counted for nothing compared with Cedric Butterworth's crucial advice to his Minister, who just might swing Anthony Eden against the invasion of Egypt, if not the invasion of Christ Church Meadow. And she wasn't about to have Butterworth so easily traduced after that, as '*only* a Dick's man, and a civil servant'.

"I'm sorry, John. But what matters more is that, whatever Cedric Butterworth is *for* . . . he's *against* invading Egypt." She replaced *Agenda One* in its envelope. "So –"

"What's wrong with invading Egypt?" He stiffened again.

"It won't work, John dear."

"No? But . . . didn't we invade *Europe* just a few years back? And we didn't do so badly then, I seem to remember."

"But the Americans were on our side then. And the Russians." She gestured wearily. "But I'm not going to argue with you – not here, anyway."

He stared at her. Then he looked down at the desk. And then he looked up, and shrugged. "OK, Godmother! If you must have it your own way!" His mouth twisted downwards. "You're right: we'd better get to hell out of here before Mr Baskerville comes back – you're right!"

She stared back at him, slightly surprised by his surrender.

He nodded towards the curtains. "Go and have a look-see at the quad, just in case –"

She moved towards the curtain. "There's no one there, dear."

"Have a good look. He could be lurking in one of the staircase entrances. And . . . is old Guy waiting under the archway?"

The quad was empty. But there was a pair of feet in the archway. And, as she observed them, they became legs. And then Guy. "Yes, dear – Guy's waiting."

The light went out behind her. "OK, then . . . You lock up

here, Godmother. And I'll check the staircase entrances, in case Baskerville is lurking in one of them – OK?" He was suddenly urgent. "Be quick, Godmother darling. I'll signal from across the quad. OK?"

"OK, dear." For a moment she thought he was scared at last. But then she knew better. Because he was his father's son, as well as her beloved godson.

That other time –

Talk of the devil, indeed!

Rigby watched the capped-and-gowned figure approach them, stalking magisterially with hands hidden in the flowing black robes. And it was a devil she knew, of course – even though Professor John Anstey hadn't talked of him at all.

"Smile sweetly, Rigby." Professor Anstey, whose nappy she had once changed when she was a teenage godmother, and whose running nose and bloody knees she had wiped during those brief intervals in her hot war, and whose pocket money and bank balance she had augmented in the long Cold War afterwards . . . that same John didn't look at her as he acknowledged the distinguished devil (no devil!) about whom he hadn't talked. "Good evening, Master. And a fine evening, too!"

"Good evening, Professor Anstey." The tasselled mortarboard cap was politely doffed in Rigby's direction. "And a fine evening, too: the city and the University are both looking well this autumn, I think."

"Yes, Master." The Professor turned to her. "Rigby, I don't believe you've met the Master of King's College, Sir Cedric Butterworth?" The professorial smile was also a conspiratorial one as it left her. "Master, may I present the best of godmothers, Miss Dorothy Rigby –?"

"You may, Professor Anstey." The Master added a small bow to his initial cap-doffing. "But in supposing that we have never met . . . you err, Professor Anstey –" To the cap and the bow the Master finally added a thin academic smile. "Miss Rigby and I are old acquaintances . . . dare I say 'old friends'?"

Rigby inclined her head. "Old friends – of course, Sir Cedric."

"But in another life? Another . . . incarnation?" The smile twitched slightly. "For me, anyway?"

Rigby tried to match the smile. "I was pleased to read of your honour, Sir Cedric – of your double honour, if I may include your election to be Master of King's."

"Thank you, Miss Rigby. The reward of longevity, rather than distinction, I fear . . . But you –? What brings you once more to Oxford? To St Antony's College, I presume? To converse with your peers –? For that is where the – ah – the senior *alumni* of the Secret Service gather now, I believe?"

"I have retired now, Sir Cedric. I am simply visiting my godson."

"Ah, yes! Just visiting? Well . . . forgive me, but I must be on my way. We have our college Gaudy this evening – *Stet fortuna domus*, and all that – so I must be away now, if I am not to be late for my own party, as it were . . . Your servant, Professor Anstey – and your admiring former *civil* servant, Miss Rigby –"

Rigby watched the robed figure diminish in the distance: Sir Cedric Butterworth, K.C.B., C.B., D.Phil. (and many other honorary doctorates, native and foreign), M.A. (Oxon), Master of King's College, Oxford, and *ci-devant* promising young Civil Servant: he was all there, in *Who's Who*, together with his numerous publications.

But not his most important unpublished work, she thought. And that thought aroused all the mischief in her.

"He could have had a great career in the Civil Service, you know, John." She watched the figure swing, gown flowing liquidly, towards the path between Merton and Corpus Christi, towards another Gaudy in Dick's – King Richard's College. "He could have been in the Lords by now."

"Mmm . . . But he didn't do so badly, did he?" John sounded uneasy.

"A fellowship at All Souls College, after Suez? After his Minister went to the wall? No . . . perhaps not." The figure was small now. Soon it would disappear, beside the Merton memorial at the back of Grove Building, to forgotten Andrew Irvine, Mallory's fellow-climber, who might (or might-not) have been the first man to scale Mount Everest, twenty-nine years before Hillary and Tenzing . . . and thirty-two years before the abortive landings at Suez. "They do themselves well in Dick's, do they? On Gaudy nights?"

He didn't reply. But, she judged, it was now or never.

"Where are you taking me tonight, John dear? Le Manoir aux Quat' Saisons?"

He drew a deep breath. "Rigby . . . Godmother *darling* . . . I have a confession to make."

It was going to be now. "Yes, dear?"

He took in his Meadow, from Magdalen to the Cathedral, to fortify himself. "That time . . . the time we burgled Butterworth's room in Dick's –?"

"Of course I remember, dear. And . . . I saw just recently in the *Financial Times* that your friend Guy has done well for himself – winning that take-over bid in the City?" But that was enough, she judged finally: because of his guilt he had believed all these years that he had done a bad thing, when he hadn't. The only bad thing, really, was that she had let him go on thinking it. "And I remember also what you did, John."

"What . . . I did?" He was looking at her, while she was looking at Magdalen tower, and Merton, and Corpus Christi, and Christ Church itself.

"Yes." She nodded towards Oxford. "While I was looking out of the window, between the curtains . . . you swopped the contents of those two envelopes – the *Oxford Roads* answers and the *Egypt/Suez* ones." The mist was drifting across Broad Walk now, from Christ Church Meadow into Merton Field. And the grass was very green under the old city wall. And it was gloriously quiet. "You swopped *Item One* with *Item Two*."

For a long moment he added to the silence. "How long have you known?"

She could lie, or she could be honest. But lies were always unsatisfactory between friends, and even more so between godmothers and godsons. So only the truth would do now. "For thirty-two years, dear – almost from the moment you did it. Or . . . perhaps even before you did it. You were so transparent when you made me look away, through those curtains. And . . . there was that War Memorial, under the archway – that was what made me certain."

"The . . . War Memorial?"

The bells were beginning to ring now, over Oxford, as though to order, in sweet celebration.

" 'The college comes first' – and Oxford comes first . . . even before war and peace." She smiled at him. "You were very young. And Oxford – your Meadow – was very beautiful . . . And you thought it would only be a very *little* war. And you'd grown up during such a big one . . . So I've never really blamed you."

He didn't speak. Or maybe he couldn't speak.

"And, besides, you didn't really *do* anything, you see, John." This might be cruel, but it was only the fullness of truth. So she swept her hand from left to right, from Magdalen to Christ Church. "If this is anyone's work, it's mine. Or . . . your *intention* . . . but my *execution*, anyway."

"Yours –?" He blinked at her. *"Yours?"*

"Yes, dear. Because I swopped the contents of the envelopes back. Only . . . you see, I wasn't as clever as I thought I was: I only thought about *you*, not about the British Cabinet in September 1956. And they were nearly all Oxford men – Duncan Sandys was a Magdalen man so he wanted the road here, to free Magdalen from the traffic . . . and Harold Macmillan was just biding his time, because he was Balliol, and didn't much care . . . And Anthony Eden was too worried about Egypt to worry about Oxford, even though he was a Christ Church man – 'in spite of his background'. But there were four other Christ Church men. And when Butterworth's Minister supported them –" She turned for a moment, but the Master of King's had disappeared now "– perhaps Butterworth loves the Meadow as much as you do, since he still walks in it. Even though he is . . . 'only a Dick's man'?"

This time he didn't blink. *"Item One* on the Cabinet agenda was a discussion of the Oxford roads problem? And . . . *Item Two* was . . . the invasion of Egypt? You got them wrong, Godmother?"

"I got them wrong, Godson: I failed to take account of the priorities of Oxford men – in spite of all the evidence to the contrary. Yes." For some reason she couldn't shrug. "But I expect it would all have turned out the same, whatever either of us did. 'In the longer view', as Butterworth's Minister used to put it –?"

He stared at her. And then at the Meadow. "No, Godmother darling. In '56, you know, they just might have put a road through here. It was the sort of thing they did in those days, before there were Green parties, and Friends of the Earth. And even Mrs Thatcher is *environmental* now –"

Margaret Hilda Thatcher, née Roberts, remembered Rigby. Somerville College, Oxford, 1943-47. They were all still Oxford, for better or worse!

"But they just might have done it then, by God!" He gave his Meadow and his Oxford one last nod. Then he came back to her. "*Si monumentum requiris – circumspice*, best and dearest of godmothers!"

He was lost to her altogether now, even more Oxford than in 1956, in so far as that was possible. "Dear John – Professor Anstey – you know my Latin is vestigial!"

"Is it? I didn't know that!" Like any good Oxford don he assimilated this new fact. "Well, let's translate it to the full, as it was meant to refer to Sir Christopher Wren, in the midst of his cathedral of St Paul's: If you're looking for the best thing I ever did in life – just look at all this, and give thanks. How about that?"

———

Rigby was delighted to have Anthony Price assigned to this chapter of her life. Price is an Oxford man through and through. An undergraduate at Merton he went on to become, in 1972, the editor of the *Oxford Times*. He relinquished this job in 1988 in order to be able to devote more time to the thrillers for which he is already well known.

As editor, he published an article on March 4th, 1988, from which he has allowed me to quote. It is a brief passage, after which there is really nothing more to say: "During his study of Oxford's Meadow Road controversy, Dr Newman discovered this agenda for a meeting of the Cabinet in 1956: 'ITEM ONE – Christ Church Meadow Road. ITEM TWO – Seizure of Suez Canal (if time permits)'."

When I showed it to Rigby she smirked.

"Told you so," she said.

John Ehrlichman

AN AFFAIR OF THE COUCH

Rigby was a friend of the United States ever since that first war-time visit to Los Alamos. In a professional sense her special relationship never really recovered after the departure of Eisenhower and the assassinations of Jack and Bobby Kennedy. She refused to go all the way with L.B.J., whom she considered a vulgarian, and she despised Carter, Ford and Reagan for wimpishness in the first case and lack of intellect in the second and third.

For Richard Nixon she had a certain grudging respect. She had known him when he was Ike's Vice-President and had been present in Moscow during his famous Khrushchev-inspired visit. When he became President in 1968 however, she had no first-hand dealings with the White House. She was nearing fifty and, though still a strikingly handsome woman who kept herself fit with regular and competitive exercise, her excursions into active service were becoming fewer and farther between.

However, there was just the one Rigby intervention during the Nixon era, and it is particularly appropriate that John Ehrlichman should be the man entrusted with writing it up. Ehrlichman, now, like Dick Stern, a resident of New Mexico, was a crucial part of the Nixon White House. He was Tour Manager of Nixon's Presidential Campaign, Counsel to the President and, from 1970 to 1973, Assistant to the President for Domestic Affairs, a member of the Council on International Economic Policy, the President's Property Review Board and Staff Director of the Domestic Council. From 1976 to 1978 he was in a Federal prison camp for his part in the Watergate scandal. He seemed an ideal author for this episode in Rigby's life.

"Bob," the President said, "something must be done. Henry was just in here for an hour, pounding away on me again. It can't go on. I have very reluctantly decided to send him away."

Richard Nixon was sitting in the half-light, cast so evenly from the soffit that there was barely a shadow in the Oval Office. H. R. Haldeman sat forward on the period chair beside the President's desk, his hand resting on a yellow pad of paper.

"Can you really do away with him now?" Haldeman asked rhetorically. "There's China and Vietnam and so much going on with the Russians right now. Who could step in, Al Haig?"

"Yes, I think Al could do it, and he would certainly be easier on me," Nixon mused. He looked sharply at Haldeman. "Do you think Henry is nuts?" he asked. "He comes in here and whines about Bill Rogers and complains about Shultz and demands that I fire some ambassador I never heard of. I think he's psychotic, for God's sake. Understand: if he has mental problems, I'm very sympathetic. He should have the best of care; can we send him to the Army doctors at Walter Reed Hospital?"

"I suppose you could, but do you really want to? It would surely leak and the Press would have a field day."

"Of course, you're right; Walter Reed is impossible. But you've got to do something, Bob. The President should not be subjected to such continual craziness. Henry suspects Rogers is having him followed now. Is that true? Rogers has a lot of security men over there at State, but is he tailing Henry? Do we know? Can we find out?"

"I suppose we can, but do we care?"

"Ha! I don't care, but Henry does. When you think about it, everything he does is in the *Post* the next day, so who needs to follow him? If Henry is worried about Rogers knowing what he does, Henry should quit talking to Kay Graham and her reporters." Nixon smiled, an instantaneous grimace that was gone in a blink. "Let's talk about what needs to be done. Someone will have to talk to Henry about his problem. I think you should do that, Bob, don't you think so?"

"I can do that, but what if he denies it?"

"Of course he'll deny it. They all deny that they have mental problems. You need to say: 'The President knows about such things, Henry. He has had some experience in these matters. He is worried . . .' No, you'd better say: 'The President is very concerned for your health. Nothing is more important to him than your well-being. You've been working so very hard, and he knows it and appreciates it. The President is well aware of the strain and stress some of you fellows work under, da dadda, da dadda, da da.' You know what to say, Bob."

"I know." Haldeman shifted uneasily in his chair.

"It must be one of two ways: either he gets some psychiatric treatment, so he calms down and gets over that awful paranoia – that's what it is, I think, a persecution complex – or he must resign. The President just must not be subjected to that kind of raving. It's bad for my health. Ha!" Nixon barked a self-denying laugh.

Haldeman shook his head as he made notes on his pad. Note-taking reassured Nixon that his staff took his instructions seriously. "I'll see what I can do," Haldeman said, "but I'm not optimistic. Henry is going to be very upset."

"Just tell him, don't ask him. Tell him: he sees a psychiatrist or he is out. Period. No appeal. Just tell him that."

"I'll tell him," Bob Haldeman said.

"We have a simply excellent woman in Washington now," Portland asserted. "I feel sure she will help you. In point of fact, she is not a member of the Services, although I have spoken to her about it. Perhaps you can persuade her. I believe you know her."

Portland poured Rigby a second cup of tea and pushed it about an inch toward her. The gesture was born of a well-inculcated obligation of hospitality but was, at the same time, inhibited by the public servant's keen sense of who was superior in rank to whom. "She was at one time," he said in a near whisper, "Churchill's daughter-in-law."

Rigby showed none of her surprise. She sipped her tea, put the cup gently into its saucer and dabbed her lips with the small linen napkin. "Panto, is it?" she asked.

"It's Pamela, née Digby, Churchill."

"Of course; Panto. I thought she was in Hollywood, married to some film producer. Is she in Washington?"

Portland nodded. "She is widowed, wealthy and married to old Averell Harriman."

Rigby smiled broadly and shook her head. "Out of the honey pot and into the jam. Panto always knew what she wanted and how to get it."

"Do you know her well enough to ask her for help, or shall I . . . ?"

"I should think I do. It was Digby and Rigby at school, wasn't it? We were really quite good friends."

Portland was never direct with Rigby about the problems involved in an assignment. He liked to skim off the easy parts, leaving the difficulties until last, and Rigby had learned to wait patiently for the bad news.

"Do you have a deadline for results in this project?" she asked, looking toward the leaded window which opened to a courtyard in the old building. She had never been comfortable with Portland. It had been obvious that he was in love with her years before, but they had never been friends. In those early days of their relationship she had pushed him away gently, without citing the reasons why she did not find his affection welcome. Yet, she was sure, he had been hurt and resentful. She did not see him often but, when she did, she believed his ardour to be on a hair trigger, always there, only waiting for some signal from her to guarantee that he would not be hurt again if he took to his knees.

"Deadline? Rather soon, I think. The Americans are up to something in a big way, and we fear it has to do with Hong Kong. The question is: are we being sold out to the Chinese?"

"Sold out? How can the Americans sell us out of Hong Kong?"

"So far the U.S. has backed us there. But if American policy should change to 'Hong Kong for the Chinese' and all of that rot, Her Majesty's Government couldn't hold the line alone. Do you see? We need a strong ally out there. We are counting on the Americans as we negotiate with the Chinks."

"Is there evidence of a change of their policy?"

"Not as such. But there are a few curious events that make us wonder. A White House staff man who works for Henry Kissinger has been seen recently in Hong Kong. Our people think he has tiptoed into the People's Republic several times. In Hong Kong he consorts with P.R.C. agents. His name is Matthew Thompson."

Portland opened a folder and laid a thin dossier in front of Rigby. She resisted the temptation to leaf through it. The young man's photograph on the cover sheet showed him to be tall, strong and good-looking.

"I am to seduce Matthew Thompson?" she asked wryly. "Panto is the one with the irresistible shoulders. Perhaps she is the seductress?"

"Not at all." Portland shook his head seriously. "I fear you are both a bit too . . . ah . . . mature for Thompson. No, your target is Kissinger himself. He alone will possess the knowledge we require."

"Ah, dear little Henry," Rigby mused.

"Do you know him?"

"Afraid not. But these days they must have him surrounded by miles of concertina wire."

"A few bodyguards, of course, but he is very social. It's my guess that Pamela Churchill knows him. If not, she can get you an introduction."

"Perhaps."

"Here is our Kissinger book." Portland produced a thick, blue notebook from the end table beside him. "You'll find it interesting reading; he is a very unusual person. On the one hand he is brilliant, a genius in international affairs. But you'll read what his former wife has to say about him, too. As a personality he is something of a mess. He is seen socially with young and beautiful actresses. It is as if he is publicly trying to validate his manhood." Portland smiled and shrugged. "An alienist was engaged to prepare an analysis which you will find in there. He suggests that Dr Kissinger may be suffering from a personality disorder."

"And what shall I do with that, sir? Shall I be the mother he never had?"

"No, he had quite a loving mother, you know. But perhaps he needs a friend?"

"A friend! A mature friend, as you say. It sounds unlikely. But I'll get on over there and see."

"Please do not contact our embassy, Rigby. Lord Cromer and his people are thought to be friendly with Kissinger, and someone might slip."

Rigby nodded, gathered the blue notebook, the Thompson dossier and her handbag. "I shall leave on Friday," she said. "That will give me the weekend to renew my recollections of Washington."

When Rigby checked into the Alban Towers, her usual hotel in Washington, she was handed a cable. After unpacking and carefully examining her room for listening devices, she sat at the little desk to read it. From her handbag she took a small missal and a magnifying glass. Quickly she decoded the wire, turning from page to page in the High Church Mass to find the needed equivalents. The message, from Portland, read: "Our insider says K. is reluctantly seeking a discreet and safe psychiatrist for consultation. Daniels en route to assist, carrying your licence, diplomas, *indicia* of qualifications as psychiatrist." She smiled. Doctor Rigby, at your service, she mused. Not half bad.

When one looks at the front of the two adjoining houses which comprise the Harriman mansion on N Street Northwest, in the Georgetown section of Washington, D.C., they appear to be tall and modest brick colonials. But a glance from the side shows them to be as wide and deep as airplane hangars. The capacious Harriman rooms were richly furnished in the colonial style, accented with paintings by great masters. In the room to which she was escorted by a butler Rigby identified a Van Gogh, two Renoirs and a small Cassatt. The wait was no more than three minutes. Then, without announcement, Pamela Digby Churchill Hayward Harriman appeared in a white sweater and brown tweed skirt, smiling, her hand outstretched.

She had changed, Rigby realised. At school she had been a country maid, tweedy, a horse lover, unworldly. Since then she had been old Winston Churchill's confidante, the companion of Edward R. Murrow, Elie de Rothschild, Jock Whitney, Gianni Agnelli and Ali Khan. Her husbands were also men of the world. Now she shone with a cultured patina, rather ageless, at home in a room hung with great and expensive paintings, comfortable with priceless antique furniture.

"Digby!"

"Rigby!"

"It really is you! It's been thirty years, hasn't it? You look marvellous."

"I was so pleased that you thought to call me. I have lost track of everyone from school. Will you have tea?"

This was no mere school chum, Rigby thought. Panto Digby was now a genuine social doyenne, endowed by her rich and aged husband with a seat of power and comfort from which to meet the world. She appeared to have no unmet needs. Her firm body had an aura of muliebrity. Her face lines were graceful, even beautiful. How did one recruit for the Services a bright and independent woman who lacked fears or desires?

Pamela Harriman poured tea and talked about her new husband and old lover with animation.

Rigby saw her opening when Pamela mentioned "the P.M."

"You did service for him, I know. I've read your dossier."

"Dossier?"

"Dossier. You know I am with the Intelligence Services, don't you?"

"Someone told me that. I'll just close that door so we won't be disturbed."

"Good idea, Panto."

Mrs Harriman walked quickly to the white double doors, drew them closed and snapped a brass lever into place to lock them. "What did you read?" she asked as she returned to the flowered couch.

"That you were a very efficient conduit for all kinds of information. I was surprised at how successful you had been with the reporter, Edward Murrow. He really did know so much of what was going on, didn't he?"

"Hmmm," Pamela replied noncommittally. "I had no official role, you know."

"I know. I think that made you ever so much more effective, Panto. You were better than some of our best commissioned agents. Even when you went to Paris after the war, you were marvellous."

At the mention of Paris, Pamela Harriman's cordiality seemed to disappear. The smile became a hard mouth. "What do you – what does Portland – want?" she asked levelly. "I doubt that I am available."

"Actually, I need just a very small bit of help, dear. I should be ever so grateful if you would tell me about dear Dr Kissinger and arrange for me to become acquainted with him. That is not so very difficult, now is it?"

"I really know him only slightly, Rigby. My late husband, Leland, had him to a party, I believe. Of course Ave knows him, but he doesn't care for Kissinger at all."

"I'm sure. But perhaps he'd come if your husband invited him to a little party?"

"He'd come, I have no doubt. Do you have a message for him?"

"No. As a matter of fact, I'd like you to introduce me to everyone – including your husband – as Dr Mary Whitechurch. I am a rather well-established psychiatrist who practises in the West End, you see, and I am here to lecture for a month at Johns Hopkins University. Would it be convenient for me to be seated next to Dr Kissinger at lunch or dinner?"

Pamela Harriman's eyebrows had elevated slowly, rising with each new part of Rigby's scenario. "My God, Rigby, what do you intend to do to Kissinger?"

"Just listen, my dear. No harm will befall him, I assure you. I intend to become his friend and confidante, and that is all."

"I must speak to Ave about you. I'm new in this house, you understand, and I must be circumspect. The Governor is surrounded by staff and family who would have every right to resent me if I moved – if I were not sensitive to their relationships with the Governor. But I'll speak to him, and there will be a little luncheon for Dr Whitechurch and Dr Kissinger. But then there must be nothing more; in my new situation I can do no more for the Services, or Portland, or you. That must be understood. Before long I intend to become a United States citizen."

"Oh? Very nice, I'm sure, Panto. Don't you have to study a great deal for an exam?"

Henry Kissinger accepted Pamela Harriman's invitation to Saturday luncheon for reasons of State. The Federal Bureau of Investigation had recently reported that Averell Harriman had begun seeing the Soviet ambassador again, after a hiatus of nearly a year. Before he was widowed, Harriman had frequent lunch meetings with Anatoly Dobrynin. But with the death of his wife, Marie, Harriman withdrew from public affairs, moved to the seashore and vegetated.

Harriman had developed deep ties with the Soviet hierarchy during the Second World War when he administered lend-lease and other aid programmes. For years he was an unofficial conduit between the Soviets and various Democrat presidents. Although Kissinger considered his relations with Dobrynin to be good, he had become deeply curious about Harriman's new role in the complex relations between the United States and the Soviet Union.

And so Dr Kissinger was disappointed to discover, upon his arrival at the N Street mansion, that Governor Harriman was having one of his 'bad days' and would not be joining the luncheon party. Pamela Harriman introduced the President's national security advisor to the other two guests while a white-jacketed butler passed drinks.

The man was a young playwright from California whose first successful play was in try-outs at the National Theater in Washington. Kissinger had a vague recollection of reading about the play in the *Washington Post*, but had no interest in the man or his play. The other guest was a middle-aged English woman from London who engaged in psychiatry. Kissinger was told that Dr Whitechurch had been invited to lecture at Johns Hopkins Medical School, and that fact informed him that she was competent and of good reputation.

The guests paired off because it was evident that the Californian had been a protégé and client of Pamela Harriman's late husband, Leland Hayward, an agent and producer. She drew the young man aside to talk about his play and his next work in progress.

It seemed fortuitous that a psychiatrist from another place

should be delivered to Dr Kissinger's hand at the very time when H. R. Haldeman was demanding that Kissinger seek psychiatric care. A few days before, after the morning senior staff meeting, Haldeman had delivered an ultimatum which – he claimed – came from the President.

"Henry," Haldeman had said, "please stay. I have something very important to tell you."

Kissinger sat back down at the conference table. Haldeman took several pages of handwritten notes from his desk and turned his chair to face Kissinger.

"The President asked me to have this talk with you. I think you'd better listen to the message I have to give you; then we can talk about it."

The demand was preceded by an explanation which Kissinger found to be insulting and invalid. With the President's best interests at heart, he had warned Nixon of the perfidy of his Secretary of State, William Rogers. His thanks was a non-negotiable admonition to get mental care. If conditions were somewhat different – if the China project and the Vietnam wind-down were farther along, and if the future course of his personal career could be better defined – Kissinger would have quit at once in disgust. But things were only beginning to jell. It would be a bad time to leave the White House just then. So he had agreed to see a private psychiatrist, against his desires and better judgment. Now here was this Englishwoman, not unattractive, competent and not involved in American politics. He found it humiliating that Nixon or Haldeman, or both, would suggest he had mental problems. It was degrading that they could compel him to seek care. He wanted no one to know.

"Are you seeing patients while you are in this country, Doctor?" Kissinger asked quietly, as lunch was being served.

"No, I haven't any patients here, you see."

"Could you see someone on a very confidential basis?"

"Oh, everything is very confidential, Doctor. Even whom I see. I never disclose the identity of a patient. Is it a friend?"

"I think I would like to come to talk with you, if you are available."

"Of course, Doctor. I have the use of a little office to which you might come."

Kissinger nodded. He hated everything about seeing a psychiatrist but this woman looked like someone he could trust.

"Al," Kissinger motioned his aide into his corner office at the White House. "I need a favour from the British Intelligence Services. Ask them to give us a dossier on a London psychiatrist named Dr Mary Whitechurch."

"Timing?" Al Haig asked.

"Urgent. I need something by tomorrow if possible. It's a woman I met at Harriman's."

"Right away," said Al Haig.

Rigby charged Daniels with the establishment of a credible psychiatrist's office in forty-eight hours. With his customary effectiveness, Daniels located a three-room suite in an old office building out on Massachusetts Avenue, not far from the Alban Towers. Beyond a very small reception room were two identical offices occupied by several Christian Science practitioners who shared the space on a temporal basis, so to speak. Daniels rented the offices furnished, for seven days, at a rental which enabled the good ladies to take a week's vacation from their healing pursuits.

Speedily he installed a rented couch and easy chair in the left-hand office and several cases of audio and video equipment in the other office. By Sunday evening the portraits of Mary Baker Eddy were gone, the telephones had been disconnected and a high resolution camera was invisibly installed to film through a tiny hole in the wall between the offices.

After her Sunday dinner, Rigby inspected Dr Whitechurch's temporary office and tried out her easy chair beside the commodious couch.

"I think this will do very well, Daniels," she declared, swivelling from side to side. "He's coming tomorrow evening – after dark – and we seem well prepared to offer him the care he requires. Now, I must go to The Towers. I have several books on psychiatric practice I wish to read before tomorrow night. I trust your equipment works silently?"

"It's very quiet, Rigby, and I'll operate it myself. I intend to arrive mid-afternoon tomorrow."

"Excellent. I'll be here at six p.m. Our patient is due at

eight. Now I must go and purchase a notepad and a small clock. Mustn't keep the patient overtime, must we?"

Henry Kissinger rarely rode in taxicabs. But he suspected that H. R. Haldeman's assistant, Larry Higby, reviewed all of the trip logs for the White House limousines, and he wanted no one to know where, and when, he had gone that evening. Once, a few months before, Kissinger had spent an evening with a young film actress who had been introduced to him by a Paramount producer, and two days later the whole White House staff knew all about it. Only the President would know of the visit to this psychiatrist, Kissinger resolved.

The taxi left Dr Kissinger at the corner of Massachusetts Avenue and Bell Lane, a half-block from the address Dr Whitechurch had given him. As he stood alone on the darkening corner the professor debated again the wisdom of this errand. If he did not visit this mind doctor, Nixon would surely discharge him; of that Kissinger had become convinced when he tried to get Nixon to corroborate Haldeman's demands. The President had silenced him curtly. "I'm sorry, Henry, but Bob has said everything there is to say. It's an ultimatum. It has to be that way, for the sake of everyone's sanity, including the President's. It's final."

But psychiatry meant countless hours of treatment. And if word got out that he was seeing a shrink, Kissinger knew, he was finished at the White House. The Press would destroy him. It was entirely possible that Haldeman and the others would leak it just to get rid of him. The bastards were devious.

He was doomed either way, and he was totally at the mercy of Richard Nixon's whim. If only he were in a position to resign right now! But if he quit they would leak that they had fired him because he had mental problems. All the choices were impossibly bad.

He determined to try this Dr Whitechurch, deferring all final decisions until after the initial session. As he opened the office door he heard a buzzer behind the closed door of an inner room. In a moment Rigby opened it and greeted him warmly.

For a few minutes they sat at the desk while Rigby-Whitechurch explained her method of consultation and gentled the professor out of his jacket and striped necktie. Henry Kissinger found Dr Whitechurch's manner to be professional but, at the same time, soothing and reassuring. She again guaranteed that the very fact of his seeing her, along with whatever might be said, would be totally confidential. Kissinger was relaxed and assured as he moved to the doctor's couch and stretched out.

"Would you be more comfortable with your shoes off?" she asked.

"No, my feet get chilled easily," he rumbled.

"Very well; it is entirely your choice. I would like you to begin by telling me what you remember of your childhood in Fürth."

Kissinger smiled. "You have read my biography in *Who's Who*?"

"I confess I have. Just tell me what best you can recall."

Kissinger talked at length about his early life in Nazi Germany, with Rigby's occasional interjection. After a few minutes Kissinger's voice began to rasp.

"Are you thirsty?" she asked. "There's water on the table."

Kissinger raised himself, half turned, reached for the tall glass and drank deeply. "Terrible tasting water Washington has," he said, lying back on the couch.

"Tell me about your family, please. What kind of man was your father?"

"He is still alive," Kissinger began, "and both my brother and I are . . ."

Kissinger felt very tired. It was impossible for him to keep his eyes open. He intended to tell the doctor about his admiration for his father but it seemed a good idea to rest, perhaps to sleep a little while before going on with his narration. He would do a much better job if he were refreshed.

When Kissinger's eyes closed, Rigby leaned forward and spoke urgently into his left ear. "Before you tell me about your father, Henry, I will ask you some other questions. When you have answered them I will once again ask you about your father. You will answer me, but you will remember neither my other questions nor your answers. Do you understand?"

"Yes," Kissinger mumbled.

"Have you ever been to Hong Kong?"

"Yes."

"Recently?"

"Passing through."

"Did you send Matthew Thompson there?"

After a long pause, Kissinger said "No" rather loudly.

"What was he doing there?"

"I don't know."

"He works for you?"

"Yes. Supposedly. He is working for others against me, I think."

"Do you think the President sent him?"

"Yes, the bastard."

"Is the President playing a double game?"

"Probably."

"Will he give away Hong Kong?"

"No, that's not it."

"What's the game?"

"China."

"He is negotiating with China?"

"He will."

"About Hong Kong?"

"No. Maybe. About everything."

Rigby scratched her head and shrugged. She looked towards the hole in the wall and the camera she knew to be hidden there.

"What does he want from China?" she continued.

"Alliance," Kissinger slurred.

"Against Russia?"

"Yes."

"Will he have it soon?" Rigby pressed.

"Probably." Kissinger stirred restlessly on the couch.

Rigby feared the effect of Portland's drug was waning. She decided to bring her patient back before he recovered on his own. One could never rely on British pharmaceuticals since the advent of the National Health Service, she reflected.

"Was your father kind to you?" Dr Whitechurch asked.

"Yes; he gave me a little carved bear and he gave my brother a pencil. I love him."

"Of course you do, Henry. Is your father kind to your mother?"

"He is sometimes angry with her and that makes me cry in my bed at night, but she comes to me and kisses me."

"Open your eyes, please, Doctor. You had a little nap, which is not unusual. Patients of mine occasionally doze off, and I take that as a compliment. It shows that they are comfortable with me. You are, aren't you?"

Kissinger nodded. It had been a deep and nurturing sleep and he did feel very much at ease with this doctor in the long, white jacket.

"I'm afraid our time has quite flown away," she said. "Shall we talk about the future?"

"Yes," Kissinger said. He swung his feet off the couch and pulled at his shirt cuffs. "Can I see you again?" he asked. His throat seemed congested.

"I'm afraid not, Henry," Rigby said sadly. "I should so much like to help you, but I must return home sooner than I had expected. A patient of mine – a very prominent person at home – has experienced some quite severe difficulties. I have a professional responsibility to him, you understand."

"Of course."

"But I do think you should find a local person to see. I think perhaps therapy is indicated, and you should be with someone who can see you regularly, on into the future."

"I see."

"Will you do that? Would you like me to find you someone?"

"Perhaps I can let you know?"

"I will be at the Alban Towers until Wednesday morning. Please call me."

"Yes. I would like to pay you."

"Oh, my, no. It has been a privilege to see such a distinguished statesman. This hour has been my contribution to world peace, let us say."

Kissinger tied his necktie and shrugged into his blue blazer. "Dr Whitechurch, may I call upon you when I am in London?" he smiled.

It's probably that transference syndrome I read about, Rigby thought to herself. "Of course, Dr Kissinger. I shall just jot down my private number here." She wrote and handed him a slip of paper. "It would be jolly good fun to see you socially in my own city. Do call if you can."

Rigby moved Kissinger gently towards the door. "Are you feeling quite all right, Henry?"

"Yes, in fact I feel very rested and relaxed."

"Oh, I am so glad. Well, goodbye, then."

"Yes, goodbye and thank you," Kissinger said.

When the door closed Rigby went to the little desk and wrote:

> Portland.
>
> It is China and the U.S. in a rapprochement. HKong is only incidental. If Henry calls Dr Whitechurch at 247-3911 cover for her. It is spring and we're in love.
>
> Rigby.

Daniels poked his head in the door and looked around. "All clear," he said. "Your patient caught a passing cab out front and sped away."

"Did the recorders work?"

"Perfectly. I say, that potion does the job, doesn't it? He had no idea."

Miss Rigby nodded. "The Americans monitor all overseas calls and cables, so I want you to get this note and your recordings into tonight's diplomatic pouch at the embassy. I have a few thank-you notes to write, then I shall be disappearing."

"Right," said Daniels. "I'll have all the equipment out of here in an hour."

"No. Send the recordings and note now. Clear out after."

"Very well. Goodnight, Dr Whitechurch."

"I was prepared for Dr Whitechurch to vanish," Rigby said, "but it may be that she has attracted a swain. Now, she will just have to stay in my closet until the telephone rings. Who knows? Perhaps some evening it will be kidneys with Kissinger in the Strand. Wouldn't that be jolly?"

"Not my choice," Daniels said gruffly.

"Oh, it will be all in the line of duty, of course. Henry is sweet, but so Teutonic. He is really not my type, I am afraid. Hurry along now, Daniels; we mustn't keep Portland waiting for the news, must we? Imagine Richard Nixon dealing with Communist China! Whatever will he do next?"

Rigby said that Henry Kissinger did make several subsequent efforts to contact 'Dr Whitechurch' and even sent a dozen red roses from Moyses Stevens. But kidneys in the Strand with the good Doctor never quite materialised. "Shame in a way," said Rigby, "but in our business one should never push one's luck."

Minette Marrin

A MAN OF GOD

Rigby was never, even in childhood, really Christian. Vestigial traces of religion attached themselves – she was fond of her mother's friend, old Father Keen, the Jesuit; she also loved the language of *The Book of Common Prayer*, the Authorised Version of the Bible, and *Hymns Ancient and Modern*. She could never resist a village church at Evensong and, on slack London days, she could sometimes be found at the back of the Brompton Oratory absorbing the Mass and the incense. But Christian – no.

One day I found myself on a train to Bristol with Minette Marrin, a freelance journalist whose first novel had just been published, and who was to be my fellow guest on a radio chat show. Our conversation soon turned to 'work in progress' and I told her about Rigby.

She frowned. "Rigby?" she said, "not Dorothy Rigby?"

It transpired that Minette had worked for B.B.C. Television's Religious Programmes in the late Seventies and early Eighties. While she was there Dorothy Rigby, or a woman very much like her, suddenly appeared in the department on some sort of special secondment and struck up an odd relationship with a musty old Anglican divine called the Reverend Gavin Sopwith. The friendship had always intrigued Minette. The pair had seemed to have so little in common and yet for a time they were so close. She knew where Gavin Sopwith was living. Would I like her to investigate? Naturally I agreed.

Months later, when I had almost forgotten this casual commission, my doorbell rang and a rather breathless Minette was standing there, clutching a nineteen-page typescript. Against all the odds she had managed to get the Reverend Gavin Sopwith to spill the beans. And this was his story.

I had the privilege of knowing Dorothy Rigby during the summer and the beautiful early autumn of 1978 and was, by some curious dispensation of Providence, a first-hand observer, indeed a collaborator, in a remarkable episode in her life. H.M.G. and the Broadcasting Corporation may have succeeded in 'hushing up' the more sensational aspects of the incident, as far as Rigby's participation went, but its long-term international repercussions are well outside their control and have yet to be felt. As for my own uncharacteristic conduct, I feel I have little with which to reproach myself, but my prayers have offered me scant reassurance that my fascination with Dorothy Rigby was based simply upon our shared devotion to Queen and country.

I realised that Miss Rigby was not quite an ordinary recruit to Religious Programmes when she pulled a gun on me, as I believe they say in detective fiction. Passions do run high in television, and even sometimes in religion, but it is not every day that a man of the cloth finds himself looking into the barrel of a pearl-handled miniature revolver. I should say, by way of preamble, which those who know the Television Centre will appreciate, that the architecture lends itself to confusion; among those labyrinthine circular passages it is easy to believe one is on the fifth floor when one is on the identical third, or to mistake one grey door for another. My colleagues, in the past, have unkindly said that I have exploited this fact to creep up on them unawares. Be that as it may, I did unwittingly open Miss Rigby's door, quietly and without knocking, expecting to find Scenic Ops.

Instead, to my surprise, I saw a tall and elegant figure with her back to me, framed in silhouette against a bright window. In the circumstances I followed my lifetime's habit of making a little scratching noise on the door, rather in the manner of Versailles, a sound which can warn without alarming. Ill judged! With astonishing speed, the creature whipped round to face me with a little pistol half hidden under her Filofax. I

was later to learn that Rigby's crocodile skin Filofax was
actually a holster, with ring binders which had been specially
adapted – not a use to which that ingenious little accessory
has often been put, I imagine. But I digress.

Above the little gun were the face and shoulders of an
elegant, hard-eyed woman of about forty-five. She signalled
me into the room, turning slightly as she did so, and when the
light fell full on her face I could see she was actually very
nearly sixty. She had the kind of understated beauty which
carries a face rather gallantly through the ravages of time,
and either her skin or the woman herself retained a kind of
luminosity. But despite all the ambiguous traces of youth, she
was unmistakably approaching old age. I have never seen a
lovelier woman.

I recognised her then, of course, from departmental meetings.
She must at that time have been with us for at least a month
as an Interdenominational Programme Consultant: one, I had
imagined, of a long line of otherwise unemployable people (not
entirely unlike myself) upon whom someone in the religious
establishment had taken pity, and given a job title (if not a
job) in the protected territory of religious broadcasting. Her
unimpressive status had led me to imagine, in short, that she
had somehow been put out to grass. How wrong I was! Rigby
will die in harness, to continue the metaphor, and splendidly.

I asked her, in the mildest tones, to put away her weapon.
Something about my manner (as I have all too often had
occasion to realise) caused her to smile slightly and she
snapped the thing up in its crocodile skin case and invited me
to sit down.

"Forgive me," she said coolly. "Old habits die hard. I once
worked for the Government, long ago, and I've been a little
nervous recently. That sound reminded me of something. I
am so sorry."

"My dear," I began, overcome by the quality of her voice.
"I ask no explanations. I am a man of the cloth, a member of
the Anglican Communion. I can assure you, you have nothing
to fear from me. Render unto Caesar, I say. Whatever it may
be, my dear Miss Rigby, your secret is safe with me."

I could see that she believed me. It is perhaps one of God's
little booby prizes for losing in so many of life's other races,

that people always do believe me. And since I had innocently broken Rigby's cover, I became a confidant, a fellow conspirator as it later seemed, a humble Sancho Panza to her Doña Quixote. What windmills we tilted at, to establish her cover! What curious little episodes we lived through in those few weeks! And what a strange and sad ending there was to it all.

She began by admitting that she still did work for the Government – a very apt euphemism, I have always felt. She told me that a number of her superiors were concerned about the political flavour of broadcasting – secret security checks on staff had revealed some alarming facts – and that she had been sent to investigate leftist bias and subversion in the Corporation.

"Not my most inspiring brief, perhaps, but at my age it's nice to be asked at all."

"And not a moment too soon," I replied, with feeling. "But Religious Programmes is hardly the epicentre of television affairs. Surely what you are looking for exists much more in News and General Features, than in our humble little outpost?"

Rigby looked at me rather sharply then.

"You are right, of course, my dear Sopwith, but it is so much easier to establish oneself here and go unnoticed." At this she gave me the first of those unforgettable, conspiratorial smiles.

She had a way, perhaps slightly too facile in retrospect, of suggesting that you and she alone shared a private understanding of the world. It appeared in her slightest mannerisms; she instinctively called me Sopwith, seeming to know that I have always hated the alacrity with which people here resort to Christian names; while I am now used to being called Gavin by one and all, I draw the line at Gavvers.

"Frightfully vulgar," Rigby would say, in private. In public she was different.

"Call me Dottie," she would say disingenuously to her patronising young colleagues. I can see her now, queuing in the canteen on the third floor.

"Call me Dottie."

Dottie? My Doña Dorothea? Hardly. But I cannot deny that she did take on, in the most disturbing way, the persona of the foolish female with which the Church is all too often afflicted.

* * *

Rigby's masters had arranged for her to begin on *Paeans of Praise* as a consultant and trainee producer; I therefore talked to her quite openly, in my work as peripatetic technical advisor, a teaching and counselling role which signals all too often a desire on the part of management to deny any role at all, without the will actually to sever the bond. We met regularly, and it was I who guided her first steps in television research and outside broadcasts. She showed a natural aptitude for it all, as she did, I believe, for everything she undertook.

As late spring wore on into early summer, Rigby toured the country for *Paeans of Praise*; she went questing to Southend, Scunthorpe, Giggleswick and Burton Bradstock, hither and yon, seeking out the faithful and their favourite hymns. Every Sunday the fruits of her labours would be broadcast: 'Breathe on Me, Breath of God' from the church warden at Ryme Intrinseca; 'Fight the Good Fight' from a widow at Derwent Water. I think Rigby loved it in her discreet, agnostic way; born an Anglican, always an Anglican, as my Uncle Cecil rightly said. But I digress.

Rigby picked out some very different congregations too. I well remember her coming back wearily from a black charismatic service in the centre of Birmingham, pale and pulling off her rather too stylish Burberry.

"People who really believe in God are so exhausting," she said. "Not like you, my dear."

I readily forgave her the little cruelty.

"I'm absolutely sick of people praying for my conversion. How many times have I got to be born again? Today I spent three hours on my knees, or even prostrate, while several hundred people prayed for me to find the Lord; quite a few of them went into convulsions. Can you imagine how I felt when they asked me to confess my sins? I think I must have broken all the commandments except for coveting my neighbour's wife, but I'm quite sure they wouldn't have believed me. And as for the dancing in the Lord! Well, I'm a little too old. I'm beginning to think this is a hardship posting."

The thought of Rigby, with her impeccably cut skirt and elegant legs, lying on the floor of some musty church hall, feigning convulsions and shouting Halleluia, was not one that should linger in the mind of a celibate elderly clergyman. I advised her to stick to the established faiths, and she did seem to choose less demanding congregations after that. Sometimes I went with her, taking care to introduce her to all the Corporation staff who might possibly be of use. It is surprising what one can learn from gaffers, riggers and sparks.

However, much though I enjoyed the occasional long afternoon with her, in a darkened Outside Broadcast van, parked outside some obscure provincial church, teaching her the mysteries of O.B. direction, I felt that she was too much at the periphery of things televisual.

"How can you really discover the political temperature at Television Centre, my dear Rigby, if you're always somewhere else?"

"Always the question pertinent, *hein*, my dear Sopwith?" She replied in a Hercule Poirot accent, teasing.

"Tell me, my dear, if I may ask, have you come to any conclusions about left wing bias?" I had manfully tried to remain silent about my own opinions of the vulgarians who rule the airwaves, but I suspect she knew my views.

"Well," she said, "I see stupidity, ignorance and wilful optimism, with a complete innocence about the rules of evidence, but little sign of anything more sinister; it is the right that must be watched, and particularly in religious matters, oddly enough. If there is anything sinister, it is there."

To my surprise I began to see more and more evidence that Rigby was particularly interested in Catholics. More than once I heard her talking to our splendid reference library about matters Roman and frequently on her desk I saw, without prying, Catholic directories and newspapers. At last, discretion defeated by my curiosity, and, I confess, the rooted anti-Papism of generations of Sopwiths, I challenged her.

"How is it that you are giving so much of your attention to the Whore of Babylon and obscure Italian banks? What are these piles of Vatican newsletters? These lengthy conversations with Father This and Monsignor That and the mysterious Camilla in Rome?"

She looked at me gravely. "One cannot get much past you, my friend," she said. "Very well. Come with me."

She led me out of the office, into the lift and out into the small, neglected park behind the canteen building.

"My dear, is this necessary? I am sure our office is quite obscure enough to be safe from surveillance."

For a moment I thought she might be going to take offence and it occurred to me briefly that I had paid her the discourtesy of underestimating her, of taking her at her own modest evaluation and of hinting that the world would be as uninterested in her as it has patently been in me. The slightest touch of temperament in a female has always terrified me; I was greatly relieved to see the expression disappear and to hear her say absently, "Habit, Sopwith, habit. Now listen," she went on intently. "There is a great deal I cannot tell you. Some of it's speculation anyway. But the point is you are right. I am interested in Catholicism."

"Ah," I said, enlightened at once. "You mean liberation theology, red priests in Latin America, rabble rousing in the barrios and all that. Destabilisation," I said, warming to my theme.

"No," she said, looking at me with something like pity. "Not that. Though it has something, distantly, to do with the teeming masses, perhaps. There are things I must know about the Church."

"I take it you mean the Church of Rome?" I said, rather stiffly.

"Yes," she said, and with her unfailing delicacy she smiled slightly at me. "The Whore of Babylon and her scarlet vestments."

"You already know more than I ever shall," I said, mollified. "How could I possibly help?"

"My dear Sancho Sopwith, you are indispensable to me. You have established my cover, you have been on jaunts with me, you are my eyes and ears and you know what programmes are being planned. I cannot do without you. This is what I want. I want a way into the Vatican."

"Impossible," I said immediately.

"You can do it," she said. "You must."

(In retrospect I came to know that she had wanted that all along, and that she had made a convenience of me. At the time my vanity was flattered by the thought that Dorothy Rigby believed I could help her achieve her ends, and had chosen me from among the finger-snapping optimists and youthful cliché-mongers to serve both Queen and country, unashamed of our unfashionable patriotism. I realised, too, that I was only one of a number of people she could have manipulated with equal success. Still, she knew she had my total loyalty from the first. I like to think of that.)

Gossiping with producers and directors in the department, in my unobtrusive way, I soon learned that there were no plans to make any programmes on Catholicism, as I reported back to Rigby.

"I'm afraid no one's interested in the Whore of Babylon at the moment, my dear. It's all inner cities and ecumenism."

How wrong I was. Rigby had a curious affinity with coincidence and, strangely enough, within only a few days came the news that Pope Paul VI was seriously ill. In a few more he was dead, and we in Religious Programmes had, for once, the luxury of a real ongoing news story, as my colleagues said.

The death of the Pope and all the excitement leading up towards the election of a new one provided us with a golden opportunity to storm the Vatican. The department was in a frenzy of excitement. Pope programme proposals fluttered about like confetti. In the twenty days that intervened before the somewhat surprising election of John Paul, no decisions were made, but Rigby worked almost fanatically on her files of matters Vatican. Finally our masters decided on a film profile of the new Pope.

The lucky producer was Ruggiero Hickman, an atheistical Baptist, chosen all too typically by the department for his command of Italian, of which, despite his name, he spoke not a word. (I was informed by Kevin in Accounts that Hickman owed his Christian name to his mother's preoccupation, during her pregnancy, with the works of Mazo de la Roche.) My Doña Dorothea, of course, spoke exquisite Italian, with an enchanting hint of Florentine, which immediately, through my intercessions, earned her a place on the little team.

Rigby was out a lot at this time, but she continued to work fanatically and filled her little office with ever more impressive quantities of books, news cuttings, directories and publications which seemed a very long way from the subject in hand.

"What on earth can you need with the annual reports of all these Italian banks, with their heavenly names – the Banca Cattolica del Veneto, the Banco Ambrosiano?" I playfully asked.

"You speak Italian, Sopwith?" she said sharply. (Modesty had prevented my mentioning the fact before; I am of the old school that waits to be asked.)

"I should have known. Come with me. You must arrange it in your inimitable style, and inveigle your way on to the Pope bandwagon and, incidentally . . ." She pointed at the bank reports and put a forefinger to her lips.

The following day, at about seven on a warm August evening, she paid me the very great compliment of inviting me to her home after work. We took a taxi to one of those austere red brick edifices on Marylebone High Street: it seemed a shame on such a glorious evening to be somewhere so breathless and urban; I had more than once pictured Dorothy Rigby in my mind's eye as an honoured guest, some summer evening, in the garden of my flatlet in Ealing. But it was not to be.

Rigby's flat on the top floor was like herself, elegant and understated. It revealed as little about her as she did herself. One felt instantly at home there and yet it was, I regretfully observed, the flat of a celibate: like my own home, it lacked any evidence of the living disorder of, how shall I put it, a more fruitful life. For this reason it was particularly congenial to me, of course. Installed in an extremely fine Victorian wing chair, next, I was amused to see, to a very interesting collection of Victorian novels, I was given without choice a glass of Pinot Grigio. We watched the sunset over the busy Westway, through the French windows at the back of the flat, and for a moment I was touched by a complex little fit of melancholy in contemplating my gifted friend.

"We might at least have got a more interesting Pope," I remarked cheerfully, rousing myself.

"Ah no, Sopwith. I think you're wrong. This one is a remarkable man."

"Well, even the Vatican Press Office don't really seem to

think so. Compromise choice. Sweet old boy, son of a peasant. Not too bright and so forth."

"Yes. I wonder why. In fact he is exceptionally intelligent and rather radical."

"Well how was it that he supported Pope Paul ten years ago on that dreadful nonsense over birth control? Humanae Vitae was quite the wickedest act of the Catholic Church in history. When one thinks of the misery, the destitution."

"Yes, yes," Rigby dismissed my remarks a trifle impatiently, and refilled my glass. "But with this man nothing is the way it seems. The Vatican P.R. image is one thing. Actually, he doesn't support Humanae Vitae at all. He's even talking to a delegation of American Congressmen, to discuss the merits of birth control."

"I shouldn't think the Vatican old guard is very keen on that."

"It hasn't happened yet," said Rigby. "It's for October."

It occurs to me now to wonder what astonishing sources of information she must have had, to know such a thing. At the time I scarcely noticed that this was a remarkable new direction – a "story", as the Pope team would say. In the event, of course, it never happened and we have a very different Pope.

Rigby sat musing, her delicate features sharpened by the remains of the sunlight. Suddenly she turned to me.

"I fear for him," she said. "I fear for him. He has the misfortune to be a good man, like you, my poor dear Sopwith."

"To be good," I replied, in all humility, I hope, "is not necessarily to be weak."

"No, but it is to be very vulnerable," she said, and she gave the sort of look whose compassion and sweetness have remained with me long after I have forgotten what must be called, I now see, her ruthlessness and her deviousness.

"And very exposed," she said.

"I should have thought any Pope, immured in the Vatican City, was as safe as houses."

Rigby ignored this.

"What do you know about Vatican finances, the Vatican Bank?" she asked abruptly.

I told her that I knew nothing, apart from the fact that there had always been some whiff of scandal about the Church's untold wealth. Rigby proceeded to enlighten me and I must say I have never heard a stranger or more shocking tale, or one that tested the credulity so far, scattered as it was with Hollywood personalities called the Shark, the Gorilla and the Puppet Master. It was an elaborate story, stretching from Rome to Chicago, from Switzerland to South America and back to Milan, made up of puzzling fragments; here the collapse of an Italian banking empire, there an F.B.I. investigation into counterfeit bonds on their way to the Vatican, somewhere else the murder of an Italian Government investigator. It was a vision of the Princes of the Church corrupted by greed and obsessed with usury (for what else can one call it?), and of an awesome web, enmeshing both prelates and bankers, spun from the entrails of a notorious Masonic Lodge.

It occurred to me to wonder whether my Doña Dorothea had spent too long in the worlds of secrets and conspiracies, and her mind had been in some sort corrupted, but she was, alas, only too precise in her fantastical allegations. At the time, I confess, I scarcely believed her. In fact the truth of these matters has yet to emerge, ten years later; the Vatican has taken no steps to clear the Church's name of the shameful charges laid at its gates.

"It was this," she admitted, "that I came into the department, in June, to investigate."

"*Paeans of Praise* and leftist subversion were just a little *divertissement*, then?"

"But highly enjoyable," she said. "You see, in April this year the pace started to quicken; the Bank of Italy started a secret investigation into the Banco Ambrosiano and Roberto Calvi. In May an order was made to extradite the financier Michele Sindona from the United States to face fraud charges in Italy. Our American cousins asked us for any help we could offer: hence my appearance in Religious Programmes."

I shrugged slightly.

"You understimate the value of the Corporation as a power base. As a way of obtaining information and contacts it is the envy of the entire world."

"It hasn't struck me that way," I said stiffly.

"In my father's house there are many mansions," she said kindly. "You see, in the past few weeks I have been able to talk to anyone, literally anyone in the religious establishment, as a harmless searcher after truth."

"Call me Dottie," I interrupted, understanding.

"To anyone in the secular world I have appeared even less alarming and memorable, if possible. It has been time well spent. And one of the most important things I have learned is that on the day after his election, on Sunday the 27th, Pope John Paul ordered his Secretary of State to review all the Vatican's finances."

"About time too," I said stoutly, but Rigby looked grave.

In the first few days of September, before we went to Rome, Rigby occasionally pointed out things to me, quietly in the office. I remember a clipping from *Il Mondo*, supplied by our excellent international cuttings service, openly protesting about the 'Wealth of Peter', and somewhat later a list in an organ called *L'Osservatore Politico* of all the members of the Vatican who belonged to the Masonic Lodge P2. Someone – not Rigby or myself – even pointed it out to Ruggiero Hickman.

"What's wrong with this, Gavvers?" he demanded, innocent as he was of theology.

"A nodding acquaintance with Catholicism would reveal that Catholics are not allowed to be Masons. On pain of excommunication."

"Well, there's a thing," said Ruggiero cheerfully, "and all these Cardinals and Monsignors and Bishops on the list. I don't think we'll go into any of that. We'll stick to sweetness and light. Otherwise they might not want to give us the interview." The foolish man imagined that he would somehow succeed, where all others had failed, in getting a personal television interview with a Pope.

Irritatingly enough, through the good offices of the English College in Rome, there seemed some chance that the wretched fellow would prevail. Accordingly a small team including Hickman, Rigby and myself, as Advisory Executive Producer, flew to Rome towards the end of September. We were all fortunate enough to stay at the English College, except, of course, Rigby, who stayed with her friend Camilla in Trastevere; she was hardly needed in her capacity as translator and we saw little of her for a day or two.

It was for me, at the beginning anyway, my most delightful visit ever to the Eternal City. Hidden behind a splendid pair of late seventeenth-century gates, the English College is a haven of civilised tradition and intellectual life. I found the gracious guest apartments on the second floor and the quiet, but witty, conversation of those Vatican luminaries whose help we were seeking entirely to my liking. Even Ruggiero Hickman seemed to soften his manner and, through the good offices of one or other of our hosts, acquired, by some miracle, permission to film for the first time ever a personal, one-to-one interview. I suspect the good Fathers were impressed by his entire indifference to theological niceties and Vatican politics.

"What a coup, Gavvers!" he cried yet again, in satisfaction, as we sat with Rigby and her friend, Camilla, at a little bar in Trastevere. "It calls for a celebration." And with a fistful of *gettoni* he ambled off to the telephone to call up a party, consisting of some Rome friends of his and our own little team. Camilla offered us the use of her roof-top studio flat.

"Why not fancy dress?" she went on, seeming to catch the excitement.

"Great! Fantastic!" said Ruggiero, in the idiom of his kind. Indeed it was fantastic. The Fathers at the English College had an immense dressing-up chest, and kindly lent us various priestly garments. Naturally I felt myself unable to join in, but since Ruggiero was going as a Cardinal I felt the least I could do was to sport my dog collar. The camera crew were a motley collection of clerics, not entirely convincing, but Rigby in a nun's habit, which Camilla had somehow found, was breathtakingly authentic.

To this day I cannot remember which is the Order that wears plain black with a white wimple, but its dramatic simplicity was the perfect setting for the noble spirituality of Rigby's face. I was not alone in being touched by the spectacle, though I was alone, but for Camilla, in knowing what a mistress of appearances the dear creature was.

It was after many glasses of Chianti that balmy Roman evening that someone as a joke said 'Dottie' ought to come to the Pope interview at Castel Gandolfo in her nun's costume. I cannot for the life of me remember whose idea it was, but that was Rigby's skill. Disrespectful, ridiculous and unprofessional it may sound now, but then it seemed rather a delicious joke, a harmless little snook cocked at Peter's all too worldly throne.

So it was that I found myself, on Thursday September 28th, sitting next to a modest Sister Nicodemus in a hired mini-bus driving the crew down the old Appian Way to Castel Gandolfo. I noticed she had with her a little book in Italian called *Illustrissimi*, written by Albino Luciani long before he became Pope, and was reading something written on the flyleaf, but when I glanced at it she immediately closed the cover.

When we arrived we parked in the little square and sat at a café outside the gates, visited from time to time by officials from the Vatican Press Office who told us of regrettable delays or hopeful prospects. One of them politely asked about Rigby, who was unexpected. "This is Sister Nicodemus, Father, one of our Catholic advisors in Religious Programmes and our translator here in Rome. She very much hopes she may be permitted to be present at the interview with the Holy Father," said Hickman smoothly. Sister Nicodemus, with her worn face and downcast eyes, looked so confused and hopeful, primly sitting opposite a glass of mineral water, that it is really hardly surprising her request was granted.

At last we were led past the Swiss Guard, through the great doors into a huge courtyard, into a side door, along a passage, out of another side door and into the famous garden. It was surrounded by a low wall on all sides and over it one could see a quite lovely panorama of the lake below. The lawns were empty and silent except for the playing of the fountains. At intervals among the umbrella pines and cypresses one could just make out a security guard; otherwise the impression was of deepest privacy.

Then he came. He arrived alone, without any fuss, walking from one side of the building along the gravel path, but as soon as he appeared four of his aides hurried to his side – press secretaries, assistants, I forget their titles, but they were tirelessly vigilant. They had set up a couple of battered old garden chairs for the interview and he came towards them. Introductions were made.

Rigby knelt gracefully as she kissed his ring and, when he

spoke to her, answered him in her beautiful Italian. He asked her about the name Nicodemus and quoted in English:

> "Wise Nicodemus saw such light
> As made him know his God by night."

"That is why I chose it," said Rigby, surprised, almost in her own manner.

He was, I will be the first to admit, a man with a real air of holiness, and – most remarkable in Rome – little undue sense of ceremony.

"Who is going to do the interview?" he quietly asked Ruggiero in English; there was a little flurry among his aides to answer him, but Ruggiero spoke first.

"Well, Holy Father, I have suggested myself, since it is to be in English."

But Pope John Paul, modestly decrying his English, and touched no doubt by Sister Nicodemus' lambent face, asked if he might speak in Italian to her.

"After all," he pointed out quite correctly, with a smile, "we have all seen the questions."

So it was that Rigby and the Pope were seated opposite each other on rattan chairs, and deftly 'miked up' by the sound man with little microphones pinned to their vestments.

"It's very simple, Holy Father. What we would like is the interview, and then shots of you walking around the garden by yourself," said Ruggiero.

While this was being explained, Rigby grabbed my arm and pulled me down to her level.

"Listen carefully," she said urgently, fiddling with her mike and in the process disconnecting it. "Before the walking shot, make sure they take off his mike, make sure, and then afterwards get Hickman to do a very long two-shot of John Paul and me together. Make sure everyone clears the shot and there's no sound. In that order. Lose the sound. And suggest a book for the walking shot."

I nodded, filled with alarm.

"Just let the Holy Father take his own direction, Sister Nicodemus," I said, standing up. "The original questions are only a guide." The sound man rather irritably hurried up and connected her mike for her. "Please don't touch it," he said brusquely.

So they began, talking in Italian, with everyone straining to hear. It was an excellent interview, if somewhat conventional, and lasted about twenty minutes. When the cameraman unloaded for the second time, the black garbed officials intervened again and Pope John Paul did not protest.

This was my moment to follow my first undercover instructions. I turned to Hickman. (It may seem strange that someone so ineffectual as myself should have any influence over a sharp operator like Hickman, but he was, like many amoral people, completely unprejudiced and had no objection to taking technical advice from me.) It was easy. I got him to suggest that the Pope took a book with him in the walking shot – Sister Nicodemus immediately offered her little copy of *Illustrissimi* from under her robes. Ruggiero himself deferentially removed his mike and the sound man went aside to record some sound atmosphere.

"I think you'd be well advised to get a really long shot of his Holiness and Sister Nicodemus together," I then said to Ruggiero.

"But we'll be cutting her out of the interview. We won't need her."

"Well yes, in theory, but this gives you the option either way. You may find you want to use her. More importantly it would give you a sense of the garden, and it would make lovely wallpaper." By which I meant the all-purpose pretty shots that are always useful.

"Absolutely right, Gavvers," he said, and later on he set it up just as Rigby wanted.

The ubiquitous flock of aides found it very difficult to leave the Pope alone and actually walk out of shot, to a spot several hundred feet away in which they couldn't hear what was being said. They protested repeatedly, but as the Pope did not, there was little they could do. It was clever of Rigby, of course. How else could she have spoken to a Pope entirely on his own?

I shall never know for certain what she said to him, but it was on its own merits a lovely shot, none the worse for being a cliché – the simple nun and the Supreme Pontiff, he in plain white robes and she in deepest black, equal before God in the autumn light. There was something else too, some sort of touching affinity between them. It was as plain to the eye as to the lens, and they gave the impression, as they walked slowly beside the cypresses, that they were deep in a profound conversation. It lasted not quite five minutes.

As soon as Ruggiero cried "Cut!", the shot suddenly filled with officials and in a flurry of black skirts and hasty farewells the Pope was ushered away. We were guided more leisurely back to the minibus, parked all too prosaically in the real world outside.

"Well, Dottie?" asked Ruggiero as soon as we were out of the shadow of the Vatican. "How was it?"

"Wonderful," she said. "He was superb," but she looked absolutely exhausted. Even Hickman noticed and didn't press her for any details.

"We'll talk about it later," he said cheerfully. "Well done, Dottie. Fantastic."

Back in Rome he disappeared off somewhere leaving me to escort Rigby to the flat and then later on to the airport. While I waited for her to pack her bags, I noticed the Pope's little book. The writing in the fly leaf was in Rigby's bold handwriting, in Italian: *Holy Father, Please show no surprise when I speak to you alone. There is much to tell you. I implore you to trust me.* Perhaps I should not have read it, but it makes no difference now.

She came out of the bedroom with her neat suitcase and we went to a trattoria for a late lunch; Rigby hardly spoke, but would not tell me what was troubling her. She claimed she didn't know. We caught a late afternoon plane and I went to bed early, sleeping long and sound in my Ealing refuge.

At about eight-thirty the next morning, on Friday September 29th, Rigby telephoned, summoning me urgently to the cutting room. When I arrived the film editor was sitting about idly, drinking coffee, and chatting on the telephone.

Rigby took me into the corridor.

"I've just been talking to Film Operations. There's been some terrible, well, some terrible mistake. There's no sound. They've lost the sound."

"How do you mean?"

"That's what I want to ask you. How could they lose the sound?"

"Well," I said, "normal procedure is that the cameramen and the sound recordists guard their cans of film and tape religiously and take them personally to the airport and check them in as air freight; in this case they'd go straight from the plane to our Heathrow Shipping Office. Shipping would redirect the film cans to whichever laboratory we'd booked and send the sound tape to a transfer suite."

"What?" she asked impatiently.

"They'd send the sound tape to a special machine, here, to transfer the sound on to a sixteen-millimetre mag track which the film editor would use. Where was it lost?"

"I don't know," she said. "I can't understand the way they talk."

I rang Film Operations for her and she listened in on an extension.

"Yes, the sound has definitely been lost."

"Where was it lost?" I asked somewhat foolishly. "What does Shipping say?"

"Oh, we've got the quarter-inch tape here," the fellow said. "It's just that there's no sound on it. Technical fault possibly. The sound recordist's coming in now. If I had to guess, I'd say that those daft Italian buggers had wiped it by mistake in Rome. Anyway, Ruggiero Hickman's called a meeting. I shouldn't like to meet him in that mood."

Rigby made signs to me to come outside.

"Where's the safest place to talk?"

"Curiously enough," I said, "an unused recording studio," and I took her to a nearby drama studio, which was filled with empty soap opera sets.

"Tell me," she asked in great distress, "could it conceivably have been an accident?"

"It is quite possible," I said. "These things do happen."

"If it wasn't," she said, "it shows that someone is rather desperate."

"Well, what was on the sound tape?"

"It can't possibly have been the interview," she said, thinking aloud. "He was very careful, very diplomatic. No abrupt changes of direction, no startling announcements. I think they were afraid that what he and I said in private was being recorded."

"Well it wasn't," I said indignantly. "You specially told me."

"*You* know that," she said, "with your knowledge of filming, but would they?"

I thought back. Ruggiero had himself removed the Pope's mike when he was talking to John Paul about the walking shot. They might have missed that. And during Rigby's private conversation with the Pope, the sound man had been recording atmosphere; that's why he had kept his earphones on and had more than once asked us to be quiet. Perhaps they thought he was recording the conversation.

"They might have been uncertain," I agreed. "Wondering about directional mikes or other technical innovations. My dear, what did you say to him?"

"I told him his life was in danger," she said, reluctantly.

"What was his reply?"

"He didn't seem in the least surprised," she said. "He knows a great deal more than we ever imagined possible. Much too much for safety. And he intends to act."

There was little more to say. I pressed her hand and we went back to the cutting room.

We spent most of the morning withstanding Ruggiero's undirected fury, and our own misgivings. All we learnt of any importance was that the assistant cameraman had noticed one of the Vatican security men at the airport. Finally, after a few hours, rumours at last began to reach us. The Pope was dead. He had been in office just thirty-three days.

The powers that be in the Corporation did not immediately know that the obscure Ruggiero Hickman had somehow charmed the Vatican into an interview with the Pope; he had been keeping his scoop under wraps, as he characteristically put it. But the news of John Paul's death naturally sent reporters from the Newsroom scurrying round to our little enclave in Religious Programmes for 'situationers' and before long the shameful secret was out: we had filmed the first personal interview with a Pope ever, on the eve of his death, using an amateur dressed up as a nun and we had lost the sound. The entire thing was untransmittable. The sound recordist, desperate to protect his reputation, and unable, naturally enough, to imagine what had happened, made a formal complaint against Rigby for interfering with his equipment (as she had) and for unprofessional behaviour. Ruggiero Hickman backed him up and Rigby offered no explanation in self-defence.

Naturally enough, Rigby disappeared immediately from the corridors of Religious Programmes and her name was scarcely mentioned again. Those who did not know her were content to think that she had taken early retirement, a fate which fell to my lot, much to the gratification of the Personnel Department who had been pressing it upon me for so long. Ruggiero Hickman was most unusually discreet and within days the waters had closed up silently behind Rigby, as though she had never passed that way.

I missed her sadly and tried repeatedly to get in touch. I even overstepped good manners far enough to visit her flat without an invitation, since I had no telephone number, but she was not there. It was she who got in touch with me, in June four years later. She invited me to tea at Richoux in Knightsbridge; it was the day after the discovery of the financier, Roberto Calvi, hanging like a broken puppet from Blackfriars Bridge. He was, of course, the director of Banco Ambrosiano which Rigby had been investigating so closely, and had earned the nickname of 'God's Banker' because of his close ties with the Vatican.

Naturally I could scarcely contain my curiosity about this development.

"It can't have been suicide, can it?" I asked.

"Of course not," she said, but without her former conspiratorial tone.

Imperceptibly, with every remark, she was slipping away from me.

"My dear Sopwith, the best thing you can do is forget everything about our time together. Sooner or later the truth about these things will emerge and in the meantime a lot of people remain in danger."

"Of course, my dear, you know my lips are sealed." I replied with ardour.

It was foolish of me, perhaps, to mention sentimentally

that far from disposing of the film cans of her extraordinary interview, I had kept them as a secret souvenir. It was this that precipitated the little coldness that ended our friendship.

"You must destroy them at once," she said sharply and she actually passed me a document across the tea and cakes, insisting rather brusquely that I should sign it. It was the Official Secrets Act, of course. She need not have asked me.

"I shall have to look for some other windmills, my dear," I said sadly, as she got up to go.

"So shall I," she said, with her ageless and lovely smile, and then she left.

Postscript. I do not intend to embroil myself further in matters which others, more courageous than myself, have latterly done so much to bring to public attention. It is not for me to take on the might of the Vatican and in any case I have signed the Official Secrets Act. However, I think it quite in order to point out that at the time of his death, allegedly from 'acute myocardial infarction', Pope John Paul was in excellent health except for his chronic low blood pressure, a condition incompatible with what is commonly known as a heart attack. Furthermore the ill-fated Roberto Calvi of the Banco Ambrosiano, whose misdeeds and whose bizarre death hold so many of the clues to this complex mystery, continues to haunt the evil doers. In January 1989, for the first time, an Italian court found that he did not die by his own hand. The mills of God may grind small, but they grind exceeding slow.

Minette and I assume that Mr. Sopwith's postscript refers to the book *In God's Name* by David Yallop which was published in 1984.

Naturally I passed the story to Rigby for corroboration but she was uncharacteristically reticent about it. In fact her only comment was "Poor dear Sopwith".

I took this to mean that the account, even if partial and biassed, is substantially accurate. So I have left it as it is.

Tim Heald

WE ARE NOT AMUSED

It is not customary in British Intelligence to send officers into the field after they have reached fifty. For two years in the early Seventies Rigby was head of station in Washington, with the rank of First Secretary. Then she was sent to run the Spy School in Lyme Regis. When Portland had a serious heart attack in 1976 she filled his shoes with a predictable competence, though she hated being stuck in Whitehall. So much of the job was shuffling paper and briefing ministers who seemed to her increasingly oafish and incompetent.

Unlike other Intelligence officers – vide Peter Wright – Rigby had always rated Harold Wilson. She was no great admirer of his Prime Ministerial record, but she respected his intelligence and political skills. As far as she was concerned his successor, James Callaghan, was not in the same league. Her personal relations with him were distant and frosty and his public performance was, in the main, as dismal as she had predicted.

In 1979 he was forced into a General Election.

Normally this would have had relatively little impact on Rigby, but on this occasion events conspired to drag her out from behind her desk and into what appears to me to be Rigby's Last Case. Rigby, incidentally, was not keen to talk about this assignment. However, my friend the Brigadier had dropped a heavy hint about it during our seminal lunch at White's and my interest was further heightened by a note from the writer, George MacDonald Fraser of 'Flashman' fame. He too, presumably through his Buckingham Palace connections, was aware of the incident and he urged me to write it up.

I took on this assignment personally because of its extremely sensitive nature.

"For God's sake, Humphrey, she was born on October 13th, 1925. I'm five years older than the woman. Almost six to be precise."

The Brigadier, though he was only a Colonel then, shifted uneasily in Rigby's regulation Whitehall armchair, guests for the use of. As Acting Head of 'Q' Rigby got two of these armchairs plus a boardroom table with eight upright chairs, an Anglepoise lamp, a swivel chair of her own, a drinks cupboard and a view of St James's Park. There was a bottle of Talisker and another of Malvern Water on the desk. It was well after conventional working hours.

"My dear Aunt, you know perfectly well that you don't look a day over forty."

"Don't be silly."

"All right, fifty if you insist. In any case you're in a damn sight better shape than she is and you know it."

Rigby did know this. Tennis three times a week; a daily half an hour of what at Cheltenham had been called 'physical jerks' and a sensible diet. She was in good shape. She also had natural good taste. Her clothes, make up and jewellery all accentuated her lean, healthy, fine-boned good-looks. No frills and silly hats for Rigby.

"But I don't look remotely like her."

"My chaps will take care of that. That's if your chaps can't. They've always managed in the past."

Rigby rose and walked to the window. It was a clear bright April evening. Half moon and evening star. Pelicans in the park bedded down for the night. Out of sight, a few hundred yards to the left, Her Majesty would probably be doing her boxes in the Palace, attended by her recently promoted private secretary.

Rigby sipped her malt and thought of England.

"Philip Moore's bound to recognise me." Sir Philip, the Queen's secretary, was a year her junior and had been at Cheltenham Boys' school while she was at the Ladies'. His father had been in the Indian Civil Service and was a friend of her father, Harry. They had known each other since childhood.

"We'll make sure he's out of the way," said the Colonel. "You won't have any trouble with Bill Heseltine. He's Australian after all, not the genuine article." Heseltine was Sir Philip's deputy.

"But dammit, Humphrey, you're asking me to subvert the whole democratic process. It's not a proper way for me to behave. The people must decide. We have to be politically neutral. That's the rule."

"With respect," said the Colonel, "my masters believe they have to act in the best interests of the country. And the best interests of the country are that the Labour Government cannot be allowed to continue. We practically ground to a halt last winter."

This was perfectly true. Even the Archbishop of Canterbury had been moved to protest about the industrial unrest, the worst since the General Strike of 1926. Food rotted in the docks, the dead went unburied, the sick untreated. "Enough is enough," the Archbishop said. Yet when Prime Minister Callaghan came home from a holiday in Guadeloupe he had asked, "Crisis, what crisis?"

Even so, when the motion of no-confidence was finally passed after the House of Commons debate on March 30th there was only a single vote in it. If poor old Sir Alfred Broughton hadn't missed out because of the heart attack which killed him a few days later, Labour might still have hung on. And now that the election campaign was underway, it looked like being a far closer call than would have seemed possible a few months earlier.

The problem was that while people were dissatisfied with the jaded performance of 'Smiling Jim' Callaghan, many of them were alarmed by the vituperative shrewishness of the woman they called 'the Leaderene'. She revelled in her new Soviet-inspired nickname, 'The Iron Lady'. Under her, the police were no longer to be affable peelers who helped old ladies cross the road and told you the time on request. Instead they were to become 'a barrier of steel'. She wanted the death penalty back; she wanted socialism destroyed. Above all, she wanted to curb immigration. "People are really rather afraid," she said in a carefully coded message to the electorate, "that this country might be swamped by people with a different culture." Her message was that "We are a British nation with British characteristics". Her policy was to make sure that Britain remained British.

By this she was widely assumed, by friends and enemies alike, to mean that while she was Prime Minister, Britain would remain white. To some people she was looking ominously like Sir Oswald Mosley in drag. And the fact that she was determined to make the trains run on time only reminded older voters of the Duce.

Nowhere was apprehension greater than at Buckingham Palace.

"My information is that the situation is becoming quite dangerous," said the Colonel.

"What do you mean by that exactly?" Rigby wanted to know.

"One can't be certain," he said carefully, "but my sources are that the Monarch would look extremely unfavourably on a Thatcher victory."

"Me too, to be frank. But *tant pis*. There's nothing one can do about it. It's a democracy. If the people want Thatcher as Prime Minister, that's their problem. For my part it's 'out of the igloo and onto the glacier,' to quote Bernard Levin. But if she gets the votes, she gets the votes."

"My sources," said the Colonel, carefully, "say that the Monarch might not see it quite like that."

"Also too bad," said Rigby. "She and the family will just have to lump it, like the rest of us. After all, she has three rights: to consult, to encourage and to warn. I'm sure you know your Bagehot."

The Colonel was a civilised man with an Honours degree to prove it.

"My dear Aunt," he said, "the only two people who still believe in Bagehot are Norman St John Stevas and the Literary Editor of *The Times*. I'm talking real life here, not the bar at the Garrick."

"Hmmm." Rigby imitated a straight bat defensive block with her left hand. "You're suggesting that H.M.Q. and her team might actually *do* something to prevent the woman becoming Prime Minister, even if lawfully elected."

"In a nutshell."

"Such as what?" Rigby sat down and swivelled, once to the right and once to the left.

"Pull some stunt involving the Privy Council. Invoke the Commonwealth. They're all nutty about the Commonwealth. Maybe just suspend Parliament and declare a state of emergency. It's been done before, and after the Jubilee she could get away with murder. They're a very popular act, the House of Windsor. Could be dangerous if they cut loose. They'd have support. No question. If it came to a choice, ninety per cent of the Armed Forces would back the Monarchy against Parliament."

Rigby took a flat Turkish cigarette from the silver box on her desk – a present from Ernie Bevin. She smoked about one a month in moments of stress.

"You're seriously telling me that Buck House is that hostile to the woman?"

"My masters and I believe there to be a risk."

"So you want me to dress up as the woman and have an agreeable talk with Her Majesty to set her mind at rest."

"Correct."

"Why not get the woman to do it herself?"

The Colonel sighed. "Out of the question. A, she wouldn't and B, she couldn't."

Rigby ground out the barely started cigarette.

"I suppose that means I'll have to carry one of those absurd handbags and wear a blue dress with a bloody great bow at the neck."

The Colonel relaxed.

"Good egg, Aunty," he said, "I knew we could count on you."

Rigby hadn't done a serious impersonation in years and even when she had been disguised, she had usually created an entirely original persona like the Vicereine's lady's maid, back in Delhi all those years ago, or Henry Kissinger's friendly visiting shrink, Dr Whitechurch. Passing yourself off as a real person, especially one as visible as the favoured candidate in a British General Election campaign, was a tallish order.

On the other hand Rigby relished nothing more than a challenge.

The physical side was easy enough. Rigby's hair, short cropped and silver streaked, fitted snugly under a brilliant straw-coloured candy-floss confection which 'wigs' knocked up in twenty-four hours. 'Wardrobe' came up with a perfect ill-fitting boxy jacket to be worn buttoned up over a Conservative Blue blouse with an outsize little-girl bow tie. The charcoal skirt matched the jacket, was heavily pleated and came down to around mid-calf. The shoes were plain, black sensible and the navy blue handbag was big enough to contain a three course lunch and a complete change of clothing. No problems there.

Rigby was taller and thinner, but judicious padding in the top half of the skirt added a good half stone and you could lose six inches of height with a well-judged slouch. The candidate's posture was surprisingly round-shouldered considering her schoolmarmish manner so, although it went against the grain, Rigby cultivated a deliberate sag.

The facial difficulties centred on the nose and teeth. 'Cosmetics' fattened her face quite easily, and a clever use of make-up gave the eyes a characteristic down turn at the corners, which could be helped by Rigby deliberately narrowing them to cultivate a crinkled effect. Enlarging the nose was not so easy. Rigby's nose was rather delicate and *retroussé*. The candidate's was not.

"Ideally," said Mahdur Singh, Director of Cosmetics (Q), "I'd recommend proper plastic surgery for this."

"Certainly not," said Rigby. "No time. Besides I like my nose as it is."

Mahdur Singh tut-tutted at this, but said that his department had just taken delivery of a new facial moulding substance pioneered on behalf of Bulgarian Intelligence. There had been some spectacular results. Rigby would have to be careful about moving her nose while in disguise. A sneeze would almost certainly blow her cover completely. Rigby said she seldom sneezed and would be sure to avoid sudden nasal movements.

Callendar, Head of Dentistry, was equally tentative. He was all for taking Rigby's even, well-preserved teeth out altogether and substituting a complete set of large irregular ones with gaps. But again Rigby was adamant and Callendar, muttering crossly, agreed to do what he could with the latest quick drying dental cement.

"But I'd advise strongly against any eating," he said.

Rigby said that she wasn't anticipating a meal at the Palace. A glass of sherry or a cup of tea seemed the likely limit.

She watched all the available film over and over again. And the Colonel arranged for her to be given an official Press pass for one of the candidate's factory tours. The candidate was doing a heavy number on factories. She was impressive when confronted with complex machinery, whether it turned out chocolate drops or computers. The briefings were thorough and she would display a seemingly genuine enthusiasm when people explained their jobs. When she asked questions they were informed and to the point. Rigby noted the way she held her head to one side, and how forceful arguments, particularly when not likely to correspond with a listener's point of view, were invariably signposted by "My goodness me" or "Good gracious, you know". Thus, when a woman in Rickmansworth said her husband would never vote for a woman, the candidate narrowed her eyes, smiled patronisingly and compared herself to Elizabeth I, remarking, "If your husband had been in that time, my goodness, if he had thought the same then, we might never have beaten the Spanish Armada".

Rigby practised in front of a mirror. "My Goodness Me, Your Majesty, you mustn't think that just because I told Robin Day . . ." and "Good Gracious, you know, Ma'am, they may call me the Iron Lady, but I'm really just a Tin Woman at heart". On second thoughts Rigby decided the allusion to the Wizard of Oz was too obscure to be effective.

Rigby's preparations were complicated by the fact that the Leaderene's image was changing almost daily. For more than a year she had been being advised by Gordon – later Sir Gordon – Reece, a suave Svengali who had been a television producer and made a reputation out of advising some of the country's leading comedians on how to improve their acts. Reece was trying – successfully – to change the Leaderene from a fussy-looking housewife, suitable for the Finchley electorate, into something approaching an authentic public figure. He was also getting her to lower her voice and slow her delivery so that she sounded less like a yappy Corgi attacking the postman's ankles and more – 'Churchillian' was the word that kept cropping up. Every day the timbre of the candidate's voice assumed a more mellifluous resonance. Rigby gargled with honey and blackcurrant and tried singing male parts from Gilbert and Sullivan. The Tories had also engaged the Saatchi Brothers, the new *wunderkinder* of the British advertising industry, to help them defeat Labour. They, too, were having a conspicuous effect on the Leaderene's style.

By the end of the fifth day, however, Rigby felt confident enough to invite the Colonel round for another glass of Talisker.

"Well, Humphrey," she said, yanking up her enormous handbag and making as if to clout him with it, "I think we're up and running." And then, lowering her voice an octave or two she said, very seriously, smiling in a long-suffering, understanding, rather patronising manner, "You know, Humphrey, many people in this country are afraid that I will be a divisive Prime Minister but, Goodness, that's not at all what I aim to be. I want to put the Great back into Britain and set the people free. And, Humphrey, I'd just like to say to you 'Where there is discord may we bring harmony, where there is error may we bring truth, where there is doubt may we bring faith, and where there is despair may we bring hope'."

The Colonel stood transfixed.

"Brilliant," he said, at last, "bloody brilliant. Where does all that stuff about discord and harmony come from?"

"Francis of Assisi." Rigby grinned. "Rupert Denham, my first boss, used to have it stuck up behind his desk."

"Bloody Good!" The Colonel struck his pin-striped thigh with the flat of his hand. "I must tell Maurice Saatchi, he'll love it. We'll get Chris Patten to put it in one of her speeches." (The infiltration and bugging of Saatchi and Saatchi by British Intelligence during the 1979 election campaign is worth several volumes on its own. It helped Rigby's deception, of course, but Rigby wanted one-way traffic. She wasn't interested in any *quid pro quo*.)

"Steady on." Rigby poured drinks. Stiff ones. Heavy on the Scotch, light on the Malvern. "Don't you dare let the woman spout those lines until I've had my session with Her Majesty. They're for her ears only. Evidence of a conciliatory consensus approach to government – the Leaderene as Butskellite. You agree?"

"Absolutely," the Colonel stared into his glass for a moment. "How about a quick dummy run on Monday? Then we can go for the real thing a day or two later."

"Dummy run?"

"Chum of mine's running a battalion in Armagh. He'd enormously value a visit from the future Prime Minister. All tremendously hush hush of course. No names, no pack drill, no Press."

"You're on," said Rigby and then, switching to Leaderene mode she breathed, "Goodness me, Humphrey, ask not what your country can do for you, but what you can do for your country".

"Kennedy's inaugural speech in '61," said the Colonel, "another new dawn."

"Bit of a false dawn, as it turned out." Rigby drained her glass. Her eyes clouded. "Alas," she said, "poor Jack!"

Rigby wasn't sure about helicopters. The Lynx had picked her up at Aldergrove off the unscheduled military flight from Northolt which, thanks to a personal history dating back almost forty years, she still thought of as *the* London Airport. Wedged into the back alongside the Colonel, she looked out through an Ulster mist to a quilt of miniature fields peppered with small cottages and farm buildings. The landscape had an old-fashioned monochrome quality viewed from the perspex bubble, which shook and bucketed in the light wind. It was almost like being at an old film. She in her twinset with the bow and the blonde wig and the enormous handbag, and the action racing past a few hundred feet below at ground level. She felt curiously detached and yet, objectively, she knew that South Armagh was Indian country. The enemy was down there with their Armalites and plastic explosive. Even up here, bouncing around in their khaki four-seater, they were within easy range of a well-aimed Sam 7.

She wanted to ask Humphrey if her hair was all right, but all four of them were plugged into headsets and mouthpieces and she didn't think enquiries about her coiffure were quite the thing to put out over the airwaves.

Presently they came across a small complex of Nissen huts with parade ground, union flag waving, an array of Land Rovers, trucks and half tracks. A platoon of men in camouflaged combat gear was drawn up alongside a landing pad. The pilot circled once, turned the Lynx on one side, straightened and came in gently, dead on target. They waited for the engines to die and the blades to stop turning, then the Commanding Officer came across smartly, opened the door and handed her out.

"Welcome to Ballypaisley, Ma'am. Very good of you to come. We appreciate it."

Rigby smiled. "Not at all, Colonel. Goodness me, it's a jolly poor Prime Minister who sends people to places she's not prepared to go to herself."

The Colonel smiled, then saluted and shook hands with Humphrey.

"Good to see you, Bill," said Humphrey. "I'm afraid we're on a pretty tight schedule, but we'll cram in as much as we can. I think it's important we meet as many of the chaps as possible."

"Absolutely, Colonel," said Rigby, thinking that she could grow into the part but longing to be out of these ridiculous togs and into combat gear herself. She wondered if they'd let her fire one of the new rocket launchers or play with the latest stun grenades. Then she remembered that she was an aspiring Prime Minister and not supposed to know about such things at first hand.

"I think you're doing an absolutely marvellous job out here," she said. "We simply must not give in to terrorism."

For herself Rigby thought – knew indeed – that life was a good deal more complex than that, but she was playing a role and she knew that the Leaderene was not one for grey areas and seeing both sides of a question.

The C.O. introduced his Adjutant and a couple of other officers, then led Rigby along the lines of men at a brisk light infantry pace. Rigby occasionally paused for what she hoped were suitable pleasantries. The men seemed gratifyingly pleased to see her, but she was irritated at having to deal in relative platitudes.

She had just finished the inspection when a Land Rover drove into camp and came to a skidding stop in a swirl of mud.

A young Lieutenant jumped out, strode over to them and gave a brisk salute.

"This is Lieutenant Carpenter," said the C.O., "whom I believe you know already."

Rigby's brain went into overdrive. Why in God's name hadn't Humphrey briefed her properly? Who was this person?

For a second she froze. Thank God the young Lieutenant had been properly brought up.

"Kevin Carpenter," he said. "I was at school with Mark. You very kindly bought me champagne after the Eton match two years ago."

"Of course," said Rigby. "You made that marvellous century. I'm afraid I didn't recognise you out of context." Thank heaven Rigby followed her cricket so assiduously. It had been a remarkable innings eulogised by Jim Swanton in the *Daily Telegraph*. She remembered the description vividly. Swanton said he'd seen no finer schoolboy performance since P.B.H. May was at Charterhouse. It was the May comparison that made it stick in Rigby's memory. Thank heaven for Swanton and May.

"How *is* Mark?" asked young Carpenter.

"Still in bed when I left home this morning." Rigby laughed and the Lieutenant laughed with her. Bulls-eye, she thought to herself.

"And Carol?"

"She's back from Australia for the election. In wonderful form."

"Do give her my love." Rigby looked quizzically to see if Lieutenant Carpenter was a potential suitor for the Leaderene's twin daughter. Quite possibly.

"Of course," she put a hand on the young man's shoulder. "And next time you're on leave, dear, do come and see us. We'd like that very much."

Beside her, Humphrey looked pointedly at his watch and the C.O. took the hint. "Tight schedule I'm afraid, Kevin," he said, "we've just got time for a quick shufti down to the border, then I'm afraid our distinguished visitor has some important engagements back home."

The Lieutenant saluted and Rigby relaxed. It had been an unpleasant moment.

The border was only a couple of miles away and the C.O. thought his guest might like to meet the men who manned an isolated look-out post on a small hillock at a place called Saint Bridey's Mount. The guest said she was game and they set off in a couple of Range Rovers. Humphrey rode with two armed Sergeants in the first and Rigby was in the second, with Colonel Bill and the Adjutant.

The weather had cleared now and a sheepish sun was peeping through the cloud. The look-out post turned out to be an abandoned barn – cold, damp and draughty but with good views over the valley to the south. About a hundred yards away a tarmac road snaked, black and moist, from East to West.

"The road's on the Republic side," said the Sergeant in charge. "It goes into Castleblaney from nowhere in particular. Just peters out at a farmhouse a couple of miles over the horizon, so there's not much traffic."

They stood outside the barn, gazing south. From the west there came the sound of a motorcar, elderly and infirm to judge by the intermittent burps coming from the exhaust. The Sergeant passed Rigby his binoculars and she focussed, then picked up the car which had just appeared over the hill and was heading east at an almost reckless speed. It was an old Morris with a bulldog nose and there were two men in front; another in the back. Rigby watched with mild interest as the passenger in the back rolled down the window on their side. Local farmers on their way into town for an alcoholic lunch, she surmised.

The car was almost opposite them when Rigby saw the sun glint off something metallic in the back of the car and at the same instant there was a light puff of blue smoke, a quick burst of tinny little explosions and a flurry of activity all round them. The Sergeant was shouting, the men were loosing off automatic rifle fire at the now fast retreating car and Rigby was the only person standing.

Colonel Humphrey and Colonel Bill scrambled to their feet, brushing mud off their knees.

"Ma'am, I really must ask you to take cover," said Colonel Bill.

"Bit late now," said Rigby, handing the binoculars back to

the Sergeant who had also got to his feet. "In any case only one of them was armed and it was just a handgun. He'd have to have been a bloody good shot to have picked any of us off at a hundred yards from a car moving at fifty m.p.h. Besides the gun was practically an antique."

Rigby was suddenly aware that the Colonel and his men were looking at her with amazement, and that she was not sounding quite as one would expect a Finchley housewife with political aspirations. Even an Iron Lady.

"Good Gracious, Colonel," she said, flashing what she hoped looked like one of her famous smiles, "you don't expect me to be intimidated by a car load of terrorists, surely? That would be playing into their hands."

The Colonel cleared his throat. "Er . . ." he said, "er . . . quite. But even so I think it might be politic if we moved on now. I know how tight your schedule is."

Later, on the flight back to Northolt, Rigby and Colonel Humphrey engaged in a tactical debrief.

"Nasty moment that," said the Colonel.

"I thought I'd had it," said Rigby.

"It did cross my mind, too." Now that the episode was over the Colonel could afford to be laconic.

"Thank God he told me his name and gave me the Eton clue. Harrovians are obviously better brought up than I thought."

"Oh, Aunt, you are impossible." The Colonel laughed, though without a lot of humour. "I meant the shooting. You could have been killed. You were an absolute sitting target."

"Oh *that*," said Rigby.

The Buckingham Palace appointment was fixed for noon in two days' time. The Palace suggested earlier, but Rigby had no intention of arriving until the daily guard-changing was over and the tourists had all dispersed. Arranging the meeting required all the Colonel's and Rigby's guile and contacts. The only aspect that eased their problems – like the visit to Ulster – was the obvious need for extreme secrecy. Neither Queen nor Candidate wished anyone, anyone at all, to know that this meeting was taking place. It was unthinkable, in the run-up to a British General Election, that any candidate could be seen having private audiences with the Monarch. Yet, if what the Colonel said was true, it was essential that the two should meet.

On the day in question the real Leaderene was due to take the usual morning Press Conference at Conservative Party H.Q. in Smith Square. The Colonel and Rigby had then established that she would be making the short trip to her home in Flood Street, Chelsea, where she would be working on an important speech before a private lunch at the House with senior Tory Party officials. She would not be appearing in public until a tour of a hairbrush factory in mid-afternoon, followed by an evening in her Finchley constituency.

So for several crucial hours she would be out of the public eye and free, in theory, to undertake clandestine visits to Buckingham Palace.

Sir Philip Moore had just gone down with an unexpected, but nasty, bout of 'flu, thanks to Q's Pharmaceuticals Division and a gentleman with an unusual umbrella who had stood next to him one evening at St James's Park tube station.

At eleven-fifteen Rigby was chauffeured, heavily muffled, in an anonymous official Ford Cortina to Chelsea where she slipped as surreptitiously as possible into a Rover, identical in every respect, including numberplates, to that of the Leaderene herself. For the Colonel and Rigby such things were easy to arrange. She eased out of the trench coat and Hermés scarf, adjusted her big blue bow, patted her wig and applied just a smidgeon of extra lipstick to her mouth. Then she pulled out her papers and eased back into the light brown leather seat.

At eleven-fifty-five the car rounded the vast, fussy memorial to Queen Victoria and turned into the gateway at the northern end of the Buckingham Palace railings. The uniformed constable consulted his notes, made a brief telephone call, and the gates swung open. The car swept over the gravel and came to a halt by the Privy Purse Entrance. The chauffeur opened the door and Rigby alighted. Inside, the burly retired Guards Sergeant-Major, in dark suit and regimental tie, opened the door, invited Rigby to sign the visitors' book and then to sit on one of the uncomfortable velvet and gilt armchairs while he announced her arrival.

Two minutes later, with the cat-like tread of a career

courtier, a shortish dark-haired man in a pin-stripe suit with incredibly highly polished black shoes, approached her and said, in a voice only slightly tinged with an Australian accent, that if Rigby would care to come with him the Queen would see her now.

Thirty-five minutes later Rigby was shown out to her car by the same gentleman. Both were smiling broadly.

At one-fifteen p.m. she was back in her office, dialling a private and confidential number. "Humphrey dear," she said when a familiar voice, in a very small basement office only a few hundred yards away, answered, "I've had a most agreeable meeting. If you'd like to discuss it perhaps you'd care to step round after six."

The rest, of course, is history. On May 4th, 1979 Mrs Thatcher was elected Prime Minister of Great Britain with an overall majority of forty-three seats. The Monarch made no objection either in public or private. There was, of course, no reason to, in view of certain undertakings made in private the previous week. The transcript and tapes of these were stored in one of Mr Chubb's safes at the Palace. The ritual kissing of hands passed off very pleasantly and, after a forty-five minute chat with the Queen, the new Prime Minister returned to 10 Downing Street where she faced the crowd and quoted from St Francis of Assisi: "Where there is discord may we bring harmony, where there is error may we bring truth, where there is doubt may we bring faith, and where there is despair may we bring hope".

Rigby, watching on television, allowed herself the luxury of a single raised eyebrow.

That evening she was working late when the duty officer came in with an envelope which had just been delivered by hand. On the back was the familiar magenta of the Royal Coat of Arms.

Rigby knifed it open with her father's kukri.

"Dear Miss Rigby," it said, in the huge Roman typewriting favoured by the Palace, "Her Majesty has asked me to say how much she appreciated your visit last week. She was much impressed and amused. She has also asked me to say that, in view of her considerable workload, she would be most grateful if you were prepared to consider accepting occasional assignments on her own behalf. If so perhaps you would be good enough to telephone me at your convenience."

Rigby looked at the signature and laughed softly. "Touché," she said, "I might just take you up on that."

Rigby adamantly refuses to be drawn about whether she ever rose to the royal challenge. Indeed she regretted mentioning the letter as soon as she had told me. Now that I know about it I look back, for instance, to one or two of the Christmas Broadcasts and to royal visits to the less agreeable parts of the globe, and I can't help wondering. Difficult, though, to prove.

It is true that Mrs Thatcher enjoys a reputation in the British Army for having considerable physical courage. I like to think that the beginning of this legend can be traced back to the morning Rigby was shot at on Ulster's border with the Republic.

Rigby's retirement was due on her sixtieth birthday, only a few months after the events described in the previous episode. She says that on January 28th, 1980 she was finally pensioned off and that she lived quietly and happily ever after in the cottage in Sussex, only coming to London to watch cricket at Lord's where she was the first ever lady member of the M.C.C. If that is what she says, then I am in no position to do other than accept it. But I would enter a modest *caveat* and say that Rigby's does not strike me as a retiring nature.

Epilogue

The final deadline for contributions to *The Rigby File* was January 5th. By the end of the month I'd sorted out the editing and sent the material to Ion Trewin, the Editorial Director of the publishers, Hodder and Stoughton. Ion's a fast reader and on February 6th, a Monday, he rang to say he'd been through it at the weekend. There were a couple of minor queries, but generally speaking he was well pleased. Hodder would probably publish in the early autumn; we must decide on a jacket design; they'd take an ad. in *The Bookseller*; was there any chance of Rigby going on *Wogan*? Etcetera etcetera. It was all publisher talk, the sort of thing all good editors (and there still are some) say when they accept a book.

As soon as we'd finished, I dialled Rigby in Sussex to tell her the good news. She said 'no' to *Wogan*, as I knew she would. In fact she said she'd not give any interviews: the book would have to stand on its own two feet or not at all. She didn't trust the media to get things right, and if they misquoted her then there was a good chance everyone would end up in the dock and we didn't want that did we?

Well, no, we didn't.

It seemed to me that the successful conclusion of our part in the proceedings called for some celebration. Only the best champagne would do and, since it's not a subject I know much about, I sought expert advice. David Marchwood, who runs Moët and Chandon over here, suggested I couldn't do better than take a bottle of Dom Perignon. "The '82," he said. "The greatest vintage of the century." (I would have asked John Cleveley at Clicquot, but he was in Australia.)

So that Saturday afternoon I drove down with my bottle in a chilled picnic box and parked by Rigby's garden gate. Everything looked neat and tidy and bedded down for winter, much as it had a year before when I'd been driven down for the first time by Sidey in the Brigadier's unmarked car. I walked down the garden path and then a funny thing happened.

A dog barked.

Rigby didn't have a dog.

Next thing the front door opened and out shot a yappy little Jack Russell which made straight for my trouser legs and started tugging at my turn-ups. And there in the doorway stood a short, ferrety-looking chap in cavalry twills, a tweed jacket, yellow cardigan and a Gunner tie.

"Yes?" he said.

"I've come to see Miss Rigby," I said.

"Well you've come to the wrong place," he said.

"I'm sorry," I said, "I've been coming here regularly for the past year. This is Dorothy Rigby's house."

"It most certainly is not," said the ferrety man. "This is my house and it's been my house for the last seven years."

This was perplexing.

"Your name's not Rigby?" I tried, tentatively.

"Certainly not. My name is Bott."

"Well, Mr Bott, there must be some mistake."

"Major Bott," he said.

"Well, Major, I'm terribly sorry but I can only say that I've been coming here regularly and every time I've been I've met Dorothy Rigby. Perhaps I didn't understand. Does she live with you?"

"Most certainly not. The only other person who lives here is Mrs Bott."

The Major had a runny nose. A drop fell from his left nostril and lodged in his pepper and salt moustache. Behind him a square woman in a grey skirt and a blue cardigan appeared and said, "Do come in and shut the door, darling. It's deathly cold."

Well, to cut a long story short, they let me into the house and everything was different. No signed photographs of Ike and Monty; no Burmese cat on the hearth; no grandmother clock. And very definitely no Rigby.

I couldn't shake them. They behaved as if I was totally round the bend and in the end the Major asked me to leave. He did it quite politely and to be honest I couldn't see any alternative.

As soon as I got back I rang the Brigadier on his home number. I didn't want to discuss it over the phone, not to seem too frantic. He had a free lunch on Thursday. I don't have a club so we arranged to meet at the Charing Cross Hotel. It's the same sort of food: anonymous and discreet. The tables are too far apart for eavesdropping, provided you don't shout. I waited until we'd finished the soup and we'd both chosen the roast beef from the carvery. Then I took a slug of the house claret for courage and gave him my best Old School Tie stare right between the eyes.

"Look," I said, "what's happened to Dorothy Rigby?"

He gave the gaze back with good measure, quite unblinking. He was chewing on the beef. When he'd swallowed he too took a sip of the claret.

"I'm sorry," he said, "who?"